WHO HE IS

BOOK 1
FIRENINE TRILOGY

Shanora Williams
writing as
S. Q. Williams

T0298057

Edited by Cassie McCown of Gathering Leaves Editing
Cover design by Regina Wamba of Mae I Design
Formatting by Amanda Heath of Little Dove Formatting

Table of Contents

Dedicated to one of the closest friends/family members
I have:
Taylor Little.
I adore you, I love you, and I appreciate all you've
done for me. My life would be so boring without you. I'm
so glad you can finally be the *real* you.

"Character cannot be developed in ease and quiet.
Only through experience of trial and suffering can the soul
be strengthened, ambition inspired, and success achieved."
~ Helen Keller

PROLOGUE

I heaved, clamping my chest, staring intently into the demented green eyes. There was a cloud of darkness behind them—anger, frustration, and a menacing glare. Those eyes frightened me every night, yet I'd dealt with it for years. His deep voice grumbled something I could hardly make out because of the blood racing around in my skull. His voice was toxic, deadly.

Through the darkness, I adjusted, but I could see her watching eyes, her partial, wicked smile from the bedroom door. I lay on top of the rough carpet and stretched out my arm, begging her to help me. Instead, she stared, watching as he picked me up from the floor and shoved me against the nearest wall. I winced, trying to keep myself steady,

S. Q. WILLIAMS

but instead I collapsed against the carpet again, burning my knees and the palms of my sensitive hands.

"Mama, please." My voice was raspy from my previous yelling—from the excruciating pain he provided. The severity of his wrath left me bruised, tattered. My head hung and my cheek smashed against the carpet. For a moment I felt safe as the room became quiet and spun around me.

Finally *she* spoke up, her voice almost a whisper. "I'm sorry, Liza, but you knew this was important. When we need money, it's not a joke. Should've done what was asked of you."

A tear escaped from beneath my swollen eyelids and then I opened them, watching her turn around quickly. I called after her desperately, begging her not to leave me alone with that bastard. More tears fell, cigarette smoke drifted into the room, and then he yelled for me to get up, yanking on my arm.

My knees buckled again and my face slammed into the floor. Blood spilled from my nose and my forehead burned from scraping against the carpet. He threatened that if I didn't get up, he was going to make the punishment worse, but I couldn't. I was weak. I didn't have the strength within me to move anymore. I was blank, nothing, like a thin sheet of paper. Unmoving unless blown by the wind or picked up by someone.

I wanted to dissolve into dust and blend in with the floor to become anything—anyone—but Eliza Smith.

I prayed and wished it would stop, but as he chuckled eerily and muttered something threatening beneath his breath, I knew it was coming. Heavy leather stung the backs of my legs, my hips, my back, my arms, and even my face countless times. I cried out repeatedly, digging my fingernails into the carpet with thick tears streaming, hoping soon I would numb to the pain.

I did eventually.

FUDGE SUNDAE

Gage Grendel...

There were only a few words that could describe him: hot, mouthwatering, and way out of my league. He *and* his band were out of my league, but apparently not my dad's. He was their manager, and this summer things were really starting to kick off for them.

I remember exactly how my dad announced the tour to me:

"You need to start packing. We're going on tour with FireNine!" he said over dinner.

I looked at him, a frown taking hold of my features, before digging into my mashed potatoes. "You mean *you're* going on tour. I'd rather stay home."

"Why? You need to get out and have some fun, Eliza."

My dad's personality made me feel so boring. He was spunky, hip, great taste, young-at-heart, all the above. When I'd moved in with him, he took me shopping first thing. He literally ran me to the mall because he said I looked "terrible."

Apparently he didn't approve of my sweatpants and the brown T-shirt I'd gotten from summer camp when I was twelve years old. I admit, by the age of sixteen it had gotten a little small on me, but I didn't mind. I was twenty-one and would still wear it whenever I could because it was my favorite tee. It was a summer I was free of the hellhole.

"Come on, Liza Bear," he begged. "It'll be fun. I know you get tired of this house. You do the same thing every day. Eat. Draw. Paint. Sleep. You aren't tired of that routine?"

"Not really."

His brown eyes scanned me and then he smirked. "I think I know what it is." He placed his fork on the table and tucked a lock of his perfectly trimmed hair behind his ear. My dad and I had the same natural platinum-blond hair. The fact that my skin was paler than a blank sheet of paper didn't make it any better for me. He'd told me once before that I could pass for an albino if my eyelashes and eyebrows were a paler blond.

My dad pulled it off, though. He classified himself as "HOT" and I agreed. He worked out every day and had straight white teeth; his hair, parted at the crown of his head, just touched his shoulders. He naturally had more fashion sense than me, which was quite embarrassing sometimes.

"What do you mean?" I asked as he crossed his arms.

"It's Gage, isn't it?"

Hearing Gage's name caused me to tear away my gaze. "What about him?"

"I notice the way you practically run to your room to hide when he and the band come over to practice now. You're such a little girl."

"Am not." I stuck out my tongue and he laughed. "Besides, they've only been here twice." A smile touched my lips as I slid away from the table, grabbing my plate. I took his as well, then made my way toward the kitchen. Our house was nice and somewhat simple. The kitchen was always clean. We had tan marble counters with grey and silver flecks, dark-brown cabinets with brushed nickel knobs, and an island in the center, surrounded by six bar stools.

I remember Gage sitting on one of those barstools and since then, I haven't touched it. There's just something about his presence that makes me nervous.

My dad stepped into the kitchen as I dropped the plates in the sink. "You really aren't going to come with me, Liza? I want you out of the house. You're twenty-one, and you spend every summer trapped here. It's time to get out and live a little, don't you think?"

"I'm sorry, Dad—"

"Ben," he corrected. That was one thing he couldn't stand. Being called "dad." It supposedly made him feel old, and he was the type who would rather feel like a brother than a father.

"Well, *Ben*," I said, rolling my eyes and plugging the sink, "I don't think going on tour with FireNine will be such a great idea. It's just a bunch of guys on a bus, drinking beer and doing God knows what else. That's not my kind of crowd."

"What is your crowd, exactly?" he asked, narrowing his eyes and leaning his elbows on the counter.

"I'm my own crowd." I winked over my shoulder. I rinsed the suds off the plates and placed them into the dish rack as he laughed.

"All right, let's make a deal." He clasped his hands. "If I give you a gift card to a bookstore, buy you some cute clothes, and even take you to get your hair done, will you go?"

I shrugged. "I like the bookstore part. As for the clothes and hair, that was kind of a downfall."

"Well, shit! You can get all the books you want. Just please come, Eliza. I swear it'll be worth your time. We're making tons of stops during the tour so there'll always be something to do. It gets boring here in Virginia after a while, and you know it."

I could agree with him there. There wasn't really much to do in Suffolk unless someone had a party of some sort, but parties weren't really my thing. Nothing was really my thing. I stayed cooped up in my house so much I think I missed out on most of the fun as a teenager. Even while enrolled in college, all I did was go to class or hide in my dorm. My roommate was trashy so I hardly ever saw her, which was a good thing most of the time because I couldn't stand her.

"Okay." I sighed as Ben's large brown eyes looked me over. "I'll go, but I don't wanna be on the same bus as the band."

"Oh, sweetie, you won't be," he assured, stepping around the counter to stand next to me. "You'll be on a separate bus with me. You'll have all the alone time you need. I wouldn't put you on a bus with a bunch of boys like them. That's just… ew. Gross. The things those boys do. Ugh!"

"Okay, okay." I giggled, lifting my hands in surrender mode. "I'll go—mainly because I do like their music and because I think it'd be cool to watch the cities go by. I can snap a few pictures or something." I shrugged, sighing. "Why the hell not?"

"That's my Liza." He kissed my cheek and then pulled me in for a hug. I hugged him back quickly before pulling away to get to the dishes again. "Tomorrow we'll go shopping."

"Cool."

The doorbell rang a few seconds later and Ben grinned as he braced himself, wiping his hands on his peachy button-up shirt. "Oh, great. The boys are here."

My eyebrows knitted as I stared out of the kitchen. "The boys?"

"Yes. FireNine. They're practicing in the garage tonight since their producer's out of town. They have a new song, and I've been dying to hear it. Perks of being the manager, huh?"

I swallowed. "Um… yeah. Sure."

Winking, my dad trailed out the kitchen, but I pulled my hands from the dishwater, dried them off with a dishtowel, and then dashed for my bedroom in a heartbeat, shutting my door behind me. I hated when they made random appearances, especially when I looked like complete trash.

As I stepped forward, I kneeled down on my knees and pulled out one of my sketchpads from beneath the bed. I then grabbed a pencil and sat at the desk in the corner of my room. Deep voices echoed through the hall, and I tried to concentrate, but it was extremely difficult. The hardest part about it was hearing Gage Grendel's deep, bedroom-like voice. It was humming through me, almost luring me in his direction. At one point, I had to fight myself to not get up and steal a peek at him. His voice was completely irresistible.

"I'll be in there once I find the bathroom," Gage called. His footsteps sounded heavier than normal and my pencil stopped sketching as he got closer and closer to my bedroom. The bathroom was a door down from mine and knowing how one could confuse the two doors scared the shit out of me. I knew it was coming. I knew *he* was coming.

My doorknob jiggled and, slowly, the door creaked open. I tensed, but I kept my gaze down and focused on my sketchpad. "Oh, damn. Wrong room."

I glanced over my shoulder, bracing myself before taking in the full sight of him. His attire was nowhere near preppy or perfect. His casual demeanor suited him. He had on black Chuck Taylor's, a black tank top that clung to his firm upper body, and a pair of near-skinny, dark-blue jeans. His hazel eyes were smiling, specks of green and yellow sparkling within. I could make out the hints of colors in his irises from a mile away. His silky, dark-brown hair had been trimmed to a messier look, curly in a few untamed places, and defined him even more. A sleeve of unique tattoos smothered both his arms—some were tribal ink, a few names, and even some Bible verses were written in cursive. There was even the band's name right below his neck.

"You look familiar," Gage said, snapping me out of my admiration.

"Probably because we went to school together," I said. *Oh shit, there goes my sarcastic side.* I was glad he disregarded it.

"That so?" He raised a suave eyebrow and I nodded.

"Yeah. You graduated three years before I did."

"Oh. Explains why I can't remember you... but you do ring a bell. What's your name?"

"Eliza Smith," I said, as if it were going to actually ring his bell.

Surprisingly, it did.

"Holy sh—no way! *You're* Benny's daughter?"

"Yes," I said defensively. I wasn't sure if he meant it insultingly. "Obviously, if I'm in a bedroom of his home..."

"That's pretty awesome. You're hotter than I expected you to be." His tone was absurdly nonchalant. "Benny talks about you nonstop. Why don't I ever see you around?"

"We're opposites I guess." I shrugged. I turned around slowly and began sketching again, but I could still feel Gage scanning me from across the room and I was starting to wonder why the hell he wasn't leaving. "The bathroom is the next door down, in case you're wondering," I said without looking back. I couldn't look back. If I did, I would have dragged him into my room and locked him in with me.

"Cool," he said. "Thanks, *Eliza*… Actually, I think I'll call you Ellie. Just came up with it. Sounds better. Fits you."

"But that's not my na—"

The door shut quickly and I was glad because hearing Gage say my name like that nearly caused me to melt inside, and him leaving saved me from embarrassing myself. *Ellie?* I'd never been called that before.

It was hypnotic. Gage saying my name and even giving me a nickname was like vanilla ice cream, and the addition of his deep, bedroom-like voice was the drizzle of warm fudge that completed it and made me totally devour it. He'd created a freaking ice cream sundae with extra-hot fudge just by uttering *my name*.

Gage was beyond the word hot. He was sexy but extremely deadly toward any girl's emotions. He could break a girl's heart in two and not care about it. It was always that way in high school. He'd hook up with a girl one day; the next she'd come into class with smeared mascara. That was one thing that agitated me about guys in rock bands. It seemed as if they were all the same—all aiming to have sex and then forget about it the next day.

I didn't want to be a witness to him or any of the other guys bringing countless girls on and off their bus, but a part of me wanted to finally get out. Ben was right about living it up. I wanted to do it for myself, even if it were something new to me. It was time for me to challenge myself. Time for me to open up.

Ben gave me a makeover and I guess Gage noticed. Even though I was the only breathing organism in the room, he actually looked at me as if I were a person. In school, when he was around, I always wore my hair in a ponytail. I never wore makeup (unless someone would consider lip balm makeup), and I wore nothing but T-shirts and jeans every day and maybe a hoodie when it was cold, but when I moved in with Ben, he stopped me from wearing my—as he put it—"ugly boy clothes." He made sure I dressed to impress. He never allowed me to wear a T-shirt with jeans again unless I was staying inside the house. Too bad I started looking nicer after Gage graduated. Maybe he would've noticed me in school.

I moved in with Ben during the second semester of my junior year, when I was seventeen. I was recognized by others for my looks and the drastic Ben-makeover and it was an odd feeling, so I always rejected the guys who came along. It never felt right to date anyone when things were just starting to make a little sense in my crazy life.

High school just seemed too young to start anything official and so was college—not that I wasn't looking. I just wanted something playful. Nothing serious. I didn't have much time for anything serious. I guess that was another reason I wanted to actually go with Ben. Because I wanted to possibly meet someone on the road who had the same interests as me. Someone who loved to absorb the feel of creativity and just breathe it. Someone who could be just as free and down to earth as me. Someone who didn't care about anyone's opinion but his own. Someone who knew how to have fun while also keeping his feelings to himself.

I was expecting too much, but if I were to have any kind of fun with someone, he had to be worth it.

GRENDEL THE FLIRT

The tour bus Ben told me to board was nice. It was larger on the inside than I thought and as I stepped in completely, there was a grand living room setting and a kitchen to my left. The living room was comprised of black suede couches directly across from each other, a coffee table in between the sofas, and a wide flat-screen TV set up on the north wall.

Gripping the handles of my suitcase and bag, I made my way down the hall and kicked open one of the doors with the tip of my running shoe. A mattress lay on the floor and a window was above it. Looking at it made me shake my head and move along to see what the next room had in store.

To my luck, the next room was perfect.

A queen-sized bed was against the wall, one square window above it. The walls were painted a gentle shade of lavender and the floor was covered with smooth, tan carpet.

I dropped my bags, gazing around with a smile. It would do for the tour. Ben told me a few days before that the tour was going to last two months, but he was going to make sure I was back in Virginia for school. I couldn't afford to miss out, especially when I had an academic scholarship I worked tremendously hard for. I wanted to get a bachelor's degree in art and then explore the world. I wanted to start a life of my own and chase my dreams.

Graduating from the University of Virginia had always been a goal of mine. After being told I would never make it anywhere in life by my so-called "mom," I wanted to graduate and prove her wrong. I figured being on a tour bus was the perfect way to start my dreams. If I had experience with traveling, taking pictures, and painting what I came across, it would make it so much easier for me to create a creative portfolio.

A few heavy grunts came from the front of the bus. Figuring it was Ben, I stepped out to check but was caught by surprise at the sight of Gage with at least four suitcases—one in each hand and one beneath the pit of each arm. "Do you need help?" I asked as he kicked the screen door to keep it open, dragging another case inside.

He looked up at me, his hazel eyes narrowing and trying to figure out who the voice had come from. "Oh, Ellie." He grinned. "It'd be nice if I could get your help."

I stepped forward, grabbed the two suitcases out of his hands, and placed them near the sofas. Gage stepped around me and dropped the bags with a heavy sigh. "Sorry. My dad packs more stuff than he needs." I laughed

He chuckled. "I can see that." He took in the interior of the bus and his eyes widened. "Wow, never been on this bus before. Ben has it good—way better than us."

"Yeah." I forced a smile before looking down, realizing how close we were. His firm arm was brushing against mine, so I took a step away. He looked at me, his gaze a bit confused, and then rocked on his heels.

"So since you're on this tour, it means I'm gonna be seeing more of you," he said.

I twisted my fingers in front of me, forcing a smile. I think it came off as uneasy. "I suppose."

His head tilted and a small smile graced his lips. "You don't seem too happy about it. I bet it's every girl's dream to be next to the lead singer of FireNine."

He nudged me gently on the ribcage with his elbow and I laughed dryly, taking another step away from him. "I forgot how arrogant you are. I'm not every girl. I'm Eliza. I like your music... but that's probably about it."

Gage's features fell as he stared at me. Before he could make it too noticeable, he blinked quickly and flashed a smile, as if what I said meant nothing to him. "We'll see about that, Ellie. Maybe I can get you to like more about me than just my music."

"Yeah, okay," I scoffed. I was surprised I was so confident while talking to him. It felt good to pretend I didn't have the biggest crush on him. I didn't want him to know, with one simple touch, he could probably make me weak in the knees. Gage seemed to have that kind of power over girls. He was the lead singer of a popular band, for heaven's sake. He was probably right about him being every girl's dream because sometimes he appeared in mine.

"Gage! We're waiting on you!" someone shouted from the door. "Bring your ass on!"

"Yeah, let's get this show on the road!" I heard Ben yell, clapping his hands. "Terri, I want you to make sure everyone and everything is on board before we leave. You have five minutes."

After some quick yelling at a few others, Ben stepped onto the bus and looked directly at Gage. "Thanks for dropping my bags off. Things are always so hectic at the beginning of tours. New staff and they don't know a damn thing." He rolled his eyes, making his way toward his suitcases.

Gage nodded at Ben and then looked at me. As he stepped past, he winked, but I looked away and aimed to keep my heart at a steady pace. I failed terribly but was glad no one could hear the clambering through my chest because of all the commotion going on from outside. "See you later, Ellie," Gage said, his voice a bit silkier than usual.

He took his last step off the bus and then hollered at someone, making my ears ring. I looked out of the thin window in front of me and watched as he bumped chests with Roy Sykes, the lead guitarist. Roy was way taller than the rest of the boys of the band and had shaggy hair that hung in his eyes. He had a lean stature and was covered in ink—way more ink than Gage.

Roy was hot and definitely something to look at as well, but from what I'd heard about him, he was soft spoken. He was comfortable with his band (by the way he was jumping and bumping fists with Gage, I could tell), but when it came to outsiders, he hardly said a thing. I don't think anyone had ever caught an interview with Roy Sykes. He was the mystery man of FireNine.

Gage and Roy boarded their tour bus, which I noticed had **FIRENINE** printed in a fierce orange on top of the black chrome. Ben cleared his throat obnoxiously from behind me, snapping me out of my daze. I turned around and his arms were folded across his chest, his eyes glued on me.

"What?" I asked, my cheeks sparking.

"Ellie, huh? He's given you a nickname... and you're blushing? How adorable."

I smirked and rolled my eyes. "I don't know why he calls me that."

He laughed. "You like it. Don't act like you don't."

"It's just a name, Ben. He's a cool guy."

"Yeah, whatever, sweetie. I've heard it all." He walked for the stairs and laughed as he stepped off the bus again. He yelled at a few of the crewmembers and told them to get everything in order, and I sighed, going for my room of the bus.

I slumped on the edge of the bed and it sank beneath my weight. How the hell was I actually going to survive the tour without being around Gage so much? I didn't know if I was going to be able to act like the careless chick—I mean, I didn't care much, but for some reason I knew I would start soon.

Gage was my high school crush. I'd fantasized about him since day one of seeing him. I always wondered what it would be like to date him… but then he got famous and that thought vanished. I knew it was never going to happen. I was sure he had his girls lined up and his picks ready. I didn't want to be one of those girls who did stupid things for a boy's attention, so I decided for the entire tour to just play it cool.

I decided to act like Eliza Smith. It's what I was best at anyway.

The next morning I woke up gasping and drenched in sweat. I shoved my blankets away, pushing myself up to lean my back against the headboard. The nightmare I had wasn't pleasant. All I could remember was a large, filthy hand gripping my neck, pinning me against the wall, and... someone cackling. A clatter from the kitchen startled me and I stepped out of bed, pushing the nightmare aside. I had to get over it. I had to be strong.

As I entered the kitchen, Ben, wearing a sky-blue robe, was humming over the stove with a spatula in hand. His hair was most likely wet and ridiculously wavy from a shower. I then realized I was still sweating. Perhaps it wasn't just my nightmare that left me that way.

"Good morning," I sighed.

He turned around, facing me quickly. Laughing, he watched me run the back of my hand over my sticky forehead before scrambling his eggs again. "We're in New Mexico, Liza," he said, chuckling. "The air-conditioning unit isn't running, but I'm having someone work on it as we speak."

"It's so hot." I reached for a loose sheet of paper on the counter and fanned myself, glad he thought I was flushed over the heat instead of my night terror.

"Well, how about you take a cold shower and I'll make you some eggs for breakfast? The boys have a show tonight, but we have to be there in two hours so they can practice and so the crew can make sure the setup is okay."

I nodded, turning around. "I'll be ready in a few minutes."

After taking an extremely cool shower, blow-drying my hair, and then stuffing my face with cheesy eggs, Ben and I were stepping off the bus to make our way to a pearly white Lincoln Navigator parked at the curb.

"That's what we're riding in?" I asked, stunned. I couldn't pull my eyes from the truck. It was sparkling all over and with the sun hovering above it, providing the truck a personal twinkle, it was pretty much in the limelight.

"Yes, Liza! Gotta make ourselves look just as extravagant." He winked over his shoulder, and I couldn't help but stare. I'd never been on a tour with Ben before so I didn't know what it was like to have a chauffeur or to even be taken to a show. I *did* know I was going to be backstage, up close and personal with the band.

Ben swung the door open and I climbed inside. He slid in after me, but a familiar voice called his name, causing my pulse to pick up. "Benny!" Gage yelled as Ben looked his way. Ben shut his door but rolled down his window with a heavy sigh.

"What is it, Gage?" Ben snapped impatiently. "We have to be there in thirty minutes and it's a twenty-five minute drive."

"Whoa now." Gage held up his hands innocently, smirking. "We'll get there in time. They have to wait for us regardless, right?"

Ben pressed his lips together, rolling his eyes at the statement.

"I just wanted to say good morning to you and your *beautiful* daughter Ellie."

My eyes stretched, heat bombarding my stomach. Ben glanced over his shoulder at me and I forced a smile before looking away and placing my sunglasses on the bridge of my nose. "You can flirt later." Ben rolled his eyes again. "Focus on the show tonight."

"Oh, we've got this shit in the bag!" Gage yelled, taking quick steps backward as I looked in his direction. Gage's attire was simple again. Chuck Taylor shoes, a white T-shirt with his band's name on it, and his hair? Still untamed and all over the place yet dangerously sexy.

With another exaggerated sigh, Ben rolled up his window and told the driver to go before we ended up late. He then looked at me and I smiled innocently, shaking my head. "He's... funny."

"And a handful, yes," Ben added.

I waited for Ben to strike up a conversation about Gage calling me *beautiful,* but he didn't. Instead, he pulled out his phone and called someone, asking them how the stage setup was going. He was ready to get to the arena and was too focused on work to be thinking about it. I doubt he put as much thought into it as I did, anyway. I don't know why, but I couldn't really stop myself from obsessing over his flirtatious tone. In my head, I'd always considered Gage Grendel the stunning one. The hot-ass guy with the sexy-ass body. There was no doubt he had everything a girl needed... except sympathy of the heart.

CONFIDENCE

The first show was amazing. Gage's vocal chords were like no other. He had a distinct voice that would let you know it was him from a mile away. It was undeniably beautiful. The way his lips parted and barely touched the microphone. The way he sang softly when the bass would drop. I just wanted to get wrapped up in it—tangled between his words. If I were someone who went through with her own thoughts, I would've dragged him off stage just to be alone with him. He sang with such grace it almost seemed unreal. He smiled behind the mic so much—so playfully—I couldn't help but smile with him. He was flirting with the crowd, blowing air kisses, grabbing hands of miscellaneous FireNine fangirls.

As soon as the boys performed their last set, they pushed through the curtain to get backstage. Roy Sykes and Montana Delray stepped back first. Montana was the bassists and had blond hair that was cut and gelled into a spiky mohawk. His right eyebrow and the right corner of his bottom lip were pierced with studs, and from what I'd heard, he was the showboat of them all. He craved the attention, knowing he could never get more than Gage did. In my perspective, Gage was hotter, but Montana was extremely close.

"We've got a live one back here already," Montana said, his eyes hard on me as he placed his red bass guitar against a crate. "I call dibs."

He winked at me, but I swallowed hard, keeping my chin up. Ben told me not to look weak in front of the boys, and I was following through with his advice. I hadn't been introduced to any of the boys except Gage. He repeated over and over how the boys loved to tease, and I had to suck it up and deal with it because they never held back.

Montana stepped toward me, his light-blue eyes lax and observing me in my skinny jeans and white blouse Ben and I bought during our shopping spree for the tour. "Can I get a name?" he asked, pierced eyebrow lifting.

"Eliza Smith."

"Eliza Smith," he repeated, grinning as he rolled my name off his tongue. "I like that. Cute."

I sighed and took a step back. Montana's eyes narrowed as he stared at me. "What brings you backstage? Which one of us were you hoping to run into?"

Just as he asked, Gage came stumbling back with Dedrick Parsley, aka Deed P., the drummer, along with a whopping of screaming and shouting from the overly excited FireNine fans. As soon as Gage caught sight of Montana near me, his head slanted. "What's up?" he asked, looking from me to Montana.

"I called dibs," Montana stated, smiling. "She's cute."

"I'm not a pick for tonight, Montana," I told him, lifting my hands and shrugging. "Sorry."

"You aren't? What are you, then?"

"I'm only back here because *my* dad is *your* manager."

Montana's eyes stretched and Gage chuckled, clapping Montana's shoulder. "Step off, Montana. Even if she were an after-party groupie, I'd be the one calling dibs. Not you."

"Oh, you think so?"

"Know so, buddy."

Montana snorted a laugh and then took a step back. "Let's hear it from Miss Eliza. If you were a groupie, who would you be waiting for right now?"

I hesitated as all eyes turned on me. Even Roy and Deed looked at me, waiting for an answer. I had to remain confident. I wanted to keep the teasing atmosphere going so I said, "Roy Sykes. I find him handsome and unique among you all."

Gage's eyes widened and Montana yelled, "Hilarious!" while chuckling.

Roy stared at me, his dark eyes wider than I'd ever seen them beneath his shaggy hair, and then he turned around, clutching his guitar a little too tightly, causing his knuckles to pale. My smile fell rapidly as he hurried for his dressing room and slammed the door shut behind him.

"She's funny as hell. I like her," Montana said, still laughing. "Don't mind Roy. It's been a while since he's had a girl. He's the weird one, if you haven't noticed already."

"Yeah." I forced a laugh, but I couldn't help but worry for Roy. I didn't think I said anything bad.

Montana turned around and trailed off to his dressing room. "Time to get ready for the real ladies, then!" he hollered right before slamming his door behind him.

Deed and Gage were still standing in front of me, and as Deed realized how awkward it was becoming, he ran a hand through his cropped, gelled black hair and turned around, his drumsticks still in hand. Deed was more slender than the other boys. I was sure he had a nice body as well; he just seemed a bit more boyish than the others.

"Yeah, so, I'm just gonna... go." He hesitated, switching glances between me and Gage. He then hurried down the hall and his door clicked shut behind him. Gage watched him disappear before chuckling and looking at me again.

"Did I say something wrong?" I asked.

"Like Montana said, Roy's the weird one. He doesn't like to deal with compliments... or girls." He laughed. "He likes to remain *ghostly*."

"Oh." I figured that was kind of impossible since he was the lead guitarist and all, but whatever.

"It's funny, though, Ellie." Gage sighed, taking a step toward me. "I thought you were going to pick me." He reached up, placing a finger on my chin, and as his skin connected with mine, my breath hitched. A zap of lightning struck my core, causing me to practically melt. I'd never known what it would be like for him to touch me, for his liquid eyes to only be on mine. It was a feeling I wanted to hang on to forever. He was so close I could smell his cologne—spicy, yet pleasing to the senses. Gage then tapped my chin twice, his eyes hard on me. "But since you're a bigger fan of Roy... well... all I can say is good luck with that." He winked, pulling his warm, slightly calloused fingers away. The fire that had ignited within me died down with each step he took.

His walk was dangerously sexy—his shoulders broad, hips swinging in a completely mannish way. He rounded a corner, disappearing out of sight, and I sighed, releasing the nervous air trapped in my lungs. He'd left me completely breathless with just the touch of his fingers. I didn't know how the hell he did it, but I wasn't going to deny the fact that I enjoyed it. I was just never going to let him know it. I didn't want him to figure out how he could have any control over me just by being near me.

"Liza!" Ben's voice called from behind me. I turned to find him marching toward me, a bright smile on his lips. "Don't be upset with me," he said, grinning as he stopped less than an inch from me, "but we've decided to rent a

VIP room at a club for the boys. I have some business to handle while we're in New Mexico so I won't be there, but I thought it'd be fun for you to hang with them for a while."

"Um, no." I shook my head, staring into Ben's eyes that would have been identical to mine if they were blue instead of warm chocolate-brown. "That's not happening. I think I'll just stay on the bus."

"Um, no," he mimicked, "you're not. That's not what you came on this tour for and it won't be an option tonight. You came to live it up a little, am I correct? To have fun?"

"Yeah, but you know I don't do clubs, Ben." Plus, knowing Gage was going to be there was bothering me already. I couldn't be at a club while he was around. I didn't want to find out what else he could do with those hands.

"Well, tonight will be a first night for everything. I bought you a nice dress and it's in my dressing room. I have the keys to the tour bus, and I ordered our driver to take you straight to the club no matter how much you beg him to take you to the bus. A pretty big tip came in handy." Ben winked, but I gave him the evil eye.

"You're serious?"

"As a heart attack, sweetie. Have some fun tonight." He squeezed my shoulders, his eyes sympathetic. "You can legally drink now so I guess I can't tell my baby girl to stay out of trouble anymore." He pulled away, checking his watch before stepping backward and spinning around. "I have to get going, but you know where the truck is. Don't get too crazy, and if you need anything, call me!" he called, winking over his shoulder.

I watched Ben walk down the hall and slip out the exit door. I couldn't believe him. He was forcing me to stay out. Clubbing and partying was never my thing. I just couldn't get down with the drinking and the jumping around. Seeing it on TV had always given me a headache.

I couldn't understand why he wanted me to get out so badly and I wouldn't have minded so much if I weren't going to be in a VIP section full of guys—a fucking rock band! A band with Gage Grendel as the lead singer. I could only put up with his flirting for so long. My confidence levels weren't high enough for me to endure it for an entire night.

I was definitely shit out of luck with this club situation.

DUO DANCE

I couldn't have felt more embarrassed.

Even my driver was stunned by what I wore. Going from a blouse and skinny jeans to a skintight silver halter-top dress that stopped mid-thigh and revealed all legs was obviously shocking to him—hell, it was shocking to me! It was complete chagrin.

I wanted so badly to hide out in the dressing room. If the lights weren't shut off and I wasn't told the arena would be closing in ten minutes, I'd probably still be there. Had I not been chicken-shit and afraid of how dark and quiet it had become, I still would have stayed. But I swear I heard chains rattling at one point. I had to get out of the dressing room before a murderer showed up and strangled me. I guess the club was a better and safer place than a possible murder scene... maybe.

Tugging my dress down with one hand while gripping the door handle of the truck with the other, I sighed and breathed roughly through my nostrils. I wasn't sure what was in store, but by the bass of the music and the long line of people waiting outside the door, I knew to expect what I'd always seen on TV and in movies... maybe worse.

"What time should I come back?" Marco, my chauffeur, asked before I could shut the door. His eyes scanned my backside and I scowled at him as he met my gaze.

"Don't," I muttered, slamming the door in his face. I had never worn anything this revealing in my life. I would have chosen my T-shirts and loose jeans any day over this display of skin.

The music boomed as I trudged forward in my six-inch heels. I finally figured out my dress wasn't going to reveal my ass, so I stopped tugging on it as I carried myself across the pavement. I told the bouncer at the door who I was and who I was with, and after he checked his clipboard and nodded his head, I was inside the club.

Rave lights danced across the night scene. A few women wore glowing necklaces and held sloshing drinks in their hands. The music was loud and catchy—something I would most likely listen to during one of my fast-paced painting days. It wasn't so bad... at least not yet.

I spotted Montana standing at the bar and rushed in his direction. It was a battle getting myself through the crowd. People were everywhere, grooving, shimmying, and gyrating. It boggled my mind that anyone could move so much at such a fast pace. Montana was leaning over the counter as I got closer. A female bartender giggled in front of him as she handed him a beer. He tucked a tip into her cleavage and she licked her lips, grinning and winking before he turned around.

"Montana!" I yelled after him before he could get away. He glanced over his shoulder, his eyes narrowing until he caught sight of me. He paused in his tracks, scanning me with his eyes from head to toe, making me more and more self-conscious.

"Hi," I breathed out as I met up with him.

"Hot damn, Eliza. Look at you," he said, still drinking me in.

I fidgeted before him but kept my chin up. "I'm looking for the VIP section. Just got here and would love to sit down. My feet are killing me."

He laughed, looking down at my heels. "I bet. Come on." Draping an arm across my shoulders, he turned around and made his way through the crowd.

"Oh my God, it's Montana Delray!" a girl squealed to her friend. I looked up and Montana winked, but he didn't stop to speak.

"This must make you feel important," I said over the music.

"Nah." He shrugged as we neared double glass doors. "It's not as exciting as it used to be."

I nodded as if I understood, and he grabbed the silver handle of the door to swing it open. The VIP room was nice. There were white leather couches against the wall, a table already set up with drinks in the middle, and the same music from the dance floor flowed out separate speakers.

"Welcome to the VIP room," Montana said. He grabbed the door handle again and stepped back out. "Help yourself to the drinks. I've got some fun to have."

I watched him walk away and then turned to look ahead. No one was inside except Deed P. and a girl sitting on his lap. I don't know why I worried about Gage's whereabouts, but I was hoping to actually see him—just to admire him from a distance.

The music grew louder from behind me as I took a step forward. A soft breeze brushed across my bare legs and a warm hand pressed against the small of my back, and that's when I figured out why it had gotten so loud.

Gage Grendel was stepping into the VIP room, his hazel eyes mellow and a warm smirk on his lips. His hair seemed sort of different and I couldn't figure out why. It was hotter—still messy, but hotter. As the door shut behind him, his lips stretched even more. "What brings you here? You don't seem like the kind of girl who likes to get down and party," Gage said, his eyes slightly confused.

I sighed. "I... uh... yeah... this isn't what I was up for tonight." He narrowed his eyes at me, obviously in need of a better response. "Ben forced me to come out," I explained. "I'm not really a party person."

"Well, maybe we can change that for tonight."

"How?"

"We can start with a drink," he said, lifting his hand and gesturing to the table. "We have beer, margaritas… or if you like the hard stuff, some whiskey, tequila, and vodka."

My lips pressed into a line. "I don't drink."

"Damn. Sucks. You should definitely make an exception." He leaned forward, his teeth glistening from the dim lighting above. His cologne filled my lungs and was even more alluring than before. He had on a completely different outfit from earlier—a horizontally striped blue-and-white muscle T-shirt, dark-blue jeans that weren't too skinny, and his usual black-and-white Chuck Taylor's on his feet.

I took a step back, realizing how close he was, and then looked at the table. I never drank before, but maybe Ben was right. I wanted to have fun while on the tour and try new things. Why not let loose a little with someone like Gage Grendel? I knew I would never go too far with him, so I simply nodded and faced him.

"What would you have?" I asked.

With a grin, he pressed his hand against the small of my back and my skin tingled beneath the warmth. The hairs on my back pricked and my skin crawled in the most delightful way. He led the way toward the table and grabbed a shot glass of clear liquid.

"It's not about me," he said. "For you, I suggest a shot of vodka." He handed the glass to me and I took it. "That is, if you're really looking for fun." Gage then grabbed another shot glass for himself and a part of me was relieved because I didn't want to drink alone. "Let's see. What should we make a toast to?" he asked.

"Um... for a rockin' tour?" I asked, slightly wincing at how corny I sounded.

"That could work," he said, nodding as his lips pressed to form a smile. "We could also give it up to getting acquainted, becoming great friends, and for two months full of diehard fun?"

I giggled as his eyes softened. Who knew Gage could be just as charming as he is sexy? "That sounds great."

"All right, to a rockin' tour... and all that other shit I said before." He smiled, we clinked glasses, and then I swallowed it down, and right after I pulled the shot glass from my lips, my throat burned. I was desperate to get something to cool it down with. With wide eyes, I looked from Gage to the table and picked up the tall glass of water on the edge. I took huge swallows while Gage and Deed laughed.

"You've got an amateur on your hands!" Deed yelled, still chuckling. "Sure about this one, Gage?"

I ignored Deed's comment, licking my lips and turning to face Gage, who was already looking at me. "Why is it so strong?" I gasped.

He laughed. "How else will you feel it?"

I shrugged, placing my shot glass down. As I looked up, Gage was still watching me, his head cocked to the side. His eyes were lax as he surveyed me from head to toe. "Have you ever danced before?" he asked, licking his lips.

As I fixed my mouth to tell him no, someone pulled open the glass door of the VIP room and stepped in. Her legs were the first thing I took in—long, tanned, glossy, toned... way better looking than my pale limbs could have ever been. Her red dress fit to every curve of her body. Glossy red lipstick was on her full lips and her hair was a deep brown, curly, and styled nicely against her shoulders. Her heels were a fierce red with a black tip. She put me to shame as she stepped forward with a warm smirk on her lips. I was even more humiliated as she hooked her arm around Gage's waist and he looked down at her.

Something seemed to crack inside me then. I didn't like how she'd come out of nowhere and put her hands all over him. It was rude, especially while we were talking. I should have expected it from the lead singer of a band, but when he didn't pull away—when he smiled back at her—I backed off and took a step away, grabbing another shot glass.

"Who's your friend?" the girl asked. Great, even her voice sounded like harmonious bells.

"This," Gage said, pulling the girl in tighter, "is Ellie."

"Eliza," I corrected.

Gage's eyes broadened. "Eliza," he whispered. "Smith."

"Oh. Nice to meet you, Eliza," the girl said. "I'm Penelope Binds, Gage's girlfriend."

Girlfriend? If it were possible for the DJ to feel my emotions, the music would have scratched to a stop in the background.

"Nice to meet you," I murmured, reaching a hand out to her. I couldn't be immature. I didn't even know why I expected Gage to be single. He was hot; of course there was going to be someone glued to his hip.

"Gage, I wanna dance," Penelope whined, poking out her bottom lip. I rolled my eyes and turned around. It was worse than I thought.

"Let's go, then. Oh, and Ellie," Gage called. I turned slowly, my eyebrows elevated. "Have fun tonight." He winked, taking Penelope's hand in his. My eyes followed them as they pushed out the glass door and disappeared within the crowd. A few girls squealed at the sight of Gage, but security guards stepped in the way, making sure they didn't get too close to him.

I sighed deeply because that just made my night even worse. Staring down at the shot of vodka in my hand, I finally decided to down it and grab another. I didn't drink, but I wanted to have fun. I wanted to forget about what I'd just seen. My mom always told me drinking gets rid of the problems, but she was part of the reason I never wanted to touch alcohol in my life. Ben would offer wine, but I never took it. This was the night to be different, though. I had to find out if what my mom always said was true, even though she was a terrible influence.

I looked at the door and in came Roy Sykes. He'd changed into a black button-up shirt with the sleeves rolled up, revealing the stretch of ink on his masculine arms and hands. His shaggy hair hung in his dark-brown eyes, and his jeans were black as well. His arms were just as pale as mine and covered with ink, but it fit Roy. He was really hot… just weird as hell.

As he spotted me, he came to a screeching halt, gripping the door handle a little too firmly, his knuckles turning pale. His eyes stretched and then he took a step back. He took a few more steps back and I stared at him, completely lost. What was he so afraid of? Was he still upset about earlier?

Roy finally turned around and dashed away. The door shut behind him, but I could still see him making a beeline through the bodies.

"Maybe you should go out on the dance floor," Deed said. His smile seemed kind of eerie, but I blamed it on the dim lighting above him. "It would make your night. Trust me."

"And how do you know this?" I asked, giving him a small smile.

He chuckled. "Because dancing frees the soul, girl. It sets you loose. Makes you do things you never thought you could do." He placed his hand against the small of the girl's back and whispered something into her ear. She poked her bottom lip out but nodded, standing from his lap. As she walked by, she grimaced at me. She then opened the door and sauntered out and Deed came up to me. "Would you like me to dance with you?"

"No—Deed, that's sweet of you, but I've never danced before and—"

"Eliza, is it?" he asked, cutting me off midsentence as he reached for another shot glass.

I nodded, pulling my bottom lip in to bite on it. He handed me the glass and I took it. He then grabbed a glass for himself.

"Ben sent you out here to have fun. Dancing is fun. I'll dance with you. It'll be like no one else is watching. I've got moves! Ask the boys who the best dancer is." He did a three-sixty spin, the liquid within his shot glass still inside, and I bit on a smile as he held out his hands. "The groove isn't just in my hands. It's everywhere."

I shook my head, but I couldn't hide my smile any longer. I glanced over my shoulder at the people dancing wildly. The lights had dimmed, making it hard to see anything. "Okay." I nodded. I chucked back my drink and he did the same. "Let's go for it," I said as we discarded our glasses.

With another eerie grin (*What's up with this lighting?*), Deed grabbed my hand and led the way. The music had grown ten times louder as we stepped out. A few large men in black T-shirts looked at Deed and he nodded at them before stepping toward the dance floor.

His grip was still tight around my hand as he pushed through the crowd. The music wasn't too fast, just a medium pace. The dub-step bass was thundering against the soles of my heels and soon I became lightheaded. I felt good—like an Eliza I'd never been before.

Deed finally stopped and faced me. He released my hand but turned me around to get my hips between his. It surprised me and I wanted to pull away, but I didn't. Warm fingers touched my waist and soon we began to rock. I was stunned I was actually going through with it. Deed had game—I could give him that—because he brought me out on the dance floor with no problem and had me dancing against him. This was new.

"Just go with the music, *Eliza*," he whispered in my ear. For some reason I shivered, but I didn't stop dancing against him. My movements were slow and seductive. I never thought I had it in me, but it felt nice.

Thrilling.

I shut my eyes and Deed's hands moved from my waist to my stomach. He was inching closer and closer to my breasts. It was unusual to have anyone this close. I never allowed anyone to get this close to my private areas... but I wasn't stopping Deed. His hands against me felt good. His body glued to my backside was only enticing me to bury my hips deeper against his groin, causing him to growl pleasantly.

"Deed, what the fuck?" an aggravated voice called over the music. My eyelids fluttered open, knowing exactly whom the bedroom voice belonged to. My gaze drifted up to Gage who was looking at us, his hazel eyes harder than normal. "Having fun?" he asked me, his head tilted.

"Yeah, I am, actually," I said.

Deed pulled away, chuckling as he stepped to my side and slung an arm tightly across my shoulders. I winced from his aggressiveness and he eased up a tad. "Ellie and I are just having some fun, Gage. Don't be a cock-blocker."

Gage sighed. "Don't call her Ellie, Deed. You didn't come up with that."

"But you were right," Deed said, smirking. "It fits her more."

Gage's jaw locked, but as he met my lost gaze, it slacked. "I think I'll be stealing her away from you now."

For a moment, Deed's expression was sour. His eyes locked with Gage's and I thought I caught rage, but then he pulled away from me and clapped Gage's shoulder loudly—a little too forcefully—and slipped through the crowd. I narrowed my eyes at the two, finding the whole encounter a bit off. Was Deed upset about Gage's interference?

Gage watched him walk off and then looked at me, moving in closer and grabbing my hand. As he spun me around, I swear I saw a smile spread across his lips. My back was facing his chest, his fingers curling around mine as he held me at my middle.

"You're a true lightweight," he murmured in my ear. I bit my bottom lip as he rocked his groin against me. His fingers pulled away from mine to move down my waist before hooking around my middle again. "Benny told me to watch over you tonight. I wasn't supposed to tell you I'm your undercover babysitter, but Deed... He isn't the kind of person you wanna get involved with. He carries more weight than you could probably handle."

"Oh." It was all I could manage. I was drowning in Gage's touch.

"I think I'd be better at dancing against you tonight anyway," Gage whispered in my ear. My skin pricked, the hair on my back rising. I could feel his erection caving into my back. His teeth grazed my earlobe and I shuddered, delighted.

"Why are you flirting and dancing with me when you have Penelope?" I panted.

He remained quiet, but he didn't stop working his hips. His fingers inched up and I sighed, allowing the back of my head to fall against his shoulder. He was getting closer to my breasts, just like Deed, but with Gage I could actually *feel* it. The heat of his fingers was so intense through my dress that I could have melted into a puddle. Instead of touching my breasts, though, he skipped over them to pull my hair away from my shoulders, his lips hovering over my neck, his warm breath tickling the skin. I caught goose bumps from his sweet, seductive actions. Damn it, he was too good.

He was getting harder and harder below, caving into my back, my hips. Was I really doing this to his body? He was getting turned on by me. I could tell by the way he was grunting and trying to keep his composure. He was trying his hardest not to touch me in my delicate places.

"Penelope's gone," he finally murmured.

"So you come to me when she can't see you." That caused my eyes to open and I spun around to face him. Gage was baffled but still smiling.

"I'm only taking care of you, Ellie," he said, a smirk curling at his lips.

"I'm twenty-one. I don't need a babysitter, Gage."

"In here you do." He looked around and I looked with him. I noticed then a few men licking their lips and staring straight at my ass. *Fucking hounds.* My glare twisted into disgust as I pushed past Gage. I wasn't about to be an easy fix for anyone.

I wanted to call Ben and tell him to get me a driver so I could leave. Drinking was obviously a mistake. If the buses weren't so far away, I would have walked to them. Unfortunately, I was stuck at this dumbass club with alcohol in my system. I wasn't feeling myself and it was good and bad. Good because I finally got to dance and feel sort of free, but bad because it made me go through with things I wouldn't do if I were sober.

I grabbed the handle of the door and went for one of the couches. As I dropped onto the cushion, Gage came strolling in. With each step he took, my heart banged against my chest. His liquid-hazel eyes never left mine.

He sighed, slouching down beside me. "I must have upset you."

"I'm fine." I inched away from him. He was too close.

"I thought you didn't do the party and club thing?" I looked at him and his eyebrow had elevated.

"I don't."

"But you were dancing against Deed like a pro. That's saying a little something."

"Trust me, that's new to me. I'm sure it won't happen again."

"It can happen," Gage said, sliding in closer. "Just not with Deed—or anyone like him."

"So you're telling me what to do now?"

"No."

I stilled as he slid in even closer. I couldn't understand Gage. He was flirting with me, dancing with me, but he had a girlfriend. A *hot* girlfriend. "Well, then I can dance with whomever I like."

"Did you enjoy dancing with me, Ellie?" he murmured. He touched my thigh and it was like a zap to my emotions—snapping me out of my stubbornness. Being next to him was making my stomach coil and my legs lock with pleasure. My nipples were tightening beneath my silky bra, causing less space for my breasts to breathe. *Goodness, how is he doing this to me?*

"The question is did *you* enjoy it?" I challenged.

He chuckled, pulling his hand away to rest his arm on top of the couch. He was still close; his chest was almost touching my side-boob. Yeah... pretty close.

"I know you felt that. I enjoyed it more than you think."

I burst into a laugh. "Why?"

"Did I not mention before that I find you hot? Sexy? Getting a dance from you was one of the many things I wanted from my 'what I'd like from Ellie' list."

"You have a list? What are the others?" I tempted. After I asked, I wasn't so sure I wanted the answer, but it was the alcohol speaking. The blabbering mouth belonged to the Eliza who had vodka coursing through her veins.

"I'm sure if I were to mention the others, we wouldn't be sitting here right now. In fact, a bed and handcuffs would most likely be involved."

"Handcuffs?" I laughed and he shook his head.

"You find that humorous?"

"Very."

"Don't tempt me, Ellie. All I need is your word and those handcuffs will be put to use one day." He reached a hand up to tuck a lock of hair behind my ear. His other hand came down to run across my thigh. "All I need is for you to say yes, and I swear you won't forget how good I made you feel."

His fingers slipped between my legs. I tensed, the feeling unusual, but I didn't push him away like I should have. He was extremely close to my womanhood—closer than anyone else had ever been, yet I didn't feel bothered by it.

As I bit my bottom lip, Gage leaned forward and his hot breath trickled across my shoulders. I kept my gaze down, and he brought his free hand up to tilt my chin. We stared into one another's eyes, and right then I wanted to jump on top of him and have him carry me to a damn bedroom, with handcuffs, for all I cared.

"The only thing is..." he whispered against my lips. They were close. Extremely close. What would it be like to place my lips against his? Would it live up to my expectations? I was sure it would. I'd imagined those lips against mine for a long time. "...I'm not sure if a *virgin* would be able to handle me."

I finally blinked and he pulled his hand away. The moisture had built up within my panties and I didn't even realize it. I was getting turned on *for* and *by* Gage. "How do you know I'm a virgin?" I asked quickly, putting all hormones aside.

"It's obvious. You don't drink. You've never danced on a dance floor before tonight. Signs of a virgin right there."

"I could just be an undercover freak. I could've been lying just to get you stick around."

He bellowed with laughter and I couldn't help but laugh myself. I couldn't believe I said that. "You're funny, Ellie. Adorable. It's part of the reason I shouldn't mess around with you too much."

My eyes narrowed. "Why shouldn't you?"

He tilted his head, his lips sealed. The glass door opened and in came Montana and Roy. Roy stared at me longer than expected and then frowned. "Gage, you're missing it. Chicks are revealing tits and shit out there, man!" Montana yelled, reaching for a glass of Jack Daniels. Roy grabbed a glass of water, which I found kind of odd.

Montana downed his drink and as he slammed down his glass, his face pinched a little. "Good shit." He sighed. "Come on, Gage. I need a wingman. Roy's acting all bummed out and shit."

Gage looked from Montana, who was making his way toward the door, to me again. "You'll be okay in here, right?"

I wanted to shake my head. I didn't want him to leave me alone with Roy, but just as Roy came to mind, he placed his glass down and stepped past Montana to get out of the VIP room. "Uh, yeah," I said quickly. I couldn't stop someone like Gage from doing what he normally did. I couldn't even understand why he was asking if I was going to be okay. It's not like he cared. "I think I'm just going to call Ben and tell him to call a ride for me or something. I'm kinda tired."

Standing, Gage nodded and walked backward toward the door. "Great idea."

"Come on, Gage! The ladies are getting antsy!"

With a wink at me, Gage turned around quickly and dashed out the door. I didn't blink until he was completely out of sight. Sighing, I stood and took my phone out of my bra, dialed Ben's number, and told him I was ready to go.

My ride arrived ten minutes later.

As I stepped out of the VIP room to get to the exit, I saw Montana and Gage on the middle of the dance floor with two girls who had to be drunk out of their minds dancing all up on them. The girl dancing with Gage turned around and, out of nowhere, kissed him a little too fiercely. I frowned as he hooked his arm around her waist and pulled her in closer. I was certain he didn't even know the girl, but he was kissing her back? What about Penelope? Was he really that disrespectful? I expected it from someone like Montana since he was single and had a careless demeanor about everything, but Gage? I guess I should have known.

The girl pulled away, giggling, and he laughed as he turned her around to start dancing with her again, smacking her ass a few times before bending her over to see more of her backside than anything else. Gage looked up and caught my eye as I tried to get through the crowd. I couldn't figure out why the hell I couldn't look away. My feet were moving, but my eyes were glued on him. His gaze softened as he watched me for a few moments until finally he winked and I scowled at him, rushing for the door.

S. Q. WILLIAMS

I was truly disgusted by what I saw, but I shouldn't have expected anything less from someone like him—someone who made girls feel like they had no value. I was more than certain that in the morning he would dismiss the girl he was dancing with and make her feel like shit. If I thought whatever was brewing between us in the VIP room was real, I had to slap myself, because it was just him running his game and trying to win me over. He was aiming to score my panties and I admit he was fairly close. Had Montana and Roy not come into the room, I would have most likely given in, virgin or not.

I couldn't have been more relieved we were interrupted.

WORDS

Ben said we were supposed to be hitting the road in a few minutes the next morning, but those minutes transitioned to an hour. During that time, I decided to get some sketching in. The sketching was different that day. It wasn't the normal flower nearby or even a perfect drawing of my hand. It was a face... Gage's face. I wasn't sure why I drew him. Maybe it was because he haunted my dreams the night before. He kept popping up and I wanted so badly to wake up just to get rid of the thoughts of him.

After what I'd seen last night, I knew I had to stay away from Gage. It was going to be kind of hard to do since I was on the same tour as him and had to go backstage, but I could avoid it for a while. I didn't have to attend every single show.

A knock came from my door and soon Ben stepped in. There was never a day he wasn't dressed to impress—tan khakis and a button-up green shirt with the sleeves rolled up to his elbows for a more casual look. His platinum hair was still parted in the middle but was wavier than the norm.

"Glad you're up, button bottom," he sighed. There's been a minor problem with one of the buses."

"What happened?"

"Well... it's the FireNine tour bus. Something's wrong with the engine—it's why we're running late," he said, checking his watch. "The boys will have to stay on our bus until Saturday afternoon, when the new FireNine bus arrives in Florida."

My eyes stretched as I shook my head. "No—no, Ben, they *cannot* be on here with us."

"It's only temporary," he said, running a hand through his hair. "I knew you'd react this way."

"Of course I'm going to react like this. That's a whole two days, Ben. I'm the only girl on this bus and those boys are—" I shook my head. There was no need to explain myself. The band was a load of animals. "I *can't* be around them."

"Why are you so upset? The boys told me they loved you last night."

"I... just can't be around them that long. I need my space."

Ben frowned, looking me over. I clutched my sketchbook, hoping he wouldn't realize why I was getting so upset. I wanted to keep my distance from Grendel. I didn't want him anywhere near me after what happened the night before. It was too close and God only knew what would happen while he was on the same bus with me.

"Eliza, don't worry. I'll be here, sweetie. I won't let them get too crazy." Someone called Ben's name from the front door of the bus and he turned around. "We'll talk later, Liza," he yelled over his shoulder.

I stood hastily, dropping my sketchbook on the bed and rushing out to see what was going on. Through the window, I saw the hood of the FireNine tour bus open and a few men looking beneath it. Some were scratching their heads and some were bent over working on it.

The door of the FireNine bus was wide open and the first one to step out with two suitcases in hand was Montana, stretching while yawning. After him it was Deed and then came Roy. Gage came out last with two black suitcases in hand and Ben met up with them, flagging his arms and pointing at our bus.

My heart sank as Ben stepped aside, allowing them to make their way toward our bus. I could feel my cheeks draining of color and my fingers getting cold. Gage had on a pair of sunglasses and tight black jeans. He had bedhead, which looked unbelievably hot on him. How the hell was I supposed to wake up without getting turned on at first sight of him?

The boys got closer and I rushed for my room. I slammed the door behind me and sank onto my bed, listening hard as the boys' heavy footsteps echoed and their weight caused the bus to shake.

"This shit is sweet!" Montana yelled after releasing a low whistle.

Footsteps went past my door and my heart thudded. "I know Ellie's in one of these rooms," Gage mumbled. I froze, listening as the boys went back and forth past my door to most likely find a bunk or a room they could claim as their own for the next two days.

My doorknob jiggled and I leaped up. *Damn it! Why the hell didn't I remember to lock it?* A few thoughts came to mind. One was to rush for the door and knock it closed with my shoulder while locking it. The other was to just let them walk in and then tell them to get the hell out. The last option would have most likely worked best.

The door creaked open and in came Gage. He still wore his aviator sunglasses and up close he looked even better. A smile hinted at his pink lips as he spotted me standing in front of the window. Slowly, he removed his sunglasses from his eyes, the hazel pools drinking me in even more. "Don't you look lovely," he said, smirking.

I frowned, reaching for my sketchbook to flip it over. I didn't want him to see it was *his* face that had been running through my mind all night and day. I sat on the bed, crossed my legs, and then scribbled on a loose sheet of paper. "This room's off limits, Gage."

"I don't know." I looked up and he was still smiling. "I kind of like it in here. We might have to become roommates... Maybe share the bed?" His eyebrows wiggled.

"Not likely."

"Let me guess." He placed his suitcase down outside my room and folded his arms over his broad chest. The ink on his arms stretched as he took a step forward. I almost made out a female's name near his elbow, but he turned slightly and I couldn't see it as clearly. "You're upset I left you alone last night."

"I don't really care," I lied, sitting up against the headboard. "I was kind of ready to go home anyway."

"If I stayed in the VIP room with you, would you have stayed a little longer?"

I frowned. "Gage, please get out. I'm kind of busy."

I didn't dare look up from my sketchbook after looking down. I didn't want to look into his eyes because looking into them was setting myself up.

"Ellie," Gage murmured, taking another step forward. He sat on the edge of my bed and placed his hand on top of mine, stroking the flesh around my knuckles. "Are you mad?"

"No."

"Why aren't you looking at me?"

"You're not really much to look at." That was a huge lie. Gage was all that and a bag of chips... however that saying went. His beauty stunned me sometimes. I could never figure out how someone could be so flawless and gorgeous yet so cocky and rude.

Gage laughed, and I looked up. He was closer than I expected. It would only take a few inches for our lips to touch so I leaned back. He slid in closer, gripped my hand, and a nervous spell took over me. I stared into his eyes framed with thick eyelashes. His lips were so full, the barely-there stubble surrounding them giving even more definition.

"Gage!" someone yelled.

Deed came rushing around the corner and stepped into my room. "Montana and Roy stole the extra bedrooms. Looks like we're bunking it in the hall." Deed looked at me and his head tilted. "Good morning, Eliza."

"Morning, Deed," I murmured. I still couldn't believe myself for dancing with him at the club. With Deed P. *and* Gage Grendel. It could have been any girl's dream. Unfortunately, it wasn't mine.

"Bunk it is," Gage sighed. "Unless Ellie here gets lonely and needs someone to cuddle with."

I pulled my hand away from his, shaking my head. "I'll be fine."

Gage and Deed laughed and then Gage stood from the bed. Deed walked out of the room, but Gage stayed in front of me, his sunglasses dangling between his fingers. "I like you, Ellie. You send me a vibe that's both good and bad."

"What's that supposed to mean?"

"The good I saw last night when you were dancing all over me and right after, allowing me to touch you." He bent down, getting on eyelevel with me, his palms on his knees. Blood rushed to my pale cheeks, but I remained bold, keeping my gaze connected with his. His cologne smelled stale, like an overnight mist, but it was still strong. We were so close that his nose was almost touching mine. "The bad... Well, I just feel like you don't like me very much. I've been trying to be as friendly as possible... with some minor flirting. Flirting doesn't hurt."

"We can be friends," I said.

"That's all?"

"That's all."

His lips pressed together to smile and then he stood up straight. "All right, Ellie. Friends it is, then." Gage turned for the door and the heaviness between us evaporated, allowing me to breathe again. "Just know, Eliza, that if you'd like to add something a little extra to this little friendship, I'd be more than willing. It won't be a problem." He winked, then disappeared around the corner. I hopped from the bed in a snap to shut the door. I had to control my nerves, but he was getting under my skin. Damn him and his beauty.

I knew the next two days were most likely going to be hell for me.

It wasn't so bad after a while since none of the guys bothered me again—although they were kind of loud. I'd sketched all day until my stomach started growling, begging me to feed it. I couldn't believe my circumstances. I was starving myself just so I wouldn't have to face the band. I knew there was going to come a time when I had to go out, so I figured it was best to get it over with. I had to woman up. Being the only girl on the bus meant I had to start acting like I had some sort of confidence and self-control. My self-esteem wasn't too high, but I knew how to handle myself to make it seem like it.

With a sigh, I gripped the doorknob as the boys yelled over whatever videogame they were playing. "All right, Eliza. Get a grip," I muttered to myself.

I felt kind of stupid for changing into yoga pants and a tank top. Ben bought the comfortable outfit for me a while back, and I actually loved it. Plus, it made me look somewhat decent without seeming like I was trying too hard to look nice in front of them. My hair was up in a sloppy bun and I had bedroom shoes on my feet. I wasn't trying too hard... at least I hoped not.

After I pulled open the door, I carried myself down the hallway. Beer and alcohol floated in the atmosphere, along with the stench of must and something else foul. I couldn't figure out what the extra odor was—that is until I rounded the corner and saw Montana with joint papers in his hand and grassy-looking stuff on the table in front of him. It got stronger as I got closer.

"What the hell is that?" I asked, frowning.

"Something to make me feel good," Montana said without looking at me. "Wanna join?" I shook my head as he licked one of his joint papers and then sprinkled the grassy stuff onto it. And I knew exactly what it was as he rolled it. It had so many names, and my mom smoked it constantly, so how could I not know?

Mary Jane

Weed.

Green.

Bud.

Marijuana.

Ben stepped from behind me and I scowled at him as he walked into the kitchen.

"Is this really what they do?" I hissed at him.

"Mainly Montana." Ben sighed. "Can't stop them. They're grown men, Liza. I already feel terrible about their bus since I was supposed to be the one to make sure everything was in order."

I ignored him and went for one of the cabinets to pull out a box of cereal. I leaned into the fridge and grabbed the milk, but then a throat cleared behind me, causing me to spin around quickly. I was expecting Ben, but he was walking down the hallway toward his bedroom again. Instead, as I turned, I met Gage's hazel eyes, taking in the smirk on his lips. A beer bottle was in his right hand and he'd changed into cleaner clothes—a white T-shirt and black sweat pants, to be exact.

"You know Lucky Charms is my favorite cereal?" he asked.

"No." I shook my head. "Didn't know that."

"Mind if I join you? Kinda hungry." He rubbed his stomach, smirking.

I pressed my lips together and looked toward the table. A few CDs and headphones were lying on top, but besides that, it seemed pretty clean. I grabbed two bowls from the cabinet, two spoons, and followed Gage to the table seats made like restaurant benches.

Pouring the cereal and milk would have been awkward had Deed and Roy not been yelling over their videogame. I handed Gage the box of cereal but noticed his eyes were on me. Watching me. Studying me. I refused to question his stare, although I was curious. I dug into my cereal and Gage cleared his throat, pouring his milk.

"So how has your day been so far, Ellie?" he asked.

"Great, Gage. And yours?"

"Oh, it would have been great if I didn't wake up with a hangover."

I shrugged as he placed down the milk. "Happens when you stay out late with a bunch of groupies."

He chuckled and I looked at him through my eyelashes. "You and Benny have the same sarcasm. You're almost like twins."

I laughed because it was true. I took another bite of cereal, looking at Montana, who was blowing puffs of thick, heavy smoke through his nostrils and lips, his arm resting on the back of the sofa. The smell was drifting our way and I tried my hardest not to gag. It was a strong, dank smell. I was sure the stench was going to linger, even when the boys were gone.

"You were drawing earlier?" Gage questioned, bringing my eyes back to him. "Is it something you enjoy doing a lot?"

I nodded. "It's a passion of mine. Just like singing is for you."

He raised an eyebrow, head nodding. "I can understand that."

"What makes you love singing so much, anyway?" I asked. I was beyond curious. I knew every singer had a reason behind his or her passion. Gage sang so powerfully that it seemed like he blacked out, got lost. His voice was beautiful and carefree. The deepness of it always made my legs quake and my belly roll.

He finished his cereal quickly, drinking his milk before dropping his spoon into his bowl. "I grew up singing with my sister," he said. "She was eleven years older than me, but whenever I heard her singing in front of a mirror or even in the shower, I sort of fell in love with singing in general. She had a voice—a beautiful one. I remember when I was five years old and she'd sing me to sleep." He chuckled, running a hand through his hair. His face then grew pained, as if he were reliving memories, and I grew even more curious about his past. As he brought his hand down, I caught the name tattooed near his elbow, in between the hues of green, red, and blue. *Kristina*.

"There's just something about music and singing that takes me away. It takes me to depths so deep I don't even realize how far I've gone until I'm done. Unlike them, where they can release it with their hands," he said, pointing at the boys with his thumb, "I can feel it coming *out of me*. All I've had stored within me from years before is released and… it's, like… I don't have to worry anymore, you know? It's, like… when I sing, there are no doubts. No problems. It has to be when I'm at my most peaceful— when I really just don't give a shit and can actually let it all go."

I stared, wide-eyed, as Gage looked me straight in the eyes. His response had caught me completely off guard, leaving me unsure of how to respond to him. It was deep—something I thought Grendel could never be.

"Sorry," he said, his chuckle nearly dry. "I made myself sound like a damn idiot—"

"No." I shook my head as he ran another nervous hand through his hair and lowered his gaze. "No. That was beautiful, Gage. Who would've known you had such a way with words?"

"Who do you think writes the songs?" He smirked. "Roy helps out, but most of the lyrics come from me."

"I just… wow." I laughed as I shook my head. I was speechless.

"Did you think I was that much of a dick?"

I giggled. "Well… yeah."

"Nah." He inhaled deeply, leaning back. "I don't think I'm that bad. Just have to get to know me. I'm sure you're the same way."

My head tilted, eyes narrowed. "What do you mean?"

"I know there's more to you. You seem like the kind of girl who's careful of not getting too close—the kind of girl who's always cautious. You'll take risks, but only when you're left with no other choice. Behind those eyes I see a girl who would love to let it all go and be herself for a change."

"I am myself," I argued. A part of me became afraid because he was sort of right. I was trying so hard to be casual, but to Gage I was probably transparent—especially since I retorted so quickly.

"You're yourself when you wanna be," he said matter-of-factly. "Last night showed me a little bit about you. I look at people in a different perspective. I saw you differently. Shy with a smart-ass mouth. Reserved, but you know exactly how to cut loose. Girls like you I have to watch out for. Girls like you are the deadliest ones." He winked.

That caused me to laugh. "Are you considering me a threat?"

"No. I'm considering you a *challenge*."

Gage's features solidified as he leaned forward. His eyes were hard on mine and he didn't dare look away. I couldn't force myself to look away either. How was I a challenge? To Gage, I could have been the easiest girl on the planet, but I guess I was doing something right if he considered me a *challenge*.

"Dude, Gage, keep your balls in your pants, man." Montana coughed from the couch, thick puffs of smoke spurting out as he held his chest. Gage's stare fell a little before he turned to look at Montana. He then forced a smile at me, grabbing his bowl.

"Cereal was great, Ellie. Maybe when we get to Texas I can take you out for some real southern dinner."

"Yeah," I breathed, pushing from the table and grabbing my bowl. "We could try that."

He winked after placing his bowl in the sink and then carried himself toward the couch to sit beside Montana. Roy and Deed were still focused on their videogame and I sighed, folding my arms and trudging toward my room.

I shut the door behind me, flopped onto the bed, and stared at the sketching of Gage for a little too long. No wonder he raided my dreams. Because he had a way with words. He had a way of making me melt and getting my heart to pump. I wasn't sure about what he meant by me being a challenge for him and I wasn't sure if I wanted to find out because he was too close to discovering who I used to be. What I used to do. How I used to *survive*.

I told myself I didn't want to know what he meant, but it was a lie. A part of me did want to figure it out sooner or later.

TEXAS

The next morning, I woke up in Texas. The sun was high in the sky; I could even hear roosters crowing from a mile away. It was a great feeling—a refreshing feeling, especially since I didn't have to deal with waking up in the middle of the night because of harsh memories.

It was best to get my day started early, so I pulled my blankets away, climbed out of bed, and grabbed a towel along with my toiletries. I heard snoring and figured the boys were still sleeping. As I drifted off to sleep last night, it sounded like they were all wide-awake.

I hurried down the hall, hoping no one was awake to see my morning hideousness. It was relief to see the bunks were empty. I neared the bathroom door and grabbed the knob, but it twisted before I could even move my wrist. I gasped, taking a leap back, and considered running for my room, but I didn't—only because I didn't have enough time to do so.

Montana appeared behind the door. His glassy, light-blue eyes widened at the sight of me. His toothbrush was hanging out of his mouth and his dirty-blond hair was mussed. Bedhead didn't only look good on Gage; it looked just as marvelous on Montana, too. "Morning, cutie," he said, stepping around me and gripping the handle of his toothbrush.

"Morning, Montana." I sighed.

"Where're you going so early?"

I shrugged. "I thought I'd go catch some coffee and breakfast somewhere or something. Why are *you* up so early?"

He shrugged. "Had to kick a broad out." I rolled my eyes. "Just kidding. I was hot. Couldn't go back to sleep." He ran his fingers through his hair, looking me over. "It's been a while since I've been out with someone other than the band, though." He stepped around me to get into the bathroom and spit into the sink. He rinsed out his mouth and the sink and then turned to face me. "Mind if I come with you?"

"Sure, why not?"

He raised an eyebrow, his right cheek lifting to form a smirk. "You don't sound so thrilled."

I sighed, dropping my things on the counter. "It's called sarcasm. Since girls are always throwing themselves all over you guys, you probably haven't heard it directed toward you in a while."

"Are you always this feisty in the morning?" he asked, pressing his palms on the walls outside the door and leaning in. "It's kinda hot. *You're* hot." He winked, smirking charismatically.

"I'll see you after I'm done, Montana."

I slammed the door in his face and he laughed behind it. After I showered, I wrung my hair out and then wiped the fog from the mirror. I stared at myself, the spitting image of my mother—oval-shaped face, button nose, soft, crystal-like blue eyes, naturally full lips. Sometimes I wondered where she was or what she might've been doing. I wondered if she'd gotten better over the years. It sucked knowing what she'd done to me, but oh well. I couldn't do much about it.

I rushed for my room before anyone could see me and locked the door behind me. I couldn't afford to have anyone getting a glimpse of my tits by accident. It seemed like a pretty warm day so I went with letting my hair air-dry. I grabbed a turquoise blouse Ben bought for me, some light-blue skinny jeans, and then a pair of jeweled sandals to add a little spunk. I guess I wasn't so bad at making myself look presentable.

I checked the wall mirror, sort of excited about my appearance. Ben had great taste, and the outfit was really hot on me. I had to give him some credit for making me look more like a lady than a little girl. We'd made a deal that as long as I was comfortable in the clothes, I would wear them. Of course, with the club dress he bought, I had no choice. I could've gone with what I'd worn at the show, but I felt it was too simple for a club. I didn't want to look like too much of a fool. I had to fit in somehow.

After scrambling through my suitcases for my wallet, grabbing my camera and my new sunglasses, I headed out of the room, ready to take on a new day.

Montana was already sitting on the couch, fully dressed in a tight vintage-green T-shirt, skinny jeans, and black boots. He didn't really do much with his mohawk, not that it looked bad. There were just a few loose blond pieces hanging on his forehead and the nape of his neck.

"Do you know what's around here?" I asked.

He looked up quickly and then stood. "Nope, but we have a driver with a GPS. We'll find something."

Nodding, I turned for the door and stepped out. It was blazing outside. I looked up and no clouds were around, only the sun. I placed my sunglasses over my eyes and Montana came out, his sunglasses in hand, too. He shielded his eyes as well, and then looked toward the black Escalade parked on the curb.

The driver was on the phone as we approached and as soon as he saw Montana and me getting closer, he yelled something into the phone and then pulled it from his ear, ending the call.

"Arguing with the ol' lady, huh, Stan?" Montana asked.

"Nah." Stan sighed, stepping around the car to get to the back door. He opened it for us and I climbed in first. Montana climbed in and shut the door behind him. Stan hopped in quickly with a heavier sigh. "Okay, I lied. It's the wife. She's annoying the hell out of me."

"What'd she do?" Montana asked.

"Just nagging. Obviously in need of some good ol' Stan. No worries." He grunted, sitting forward and starting the car. "As soon as I get back home, her nagging'll stop. She just misses Big Papa, that's all."

Montana laughed and rolled down his window. I couldn't help but giggle. "Keep telling that to yourself, Stan."

Stan was a round man with an evident beer belly and a bald head beneath his black chauffeur's hat. He had a meaty neck, but he had kind brown eyes, which made him seem friendlier than anything. To top it all off, he was funny and I automatically knew he was a big teddy bear who probably tried to act tough whenever his wife wasn't around. I was certain when he was alone with her, he did anything for her in a heartbeat. He just seemed like the type of guy who would kiss his woman's toes if she asked him to.

Stan looked over his shoulder. "Where to?"

"Just take us to the nearest diner, if you can," I inquired.

"You got it. I actually know of a place that's really close. They serve the best damn waffles and eggs I've ever had.

The waffles aren't too crisp or too fluffy. They're just right.
I'm tellin' ya."

Montana chuckled again, staring out the window. I
couldn't help but laugh as well. Stan was a cool guy. I
wanted him to be my driver instead of Marco's perverted
ass.

It took us about ten minutes to get to the diner. It was
pretty old-fashioned, small, but seemed really comfortable
and welcoming. As soon as we stepped inside, a woman
with grey hair smiled at us from the counter. Her lips were
smothered with pink lipstick and her makeup was a bit
dramatic for her age.

"It's you!" she squealed, rushing in our direction.

I looked up at Montana with a face full of confusion and
he frowned at the lady before looking down at me and
shaking his head. "Trust me, I do not get *that* drunk."

She continued rushing our way, but then I saw she
wasn't coming for us. She was going for Stan, who was
trailing in behind us. "Hey!" Stan boomed from the door.
Montana and I took a step to the side as they hugged.

"What brings you back to Houston?" the woman asked,
grinning up at him.

"On the road again, as usual. Got a few rockers on tour and I'm one of the drivers."

"Aw, ain't that nice." The woman patted Stan's belly and then looked in our direction. "Well, let's go fill you on up, then."

I figured out during our chat at the bar that the woman's name was Marceline. She and Stan were like siblings because Stan lived in Houston, Texas, for two years. He'd even worked at the diner with her as a chef for a short period of time.

I ordered the house famous waffles and scrambled eggs Stan mentioned and I admit he was right. The food was phenomenal, the coffee was perfect, and to top it all off, Marceline and the staff were extremely kind.

"Do you guys mind if I snap a few pictures of you?" I asked, pulling the strap of my camera over my head. "I just—I have a thing where I like to take pictures of my surroundings."

"Of course, dear," Marceline chimed, waving her hand at me. "I'm all up for makin' memories."

"Just make sure you don't drool all over the sight of me in that pic later," Montana teased, standing from his barstool. I rolled my eyes playfully and he laughed, standing on the right side of Marceline. Stan was on her left.

I snapped a few pictures of them doing a few poses and making funny faces and when I was done, I hooked the strap of my camera around my neck again. Marceline gathered our dishes while she and Stan started talking about the diner and I decided I could find a few more things outside to take pictures of, so as soon as I finished my orange juice I headed out.

"So, are you making a scrapbook or something?" Montana asked as he stepped to my side.

"Something like that."

He chuckled quietly and I looked up at him. "You're a really confidential person, you know that? It's weird because I feel like I've been around you long enough to call you a friend, yet I don't know a single thing about you."

I pursed my lips with a shrug. "I'm not that hard to figure out."

"You are to Gage," he said, chuckling.

I was about to smile, but it evaporated immediately as he said Gage's name. "How am I hard for Gage to figure out?"

"I don't know." He shrugged. "Gage is a complicated man. He's one of those guys who likes to get under people's skin by trying to figure them out completely— girls especially. He calls it a 'panty dropper thing.' Trust me, once he's figured a girl out, he'll use it as a sweet weapon against them. He's weird as fuck that way, but I can't blame him because it works every damn time."

"I'll never understand you rockers," I sighed. I turned around to find something to snap pictures of and he followed after me.

"Look, I don't want shit to get ugly so I think I should say this now."

I paused in my tracks, turning to face Montana, who'd placed his sunglasses over his eyes, his face now serious. "What are you talking about?"

"You danced with Deed the night before—at the club. I'm sure it was fun and all, but when Gage is interested in someone, I know it. I can tell. I've known Gage for years and he isn't usually one for talking about a girl repeatedly, but it's weird how he talks about you. And it's not in a way that makes it seem like he's crushing on you or even wants to get in your pants. He's just met you and for some reason he won't stop bringing you up.

"Like the night at the club, for instance. We were talking about the girls dancing on us and he'd mentioned that you might have gotten mad at him for it. He also told me he thinks Deed danced with you on purpose since Deed knows he called 'dibs' on you. Right after he said something about you, he bailed on us."

"He didn't sleep with anyone that night?" I asked, slightly relieved. Of course I tried to hide the relief.

"Nah. He called a ride and went straight to the bus. I'll be honest here. I think he was upset that you danced with Deed, but of course he wasn't gonna say it out loud to us... but I could tell."

I pretended not to care much about what Montana was telling me, but I was kind of glad to hear it. He didn't sleep with anyone that night. I thought he did since I saw a few girls getting off the FireNine bus the previous morning. I guess there were only two girls for a reason. One for Montana and one for Deed... or maybe two for Montana.

Turning slowly, I looked ahead and tried to find something to take a picture of to distract myself from these mindboggling thoughts of Grendel. Of course, Montana kept bringing it back up.

"What I wanted to say before is if any one of us tries to claim you, it should be Gage. Don't fuck with Deed. He's only doing it to get under Gage's skin."

"No one's claiming me," I said over my shoulder. I bent down to take a picture of a ladybug sitting on a dirty water bottle.

"Just saying." Montana's shadow shrugged. "I just hope he doesn't get too caught up on you—not that you're a bad girl. I just know he and Deed are supposed to be sort of partners for the tour and Deed can act like a real bitch sometimes when it comes down to going out and shit. The kid hates to be alone for some reason."

Stan came tumbling out of the diner and I was glad to see he had on his hat and his keys clutched in hand because the conversation between Montana and me was beginning to get a little awkward.

I didn't want to talk about Gage with him. I didn't really want to care. On the inside, I was excited as hell. If I would've known Gage didn't sleep with anyone the night we were at the club, I probably wouldn't have been so rude toward him the morning after. Of course I was still annoyed about him kissing a girl he didn't know while dating Penelope, but at least it wasn't me he was hurting.

At least, during his whole night, I was somewhere on his mind.

That made me kind of giddy.

IMPORTANT

Ten minutes until the show.

That's what the men kept yelling backstage, but it had been twenty minutes and no one was singing. The crowd was getting upset that FireNine wasn't out there pleasing them. The opening act did their part and had to hit the road ASAP.

"Where the hell is Deed? He should have been here an hour ago!" Ben growled through clamped teeth. "I swear if he isn't here in thirty minutes, he's getting replaced. It's only been three days and he's fucking up already?"

"Ben, I'm sure he'll be here," I whispered. "Just calm down."

There was one side of Ben I didn't like: his impatient and pissed-off side. He could definitely hold a grudge, which was why I always aimed to be on his good side. He was a bit more emotional than the normal male (for obvious reasons), but he was also about business. When it came down to it, there could be no slacking off, no disappointments. Ben was about his money and he had his reasons to be. After getting robbed of everything, he had to get it back as best as he could. He worked hard for his living.

Ben started pacing as the fans yelled and complained even louder. I think I heard every negative name in the book during our wait. "If we don't start in two minutes, the show will have to be cancelled and we'll have to give these people their money back," a man with circular glasses and a broom-like moustache said to Ben. Ben nodded and the man walked off quickly with his clipboard and walkie-talkie in hand. As soon as Ben stopped pacing, the back door swung open.

In came Deed with a pair of sunglasses over his eyes. He had on a black T-shirt with the FireNine logo printed in bright orange. His hair was gelled and spiked in a few places, but his face was hard, edgy. A tall man followed in behind him, his face harder than granite. He had salt-and-pepper hair, his face was clean, and he wore a suit, proving he was about nothing but business. Neither one of them were smiling as they met up with us.

"Found him," the man in the suit said, glaring at Deed.

"Sorry I'm late, Ben. I can explain later," Deed muttered.

"Oh, you better explain later. Right now you all need to get your asses on that stage and please this damn crowd." Ben clapped his hands and the boys gathered their instruments.

"Deed, what the fuck happened?" Montana hissed at him.

"Nothing." Deed stole a glance over his shoulder at the man in the suit who'd just slid his fingertips into his front pockets. He was staring at Deed the entire time and it was making my skin crawl. It wasn't a normal stare. It was almost like an "I'll fuck you up" stare.

The boys stopped asking questions, shaking their heads as they marched for the stage. The crowd was still yelling and beyond impatient, even when the boys were getting set up. But then Gage leaned into the microphone and his voice filled the arena.

"Good evening, Texas," Gage said, gripping the microphone with both hands. The crowd stopped ranting and went wild. There were some yelling, "I love you, Gage!" and others yelling madly over Montana, who'd winked and blew an air-kiss at the crowd, strapping his guitar around him. "There was a bit of an issue backstage, but it's nothing we couldn't handle. Shit happens, right?" The crowd hollered again, maybe louder this time, and I bit on a smile as he watched them with cheerful eyes, grinning widely. "We've got to make it up to you somehow, so I figured we could sing one of our newest songs. It hasn't even been recorded in the studio yet, but you deserve it for sticking around."

"What the hell is he doing?" Ben snapped, his hand on his chin. His foot was tapping and anger still had a hold of him, but I placed a hand on his arm, shaking my head.

"Ben, you've got to calm down. Gage is smart. I'm sure he knows what he's doing."

"This song," Gage said, his deep, bedroom voice echoing across the large arena and making the center of my legs clench, "is one we thought of while sitting in the garage. The title is 'Promised Me.' Sounds cheesy—we know." Gage chuckled, shaking his head. "But the lyrics make up for it."

Gage looked over his shoulder at his band brothers and they nodded, ready to play. Deed did a quick countdown with his drumsticks and the music blared. The crowd went wild as Gage strummed his guitar, singing into his microphone. His eyes lowered and he leaned forward, winking, singing, his fingers moving rapidly along the strings. With a few words, he'd pucker his lips and I'd melt on the inside, craving another low, deep note of his voice.

"I can't believe it," Ben said, smiling. "It's the song they were practicing in my garage. They said they weren't going to sing it for another few months!"

"It's getting a great reaction!" I yelled over the music.

"A *very* great reaction," Ben said, rubbing his hands together. "Terri!" he shouted over his shoulder.

Terri, a short guy with a large nose, square glasses, and cropped black hair, hustled his way forward to get to Ben's side. "You've got to record the performance. I'm sure Luke will love to hear this one."

"Yes, sir." Terri dashed away but returned in less than a minute, fidgeting with a video camera. My attention turned to Gage singing exquisitely. He'd dropped his guitar to wrap his fingers around the microphone. His eyes shut and as the boys slowed down the beat, his voice came out powerfully. He was giving it his all.

...You promised me
You'd let it all go.
You swore to put me first,
But all I got was your worst.

So where the hell are you?
What the hell are we?
I needed you with me,
But you continuously destroyed me.

You promised meeee... so much.

The lyrics were heart aching, incredible, but I questioned where they came from. Had Gage been in love before? He mentioned to me that he wrote most of the lyrics. I was sure this song was his as well.

There was a lot about Gage that left me curious. I asked myself more and more questions about him each day. He had more within him that he wasn't showing and I couldn't help but think there was a reason behind it all. What was he hiding?

The boys were going out to another club, but this time I beat Ben before he could pull another mandatory night out. I told Marco to drop me off at the bus, deciding a little painting would do for the night.

I only painted when there was absolute silence or with extremely loud music. I didn't know where Ben was, but I knew he wasn't going to show up for another few hours.

The bus was quieter than usual, and with the crickets chirping outside the window, it made the night even better. It was peaceful. Humble.

When I started, I couldn't stop. I finger-painted a lot. It was a unique technique I'd learned the previous semester. It wasn't the simple child's finger painting, either. There was complexity of my fingernails, the back of my hand to make it look rougher, and even the palm of my hand to smooth edges. There was a flowerpot full of tulips on the table next to my dresser so I went with painting that.

But then the front door of the bus creaked open and I paused on my next finger stroke. It slammed behind whoever stepped inside and then heavy footsteps started down the hallway. I knew there were a few security guards parked outside the bus so I got rid of the thought that maybe it was burglar or a murderer.

A heavy grunt filled the silence and I stood, placing my paint on the floor and going for the door. I wiped my hands on my apron as much as I could to get rid of the paint before twisting the doorknob and swinging the door open. As I looked out, a pair of legs dangled from the top bunk of the hallway.

"Gage?" I called, my eyebrows knitted.

Gage turned around quickly and nearly hit his head on the ceiling. "Ellie," he breathed.

"What are you doing?" I laughed.

"Came to change clothes, but my suitcase fell behind the bed." He turned around again and grunted as he pulled up his suitcase. "Got it."

"Oh, okay." I started to step back and close the door, but then Gage called my name and I paused.

"What are you doing tonight?" he asked, his eyebrow arched.

"I was just getting some painting done."

"You really don't go out much, huh?" he teased.

"Not really. I told you clubs and parties aren't really for me."

Pressing his lips, he dropped his suitcase on the floor before jumping from the top bunk and landing beside it. "There's a place here where they square dance every Saturday night. It's fun."

I frowned. "I've never square danced before."

"Let's change that." He grunted, bending down to unzip his suitcase. His eyes never left mine. "Come with me."

"Don't you have to wear something cowboy-ish to an event like that?"

He smiled boyishly. "It's not required, but it makes the night much more fun when you do."

"Oh, well, that's too bad." I shrugged. "I don't own any rodeo or square-dancing clothes."

Gage stood up straight and cocked his head at me. He then dug into his back pocket for his cell phone. "Most places down here don't close for another hour or so," he said, checking the time. "We have just enough time to buy something nice and make it there. Square dancing doesn't start until ten."

"Gage…" I giggled. "Seriously, it's nice of you, but no."

He frowned. "What's your excuse?"

"For one, I have paint all over me," I said, holding out my hands. "And two, it's just really one of the nights where I wanna relax and enjoy the quiet. I know when the boys get back it's going to be a damn circus in here."

"Ellie," Gage murmured, taking a step toward me. He grabbed my right hand and looked down at it. "The paint will always be here. Square dancing in Texas only comes around every once in a while. We're only staying here for one night. Why not embrace it?"

"I can always come back to Texas when I wanna square dance," I whispered, trying my best to keep my breath from hitching.

He took another step near me, reaching a hand up to cap my shoulder. "It'll be fun, Eliza. I swear. Come with me."

I noticed then that Gage only called me by my real name when he was being serious. It made me feel kind of important… in an odd sort of way.

I stared into his pleading hazel eyes and soon the guilt surfaced. Groaning, I removed my hand from his and took a step back. "Fine," I sighed. "Just let me wash up."

"Take your time, Ellie." He winked at me before going for his suitcase again and I slowly made my way toward the bathroom, wondering how this night was going to turn out.

HOEDOWN

I felt so silly—actually beyond it. Gage and I went shopping for something to wear for square dancing, and I ended up getting a blue-and-red gingham dress. Gage got a red-and-blue plaid button-up, some boot-cut jeans, and he'd even gotten us a pair of matching brown cowboy boots. I found it ridiculous but cute. I'd even gotten him to buy himself a brown cowboy hat... and damn if he didn't look hotter than hell...

"Look at you, Ellie, looking like a million bucks," Gage said as he held the back door open for me. I looked at him beneath my eyelashes and he shut the door behind me. He tapped the window twice and Stan pulled off.

"You really had to insist that the woman give me pigtails, huh?" I giggled, toying with my hair. "She was enjoying playing dress-up with me."

"The pigtails look good on you. Fits the theme. You look like Rodeo Barbie." Gage winked and then held his elbow out and I hooked my arm through his. The pavement led to a tall red barn, and a few monster trucks and classic cars were parked outside. Lanterns were hanging outside the barn, the light stretching across the dewy grass, and a large green tractor was parked in front.

"What's the tractor for?" I asked, my vision tunneling in on it. "It's blocking the entrance."

"Oh yeah!" Gage yelled, laughing. "That's the thing about these people. They can get a little wild. Before we're allowed in, we have to race another couple on riding lawn mowers."

"What?" I squealed. "That's insane."

"It's Texas, baby!" someone yelled from beside the tractor. I looked up quickly to figure out who the deep voice belonged to and a tall man with a black cowboy hat, a belt with a large silver buckle, and a white button-up revealed himself. He was smiling as a woman with blond hair stepped by his side.

Gage tilted down his cowboy hat and the man did the same. "Lawn racin' is the only way you can get in," the man said, grinning. "Well—all right, I'm lyin', but we'd prefer it to liven the atmosphere a bit. We want y'all to have some fun."

"Trust me, Ellie, it's fun," Gage murmured in my ear. "I'll be the driver. You just ride and be my little cheerleader." Gage looked at the man and woman who were standing hand-in-hand. "All right. Where's our mower?"

The man chuckled and the woman ran from his side to go behind the barn. She returned in less than a minute, riding on a chrome red mower. "Here's yours," she chimed, her southern accent thick.

"I take it you ain't been 'round here before," the man said to me, hopping onto the green mower beside the tractor.

"No," I replied, shaking my head. "First time in Texas."

"Well, I hope you're havin' a ball. If not, this should make up for it. It's the best part of the night. I think it's the only reason people still even attend these hoedown joints."

Gage climbed onto the red riding mower and as he got situated, he looked at me. "Come on, Ellie," he said, offering his hand. I looked over at the petite woman hopping on behind the man with the cowboy hat and then looked at Gage again. I couldn't believe it. They were serious. They were really about to race... on riding lawn mowers?

I hurried forward, reaching for Gage's hand anyway. "Aren't lawn mowers kind of... slow?" I whispered in his ear. If they were, it was going to be one boring-ass race.

Gage chuckled. "These aren't just ordinary mowers. For one, they boost them to make them faster. *John Deere* is already a good brand, but giving them a boost—" Gage's head shook as he gripped the wheel. He wasn't even looking at me and knew for a fact I was completely lost on what he was talking about. "Just know we're in for some fun, Ellie. You actually might wanna hang on."

I hooked my arms around Gage's middle without hesitation. I knew he had no reason to lie. Gage started the mower and it rumbled deeply, causing my entire body to vibrate. He was still smiling as he looked over at the man and woman on their mower. They started theirs and their mower rumbled even louder.

A few people came out from the back of the barn to watch and I got a little more excited. It was almost like drag racing... only on mowers. Gage pressed his pedal and lined up by our competitors.

"Just follow the path ahead!" the man yelled over the roar of the engines. "We'll start on three!"

Gage tipped his hat again and then gripped his wheel.

"One!"

It was starting! My heart beat a little louder.

"Two!"

I clung on even tighter. I knew it was coming. I was nervous. Thrilled. Fucking insane. Adrenaline coursed through me and we hadn't even started yet. *Why the hell am I so amped for this?*

"Three!"

Gage took off, the engines roaring even louder, and let out a, "Hell yeah!" once he realized we were already in the lead. A tree came up ahead and Gage whipped his wheel, but he didn't stop. I hung on tighter and wanted to shut my eyes, but I didn't. It was fun to see everything coming at me.

The path curved and Gage turned his wheel a little too sharply. We jerked to the side and I gasped, thinking we were about to flip over. He rotated the wheel to the left and got back on track, bellowing with laughter as I clung to the front of his shirt.

"I got you, Ellie," he said over his shoulder.

I glanced over mine and saw the man and woman getting closer. "Gage, they're coming!" I squealed.

Another tree appeared ahead and he took the right side, the man and woman taking the left. We were neck and neck and the finish line was only a few feet away. I couldn't tell which one of us was taking the lead.

The wind grew harsher, causing my pigtails to flap and my cheeks to burn, and Gage pressed his pedal to the max the closer we got to the finish line. I squeezed my eyes shut and rested my cheek against his back. I couldn't look. I wanted to, but I couldn't.

Cheers and hollers from the crowd got closer and soon the cheering died down and the mower jerked forward before coming to a screeching halt. Silence rang in my ears and then Gage sat back, laughing.

"Oh shit! That was fun!" he said, chuckling. "We won, Ellie. You can open your eyes now." My eyelids opened slowly, but I was still glued to Gage's back.

He took one of my hands and helped me off the mower. My butt felt numb and my legs wobbled like spaghetti, but I managed to stand anyway.

"Woo-wee!" the man we raced yelled as he jogged in our direction. "That was some ride!"

"It was!" Gage laughed. His eyes chinked as he stared at the man and I hadn't noticed before, but that kind of smile made him look younger. Adorable.

"Well, you got your ticket in. I'm Darrell, by the way. It was fun racing with ya. Square dancin' starts in five." Darrell looked at me and winked. "Have fun, lil' lady."

I smiled. "I will. Thanks."

Darrell walked off and Gage turned to look at me. He held his elbow out again and I hooked my arm through his.

"You okay?" he asked.

I shrugged. "Is it bad that I feel like I'm made of Jell-O right now?" I asked, grinning.

He let out a deep laugh as we neared the door, the tractor moving forward to let us in. "First time's always like that."

"How many times have you been here?"

"My family and I used to live in Texas for a while— before my dad moved his business to Virginia."

"Oh." He brought up his family a lot, but I wasn't sure if I should ask about them. He always spoke in the past tense, as if they were no longer living.

Good thing we entered the barn and a few people were already in the middle dancing, providing a distraction from our conversation. Some people were chatting and some stood next to the table of food with plates and cups in hand. "Want a drink? Beer?"

I laughed dryly. "I've never had beer before."

His eyes expanded. "Never? How the hell are you enjoying life right now? Didn't you say you're twenty-one?"

"Yes."

"When did you turn twenty-one?" he asked, leading the way toward a decorated table with wide silver pails on top.

"January fourteenth."

"It's June and you've never had a beer before? I know Ben drinks them. You've never tried to sneak one?"

"Nope," I said, popping my lips.

"I guess that's another thing to change tonight." Gage dug into the wide pail filled with ice and pulled out two beers. Uncapping them, he handed one to me before taking a sip of his.

I sniffed it and my nose pinched. "Smells like piss."

He laughed. "Tastes like heaven. Try it."

I stared at my bottle for a second before lifting the rim to my lips. It tasted bland at first, but as I took a few more sips, it wasn't so bad. It cooled me down after the intense lawn mower race that'd taken place seconds ago.

"See," Gage said, lifting his bottle, "not so bad right?"

"It's okay." I smiled at him before turning to face the crowd, and for once I didn't feel out of place. The women there had on the same kind of gingham dresses. Most of them wore their hair in pigtails just like mine, but they had on tons of makeup. The men were dressed like Gage—plaid button-up shirts, cowboy boots, and a hat to match. On Gage, it was sexy as hell. Who knew the country-boy style could look so good on him? I wanted to devour him even more, if that were humanly possible.

"All righty!" a woman yelled through a microphone from the DJ stand. "Round those partners up 'cause the square dancing is about to begin. Ladies, get pretty. Fellas, get sexy. It's time to have a ball!"

I looked at Gage nervously, biting my lip. "How am I supposed to know what to do?" I asked.

"I'll lead you." He grabbed my bottle and set it on the table, leading me out onto the dance floor. "Just listen to the calls," he murmured. Fiddles started playing and I became more and more nervous. A hand moved in my peripheral and I looked down at it.

"G'evening again, lil' lady," the familiar deep voice said. I looked up and sure enough it was Darrell. "Lookin' mighty worried. Don't sweat it. After the first try, it gets easier."

The fiddles grew louder as a man yelled through the mic to call everyone in for the last time. Unease consumed me, but as Gage pressed a hand against the small of my back and I looked up at him, I calmed down a bit. "It's not so bad," he said, winking. "Trust me."

"All right, go ahead and give a bow to ya partner," the man at the mic called. Gage's hand was still in mine and he bowed, tipping his hat down a little. Giggling, I bowed back. "Okay, now bow to the other."

I looked at Darrell who bowed at the same time as me. Okay, it was pretty easy so far. "Now join hands and circle around. Gone 'head, take it on 'round," the man sang.

The music picked up and blared through the speakers and Gage moved left while I moved with him. Our hands were still glued together and the room shifted with each step I took. *Okay. Still easy.*

"Swing that partner high and low!"

The spinning circle stopped and Gage came forward to hook his arm around my waist, the other holding up my hand. He spun in small circles, grinning at me. I placed my arm on top of his shoulder and laughed as he winked.

"Now all our ladies step to the middle, then back it on up. Now step back and let the gentleman take over."

Gage released me and I turned around to step in the middle. I couldn't help but smile even more because all the women were excited. I rushed back to Gage's side before he stepped forward, tipping his hat at the man in front of him.

He came back and the man yelled, "Go promenade around the ring." With that, Gage hung on to my waist and spun in circles again. Our free hands were clasped together in the air for the second time.

"Having fun?" he asked.

I nodded and then he lifted my arm to spin me in a quick three-sixty.

"Now join hands and swing it on 'round." We did as commanded. "Now promenade to cool it down."

I couldn't believe how much fun I was having doing a *square dance*. With Gage, it felt even more enjoyable. I wasn't sure how, but he made me smile the entire time. I don't think the smile ever left my glee-filled face.

The man told us to take a break after our fourth set and we laughed as we went for another round of beers. "I don't know how I've missed out on this before," I said before taking a gulp of my beer.

"Well, when you stay cooped up in your room that's what happens," Gage said, leaning against the wall. "You miss out on fun opportunities."

"I have fun," I argued.

He smirked. "Doing what exactly?"

"Drawing. Painting. Taking pictures."

"So you're really on the creative side?" he asked, amused.

"I am. I love art. I wanna make it my career."

"Maybe you should take some pictures of the band. You could make a ton of money off them—you could even become a graphic designer for us. All you need is my word. I can hook it up for you."

I narrowed my eyes at him. "I don't think I want my future in your hands."

He laughed. "What, do you think I'd forget about hooking you up?"

"No... well, yeah," I stated honestly.

Gage laughed again before downing his beer. "If there's one thing I don't fuck with, it's someone's future and career. You seem passionate about it. If you really want it, I can give it to you." His eyes softened and then he looked from my eyes to my cleavage. "I mean that in more ways than one, though."

"Stop." I slapped his arm playfully. "We're just friends. Remember?"

"Well, yeah. Only because that's what you want. I can respect that, but it doesn't mean I wouldn't do more with your body if I were given permission."

I smirked at him before taking another sip of beer. "I'd love to be a graphic designer for FireNine. I could create your next CD cover—maybe even the band's T-shirts?"

"You could create a whole damn store for us if you want, Ellie." He smirked. "I'm sure it would sell."

I put down my beer, squaring my shoulders at Gage. He looked into my eyes, his eyebrows stitching as his lips pressed thin. "You'd really do that for me, Gage? Let me become a designer for you, I mean."

"Is it something you'll agree to keep doing?" he asked, leaning his shoulder against the wall and folding his arms. "'Cause that's what a career is all about. I don't like quitters."

"If I had an opportunity like that, I'd do my best to keep it."

His right cheek lifted into a smirk as he studied my eyes. He was most likely trying to figure out if I was being serious. I was serious as hell. That was a dream job for me—to paint and draw and then see it as a final product. It was something I'd craved since I was a child.

"All right." He sighed. "I'll see what I can do. Of course, you'll have to talk to Ben about it, too. He may know more people than me that could help you out a bit."

"Oh my gosh! Really?" I squealed, grabbing his hands.

"Really." He winked before tossing his empty beer bottle. "Wanna go for some fresh air?" he asked, cocking his head toward the exit.

I nodded quickly. I was excited. I could see in his eyes that he was being serious. I knew he joked around a lot and could be really irresponsible, but this was one thing I wanted to trust him with.

I hooked my arm through his and we stepped through the crowd to get outside. "You don't find it weird that none of those people in there knew you?" I asked.

"Not really." He shrugged. "Most of them are real down-to-earth country people. They'll listen to nothing but the country genre. FireNine is more of a rock-slash-alternative kind of band—plus we're just starting to become popular. Our music isn't too hardcore or too soft. We're, like, right in between."

I nodded, my lips pressed together. "Makes sense." We continued walking and silence crept up on us. There was one question that had been on my mind since his performance earlier and I had to get an answer. "Have you ever been in love before?" I blurted. Right after asking, my cheeks burned and I lowered my head a little.

Gage looked down at me, his eyes narrowed. "What makes you ask that?"

"Well… your song you sang earlier—the new one from the garage—you told me the other night that you write most of the songs. Did you write that one?"

He shrugged. "Yeah."

"The lyrics seemed to be about a broken heart..." I trailed off as he looked at me, smirking. "Never mind." I sighed, feeling completely idiotic for bringing it up.

"No, it's cool." He tucked his fingers into his back pockets. "I've never been in love before. It's odd, though, how one would think it's always a boyfriend or girlfriend who's broken someone's heart. Sometimes it's the ones closest to us who can destroy us most. Sometimes it's friends... *family*. It's not always a romantic relationship that can leave us with a broken heart."

I nodded, speechless. His way with words was really, really getting to me. How could he be so deep and emotional yet one of the most ruthless rockers I'd ever known? It confused me and I thought on it as we continued walking—that is until Gage lightened up and looked at me. "So tell me about you, Sweet Ellie," he said. "Besides your crazy, mad obsession with art, what else do you like to do?"

I thought hard on his question as I looked ahead. I knew he was trying to change the subject and I was glad, because knowing me, I would have asked him to clear my confusion. I wanted to know who exactly broke his heart.

The path was continuing between a cut of trees, but the moonlight was seeping through, giving us enough light to see where we were going. "I like music," I said. "And watching cartoons sometimes."

Gage laughed at me. "And, again, you say you're twenty-one, right?"

"Yes, I am," I said matter-of-factly. "Cartoons will never get old—especially the classics."

He laughed again. "Okay, okay." I pulled my arm from his to give him some space. It felt nice to be close to him, but I knew sooner or later me clinging to his arm was going to turn into something outside of being friends. I couldn't afford it. "So what about your future? Do you have a boyfriend you swear you're going to marry one day like most girls do?" he teased, winking.

"Nope." My lips popped. "I'm a single dove right now."

"I like that. Single dove," he noted, eyes connecting with mine.

"Really?" I folded my fingers in front of me and a creek came into view. "You should make a song out of it... even though you aren't single—but you do live the single life."

He laughed. "What's that supposed to mean?"

I rolled my eyes. "I think it's obvious what it means, Gage."

"Oh, Ellie," he said, his deep voice causing my stomach to coil. "So impudent, aren't you?"

I smiled, looking up into the hazel eyes that were already looking down at me. "Actually, I can be really coy."

"I can see that. You're one of those people who doesn't give too much away."

"Is that a bad thing?" I asked, biting the corner of my bottom lip.

"Not at all. Not when you're someone like *you*."

My eyebrows drew in and an innocent frown took hold of my features. "That made no sense at all," I scoffed.

Gage took off his cowboy hat and ran a hand through his messy hair as he stopped walking. His dark hair rustled with the gentle breeze and as a strand fell onto his forehead, I bit my lower lip again, fighting the urge to push it back and get a clear view of his gorgeous face. Good thing his head was turned and he wasn't looking at me admiring him.

"Would you like me to explain it to you?" he asked, meeting my eyes again.

"Please do, Grendel."

He laughed at that. "Okay. Someone like you is… innocent—but knows how to have a good time. You're someone who can create a smile without even trying. I've noticed it lately. I'm not really sure if it's your innocence that makes people automatically fond of you or if it's just that smile of yours that always seems so wide, yet so much is hidden behind it." Gage's smile fell the same time mine did. For some reason, I couldn't look away from him. His eyes sparkled from the light of the moon, and as he blinked, I finally lowered my head to look anywhere but at him.

"You're someone who I can tell doesn't trust easily. Love easily. Fall easily. Someone who knows how to step away from stupidity and nonsense instead of lingering around it. You're the kind of person who knows she deserves it all because you're strong, knowledgeable, and mature for your age. I find it nice, really," he said, grinning, but I could still feel him looking at me. He then did the unexpected.

He took a step forward, bringing his hand up and pulling me in by my waist. My heart throbbed and a trickle of heat ran from my throat to my stomach as he tilted my chin up with his forefinger. "I find *you* nice, Ellie. I see a whole lot more within you than you think I do."

I couldn't breathe. Usually that's a bad thing, but in this circumstance, it was good. Gage's lips hovered above mine and his warm breath tickled my cheek. The warmth of his free hand was at my waist and his eyelids lowered as he looked from my eyes and then down to my lips again.

I bit on my bottom lip and his parted as he brought his hand up to cup my cheek. The touch of his skin on mine sent me over the edge. He was so close. Even with the few gusts of wind blowing against us, I was burning up on the inside, yearning for at least one kiss. It didn't have to happen again after this night, but at this very moment, it was the perfect time to go in for a taste of him. But how was I to go about it? What if it wasn't the time yet? It felt wrong... but my body was screaming that it was so right.

"Gage—"

He cut me off before I could finish speaking, placing his finger against the fold of my lips. "Don't," he whispered. He moved in even closer and I stifled a breath. My heart was pounding the closer he got. He removed his finger from my lips to get full view of them again and a slow, sensual smile weaved its way across his lips. *Oh, God.* He was so beautiful.

So. Damn. Beautiful.

But just as he was about to place his lips on mine, a buzzing noise came out of nowhere and Gage stopped, but he was so close. He was almost there, but the vibrating disturbed it all. He then looked down and pulled away. "Your phone's ringing, Eliza," he murmured.

I blinked quickly, taking a step back and snapping out of my daze. I'd forgotten about everything else that was going on outside of us. I quickly pulled the phone out of the pocket of my dress and saw Ben's name on the screen.

"Hello?"

"Liza, where are you?" Ben asked.

"I'm out... with Gage," I said, taking a brief glance at him. Gage forced a smile.

"Ohhh," Ben sang. "Hope you're having fun. I just wanted to check on you. I went by the bus and didn't see you there. I knew you weren't at the club." He laughed, teasing me.

"Hardy-har-har," I said sarcastically, biting on a smile.

"Well, have fun. I'll be out with a few friends tonight so don't wait up for me. Hugs and kisses." Ben hung up and I slid the phone back into the pocket of my dress before turning slowly to look at Gage. I took a step back and he looked me over, confused by the space I allowed to grow between us. He turned his head, breathing strongly through his nostrils. His features became aggravated, frustrated. His jaw ticked and his grip around his cowboy hat grew tighter.

"Should we get out of here?" he asked, forcing another smile as he finally looked me in the eyes.

"Yeah," I breathed as I stepped to his side.

His eyes softened and the walk to the barn was quicker, but only because Gage was pacing forward. During our walk, he called Stan and told him to come and get us. We waited in the barn for only ten minutes, quietly watching the people square dance, before Gage checked his phone and then told me to come on.

The ride back to the bus was worse.

Ten times worse.

If Stan wouldn't have had his jazz music playing, the ride would've been dead silent and way too awkward. The night was ending in the wrong way, but I didn't care because it was way too close. I'd gotten too close to Gage.

Stan pulled up in front of the tour bus and I climbed out quickly. Gage got out, but before he shut the door behind him, he told Stan to wait. One of the security guards hopped out of one of the trailers behind the bus with a bundle of keys in hand. He unlocked the door, nodded at me, and then hurried back.

I sped for my room, latching the door behind me. I slipped out of the boots, the dress, and removed the pigtails before sliding into some pajama shorts and a tank top.

Zippers zipped and Gage grunted a few times on the other side of the door. It was too damn quiet and I was starting to get annoyed by it.

I pulled my door open to look out, but my forehead creased as Gage sprayed some cologne over his fresh clothes. I expected pajamas, but instead he'd changed into some black jeans, a tight blue T-shirt, and his usual Chuck Taylor's.

"Where are you going?" I asked.

"Out," he said without looking at me.

"Again?"

He looked at me, his jaw locking. "Something wrong with that?"

"No, I just thought you were tired or something—" I broke off as he kicked his suitcase beneath the bunks, causing a loud scraping across the floor that overpowered my voice.

"FireNine never sleeps, Ellie," he said, stepping past me. "We do whatever the hell we want. Remember that. Now, excuse me. I have someone to meet." He continued down the hallway and after only a second, the door slammed shut behind him. I slammed my door as well, hating myself for even bothering to ask.

What the hell was his problem? Was he mad that I didn't finish the kiss? To be honest, I was glad we didn't kiss. I was glad to be interrupted because if I would've kissed him, feelings would have gotten involved between us, and I didn't want any feelings. I couldn't afford them. Feelings and emotions sucked and I wasn't about to start letting them get to me because of him.

I slumped into my bed, yanking my blanket over me and turning off the lamp. I wanted to sleep, but I kept tossing and turning, thinking about how much fun we had dancing at the barn and even about us almost kissing... and then him leaving to most likely go to a club—to most likely kiss another trashy girl or maybe even meet Penelope. *How the hell is she getting around anyway?*

It frustrated me how worked up I was, but I couldn't seem to let it go. And the only reason I didn't let it go was because his actions were my fault. He'd gotten so silent and rushed away from me, as if I were carrying some kind of disease. He shouldn't have been upset anyway. He's Gage Grendel. His motto was always "I don't give a shit," even during high school. What was one kiss from me anyway? I'm pretty sure it was *nothing*.

There was one thing I was sure about, though: I was never going to figure him out, no matter how hard I tried.

NEW ARRIVAL

Obnoxious giggling woke me out of my sleep. I groaned, pushing the blankets off my head as the sun spilled down from the window above. The giggling started again and I shook my head, knowing for sure one of the boys had a girl with them.

My stomach grumbled and I cursed myself. I didn't want to go out there and see any of them. I definitely didn't want to see any of them with a girl on top of them or even beneath them. I wasn't up for being scarred.

I went with being bold. Fuck the band and the girls with them. This was my bus first. I had to hand it to myself; my confidence was rising. I guess it was because the boys never bothered me like I thought they would.

Sliding into my slippers and grabbing my toothbrush, I opened my door and went for the bathroom. I couldn't help but stare at Gage's empty bunk as I walked past. After brushing my teeth and tossing my hair into a sloppy bun, I headed for the kitchen, but the giggling started again and I should have never looked. I should've slapped myself for even giving it the time of day.

What I expected was to see Montana or even Deed with a girl. It wasn't either of them. In fact, none of the boys were in the living room... except Gage... and his girlfriend Penelope. At first sight of them, my mouth hung open, but I clamped it shut quickly before Gage glanced up at me. I guess I was right about him going to meet Penelope last night. *Fuck, did he hold off on hanging out with her for me?* No wonder he was upset... I wasted his time.

"Oh, good morning, Eliza," Penelope said, smiling. She was sitting on Gage's lap.

Gage smirked. "Morning, Ellie."

If it were possible, darts would've been flying from my eyes and right for Gage's head... or maybe his balls. Either way, it would teach him a lesson.

"Good morning." I sighed, stepping ahead to get into the kitchen. I couldn't let it get to me. Penelope was his girlfriend, but why the hell did he have to come back to the bus with her? Why didn't he just stay out and get a hotel like the other boys did? It was like he was trying to get under my skin.

"Gage, stop it," Penelope giggled.

I rolled my eyes as I pulled the cereal from the cabinet. Her voice was pleasant the night at the club, but it was starting to annoy me the more she talked and snickered. After dumping my cereal into a bowl, I grabbed the milk and drowned it. I then looked at Gage and Penelope, who were practically glued together—her legs wrapped around his waist, her fingers tangled in his hair, his arms around her waist, and his hands sliding beneath her waistband to touch her ass. He was looking up at her, his eyes lower and lazier than usual, as he spanked her, and then pulled his arms back to rest them on top of the couch. He had to be stoned; I could tell by the glazed-over look in his eyes, his lazy smile.

Penelope swung her head to look at me and then at my bowl. "Oh, what kind of cereal is that?" she asked, hopping off Gage's lap. "I have a serious case of the munchies." *Well, I guess I was right about the stoned part.*

Gage laughed, but I rolled my eyes again and started for my room, shoveling my cereal into my mouth. I had to bite my tongue. I could have ruined their moment by telling Penelope that Gage hung out with me before meeting her and we almost kissed, but I held off. Neither of them was worth it. Being immature wasn't worth it. If I were the old me, maybe I would have done it, but I'd calmed down. I was living life differently and I was proud of who I was becoming.

I was curious about something, though. Before I could make it down the thin hallway, I looked at them again. "Penelope?" I called.

She looked at me quickly. "Hmm?"

"How do you get to each of our locations?"

"Oh, Gage pays for me to come and go," she said, sinking onto his lap again and hooking her arms around his neck, smashing her cheek against his. He leaned back a little to kiss her cheek and a part of me cringed. I didn't want to take the next bite of my cereal, but I forced myself to swallow it down. No point in looking pathetic in front of him. It's what he wanted and I wasn't about to let him win.

"So, in other words, he only brings you around when he wants?" I asked.

"Sometimes we agree," she said.

Boy was she ditzy. And I thought the blondes like me were the crazy ones. "Hmm," I mumbled, turning around. I went down the hall, hearing more of, "Stop, Gage," and, "Oh my gosh," from Penelope. As I entered my bedroom, it got so quiet I couldn't figure out what the hell they were doing. There was shuffling, stumbling, and muttering. Why the hell was I listening anyway?

But then Penelope started moaning, and I cringed, placing my cereal on the nightstand to cover my ears. I scrambled through my suitcase for my headphones and iPod and was more than relieved to hear Hayley Williams of Paramore versus them *fucking*.

I don't think I could have been more disgusted with Gage.

I had to get out of the bus. I had to go somewhere to rid my mind of what I'd seen and heard earlier that morning. I had no right to be upset, but it seemed like he was rubbing it in my face. What was his point? Was he still mad over the measly kiss I didn't give? I was so frustrated I couldn't even see straight. When I got ready to plan a mini adventure, Gage and Penelope were already gone, and I was glad. I didn't want to see him.

Who knew anyone could be so disrespectful? And how dumb was she to sleep with him while people were around? Careless broads like her were why rockers ran over every girl that crossed their paths.

The bus was in a parking lot, but it was surrounded with trees, trees, and more trees. Trudging forward, I clutched my sketchbook beneath my arm and went straight through. A few mosquitos and gnats buzzed around my head. Some kind of water source was nearby and I wanted to find it. I kept moving forward, hoping to come across some sort of serenity. I just wanted to allow nature to consume me and help me forget and live on.

And then I found it.

Centered between tons of large boulders and hovering trees providing shade was a lake. It was a warm day and I had on my sunglasses, along with some jean shorts and an orange tank. It felt nice as I stepped beneath the shade of the trees. The grass was softer than I thought it would be so I sat and placed my sketchbook in front of me.

I didn't want to draw yet. I just wanted to take it in. The breeze was nice. In the shade it wasn't too hot. It was just right, actually. I finally decided to get started. I took a pencil out of my white satchel Ben bought for me a while ago and opened my sketchbook to a clean page. I drew the lake first and then all its surroundings. I drew the birds perched on tree branches and even on top of the boulders, the various flowers sprouting near the edge of the lake. I don't know why, but seeing one of the grey birds flying by reminded me of what I said to Gage the night before.

A single dove.

That, I certainly was and I didn't give a damn about it. I would rather be single and happy than in a relationship and miserable. The right one was coming for me. I wasn't rushing to be found or even introduced. I just had to wait for the right moment and that moment was going to be *after* I started a career and a real life for myself.

Sad to say, but I'd never been in a relationship in my entire life. I'd never kissed a boy or even held hands with one. The closest I'd gotten was with Gage at the club the first night of the tour and then after square dancing when we almost kissed. I don't even know why I allowed him, of all people, get that close to me.

I shook my head. I was fucking insane, but I had a right to be. I couldn't allow anyone to walk into my life and try and steal my heart away from me. They had to work for it. I had high standards and it may have been because my mom stooped so low and I never wanted to be like her.

Ever.

It also could've been because of all the books I read. I read so much that words were a big deal to me, almost as much as art. Words consumed me until my eyes crossed from reading too much. Plus, finding a new book boyfriend to love was always better than finding a guy in real life to fit my expectations. It was a mental thing only a few could understand.

My high expectations were probably the number one reason I was still single. Ben always said it was a good thing, but sometimes I felt like it wasn't. Sometimes I felt the need to stop being a stuck-up, picky brat and give in to someone for a change. But the person had to be at least halfway decent. I didn't want a one-night stand kind of guy. I wanted someone who would invest more if I were to actually give a relationship a try.

My surroundings became calmer as I dropped my sketchbook and took in the view of the lake again. It had really put me at ease. I was able to let some stuff go and I'd even forgotten about Gage and Penelope's little shindig on the bus.

But then a crackle came from behind me. My head whipped toward the sound and I waited for whoever or whatever it was to step out. I hoped it wasn't a large reptile or animal of some kind. I was deathly afraid of reptiles and if it were a large animal… well, I guess I was just dead.

The crackling happened again and I didn't look away. I then saw a black tennis shoe step out first. My eyes traveled up the lanky length of his legs and then his FIRENINE T-shirt. I finally met his dark-brown eyes that were just as confused as mine and then gasped, taking in the purplish bruise around his right eye.

In an instant, Deed took a step back, placing his sunglasses over his eyes rapidly. "Eliza," he said. He sounded cool, but I could tell by the bothered look on his face he was far from it.

"Deed." I stood to my feet quickly, staring at him. "W-what happened to your eye?"

"What do you mean?" he asked as if I were an idiot.

"Deed, I'm not stupid. Let me take a look at it."

"Um, no."

"Deed—"

I marched toward him, but he took a step back and shook his head. "Eliza, back the hell up and mind your own fucking business, all right?"

I ignored him. "Is that why you were late to the concert last night?"

His lips remained sealed.

"Deed, I swear you can talk to me. What happened?"

His tongue ran across his dry lips as he took another step away, shaking his head. "I don't have to explain shit to you. I didn't mean to run into you out here anyway. I'm going back—"

"Has anyone else seen your eye?"

"No, so don't go around the bus telling everyone about it. I've been blaming the sunglasses on a hangover."

"What really happened?"

He scowled. "Even if I were to tell you, what would you do about it, Eliza?"

"I—I would tell Ben or the boys. It seems like you got jumped or purposely beaten up."

He shrugged. "Shit happens."

I folded my arms. "You're being ridiculous."

"And you're being nosey."

My mouth clamped shut. I couldn't disagree and say I wasn't.

"Look, whatever you do, don't tell the band about it. It's whatever."

Before I could respond, Deed turned his back to me and took off, leaving me completely stumped. I wanted to chase after him just to find out. What could he have possibly done to get a black eye? It sort of freaked me out.

I wasn't the kind of person who brought darkness to light. I had my own closet that I never wanted to open and memories I never wanted to relive again, so instead of chasing after Deed, I grabbed my sketchbook, slid my pencil into my satchel, and headed for the bus.

"All right, let's go!" Ben yelled from the front door of the bus. Snickering, I crossed my legs on the couch and pretended to watch TV. I wasn't really a TV person—plus, the entire time I'd been listening in on Gage and Penelope arguing outside. It was sort of my entertainment.

All I could make out was her being upset that she couldn't ride with him on our bus to the next city. He'd already bought her a plane ticket to go back home. The next city stop was Orlando, Florida, and their new FireNine tour bus was waiting there. I was glad about it. I was growing tired of the boys being around… specifically Gage.

Gage stepped onto the bus with a heavy sigh. I turned slowly to look at him, but he was already looking at me. He didn't say anything, though. Instead, he turned for the hallway and the bathroom door shut behind him.

Deed, Roy, and Montana stepped onto the bus next. Deed still wore a dark pair of sunglasses. I could feel him looking at me through them, but he didn't say a thing. He most likely thought I was going to bring something up, but I knew better. I doubt I had it in me to mention it in front of everyone anyway.

"This is a twenty-hour ride so get ready, boys," Ben said, the door slamming shut behind him. The boys groaned as they parted ways. Deed went for his bunk, Roy went for his room, but Montana came for the couch across from me.

"S'up, Eliza? Didn't see you at the club last night."

"I don't really do clubs." I hated repeating myself.

Montana nodded, looking at the TV. A movie with Justin Timberlake and Mila Kunis was playing, and I found it kind of interesting. I wondered if it were possible to have benefits with a friend of the opposite sex. To have a guy I could mess around with whenever I'd like with no feelings involved until I was ready. It sounded like a good plan to me. No feelings, no problems. No attachments. Just fun.

Just as the thought came to mind, it seemed like luck had come my way. The door swung open and when I looked toward it, my jaw literally dropped. He had on dark-blue jeans, a tight black T-shirt, and his hair was dirty blond. A few pieces of hair hung in his light-green eyes, but his smile was contagious. As he looked at me briefly, I felt my knees lock and my body ooze with warm excitement. He had a rugged look about him because of his couple-day-old stubble, but it was sexy all the same.

His jawline was firm, all man, and his nose not too pointy or too crooked. Just right.

His black camera hung from his neck. A bag was slung on his shoulder and the handle of his suitcase was locked between his fingers. I didn't know who this guy was, but obviously Ben did because, from the kitchen, he yelled excitedly and rushed in the hot guy's direction.

"I'm so glad you're here, Cal!" Ben exclaimed. He ushered the phenomenal "Cal" inside and he looked around before dropping his bags in the corner.

"So where's a guy like me supposed to sleep?" he asked Ben. "I'm not too big so I don't need much space." He chuckled.

Ben laughed with him. "Don't worry. The couch is available for tonight. The boys will have their tour bus back tomorrow so the rooms will be empty for the rest of the tour. I'm so glad you've decided to take us up on the offer, though. A journalist like you is exactly what we need to get FireNine that extra buzz."

A journalist? When I found out what he was, I licked my lips. He was a man who dealt with words. Check one on the list of friends with benefits material.

"I wouldn't have missed it, Ben. I love this band's music and to get the full effect should be fun. I've been looking forward to it since you contacted me about it."

"Well, great." Ben turned around to look at me and I looked away quickly before Cal could see me staring at him. "Eliza, come here, sweetie," Ben insisted.

I hesitated. What I had on was rather hideous—a pair of black-and-red running shorts with a red T-shirt to match. I wasn't dressed to impress at all and being introduced to Cal so underdressed kind of bothered me. Meeting him for the first time meant I should've been rocking some nice jeans and a blouse that was a bit revealing. For a guy like him, I was supposed to make him do a double take, make his jaw drop, his head spin—something.

I had to remain bold, though.

I stood slowly and made my way to Ben's side. As I got closer, Ben wrapped his arm around my shoulders, looking at Cal, who was already looking at me. "Cal, I'd like you to meet my daughter, Eliza Smith."

Cal's head tilted as his eyes scanned me from head to toe. As he did, I fidgeted. Cal then took my hand and kissed the skin on top. "It's a pleasure, really." My cheeks caught on fire as he looked at me beneath his blond eyelashes. His green eyes were so clear yet hard as he observed every aspect of my face. I wondered if he found me attractive because he was attracting the hell out of me. "They call me Cal, but my full name is Calvin Avery."

"It's nice to meet you, Cal," I said boldly, although I could feel my voice wanting to waver.

"Ben!" someone shouted from the front door of the bus. It sounded like Terri. Ben pulled his arm away from my shoulders and took a step forward with a sigh.

"I'll be right back," he said hurriedly.

This was one moment I didn't want Ben to leave me alone... with Calvin Avery. A sexy Calvin Avery whom I couldn't be so confident around. He was really something to look at. Beneath his shirt I could make out the creases that defined his upper half. Through his jeans, I knew he was carrying a rather large package. He looked like he had it all.

"So, Eliza," he finally sighed. "What brought you on tour with a bunch of men?"

Finally blinking, I looked from Cal to Montana, who was currently lying on his back, his eyelids droopy, on the verge of falling asleep. "Ben thought it would be nice for me to come along with him this year. I had nothing else to do this summer so…" I shrugged. "I just went with it."

Cal nodded. "Has it been fun for you so far? You seem rather… bored." He looked around, as if we were supposed to be throwing some kind of animalistic party.

"It's been pretty chill so far. It'll probably pick up in Orlando."

"Considering that we'll be staying there for five days, it just might. It'll give me a chance to get to know each band member personally… and maybe a few others around." He winked and my cheeks heated as he bent down to grab his suitcase. I couldn't believe it. Calvin Avery was flirting with me?

"Ben?" a deep voice called from the hallway. I knew who the voice belonged to. Gage, of course.

He stepped around the corner and at first sight of Cal, his eyes narrowed. "Who are you?"

"Ho-ly shit." Cal dropped his bags and rushed for Gage. Gage looked at him, slightly inconspicuous, before shaking the hand Cal held out toward him. "I'm Calvin Avery, but you can call me Cal. I work for *It's Real* magazine, and I've been asked to write an article on you and the band in August after the tour is over. I have to say, it's going to be amazing to be up close and personal with you guys and to get the full effect. I know the readers will love to read about my adventure and road trip with you all, the ladies especially."

Gage forced a laugh, looking from Cal to me. "That's great. I can't wait to get to know you... I guess," he said, looking at Cal again. Cal nodded and Gage glanced at me once more before going for the stairs of the bus and stepping outside.

"This should be fun," Cal said, sighing as he took in the feel of the bus. He looked at Montana, who was snoring. He'd fallen asleep that fast. "So, Eliza, would you like to show me around the bus?"

I snorted a laugh. "I can, but there's not much to see." I stepped to his side and looked at the kitchen. "That's obviously the kitchen," I said, pointing at it.

He nodded, smirking. I slightly oozed on the inside, holding back on a grin.
I turned for the hallway but stepped past the first bedroom. That was the room Roy was in and I refused to go in because he always made situations awkward. He could have been cutting kittens' heads off in there... Okay, that wasn't true, but that's how much he creeped me out.

We passed the bunks and I mentioned to Cal the top bunk was Gage's and the bottom one was Deed's. My room was diagonally across from it and I swung the door open. I was slightly embarrassed as I took it in from a bystander's point of view.

The bed wasn't made. I had pencils and drawing paper all over the place. Paint was sitting in the corner, and my clothes weren't too organized in my suitcase. I grabbed the door handle and tried to shut the door after telling him it was my room, but he held up his hand and pressed his palm against it to stop me.

"Hold on now." He chuckled. "Are you embarrassed about me seeing your room?"

I shook my head as he took a step in. "No. It's just not too clean right now."

"Hey"—he shrugged—"clean isn't even in my vocabulary. I hate cleaning. It's just something I've despised for ages. And besides..." He sighed, reaching for one of the pencils on my bed. "I kind of like dirty girls."

He'd definitely lit another fire within my cheeks. He noticed the way I tried to control my girly emotions and laughed smoothly. "Shall we continue the tour?" I asked.

"We shall," he said, dropping the pencil on the bed and following me out. I led him down the hallway and showed him the bathroom. Afterward, I mentioned that the last two bedrooms belonged to Montana and Ben.

"For a bus, it's kind of big," he said as we stepped into the living room again.

"Yeah. It's big, but I kind of love it."

"A girl who loves big things," he said, smirking. "You know, Eliza, you're making me more and more interested in you by the second."

I giggled, blushing. "How?"

"It wouldn't be fair to tell you unless we get to know one another, now would it?"

"Get to know one another how, exactly?" I asked, my head tilting. I was still smiling, which shocked me a little.

"We have almost two months ahead of us. I'm sure we can figure it out way before the tour is over."

I laughed. I couldn't doubt he was flirting with me. It was obvious, and as someone who didn't really care for guys who flirted with me, I was finding it fun with Cal. He was adorable, especially when he smiled and his cheeks sank in, revealing his dimples. I couldn't deny it.

The front door of the bus swung open and in came Gage again. He looked at us and then noticed how close I stood in front of Cal. Gage's hazel eyes were like steel and, if I wasn't mistaken, held a hint of aggravation. I figured he was still upset about his argument with Penelope, but I took a step back anyway.

"Gage, you don't mind if I get a few questions in with you tonight, do you?" Cal asked, taking a step back as well. "I have some from the fans, but I won't bombard you with them. I have a few for the whole band, but it seems like everyone wants to hear what you have to say most."

Gage shrugged. "Happens when you're lead singer of a band."

"Cocky much?" I teased.

He laughed at me, running a hand through his hair. "Never that, Sweet Ellie. Never that. Just confident."

Cal laughed with him and then went for his suitcase. "Great. When would you like to start?"

"We could do it now." Gage sighed. "I have plenty of time to practice my vocals later."

"Awesome." Cal dug into his suitcase and unzipped a small black bag, fishing out a cell phone and a notebook. "At the table, shall we?" He gestured to the table.

Cal went for it quickly and Gage nodded with a sigh. As he stepped by, he paused to take a look over his shoulder and winked at me. I frowned. I was still annoyed with him and his act with Penelope; plus, I knew the interview was going to take a while so I headed for my bedroom.

I allowed drawing to consume me and even did some drawings and T-shirt designs for the band. They turned out way better than I thought they would. There weren't skulls or anything grunge. It was actually on the softer side but with a hint of masculinity.

I dug around my suitcase for my colored pencils to fill in the logo I'd created. Orange, red, and black were already the band's official colors, so I had to make do. I preferred the cool colors like blue, teal, green, and maybe a little bit of black for the boys because it fit them more, but I couldn't change much just yet. I knew even if Gage were to set something up for me, I wouldn't be able to make too many changes. I'd have a minor say-so, especially because of my age.

The night carried on with me making a ton of designs for T-shirts, their next CD cover, and even their instruments. It was fun to plan and I didn't even realize how late it became or that we were on the road again until a knock came from my door.

I looked at it quickly, wishing I could just pretend to be asleep, but I was sure they saw my light on from the dark hallway. "Who is it?" I called.

"Your enemy, I guess," Gage said from behind the door. There was humor in his tone.

I rolled my eyes before pushing up from the bed and going for the door. Swinging it open, I looked into Gage's bright eyes and folded my arms. His hands were gripping the frames of the door and his head was tilted down. He was way taller than me, which wasn't unusual at my five feet and three inches.

"I haven't talked to you much today," he said.

"And that's my fault?"

"No." He shrugged, stepping into my room. My eyebrows drew in as he looked toward my bed. He spotted the FireNine drawings and smiled as he picked up one. "You're working," he noted, smirking. "Dedication."

"I don't consider it working. Just thought it'd be fun to test some things out for you guys."

"Seems like the testing is going well. This looks like something I'd definitely wear," he said, holding up the sheet of paper. "The colors I love most. Blue... it's my favorite color. And black."

"Yeah," I scoffed. "I can tell black is." I laughed as I looked him over in his black T-shirt and black sweats.

"Are you finding my clothes a problem, Ellie?" he asked, eyebrow arching as he sat on the end of my bed.

"Not at all, Gage."

He sighed, dropping the paper back on the bed and then scooting toward me. "Can I ask you something?"

"Sure."

"Were you upset about Penelope being over earlier?"

I scowled at him, taking a step back. "Why would I be upset?"

"Maybe because you're interested in me." He smirked confidently.

"Not likely. I don't really care about you or Penelope, to be honest."

His eyebrow rose. "Really? I find that hard to believe— not about Penelope, but about you not caring about me."

"I'm just starting to know you and right now you're coming off as an arrogant ass. I don't favor people like you."

"An arrogant ass?" he repeated, chuckling with wide eyes. "You've called me arrogant twice in less than a week. That's funny."

"Is this what you came in here for? Because you think I like you and I'm jealous of your ditzy girlfriend?"

He winked. "Maybe."

I took another step back and sighed. "Well, I'm not, Gage. As I've said before, you're my *friend*. That's all."

He licked his lips, nodding slowly as he looked into my eyes. "And that's final? You're completely sure about that? You want nothing more? Not even after what was about to happen between us last night?"

I almost hesitated. I wanted to shout at him about how I'd had a crush on him since my freshman year of high school. I wanted to tell him that I fantasized about those plush lips against mine, his firm body pressed up on me for hours. I'd even fantasized about having *sex* with him. All kinds of sex. I was sure I would've gone through with all of it if he weren't so damn egotistical, but he was and I couldn't get down with that.

I couldn't get down with a guy who would sleep with a girl just for the hell of it and then forget about her. I couldn't be a part of his "yeah, I fucked her" list. I was more than certain that was the list Gage would add me to, so I finally folded my arms and said, "I'm positive."

He stared at me a little longer than expected and stood and stepped back with a nod. Gripping the doorknob, he narrowed his eyes and a forced smile across his lips. "Goodnight, Ellie."

Before I could say it back, the door was already shutting. I pitched a dry laugh because that entire conversation was pointless as hell. What was the purpose of it? Why did he care if I liked him or not anyway? And why the hell would I be jealous of fucking Penelope?

There were probably a million girls in the world that claimed to be madly in love with Gage Grendel, but he was worried about *my* opinion of him? Thinking about it as I sat down to color in a few logos caused me to laugh again.

I'd mentioned it to Ben once before, but Gage really was a character in my eyes. A truly confusing one.

NEXT QUICK FIX

I'm not sure when I fell asleep the night before, but I do know I woke up in Orlando. It was a late morning and we'd been on the road twenty hours. I had to have slept for twelve hours or more and of course I woke up in the middle of the night, gasping for breath while clinging to my chest. As I sat up, I had one of those sleep hangovers that could kill a whole day if you allowed it.

The only plus to waking up in Orlando was there was a ton of sun. I loved the sun. Anytime I could be in it, I would be. I would paint in the sun just to feel it on my skin. I could never figure out why I was so pale when all I wanted was to be around it.

A knock came from my door and right after, it opened quickly and in came Ben. He had on a collared light-pink shirt, dark-brown khaki's, and penny loafers. His hair was parted in the middle, as usual, but what confused me was the frown on his face. "Why are you still in bed?"

I groaned, pushing on my hands to climb out of the bed. "I had a long night last night."

He raised an eyebrow. "Doing?"

"Painting, drawing—the usual." *And thinking about Gage.*

Ben's lips pressed as he folded his arms. "Well, everyone's outside waiting on *you*."

"On me?" I frowned, eyes wide. "Why?"

"We've decided to go out for some breakfast." He flashed a smile and then checked his watch. "Ten minutes, button bottom."

Before I could speak, he was stepping out of my room and shutting the door behind him. I sighed, turning for my suitcase to pull out some jean shorts and a lavender tunic. I then grabbed my toiletries and rushed for the bathroom to take a quick shower. I usually hated those, but I hated it more when people were waiting on me. It kind of bothered me.

I rushed to put on my clothes, sliding the thongs of my flip-flops between my toes, grabbing my camera, and then hurrying out. I kicked open the screen door and stepped out, absorbing the sun. It felt nice against my skin, although I was a bit flustered from rushing around. I turned my head to look toward the white truck Ben and I usually rode in, but before I could even take a step ahead, Gage stepped to my side.

"Did you even bother to dry your hair?" he asked.

I frowned, reaching up to touch it, and my face fell rapidly. I jerked my hand down because my hair was soaked. My cheeks burned and I rushed away from Gage to get to the bus again. I could hear him laughing at me and felt even more embarrassed. I had a damn mop on top of my head and didn't even realize it. No wonder it felt so nice outside.

I hurried for the bathroom, wrung out my hair, dried it with a towel, and then pulled it up into a bun. I gave the mirror one last check, approving my casual demeanor, and then stepped out. As soon as I did, I ran into a broad chest.

My eyes traveled from his tan T-shirt up to his pink lips curved into a smile and then into his light-green eyes. His blond eyelashes batted at me and my breath stifled slightly as he caught me by the hip before I could fall into him any farther. "Morning, Eliza," Cal said, still smiling.

"Um, good morning," I murmured, taking a step away. "Sorry. I'm in a rush. Ben said I only had ten minutes to get ready."

Cal laughed. "There's no rush. Ben and the crew are too busy chatting about today's show."

I nodded, releasing a breath of relief. "Oh… okay."

"So I take it I'm riding with you and Ben?" he asked, turning around.

"I guess so." I took a few steps down the hallway and he followed me out the door.

He was right about not being in a rush. Ben was talking with a group of people near the FireNine tour bus. I took in the bus and noticed how different it looked from the last. It was still black, but instead of just the logo, it had each band member on the front, posing with their instrument. Gage was in the middle, behind the FireNine logo, with a mic in hand, his hazel eyes narrowed and his hair hanging over his forehead. It was an old picture because Gage had cut his hair a while back so it didn't even touch his forehead. It barely touched his ears.

And then it dawned on me. I hadn't even noticed that the boys' luggage wasn't on the bus. Their bunks were clear and made up. The band was finally going back to their own bus. I wanted to shout with joy when I figured it out, but I kept my cool, especially when Gage and Montana started coming our way.

"Eliza, is there ever a time you don't look good?" Montana asked.

I laughed.

"Seriously," he said, looking me over. "You always look hot." Gage play-punched his arm, chuckling, and I giggled.

"Thanks, Montana."

"Just stating facts." He winked.

"So where are we eating?" Cal asked.

"Cracker Barrel," Gage said, folding his arms.

"Oh, that's great." Cal's gaze shot over quickly to Montana. "Montana, do you think I could get some questions with you—I mean, since we're waiting on Ben and the crew, I thought it'd be the perfect time and all."

Montana ran a hand over his mohawk that was slicked back and then nodded. "Sure."

"Great." Cal stepped from my side to get to Montana and they walked off. Cal had pulled out his phone and every time he asked a question, he would put the phone a little too close to Montana's mouth for his response. Montana would back away, aiming to conceal a frown, and I would laugh because he was doing a horrible job at hiding his discomfort.

"Don't tell me you find that *Calvin* guy interesting," Gage said, snapping me out of my stare.

"What are you talking about?"

"You're practically drooling, Ellie." He smirked.

"No, I'm not."

"You are." Gage chuckled. "So you find guys with blond hair more interesting than me. Maybe I should bleach my hair. Will it get you to be nicer to me?"

"Gage." I laughed, shaking my head. "I'm not mean to you. And besides, blond would be really ugly on you."

He laughed smoothly. "Would it? Penelope told me I'd look good in anything."

"Well, I'm sorry to tell you, but for one, Penelope lied to you and two... it's Penelope. I'm not entirely sure what she knows outside of following your every command."

His eyes narrowed, but in only a second he smirked. "Is that jealousy I'm sensing? Did you lie to me last night?"

"Not at all. Sorry." My sarcasm with Gage was growing by the second. It was hard keeping up with this careless attitude.

Gage moved in closer, limiting the space between us. He was about to reach up and touch my cheek, but then he stopped abruptly, in midair, and shook his head, jerking down his hand. "Whatever you say, Ellie." He turned quickly, meeting up with Roy and Deed who were standing by the truck. Ben clapped his hands and yelled for everyone to get ready and I sighed, turning for our Navigator. I hopped in the backseat and Cal jumped in a minute after.

"Montana is hilarious," he said, tucking his phone into his pocket.

"Yeah," I agreed. "Montana's pretty chill."

"My boss is gonna love what I've gotten so far. I should be able to take up four whole pages for FireNine by the time the tour is over. That could make them a highlight of the magazine... maybe even get them on the front cover."

"Wow. That would be good for them."

"Yeah. These boys are underestimated. I'd love for my article to be one of the very first up-close-and-personal articles with FireNine. Not only will it take me to greater places, but it just might get them attention outside of the United States. They might not just be traveling by bus anymore." He winked.

I smiled and Ben opened the front door of the truck to get in. He glanced over his shoulder, lowering his sunglasses to wink at me. "Sorry about the wait," he said. "We've got a long day ahead of us."

"What's going on today?" I asked as Ben faced forward and Marco put the car in drive.

"The boys have a show tonight and Monday night." He sighed as the tires of the truck hit the main road. "Besides tomorrow, Sunday, and Tuesday, their weekend in Orlando is booked."

"Oh." I nodded.

"Yeah. There's supposed to be a huge turnout tonight. I had to make sure I told the drivers to get the boys there on time and make sure Deed P. is there on time as well. I still haven't figured out what the hell held him up during the last show. It almost cost us a good penny."

I stared at Ben's back before looking out my window. I had to remain quiet about Deed. I didn't know what happened to him either, but it had to be something serious if he was left with a black eye.

Marco pulled up to Cracker Barrel and I hopped out quickly. Turning back, I saw the band hopping out of their truck as well, but they had to be escorted to the door by a few security guards when a cluster of squealing girls rushed for them. It had to suck for the boys. They couldn't even go out and eat comfortably without fans hounding them.

As soon as we were inside, the woman behind the counter gave us a table immediately. Of course, she got the boys to autograph a few things for her in return, but they thought nothing of it. Ben asked for an entire section alone so people wouldn't purposely walk by our table just to get close to FireNine. Being with the band made me realize how people would do anything for an autograph. Even the employees stepped out of their way to get a few things signed.

Unfortunately, I had to sit between Ben and Gage. It kind of bothered me that Gage was sitting so close, and even when I slid his chair away from me with my foot, he always managed to get close again.

Cal sat across from Ben, engrossed in a topic about the magazine and how he was going to write the article about the band. He was really excited about his job. I couldn't wait to be like him one day—excited to work. Most people are miserable when they think of work. I didn't want to be like that. I wanted to be eager for my next day on the job.

Our food arrived and I drenched my French toast with syrup. Gage chuckled from my side and I looked up to meet his eyes. "You're like me," he noted, pointing at his plate with his fork. "You love syrup."

"I do love syrup." I cut my toast into pieces and began to eat, but it was kind of nerve-wracking to have Gage so damn close to me. His heavy arm always brushed against mine when he would cut his pancake or when he took a sip of his orange juice. He was so close I could smell his body wash hidden beneath the sheen of spicy cologne. It wasn't too strong for me so I dealt with it, but I had to get his chair to move again.

Placing the tip of my sandal against the leg, I pushed his chair forward slowly but kept my gaze on my French toast. I grabbed my drink and Gage laughed silently, his shoulders shaking as he placed his elbows on the table. "Don't you like being close to me, Ellie?" he asked, almost in a whisper.

My stomach rolled. I couldn't understand how it was possible to feel so pleasured by someone's voice. Gage's voice was so damn sexy that I couldn't deny it, no matter how much I despised the way he was.

"You're just really close," I murmured.

"You don't like when I'm close to you?"

"No."

He chuckled silently again before looking around at each person busy chatting over their breakfast. He then slid his chair in closer and my heart paused on the next beat as he placed his hand on my thigh beneath the table. He and I both knew if I were to jolt I would bang my knee against the table and draw attention, so I kept perfectly still.

His fingers moved up until they were completely between my legs. It was a gesture he'd pulled once before, but I couldn't remember much of it from last time. This time, it was as clear as day.

His fingers were warm, the palm of his hand soft as it caressed my skin. My breath kept hitching and I was glad everyone was talking because otherwise, I would've been making a fool of myself.

"It's funny how you seem to hate me so much, yet your body is reacting so positively to my touch," Gage whispered in my ear. "Maybe you do like when I'm close to you." My legs clenched around his hand and he chuckled softly so only I could hear. "There are so many things I could do to you, Ellie, if only you'd let me."

His hand recoiled and I was partially relieved, partially upset. Relieved because that was too close to me reaching a damn orgasm and upset because I kind of liked his hands on me, his fingers moving up and down my leg. Unlike the club where he had his hands on me briefly, this moment seemed longer. It was weird how no one noticed how close he was to me, and if I wasn't mistaken, he would have definitely finger-fucked me if he would've kept his hand down there a little longer.

"Liza?" Ben called.

"Hmm?" I answered quickly.

He looked down at me, his eyes narrowing as I placed my hands on my thighs. I could feel my cheeks burning with blood and heat, but I kept my eyes on him. "Cal said he's looking for an artist to draw something for him for his article. It sounds like something you'd be interested in," he said, gesturing to Cal.

"Oh." I gulped, looking from Ben to Cal. "What would it be?"

"Oh, just some minor drawings. When writing an article for *It's Real* magazine, we get to decorate our pages ourselves, but it has to match the topic. Since my article will be based on the band and music, I'd gather a ton of drawings of guitars, microphones, creative music notes... maybe even cartoon characters that are singing. I'd make it spiffy, fun." He smiled.

I nodded. "I can help with that."

Cal winked. "That'd be great, Eliza." He and Ben started talking about a bunch of junk I didn't really care about again, and I sighed heavily, reaching for my glass of apple juice to kill the fire that still seemed to be burning inside of me... because of Gage Grendel.

I dared a look at him and his fingers were folded on top of the table. He was leaning his back against his seat, a smirk on his lips, staring ahead. I wasn't sure what at, but as I looked up, I figured it out.

A girl with blond hair, a tight miniskirt, and a purple belly shirt stood at the entrance, staring directly at Gage. She batted her eyelashes at him a few times and then winked as she stepped around the corner to get to the restrooms. Was that her gesture to get him to come after her?

What surprised me most was that it worked because, clearing his throat, Gage pushed from the table and slid in his chair. No one else seemed to notice he was walking toward the restrooms but me, and that's only because the stunt he pulled was really ignorant and disgusting.

I couldn't stand it. I couldn't stand how he could make me catch on fire one second, but then right after he'd find someone else to give his attention. It confused me and I was pissed I felt anything toward him. I didn't want to feel anything because feelings hurt. I had to shut off my damn emotions and continue acting like I didn't care. I knew he was only going to continue.

Gage disappeared around the corner and didn't return for a whole fifteen minutes. No one at the table happened to notice he hadn't come back yet... no one but me, anyway. I knew what he was doing in the restrooms, most likely in a stall with the blond whore he knew nothing about. How could he just do that to himself? What if she carried a disease? I knew he was low, but I didn't think he would go as low as having sex with a completely random girl.

Everyone finished up their meals and as soon as we all stood and pushed in our chairs, out came Gage fixing his red T-shirt and jeans. His hair was mussed, way messier than just a few minutes ago, and he looked worn, as if he'd just worked out. Gage saw us getting ready to leave so he headed for the exit. As I stepped past the restrooms, the random blond whore was stepping out, applying lip-gloss to her lips curved into a satisfied smile. *Un-fucking-believable.*

"Oh shit!" Montana yelled from the knick-knack area. I turned to see him holding up a large Tootsie Roll pop. He pretended to lick it and I laughed as I stepped in, forgetting all about Gage and his gross bathroom scandal.

"Can I get a picture of you with that?" I asked.

"Anything for you, Miss Eliza." He winked. I lifted my camera off of my chest and he posed, holding the Tootsie pop against him, as if he were a kid. I giggled as I snapped two and then pulled the camera from my eye.

"So, Eliza…" Montana sighed, putting down the lollipop. "Do you have a boyfriend?"

I shook my head quickly. "No."

"Why not?"

"I don't know." I shrugged. "I'm really picky, I guess. He has to be worth dating."

Montana snorted a laugh before picking up a hand-sized water gun. "So, in other words, you're waiting on a guy you know you'll want to marry. You're that kind of chick? Old-fashioned?"

I blinked quickly because he was right on... sort of. "Kind of." I lied. The truth was yes, but it was way too early for me to be thinking about marriage, which was why I was taking my time on dating. There was no rush. I had plenty of time.

"Sounds like you wouldn't give anyone on this tour a chance, then," he said, stepping toward me and licking his lips.

"That's a definite no." I laughed as I took a step away.

"But what if one of us is willing to take the dive for you? I mean, it may not be right now exactly, but in the future."

I narrowed my eyes at him. "What are you getting at, Montana?"

"I'm not saying me," he said, raising his hands innocently. "I'm just saying... maybe I know someone who would be a good match for you."

I laughed as I scanned the shop. Everyone was looking at different things. Roy and Deed sorted through old-fashioned guitar picks and Gage messed with candy bars and candles. Ben was still talking to Cal about God knows what, and the other miscellaneous people of the crew were waiting by the door, checking their watches and phones, ready to go.

"I highly doubt anyone here is a match for me," I finally said, looking at Montana again.

"What about Gage?" he asked, lifting his eyebrows and pointing his thumb toward him. " We've talked about this before and I see the way he looks at you, the way you look at him. I wish you two would just fuck and get it over with already. The wait is killing me and I'm not even getting any ass."

"Hmm… no thanks. I've literally just gotten to know him and he's most likely unsanitary, inside and out."

Montana laughed obnoxiously. "Eliza, I'm pretty sure any guy that's a part of a band is naturally unsanitary. We like to get dirty. Being clean is for the birds." He waved his hand, slightly rolling his eyes.

"Well, dirty isn't my thing. I like clean men," I said matter-of-factly, picking up a strawberry-flavored lollipop.

"So you like douchebags like Cal over there?" he grumbled.

"Cal's sweet," I said, glancing over my shoulder to find him. He was talking to another crewmember.

Montana sighed, as if he were bored with me. "Being sweet is the new bitter."

"Oh, really?" I placed a hand on my hip. "So what's being rude, then? What's being a jerk? An asshole? I hope you aren't going to make it a reference to being sweet or cool because it isn't."

"Hey, no one said anything about being rude. I'm a pretty nice guy. I just like to have fun and the girls I come across don't realize that. I'm still young. I still have a life to live. I'm pretty sure my band brothers feel the exact same way. We aren't settlers. We just take whatever life hands us and run with it."

"Even when life hands you a random broad to fuck in the bathroom?" I countered.

He chuckled, running a hand over his slick mohawk. "You caught that, too, huh? Gage thinks he's the sneakiest bastard alive. I swear he does."

"It's gross. He didn't even know her."

"Which is the best part. When he doesn't know her, he doesn't have to worry about seeing her again, and if he does, he can pretend they've never met. We're constantly on the move, Eliza. We see so many faces that it all becomes a blur. That's one thing you have to understand. We don't have time to care for feelings outside our own. It's hard to really give a fuck about anyone but ourselves," he said, his tone nonchalant.

I sighed, turning around to get to the exit. "Well, I guess what people say about rockers is true."

"And what might that be?" Montana asked, catching up to me.

"Rockers are selfish and filthy fuckers—at least, that's what I always hear. I used to think it was a stereotype, but the more I'm around you boys, the more I think maybe it's the truth." Montana chuckled and I couldn't help but laugh with him. At least he wasn't denying his ways. I could respect that.

"You don't need to worry, Eliza. You're off limits to all of us anyway. You're around us too much and we see you every day, so if any one of us even takes the dare to try and have sex with you, we wouldn't be getting off so easily. Unlike the other girls where we can kick them out or even leave them without an excuse, you get to stay and we'll have to make one up for you and... well... that's just too much damn work. None of us wants to be nagged, so you're safe around us—plus, you're our manager's daughter. Couldn't do you like that."

I frowned as we stepped outside and Montana placed his dark sunglasses over his eyes. "Is that really how the band sees me? As a girl they know they shouldn't have sex with?"

"Not exactly that way, but somewhere near that. I'd rather have you as a buddy. I'm not sure about everyone else… especially Gage. He's been getting so close to you that it might just happen one day or another," he teased. "Gage will take the nagging as long as he's scored himself some pussy."

"Number one: I don't nag," I said, laughing. "And number two: I would never have sex with Gage after being a witness to him having sex in a public restroom with a girl he doesn't even know."

"Whatever you say, Miss Eliza." He shrugged, sighing. "There's always something that'll get a person to crack. Gage is a wise man when it comes down to it. He'll get a chick to crack in a heartbeat. He enjoys the chase."

"I think you've failed to realize that I'm not like the chicks you and Gage mess around with. I'm far from it, actually."

"How far?" he tempted.

"Pretty far."

"Mm-hmm..." He smirked, looking me over beneath his sunglasses. "Tell that to me at the end of the tour. You're still a girl. You still have desires... needs."

"Are we making a bet over Gage and my vagina?"

"How much are you willing to put on it?" he inquired, grinning slyly.

"I wouldn't put anything on my precious vagina because I know, in the end, he wouldn't be worth it."

"Who wouldn't be worth what?" Gage's voice bellowed behind me.

My heart stilled and I refused to look back. Instead, I stared straight ahead at Montana who'd just looked from Gage to me, his smile confident. "Yeah. Even though there's no money on it, I know I'm gonna win this bet," he said before turning around and walking off.

"What's that clown talking about?" Gage asked, stepping around to get in front of me.

"Uh... nothing," I muttered. He folded his arms across his chest and the ink stretched over his sculpted muscles.

"So you *are* intrigued by blonds," he said.

My eyes narrowed. "How?"

"Well, Cal has blond hair. Montana... I'm just putting two and two together here, Ellie."

"You're obviously attracted to blonds as well," I quipped.

He raised an eyebrow. "How so?"

"In bathrooms of Cracker Barrel."

"You're upset about that?"

"No," I lied. "And do you have any respect?"

Gage's features fell, his smile evaporating. I thought for a moment he was going to give in and say yes—that maybe he was going to apologize—but he didn't. Instead, he said, "I have more respect for myself now than I've ever had before. I think I've accomplished a lot in the past four years." He ran a hand through his hair, looking at the rest of the band standing by the truck. "Maybe you should listen to Montana. He's right."

"Ugh." I shook my head. "You were listening?"

He chuckled, lowering his head. "It wasn't hard to figure out you two were talking about me. You wouldn't stop looking at me." He laughed. "And besides, you should take notes from him. I'll get you to crack and open up one day... and you're gonna love the hell out of me for it, too." A cocky smirk formed on his lips as he scanned me from head to toe.

I placed a hand on my hip, not daring to back down. I knew he was trying to get under my skin, but I wasn't having it. "You know what I think?" I asked rhetorically. Gage folded his arms, still smirking. "I think you only do your nasty charades in public for show. You want someone to pay attention to you—someone to tell you how wrong you are so you can laugh at them." I folded my arms, pressing my lips. "I think you only do it so you won't have to bother yourself with reality—so you can have a little laugh—but deep down, it's not what you really want. You're not as careless as you claim to be."

For a moment, shock overtook Gage's face. His mouth hung open slightly and his eyes grew a little wider, but in a snap he clamped his mouth shut and took a step back, placing his sunglasses over his eyes. "Don't pretend you know anything about me," he muttered. "You don't and you never will." His jaw ticked, proving maybe I was right about him. No one would get that upset unless I spoke the truth. And the truth hurts.

"I'm right, aren't I?" I asked. My eyes narrowed as I aimed to look deeply into his eyes.

"Far from it, Sweet Ellie." I could tell he was lying. He was no longer looking at me.

"Yeah." I scoffed. "Whatever." I began to turn around, but before I could completely, Gage grabbed my arm and spun me back. I landed between his arms and as I tried to pull away, he held on tighter. One of his hands slid down my hips and I bit my bottom lip, trying my hardest to not moan or hitch my breath.

Gage then placed his plush lips on my ear. Tingles ran down my spine and I bit my fingers into the back of his shirt, shutting my eyes briefly, instinctively breathing him in.

"Stop fighting and make it easier on yourself," he murmured in my ear. "You want me. I see it. I *feel* it."

My lower belly sparked with heat that ran down and puddled between my legs. Ugh, I wanted to melt all over.

"Let's just settle this when we get back to the buses. Maybe it'll get you to stop denying me. And I think it'll make you happy, just like it did whatshername in there." He pulled away from me and pointed over my shoulder at Cracker Barrel, a small smirk tugging on the corner of his upper lip.

I scowled, yanking away from him and giving the middle finger before storming for the truck.

What an asshole.

WAR

I despised Gage in every way.

Every time we'd go out, he'd have a different girl on his arm—making out with her, holding her, nuzzling her neck. He'd do it right in front of me. I tried ignoring him, but after a while I realized he was running into me on purpose.

We'd all split up during our free time at the mall and were going to meet at the food court in two hours max, but somehow Gage would always find me and do something explicit with his skank in public. I would continuously scowl at him and brush past him, and each time he would chuckle to purposely get under my skin. I refused to allow him to get to me.

I'd done some shopping around in a bookstore, a department store where I found a really cute red blouse, and then headed to the food court early, hoping I wouldn't run into Gage again. Surprisingly, Montana, Roy, and Deed were already sitting at a table in the middle, surrounded by a cluster of females. I rolled my eyes, trudging forward and pushing my way through, the struggle comparable to punching bricks, just to squeeze in. None of the girls budged until Montana saw me, stood, and grabbed my arm to reel me in. He pushed some girls out of the way for me and I thanked him with my eyes, smiling half-heartedly.

"Thanks," I sighed, sitting beside him.

"Always, Miss Eliza." He winked. The boys reached over the table to sign a few things for the wild girls and even took a few pictures with them until Deed gave a signal to one of the security guards. They bustled their way through, pushing some of the girls back and telling them the boys weren't giving any more autographs. A few of them pouted their bottom lips and turned away, but some stayed, staring from a distance. The security guards shook their heads, folding their arms.

"Sorry about that." Montana sighed, fixing his spiky mohawk. "The ladies tend to get a little crazy over our asses."

I laughed. "I see."

I looked at Roy and Deed, but they were staring off, their eyebrows knitted. Deed finally looked at Roy, cocking his head to his left, and Roy nodded, standing from his seat as if he'd been waiting the entire time for the gesture. Deed stood and they went two tables down to sit. I frowned, glaring at them. What the fuck was their problem?

"Why the hell are they being like that?" I snapped at Montana.

He held up his hands innocently, his light-blue eyes wide, his eyebrow and lip piercings sparkling from the sunlight spilling in from above. "Hey... don't get mad at me. I have no clue what those fuckers' problems are. We all know Roy can be a dick, but Deed... I don't know what's been up his ass."

I sighed, dropping my hands in my lap. I was about to say something else about them, but then a girl screamed, "HOLY FUCKING HELL! IT'S GAGE FUCKING GRENDEL! OH MY GOD, I THINK I'M GONNA DIE!"

The ladies standing near the security guards squealed as they rushed for him. The security guards bustled forward, guarding Gage before he could get trampled. I wouldn't have felt bad for him or the blond skank on his arm if they were to get bulldozed. It would've given me something to laugh about. The skank smirked, knowing she didn't have to fight like they did to get his attention. She knew she had him and none of them could take him... but of course it was only for the moment.

Gage signed a few things for the raging girls and pulled away from the skank who looked defeated as he kissed one girl on the cheek while a friend took a picture. She grinned again, though, after he stepped back and hooked his arm around her. Gage gave the signal to the guards and they stepped in, backing up the girls.

As he and the skank started coming our way, my heart thudded. His eyes were hard on me, his head tilted, a smirk on his lips. I wanted to smack it off his annoyingly beautiful face. I wanted to slap her for being so silly, knowing she wasn't getting anything out of it in the end. I prayed they wouldn't sit across from me, but when they did, I lowered my head. Gage pulled the skank in close, grinning at her before looking at Montana.

"We're jet skiing today," Gage said. "Ben set it up for us."

"Holy shit." Montana rubbed his hands together. "Wait..." His face fell as he stared at Gage. "I don't have a bitch."

I gasped and the skank snickered. "Montana, don't call them that," I snapped at him, slapping his arm.

"Oh... sorry, Eliza. I always forget you're an actual lady with class. My apologies." He kissed my cheek playfully and I laughed. Gage stiffened across the table and I looked at him, slowly smirking.

And then my mindset became a little devilish. Oh, it was perfect: pretend Montana and I did have something going on just to get under Grendel's skin. He was getting under mine. It was only fair as payback, right? It was time for war.

"Well, I don't have a *chick*," Montana said, glancing at me to make sure what he said was an okay term.

"If you want, we can partner up. It's no big deal."

Montana's eyes stretched and I could feel Gage glaring holes through the side of my head. "Really? You do know jet skiing requires me sitting behind you and... well, you have the hottest ass ever, Eliza. I don't mind. It's just you I'm worried about." He grinned.

I grinned back, ignoring Gage. "That's fine. Just keep your hands in appropriate places and we're good. We'll have fun."

"It's not my hands you'll have to worry—"

"What time do you want to leave from here?" Gage asked, interrupting him. I looked at him and his eyes were hard, his glare icy as he directed it on Montana.

Montana didn't seem to notice and that made the moment even more hilarious. I was winning. I was getting under his arrogant, thick skin.

"Anytime, man. Doesn't matter. Since Miss Eliza is my date for the afternoon, I guess I should be asking her." He looked at me, smirking. "What time would you like to go, cutie?"

"Doesn't matter." I held back a laugh. Montana was so natural at flirting that I felt he played along with me to make Gage even more annoyed. Hilarious.

"Well, we should go and get ready now," Gage said, drumming his fingers on the table. "Truck's already waiting."

Montana and I nodded and Gage stood without another word. The skank followed after him, but he didn't touch her. I watched as she brushed against his side when he met up with Roy and Deed and said something to them. They nodded and followed Gage out of the mall, but he still wasn't touching the broad.

"Shall we?" Montana asked, offering his hand. I nodded, taking his hand and standing from my seat. "So does this mean I have to spend the whole afternoon with you? Not that you're a problem or anything. I just know there's going to be some hot bitches there and—"

"Montana! Stop calling them *bitches,* please." I aimed to be serious, but of course I failed terribly as he grinned goofily and knuckled my chin.

"Sorry." He laughed. "I'm just used to it. It's not like they aren't bitches. Most of 'em are stuck-up and self-centered anyway. Best ones to have sex with, though."

"They're still people," I said softly.

He smirked at me, shaking his head. "So, like I was saying... we'll be at the beach and I'll be seeing some hot..."—he hesitated, trying to find a polite word, and I laughed—"...*females.* I'm gonna get at one for myself. You know that, right?"

"I know. It's cool." I shrugged. "I don't expect you to stick with me the whole time. I'm not expecting a real date from you."

He smirked, holding the glass door open for me. I stepped out and he caught up with me, putting on his sunglasses. "I know what you're doing, Eliza. It's fucking funny as hell, too."

"What do you mean?"

"You're pissing Gage off. It's funny when he's mad. He does that whole scary glare thing and his jaw clenches a million times. He'll say he's not mad constantly when we all know he is." He laughed, sliding his fingers into his front pockets. "You're an asshole for this. You know that, right?"

I laughed. So Montana did know I was trying to get under Grendel's skin. "I'm not an asshole. I just know it's killing him to think I've rejected him for you. He's been rubbing his skank in my face all day, and it's truly annoying."

Still laughing, Montana and I climbed into the truck and took the back row with Roy. Of course Roy took a window seat, and to make things less awkward, Montana sat in the middle, but I didn't let Roy bother me like usual. This afternoon was going to be… interesting, and I was ready for Gage's reactions toward my fake date.

After picking up a striped black-and-white bathing suit from one of the stores nearby, the boys and I were at Cocoa Beach. It was beautiful, temperature blazing, and my sunglasses were definitely necessary. What weren't necessary were the millions of chicks in bikinis that the boys had invited. There were a few guys as well, but they barely stood out among the flocks of girls waiting around for attention with bottles and cups of beer in hand.

"All right, Miss Eliza," Montana said, rubbing his hands together. "Do your worst. We've gotta make this quick, though, 'cause—" Montana stopped talking rapidly as a girl in a black G-string bikini walked by, her skin shiny from tanning oils. She giggled over her shoulder, red cup in hand, as Montana stared directly at her ass. I rolled my eyes as he practically drooled. I then snapped my fingers in front of his face, breaking him out of his horny state of mind.

"Get it together, Montana," I sighed.

He shook his head, still staring at her ass. "Sorry, but that one's mine. Let's make this quick. Please?" he begged, turning around to hold on to my shoulders. Just as he'd placed his hands on me, Gage stepped by with a new chick on his arm. *Typical.*

He paused in front of us, staring at Montana's long, tanned arms stretched out toward me. His hands gripped my shoulders and we were only a few inches apart. From a bystander's point of view, it looked like we were about to kiss and then hug, and I could see in Gage's eyes that was exactly what he thought.

The girl on his arm hugged against him, probably aiming to never let go. If she were to let go, he would have most likely found another chick to fondle. It made me giggle thinking how stupid and naïve she was. It made me giggle even more as Gage frowned at Montana. "Ready?" Montana asked, hooking his arm around my shoulders.

I nodded at him, smiling. "Yep." I smiled warmly at Gage, but his eyes were stern, cold. Montana gave him a playful punch in the arm, but Gage's frown deepened. "He looks really mad," I said as soon as we were out of earshot.

"It's your point, right? To piss him off?"

"A little, but not too much. I don't want him too mad."

"Gage'll be fine. You're making him realize his balls aren't as big as he thinks they are. He's one cocky fucker." Montana released me as we met up at the jet skis. After we strapped up in our lifejackets and I pulled my hair up into a tight ponytail, Montana stepped ahead of me. "You know how to work one of these things?" he asked, fiddling with one of the handlebars.

"No." I shrugged. "But it can't be too hard. I'll give it a shot."

"Oh, good 'cause I know nothing about this shit. If we end up wrecking, you'll take full blame and Ben will pay it off."

I laughed, stepping past him to climb on. As I did, a jet ski appeared beside us and girly giggling caused me to turn. Gage floated in next to us, a cocky smile on his lips as he looked directly into my eyes. He didn't look away as he strapped on his lifejacket, ran his fingers through his hair, and then pulled the girl in by the waist. Her annoying giggles chimed again, but I rolled my eyes, gripping the bars of our jet ski.

"How about a race?" Gage asked. "It'll be just like lawn mower racing... on water." He winked at me, but I frowned, reliving our night of square dancing and the kiss that almost happened. "Hop on, baby," Gage said to the girl, his eyes still locked on mine. "You know I like it from the back."

I rolled my eyes again, looking at Montana, who was staring off. I looked back and saw the same girl with the black G-string. *Ugh, men.* "Montana, come on," I said, snapping my fingers in his face again.

"Oh, right." He climbed on behind me, hooking his arms around my middle. He placed his chin on my shoulder but kept his lower half a few inches away. "I won't get too close," he said in my ear.

I smiled over my shoulder before looking at Gage, who'd been staring at us the entire time. "So, about that race?" I asked, grinning.

He slid behind the brunette who had her fingers clutched around the handles. He then cupped her breasts with his hands, grinning over her shoulder. "Ready, baby?"

She smiled. "Of course."

He looked at me just as I had shuddered and looked away.

"All right, get ready!" Montana yelled.

I clutched the handlebars, staring ahead.

"Set... GO!"

I sped off, leaving a splash of water to resemble my dust. I squeezed the gas lever as Montana hooted and hollered. Some water splashed onto us, but it felt nice along with the wind beneath the blazing sun. I'd put Gage and his skank to shame as I circled around and rushed forward. I thought they would at least catch up, but it wasn't happening. As I looked back, it seemed the skank was whining, clutching the handle a little too tightly. She soon started complaining about her nails, waving them in the air dramatically. Gage rolled his eyes a dozen times before looking at me and narrowing his eyes as we rushed back to shore.

I laughed as we met at the shore and Montana hopped off immediately. "All right, Miss Eliza," he said, unclipping his lifejacket. "It was nice fucking with Gage, but that hot chick over there is giving me the fuck-me eyes and I can't afford to miss out. I'll catch you later, I promise."

He kissed my forehead playfully and then dashed away to get to the blonde in the G-string. I knew Gage caught Montana's playful kiss on my forehead because his deep voice asked, "You're interested in Montana?"

Gage was a few steps away, his head cocked and his eyes narrowed again. His skank was still sitting on the wave runner, sighing over her broken nail, her bottom lip poked out.

"I'm not." I smirked, climbing off, and unclipped my jacket. I pulled it over my head and sauntered toward the stand where they'd been hanging. When I hung it up and turned around, Gage stood a step away, his head tilted.

"What the hell are you doing?" he asked.

I frowned. "What are you talking about?"

"You and Montana. What is it?"

"Montana and I are just friends."

He laughed dryly, running a hand through his untamed hair. As he lifted his arms, his muscles tensed, and I inhaled to keep myself steady. He had a body to die for... ink I wanted to lick away, but I couldn't fall for it. I didn't want to. I couldn't stand him. "Friends? That's funny. Friends don't flirt."

"So you're upset we're flirting?"

"Well... yeah, 'cause you said before you weren't interested in him. Flirting means interest."

I folded my arms. "Never said I wasn't interested in him, actually."

"Seems like there's more between you two." His eyes hardened as he took another step forward. My breathing became heavier as he closed the space between us, bringing a hand up to cap my shoulder. His hand on my skin was bringing even more warmth to my body. It was hot as hell outside, but with him this close, I wouldn't have been surprised if I were to suddenly combust. "You're mad about my girls?" he asked, smiling.

"They're not *your* girls," I muttered, aiming to remain confident.

"They're my girls, all right. You could be as well."

"I want nothing to do with you, Gage. What part of 'we're friends' do you not understand?"

"Why can't you just flirt around with me like you do with Montana?"

I stifled a laugh, pulling away from him. I wonder if he realized how desperate he sounded. "Gage—"

"Ellie," he interrupted. "What's so bad about me? I'll let you know right now that Montana is ten times worse than I could ever be. You see how he left you for another chick. You really want that?"

"Montana and I are just friends, just as you and I are— and I'm sure you'd do the exact same thing he did. I don't care what either of you do. You're both my *friends*."

He pressed his lips, his hazel eyes expanding. "You always say that, but I find it hard to believe."

I frowned. "Why?"

Smirking, he leaned forward, brushing the tip of his nose across my cheek. My skin tingled, my breath catching as one of his hands moved down to my waist and then past the small of my back to cup my ass. I gasped as he chuckled. "I find it hard to believe because you're always gasping... always holding off on your next breath to see what I'll do. You may not notice it, but you always lean in, wanting some part of your body against mine." I looked down, noticing how my chest had inched forward to press against his.

"You always tense up when I touch you. What part of your body do you want me to touch most, Ellie? Your lips?" he asked, running a finger over my bottom lip. I wanted to savor that finger on my lip, lick it just because it was part of his body. "Your chest?" His finger dragged from my lip to my chest and heat boiled in my stomach. "Your full, perky breasts that I can't seem to stop staring at? If I had the chance, I'd motorboat the hell out of 'em." He smirked, his fingers expanding and reaching in for one of my breasts. Before he could grab it, I snapped out of my daze and shoved him away, scowling.

"God, you're so full of yourself."

He chuckled deeply as I pushed past him to get to the coolers of beers. "I'll be waiting, Ellie!" he called. I grimaced over my shoulder, but that grimace turned into a mask full of shock as a cluster of girls rushed for him, fighting to be on his arm for the rest of the afternoon. He simply laughed over their arguing, his eyebrow arched amusedly. His eyes then swung up to meet mine as I stopped in front of the coolers and snatched out a beer. It was hard to look away from him. "I'm ready when you are," he mouthed at me, grinning widely.

"Never, dickhead!" I mouthed back.

He simply chuckled, chose two from his collection of girls, and went off with them. Not once did he look at me as the day carried on.

When the sun had set, Montana finally came to check on me, a smile gracing his lips. "You okay, Eliza?"

"I'm great," I sighed, sitting up on my towel.

He tilted his head, his eyes softening. "I'm being a horrible date, aren't I?"

I giggled. "A very horrible one, but don't worry about it. I'll move on."

He chuckled and placed his palms on his knees to bend over. "Most of us are going to a party later. I know how you hate parties and… well… I'll be hanging with the hot chick over there for the rest of my evening." He pointed back with his thumb and I looked, seeing Miss G-string standing a few feet away with a towel on her shoulder. "Maybe you should call Ben, tell him to get you a ride back to the bus."

I nodded because the bus sounded like heaven to my ears compared to a party. "Yeah. I'll do that."

"Great." He sighed, standing up straight. "Have a good night, Miss Eliza!"

I waved at him, laughing at how nonchalant he was. Montana was sweet, but when he had plans, he didn't like to be held back. I couldn't blame him. He was living his life and doing what he wanted. I was never one to make others hold back, so I had no problem with him fleeing.

After calling Ben and hurrying for the parking lot to wait for my ride, I sighed and sat on the curb, the palms of my hands planted behind me on the concrete. Someone cleared his throat behind me and I glanced over my shoulder. Gage came into view with the blonde from the mall and the brunette he'd ridden with on the jet ski.

"No date?" he asked, smirking.

I stuck my middle finger up and turned my head. I was no longer in the mood for him.

Gage chuckled, stepping ahead with the skanks. He nuzzled the brunette's neck as they approached the truck. She giggled obnoxiously, and as the girls climbed in before him, he spanked their asses and they yelped excitedly.

I rolled my eyes, looking away. He was truly revolting.

The doors slammed shut and the truck made a U-turn to get out the parking lot. As it drove by, Gage winked at me, making kissy faces and then shouting, "Make it soon, Sweet Ellie!" Again, I gave him the middle finger and as soon as they were out of sight, my truck came and I sighed heavily, ready for the night to just be over.

WRONG TIMING

The following night the boys had a show and, of course, they knocked the ball out of the fucking park. Amazing, beautiful, and heart throbbing, as always. I hated how Gage could sing so beautifully but had one of the ugliest and cockiest personalities. I don't know why it did, but it bothered me that I'd caught on fire for his ass once again right after jet skiing.

It was two times in a row, and each time I made myself look foolish. He knew what he could do to me with his touch, how weak I could become.

Ugh.

It annoyed me.

It excited me.

It pissed me off.

It thrilled me.

It was completely enthralling, but I knew I had to keep my distance. He wasn't good for me. He expected me to become one of the many whores on his arms. *Um… not likely. Not ever.* Unlike them, I had pride and dignity in myself.

After the show ended, a few girls stormed backstage arm-in-arm, waiting on the boys to come out of their dressing rooms just to meet them. As I sat on the sofa by the wall, I couldn't help but watch them. They were giggling… a lot. They were too eager to see the boys and were even taking pictures with one another with their tongues hanging out while they waited.

I thought about why I didn't have friends, but then reality slapped me out of my stupor and told me exactly why.

"You were no good to be around."

If reality were real, that's what it would have said to me. It would have scolded me for doing what I used to do for my mom. I didn't deserve friends. I remember when I made a friend in elementary school. Her name was Teresa Talon and she wore pigtails every single day. She was a brunette with bright brown eyes and extremely tan skin. I met her during one of our recesses and we immediately became buddies.

One night, Teresa asked me to come to her house for a sleepover. I told my mom and she said I could, but only if I came back with something valuable. By valuable she meant I had to come back home with something worth a lot of money. Something she could pawn for some extra cash.

Let's just say after the sleepover, I could never play with Teresa again. I could never see her, hang with her on the playground—I couldn't even set my eyes in her direction. Those were her mom's commands. I was placed in another class and never saw Teresa again.

"OH MY GOD!" one of the girls squealed, snapping me out of my daze. "There's Gage Grendel! Oh my God, look at him! He's so fucking hot!"

I rolled my eyes because if she knew how Gage really was, her pants wouldn't have been so hot. Gage came down the hall in black jeans and a white T-shirt with black Arabic print on it. When he saw the cluster of girls bouncing up and down for him, he revealed a low, lazy smile and kept moving forward.

As soon as he was a step away, the security guards stepped in place so the girls wouldn't trample him. "Gage! Please sign this!" one of the girls screamed, holding out a poster and a Sharpie.

"Gage, I have something even better." One of the girls with bright pink hair pulled out her tit and held out a Sharpie. The security guards' eyes widened as they stared down, but they kept their arms folded and the girls back. Gage chuckled, as if it were nothing to him, and signed her tit. Gross.

"How's that?" he winked at her.

"Thanks, Gage," she said, aiming to sound seductive. I snorted a laugh.

Gage continued signing things for the group of girls and soon each band member joined him. Roy didn't stay as long as the others and I couldn't help but watch him nearly sneak out the exit door. He was one who didn't like to be seen at all. I had the urge to go after him, but I didn't. I couldn't afford to be nosey and I definitely didn't want to follow after him and witness him beheading a poor kitten or a harmless turtle.

"All right, ladies. Time for the boys to get going," one of the security guards said, pushing the girls back. "Come on. Out the door you go." He grunted, aiming to keep one of them back. The other rushed forward to help get them out and when the door had shut, they both sighed, staring at one another, their heads shaking. "I swear it's like a fucking zoo every time." One of them chuckled.

"It's the damn wild," the other added as they walked down the hall.

"So let me guess…" I sighed, pushing from the sofa. Deed, Montana, and Gage turned quickly to look at me. It was like they just noticed I was around. "You're going to the club again tonight?"

"Oh, no, Miss Eliza," Montana said, shaking his head. "Tonight we'll be hitting a house party. It's going to be epic. Tons of other famous people will be there."

I raised my eyebrows. Yet again, I was stuck with the band. Ben had taken the keys to the bus and my only ride was with them. I knew he did it on purpose, but he acted like it was an accident when I'd called him about it. I could hear him trying to conceal his snickering while on the phone.

I looked down at my clothes. Pink shorts and a solid grey T-shirt. I definitely wasn't suited for a house party— let alone a party where a ton of famous people were going to be. FireNine was already too much for me.

"Do you think your driver will drop me off somewhere else before you get there?" I asked.

"Uh, hell no," Deed snapped. "We aren't making any stops. We're going straight there. Gah, who let the *girl* tag along?" I couldn't see his eyes beneath his sunglasses, but I knew for sure they were upset.

"I don't have to go. I was just—"

"No," Gage said, interrupting me. "You're worried about your attire, but you look fine, Ellie."

"I just... I'd rather have something better on," I murmured.

"Oh, great." Deed threw his hands in the air. I was sure his eyes rolled along with it.

"Deed, cut her some fucking slack." Montana frowned at him. "The fuck is your problem anyway?"

"She's my fucking problem!" he barked. I flinched, blinking rapidly. "She's not even supposed to be with the band. If she doesn't know what we do after shows or even how to dress, she shouldn't be tagging along."

And just like that, I wanted to snap. Deed's attitude pissed me all the way off. I could have blown him up on the spot. I could have smacked his stupid sunglasses away from his eyes and showed the boys his black eye. I could have done so much... but I held off. My hands had balled into fists, but I loosened them, realizing I was turning into the Eliza I no longer wanted to be. I couldn't let it happen. I had to let it go. He wasn't worth it.

I knew I wasn't going to be able to hold my tongue for long so I turned quickly and rushed down the hall.

"Shit," Montana hissed. "Why the fuck would you say that to her?"

"Eliza," Gage called at the same time. For a moment, I thought I caught a hint of sympathy behind his voice.

I ignored both of them, though.

I pushed out the exit door and as soon as it was shut behind me, hot tears burned my eyes. I had to cool off. I had to remain calm. I had to tell myself over and over again he wasn't worth it, but I swore if it were five or six years ago, I would have blown up on him. I used to be ruthless. Reckless. I had to fight for myself so much and sometimes the girls were way bigger than Deed. I should have busted his lip for his attitude. A part of me was proud for walking away from something that could have turned deadly and ended the tour for them completely.

I drew in a deep breath, taking a slow look around the parking lot. Besides the black truck I knew was meant for the boys to ride in and the miscellaneous cars scattered about, there was absolutely nothing around. The night was young and the moon was high in the sky. The stars twinkled and a soft breeze blew by, allowing me to inhale deeply.

The door of the stadium burst open behind me and I turned around, spotting Gage coming out first, Montana right behind him. Deed was last to come out and I knew he was glaring at me, even beneath his sunglasses. I could almost make out what was really beneath them. Aggravation. Frustration. *Anger*. A black eye.

"Eliza, are you okay?" Gage asked, meeting up to me.

"I'm fine."

He blinked, taking a step back to get a clear look of my face. "You aren't going to cry, are you?" he asked. "I don't know how I would handle you... crying."

"I'm fine, Gage. Just go away. It's not like you care." He frowned, looking me over a dozen times before settling on my eyes again. His eyes then softened and he was fixing his lips to say something, but before he did, Montana hustled forward, his eyes remorseful.

"Sorry," Montana apologized. "Deed's a fucking asshole. Don't take the shit he says to heart."

I sighed, looking from Montana to Deed, who was climbing into the front seat of the truck.

"Montana, can we talk for a sec?" Gage asked, taking a few steps back while gesturing Montana to come his way.

I watched as the boys took a few more steps toward the truck while whispering to one another. Montana kept stealing glances at me as Gage hooked an arm around his shoulder, still muttering something I couldn't make out.

"All right, man." Montana capped Gage's shoulder. "See you there." Montana quickly hopped into the truck, shut the door behind him, and then they pulled off.

I frowned as Gage watched them leave before he turned around to look at me, his fingertips in his front pockets.

"What the hell? Are they coming back?" I asked.

"No. We're going to meet them there."

I frowned. "Why?"

"You want something better to wear, right? There's an outlet right around the corner. I'll even buy the clothes for you."

I shook my head. "Gage—no. I could have just gone somewhere else," I said, looking down at my clothes.

"Ellie, if Ben left you with us, you're sticking with us. We aren't letting you go somewhere else. If you wanna look more presentable, I'll take you to get dolled up." He winked. "I don't mind."

"Gage—"

"Come on." He insisted, cocking his head to his right, his elbow held out for me to hook my arm through. I wanted to tell him no. I wanted to tell him to call Montana and get them to come back... but his smile was too much. It was simple and sweet, yet deadly. It was mesmerizing, causing effortless butterflies to flutter around the pit of my stomach.

"Okay, but if I'm going with you, promise me one thing," I said, hooking my arm through his cautiously.

"What's that?"

"Try not to leave me standing around alone like Montana did. I don't wanna look stupid there."

He laughed, running a hand through his tousled hair as we stepped ahead for the sidewalk. "I'll be sure to stick by your side tonight, Sweet Ellie."

They may have stretched the truth a little about there being a ton of famous people. There were a few around, but it was more random drunk girls and guys than anyone else. It kind of took me off guard that the first thing I saw when stepping into the house was a girl vomiting grievously into a flowerpot.

"Would you like a drink?" Gage asked into my ear.

"Uh…" I stared around, debating on whether a drink was safe or not. "Sure, why not?" I shrugged.

He held out his hand and surprisingly I took it. It happened without thought, though. I didn't want to lose him through the crowd and I couldn't afford to be left alone… *Lies.*

Gage pushed through the mass, the rave lights flickering above. They danced off the walls, reflected off of the shimmering sweat within the crowd. The atmosphere was thick, hype. Some people were so close to one another they could've passed as Siamese twins.

Gage finally reached the kitchen, which was even more congested, and stopped to look around for the drinks. As soon as he found them on the island counter, he told me to stay put until he came back. I leaned against the wall, but a couple was making out right beside me and I took a leap back, frowning as I watched their tongues slide in and out of one another's mouths.

I noticed a few people standing on the patio, blowing thick puffs of smoke. Among the crowd was Montana with his mohawk slicked back again. His eyes were lower and lazier than usual and a girl was glued to his hip, his arm around her. Her hand was on his chest and she giggled a little too dramatically whenever he said something. I was more than certain she wasn't going to be giggling within the next twelve hours when Montana kicked her off the tour bus.

Gage finally returned with two plastic yellow cups and handed me one. "What's to drink tonight?" I asked, standing on my toes to get near his ear. I could hardly hear myself over the music, but he managed to hear what I said.

"Tequila." He winked. "Can't forget the salt and lime." He held out two limes and I took one. He then dipped his finger into his cup of tequila and ran it across his hand. He sprinkled salt onto it and then looked at me. "Before each shot, lick the salt away. After each one, suck the lime."

I nodded, sort of eager to try it, as I swiped liquid across the top of my hand and then sprinkled it with salt. I licked the salt away, took a sip of the tequila, and the liquid was strong—way stronger than the vodka from the club—but I kept it down and sucked my lime right after.

"Looks like you'll need a few more limes." Gage chuckled, observing my shriveled lime slice.

I nodded my head, my face puckering. "Yeah," I breathed. "Most likely."

Gage went back to grab a few more limes and with a few gasps and puckered faces, we finally finished our cups of tequila. It had to equal out to about three shots. The woozy feeling I caught was automatic. I couldn't believe how much of an amateur I was. I'd gotten drunk that fast while Gage seemed perfectly fine.

"Are you okay?" He laughed.

I grabbed his arm, nodding quickly while aiming to steady myself. "Fine. Maybe we should go dance?" *Woops*.

That couldn't have been me. Had I really asked that? I laughed at the thought and at myself for asking Gage to dance.

Chuckling, Gage placed a hand against the small of my back and his touch alone caused my skin to tingle. He grabbed my hand before stepping through the crowd. As we pushed through, I found out why everyone was having so much fun and why the crowd was so wild. Everything looked so different. Who knew tequila could get someone out of it so fast? I'd heard many things about tequila (mainly from my mom and her husband), but I never believed anything they said about it. They tried to force me to drink it once. Since then, I've hated alcohol, but this… drinking with Gage was… different.

We finally hit the middle of the dance floor and Gage turned around quickly, pulling me against him as a few people jumped up and down and bumped against us. His fingers inched along my spine, running down to my hips. Gage had bought me a purple dress that revealed a bit of cleavage and legs. It was short, but he begged me to wear it, and since he was the one buying it, I gave in. I couldn't really complain much. I guess if I wanted to fit in with the boys, I had to start getting used to wearing less clothing.

The pace of the music picked up. It was techno with a heavy dub-step bass. I turned around willingly and buried my hips between his. I don't know whether he grunted or said something, but I ignored it. I didn't want to hear anything. I just wanted to party.

His hands found their way to my waist and he pulled me closer to him. I wanted to dance then. As one of his hands moved up my stomach, the other down my thigh, I nearly melted. I was panting, grinning, and I didn't even know it. I was enjoying myself. This wasn't like the club. This was better because there were fewer lights and more people. I couldn't be seen as easily. I could actually be free without being watched or judged. Everyone was in their own little world.

Gage leaned forward, his rock-hard chest pressing against my back. He pulled my hair away to place his lips behind my ear and I brought my arms back, hooking them around his neck to keep him close. "Damn, Ellie," he murmured, causing my legs to lock just a bit. His bedroom voice heated my core. It was my motivation to keep going—to keep pressing against the thick, hard muscle in his pants. He kissed me behind the ear and my head rolled to the side. "God, I want you so much."

I smirked as he whispered in my ear. He had no idea how much or how long I'd wanted him, too. Even though he'd pissed me off to the extreme within the past forty-eight hours, I was starting to forget about it. I was having fun and there didn't need to be any hostility between us, so I dropped all anger and frustration. I decided to just go with it.

We continued dancing and soon sweat built up between us. It was getting sticky, hot, and heavy, but I didn't mind it one bit. With the people dancing around me, I couldn't seem to focus. I couldn't seem to do anything else outside of dancing, grinding, and moving against Gage. I wanted him to feel it all—to at least crave me like I craved every part of him.

"Do you think there're any open bedrooms in here?" I asked, spinning in Gage's arms. I was talking before thinking—which was bad—but a part of me wanted to take a risk. I wanted to see what it would be like to be in a room alone with Gage Grendel.

He grinned down at me and I bit my bottom lip. "I don't know, but we can try looking for one."

I nodded and he took my hand in his and pushed through the crowd. A staircase came into view and he went for it. I didn't know how the hell I was going to make it up those stairs feeling as lightheaded as I did, but I didn't care. I would have let him carry me if it came to that.

Surprisingly, I managed to make it up. The music seemed to follow us upstairs, but we didn't stop rushing ahead. Gage hissed some mild profanity beneath his breath when he saw none of the bedrooms were available. I was about to tell him never mind and to just go back to the dance floor, but before I could, he jerked me forward and rushed into one of the last rooms available.

The door slammed behind us and as soon as we were inside, he pressed against me, not even hesitating to wrap his arms around me. I laced my arms around his neck and he groaned, kissing the hollow of mine while picking me up to wrap my legs around him. We fell on the bed, but he didn't pull away from me.

He continued kissing my neck, trailing down to my chest and then the curve of my breasts. My panting increased as he came up to my lips and looked down at me, the moonlight shining on his face through the curtains. *What is he waiting on?* His lips were so close. We were so close. I could feel his cock throbbing through his pants, ready to take me. At that moment, I would have let him because I wasn't me. I wasn't in my right state of mind; therefore I didn't care much. I would have most likely regretted it the next day, but that was the now. Nothing outside of it mattered. Tomorrow didn't matter. The next hour didn't matter. All that mattered was what was sparking between us, the music blasting from downstairs, and his lips barely brushing mine.

Then, finally, Gage's lips crushed mine. I moaned, hooking my arms around his neck as he pushed up and cupped my waist to bring me to the middle of the bed. He tasted good. He felt good against me. His breathing was rigid and sounded almost painful, but he didn't stop. I knew he was having a hard time controlling himself because I definitely was. I wanted this to happen.

One of his hands crept beneath my dress to pull my panties down, the other cupping my breast.

And then he added something else to the kiss. Something smooth, wet, and laced with tequila.

His tongue.

Oh God, his tongue. It sent me into overdrive. I couldn't control myself any longer. I wanted to rip all my clothes off for him. I wanted to let my tongue play with his for the entire night. I wanted to taste him until I couldn't taste anymore. He sank between my legs, his cock digging into me and causing me to moan.

"Fuck, Eliza," he growled against my mouth. Our lips were swollen, throbbing, yet I wanted more of him. I pulled his head down to kiss him again and he kissed me back, but it wasn't as strong as before. I didn't question it—in fact, I didn't really notice it much because being near him was more than enough for me. "I just wanna take you here. Now. Damn, I want you so bad. I don't even think you realize it."

My response was a breathy moan against the hollow of his neck. A friction built up between us and soon after, he picked me up, hooking my legs around his waist again and climbing off the bed. I was amazed he'd done it so quickly. That my back had hit the wall and he was sucking on my skin greedily, thrusting against me, making sure no space was between us.

"You can't tell me you aren't feeling this," he growled. I yelped pleasurably. "You can't deny it anymore."

I shook my head because I couldn't deny it. I didn't want to. I would've done anything with Gage during this moment. I was drunk, vulnerable, and ready. I ran my fingers through his hair as our lips collided again. He spun around, placing my back on the bed and pulling my dress up to run his hands from my thighs and up to my stomach. I'd completely forgotten he'd taken off my panties. I was drenched between my legs, something I'd never felt before, but it felt good. I was ready for it. I was ready for *him*.

I'd heard a lot of things about how much it hurts to lose your virginity. I was also told that right after the pain there's pleasure, and I was seeking it. The pleasure after the pain. The satisfaction after so many years of boring celibacy. It was about time. I was a woman and it was time to test my limits.

My head swam as Gage bent down on his knees, pulled me to the edge of the bed, and kissed up my leg, his lips then touching the center of my thigh. He was so close to my entrance that I bucked against him, but he shook his head through the darkness. "Don't move. Let me," he growled, placing my feet on his shoulders.

I couldn't fight it. I lost a bit of the tension and placed the back of my head against the bed, my legs hoisted up by his large shoulders. He started from the bottom of my thigh and kissed his way up. His fingers were hooked on my waist, his head moving up gradually. I was panting, anticipating, wanting to move wildly, and he wasn't even there yet.

He groaned as his tongue slipped over one thigh before moving to the other. I moaned, squeezing his hand. He was teasing me. I could feel him laughing silently every time I shuddered. His hot tongue slid between my legs and then he pushed them apart completely, leaving me wide open.

"Get ready for me," he murmured, his warm breath running across my core. "Eliza," he whispered so faintly I thought I was imagining it. "I don't want you to lie to me again after tonight." He kissed the top of my knee, but I frowned, confused. "Don't tell me we're 'just friends' again. I'm about to show you we aren't anymore. I don't wanna be. I want more of you..."

And then, before I could even speak, his tongue leisurely slid across my clit and I gasped. The heat consumed me, warmed me, and he groaned deeply as he sucked and licked. "Tastes so good, Sweet Ellie," he murmured, his mouth still glued between my legs. I screamed, and I couldn't even count how many times I ran my hands through his silky hair or hooked my arms around his neck. I was squeezing his hand so tightly at one point I thought I was going to burst.

I began to pulsate, climax, and I'd never felt anything like this before, but it felt right. I was overheating below, my chest sinking and rising, my breath catching with each lick and flicker of his tongue. He was spinning and swirling his tongue around me, groaning and grunting as he slid a finger in and out.

"Come for me, Eliza," he grumbled, his tongue never leaving my swollen nub.

His voice was obviously all I needed to hit the ultimate climax because slowly I ruptured, he growled, and I screeched as he clutched my waist, my legs flying in the air. I bucked against his mouth again, shuddering and quaking and gripping his hands. My eyes were squeezed shut so tightly I saw stars. Had he really created that feeling for me? Had I really gone so high? I couldn't believe it. Amazing just didn't seem like a good enough word for how his mouth felt between my legs.

Gage pulled up and kissed my collarbone. "How's that for friends?" he asked, grinning. The moonlight was still reflecting off his face and I laughed, shaking my head.

"So... is this the part where you ask to take my virginity?"

In an instant he frowned. "No."

My head tilted. "Why not?"

"I can't... Someone like me can't take that away from you, Eliza."

I frowned, confused. "What do you mean?"

"I mean, I'm not the guy who should be popping your cherry," he said, as if that answered my question.

I was still confused. He had the perfect opportunity to have sex with me. From what I'd seen and heard, Gage was a sex fiend... but he was denying me? He had sex with girls he didn't even know without a problem. I felt kind of offended by that and the emotions intensified since I was nearly drunk.

I pushed up on my elbows as he stood and fixed his crumpled T-shirt. "Am I not good enough for you?" I asked.

He laughed, helping me up and then bending down to grab my panties. He placed them in my hand but pulled me forward, placing his lips against my ear. "I don't eat girls who aren't good for me," he murmured. "If I did, it would be just like eating out of the garbage. Consider yourself my... treasure for tonight."

I clenched below, delightfully of course. "I just don't get it," I muttered, tugging my panties on.

"Eliza…" He shook his head, running a hand through the dark-brown hair I'd made even messier. A few pieces had fallen onto his forehead, making him look even hotter. "I take it you wanna hear something from me that'll make you feel good about yourself right now."

My arms folded. "I do, actually."

His lips pressed, his features hardening a bit. "Okay." He then moved forward, hooking his arm around my waist and pulling me against him. His hazel eyes shimmered from the streaks of moonlight beside us, and my breath tangled with his. I couldn't seem to look away from the eyes that were so focused on mine that it would have made it awkward to look away.

"You're the first girl I've given that kind of satisfaction. I've never given pleasure without pleasing myself in return."

I waited to see if he'd smile, laugh—something. He didn't. His face was stern with a soft edge, and for some reason I believed him. "Why?" I whispered.

"Well, for one, none of the girls I sleep with are virgins." He chuckled, pulling away from me.

"Obviously," I muttered, rolling my eyes. "But that doesn't mean anything. You could have still... taken it away from me."

"I didn't want to."

"Why not?" I don't know why I was getting upset, but it really was bothering me how he could sleep with any other girl without a problem. I felt like some kind of whore for complaining, but I really needed to know what his deal was. Did I seem lame in bed? I mean I know I was a virgin and all, but I could learn.

"Eliza, I can't do that to you. I can't take something that valuable away from you. You're so innocent and I'm just... me. I'm Gage Grendel, a guy who hardly gives a fuck. You need someone who cares to take that away from you." He ran a hand through his hair. "I've been around you for a while now and it wouldn't feel right to just... take it. You're a nice girl. I don't want to turn you into one of the many whores in this world who thought their first was going to be their everything. I wouldn't even be able to live up to being your everything."

His gaze lowered and if I wasn't mistaken, I saw guilt behind his eyes. I wasn't allowed enough time to speak on it because he was reaching for my hand and pulling me toward him to cup my face. His fingers stroked my cheeks and the sensitive skin behind my ears and his lips were so close that with one tiny inch forward, I would have been kissing him again. I would be tasting the lips I used to dream about. I still couldn't believe I'd kissed Gage Grendel. "I do want more of you, trust me," he sighed. "But wait for the right time, Ellie. This isn't it. I'm not it."

I stared into his eyes and after watching the sincerity run through his, I knew he was right. "Fine," I breathed, forcing myself to pull away from him.

He smiled softly and then went for the door. Stretching an arm out, he looked at me and flicked his fingertips for me to come to him. "Let's go finish our dance," he murmured. "I wanna see what else you can do with those hips."

NO MORE THAN FRIENDS

We were laughing entirely too much, to the point it started hurting my sides. I just couldn't help myself, though. With Gage, it felt good to laugh. And to know he was actually laughing with me made me feel even better.

Gage always had a little sadness behind his eyes. He tried to cover it up with joking around, messing around, and other minor things, but I could always tell. I knew when someone carried a burden they've tried to forget about. I was one of those people, and the only reason I didn't bring it up to him was because I knew how much I hated to talk about it. I would rather keep it in the past.

Gage hooked an arm around my waist as we hurried for the FireNine bus. As we got closer, I paused, placing a hand against his chest and facing him. "Wait, Gage," I breathed, giggling.

"What?" he asked, laughing with me as his head lowered. I couldn't help but admire the chink around his eyes. The way his skin wrinkled softly. It was adorable.

"I can't go in this bus," I whispered.

He looked around quickly, then looked at me again, his head tilting. "Why not?"

"'Cause I might see naked girls in there or something." My nose crinkled in disgust and he chuckled. It was a deep, sexy chuckle. One that made my legs clench and my nipples tighten beneath the fabric of my bra. It was so damn sexy. And I was drunk, which enhanced his sexiness.

"You won't," he said. "None of the boys are here and even if they come, we'll be in my room."

I paused again. *His room?* What were we going to be doing in there? I knew I was leading Gage on. I couldn't help myself, though. It was fun to kiss someone for the first time, over and over again. I'd never experienced anyone's lips against mine or anyone's body rubbing against me. I was enjoying myself with Gage, but I knew the next morning I was going to hate myself for it. For kissing him, getting drunk with him, and almost having sex with him... *That was a close one.*

"Eliza?" Gage murmured, moving in closer. I looked up and his features were solid. His lips were pressed, but his eyes were lax. "I just—I mean... you don't have to come in if you don't want to. I don't wanna make you feel uncomfortable." He looked up toward my bus. "I can just take you to your bus if you'd like." He cocked his head to his left.

"No—no," I said quickly, feeling bad for his hesitation. I could tell he was trying to make me comfortable. "It's fine. I'll come in."

"Are you sure?"

I grinned. "Positive."

Nodding, he grabbed my hand and turned for the door. As he twisted the knob, a nervous spell took hold of me. I really wasn't sure why. Maybe the alcohol made me antsy. Perhaps it was because I didn't know what to expect with just us on the bus. At least at the party there were people around. I didn't mind getting a few more drinks into my system because I knew Gage wasn't going to want to go to a bedroom with me again.

The first thing that came into view was the large L-shaped white leather sofa facing the huge flat-screen TV that was mounted on the north wall. He complained about his bus before, but already theirs was ten times better than ours.

As he flipped on one of the light switches, I saw the floors were made of hardwood, a dining table with a matching set of grey placemats and silverware was set up in the corner across from the kitchen, and their kitchen was nice, too—black marble counters, oak cabinets. It was way bigger than ours.

"Wow, this bus is nicer than I thought."

"What'd you expect?" he asked, looking down at me with a smirk. "Stripper poles, butt-naked women, and loads of beer bottles scattered across the floor?"

I laughed. "Something like that."

"Nah. I guess they decided to get rid of the strippers and poles. There wasn't enough space anyway," he teased.

"Oh, funny," I sassed him playfully. I released Gage's hand and took a step ahead to look around. It really was nice. There was a drum set in the corner beside the TV, most likely for Deed to practice on. Three guitars—an acoustic, a bass, and a lead—sat in the opposite corner along with an amp. A few posters of naked women were on the walls (that was pretty predictable) and even some of the FireNine logos were plastered around. A neon red FireNine sign was on the wall in the kitchen.

"Wanna check out my room?" Gage asked over my shoulder. A soothing chill ran down my spine when I realized how close he was. I could feel the heat radiating from his body, ready to consume me. His breath trickled across my neck and through my hair, causing me to tingle and shudder like I never had before.

"Sure," I whispered breathily.

He chuckled softly, grabbing my hand and turning me around. He pulled me in close by my hipbone, his eyes locked on mine, his lips so close that, from a bystander's point of view, it would have looked like we were kissing. His cologne was so strong, yet sweet and delectable to me. I wanted a taste of him—anywhere. *Everywhere.*

In less than a second, I got what I wanted.

Gage moved in slowly and pressed his lips against mine, and I didn't hold back. I hooked my arms around his neck and he picked me up so my legs could circle his waist. He grunted as he held me in his arms and stumbled down the hallway. I'm not sure which bedroom he kicked open, but within no time we were inside and he'd slammed the door behind us.

My head was still swimming. I was still seeing stars from earlier and it obviously meant I was still in a pretty high state of mind. It was a pleasant high—one I never wanted to come down from because I knew coming down meant facing reality, facing everything I never wanted to recollect. I didn't want the negativity. I loved the feeling taking over me. I loved the Eliza I was while I was with the stars. While I was with Gage Grendel.

"Eliza," Gage murmured against my neck. He laid my back on the bed and climbed on top of me, pushing my legs apart with his knee to get between them, but he didn't stop kissing me. I cracked my eyelids open a little. They were heavy and low, and it was then that I realized how tired I was. I was completely drained. I wondered what time it was and how long we actually ended up staying at the party.

From the window above, the moonlight sprinkled across Gage, revealing his chiseled face. Most of his features had a soft edge. His nose wasn't too pointy or too perfect. It was slightly crooked, but one could only tell if they were up close. It fit him, though. His jawline and chin were defined, sculpted, and the stubble around his lips and on his chin was faint, but I could feel the roughness of it every time he kissed me. The only thing baby-like on Gage were his eyes. They were bordered with long, thick lashes. He seemed almost innocent with them, but I knew he was far from it. Besides his beautiful, baby-like hazel eyes, Gage was all man.

"Yes?" I finally answered him, my voice faint. I could hardly hear myself. Lying against his sheets and pillows wasn't helping the situation, either. I was so close to reaching slumber and to top it all off, my head was swimming. The feeling was like being rocked back and forth on a boat during a calm night at sea. Comforting.

Soundless.

Peaceful.

"You didn't really have anything going on with Montana, did you?" The room stilled. He was probably waiting on me to answer because he'd gotten silent right after, but I couldn't form the words. *Of course I don't have anything going on with Montana.* I was about to say it, but he started talking again. "I mean, if so, it's cool. We can stop what we're doing. Neither one of us are worth your time anyway. Our lifestyles are crazy... something you don't need. You deserve someone worthy and that's neither of us."

I frowned and my lips wanted to move and speak on it, but they wouldn't. My body was working against me, begging me to just shut my eyes already. I allowed them to close briefly, but when I opened them again, Gage was staring at me.

I finally asked, "What do you mean 'worthy of my time?'"

He sighed. "I don't know. It's hard to explain... I'll never really be the kinda guy who knows how to treat someone like you—" He stopped talking abruptly, shaking his head. He then kissed the top of my hand, my knuckles, and then moved up to lie beside me.

Pulling me against him, he sighed while stroking my hair. His fingers felt good as they ran along the edges of my hair, but he was making me even more peaceful, which meant sleepier as well. I moved in and snuggled against his chest. I wrapped my arm around his waist and he stiffened. It seemed as if he'd stopped breathing, but I ignored it and moments after, he loosened up.

"Finish what you were you going to say," I mumbled.

He didn't respond right away, but I could feel his eyes on me. His thumb was still rubbing across my forehead and his arm was still wrapped around me. I breathed him in, satisfied with where I was. I wasn't alone like usual. I was with him, and for some odd reason, it felt... good. It felt *right*.

"Never mind," he whispered in my ear, his voice deep, husky. "Get some sleep, Eliza. We've got a long day ahead of us tomorrow."

I don't know if I nodded for real or not. I may have been thinking I did, but either way I agreed and had completely sunk against his chest. His body was hard but relaxing. I'd never slept next to anyone, but being here with Gage felt nice. Satisfying.

Soon my breath evened out. Gage continued stroking the edges of my hair, placing small kisses on my forehead, and then I fell asleep.

I woke up the next morning with a dull headache. I groaned, shielding my eyes from the sun blazing in through the window above. My senses were piqued. I smelled strong cologne everywhere and even coffee lingered in the air.

Stumbling out of bed and continuing to shield my eyes, I wobbled before taking a small look around. My head hurt so badly. I knew I shouldn't have drunk so much the night before and at the thought of drinking, my eyes stretched. I yanked my hands down and took in the unfamiliar room. There were FireNine posters on each wall, all different with different colors and pictures of the boys. A few half-naked models were plastered on the walls as well and I shook my head because, unfortunately, I knew exactly where I was.

Gage's bedroom.

The door swung open and my pulse paused as Gage stepped in, his hair wet, floppy, and messy as if he'd recently taken a shower. He had to have taken one because he had on fresher clothes. As soon as he looked into my eyes, his face softened and he clutched the doorknob. "Ellie," he breathed.

"Uh... hi," I whispered. Oh, goodness, it had gotten awkward. Seeing Gage made me go over how drunk I was the night before and then I remembered how he'd licked me in a spot that had never been licked or touched before. Slow, sensuous, and delicately sweet. Thinking of how great it felt caused my face to burn from embarrassment and he took a step in, his head tilted.

"I made some coffee and there's some water right there on the nightstand." He pointed at it and I looked over my shoulder.

"I'll take the coffee," I murmured.

He nodded, looking me over twice before stepping back. I knew I looked like complete shit, without a doubt. Gage turned around and I followed him down the hallway. To my luck, no one was in the living room and I let out a sigh of relief. I didn't want the boys to see me looking like trash or even in the same attire from the previous night.

"Do you want crème?" he asked.

"Please."

"Sugar?"

"Yes, please." He nodded and I inhaled, taking a seat at the table. The coffee smelled pleasant, rich, and was already clearing my head of some of the throbbing.

Gage stirred a spoon around in a black mug and then placed it in front of me. Winking, he turned back around and went for the microwave. "I went out this morning to get some bagels from Panera. You mentioned last night how you liked the cinnamon crunch kind with hazelnut cream cheese?"

My eyes stretched. How did he remember that? I'd barely said much about it. The conversation about bagels was so minor that *I* couldn't even remember it.

Instead of questioning it, I took a sip of my coffee and nodded. "Yeah, that's my favorite," I said after swallowing the hot liquid. He smirked over his shoulder and brought the brown bag to the table. He took the seat across from me and placed one of the plastic butter knives in front of me. "You know you didn't have to do this, Gage," I said.

"I wanted to." He placed one of the sweet bagels in front of me. "I've never had Panera before."

"Well, it's really good." I grabbed my bagel, the butter knife, and then one of the packets of cream cheese. "Their broccoli cheddar soup is my favorite."

"Oh. I shoulda got you that, too." He smirked.

"No." I shook my head. "It's fine. This is more than enough... Thank you."

"My pleasure."

Gage and I ate silently for the first few minutes. I was right about it being awkward on my behalf, but he didn't seem to mind the silence. He would take a few glances at me whenever taking a bite into his bagel and I would force a smile, pretending I didn't mind. It was cute... but weird. I was having breakfast... *alone*... with Gage Grendel. Who knew?

"We're all going to the waterpark today," he said, smiling.

"A waterpark? I've never been to one before."

He gaped at me. "What?" He smiled so widely it revealed all his teeth. "You've never been to a waterpark before? What kind of childhood did you have?"

A shitty one. I shrugged it off. "Obviously one that wasn't filled with waterparks."

He laughed. "Well, today we'll be changing that. I have to say, Ellie, I feel like I've introduced you to a ton of new things lately. The club, square dancing in Texas, house parties with tequila, and now the waterpark? You really are an innocent girl."

I laughed off his statement. Innocent was far from what I was. I used to be terrible. "I guess so," I sighed.

He looked me over, folding his fingers on top of the table. He then placed a leg on his knee, leaned his back against his chair, and brought his mug to his lips. "Did you have fun with me last night?" he asked after taking a sip.

I hesitated. Hell yeah, I had fun. Too much fun. He licked me between my legs for heaven's sake. That had to be a sign of some kind of excitement. "I did."

"And you still think we're 'just friends?'"

My lips pressed and I shook my head. "Why would we be more than that, Gage?"

He frowned. "After what happened between us, why wouldn't we be?"

"Because, like you said last night, you're Gage Grendel. You don't care. Friends are all we need to be. Nothing more."

"But I showed you last night we could be way more than that. I wanna try a little something else with you."

"We were drunk, Gage. Besides, one party doesn't determine that we're more than friends. We were just having fun, right?"

He was about to say something else, but then his lips sealed. He nodded, dropping his leg to sit forward. "You're right." He huffed, his jaw ticking. "It's whatever." He placed his coffee down, then snatched the paper bag off the table to drop it into the trash bin. "Ben unlocked your bus earlier. You can go now." I stared at his back, wide-eyed, as he marched for his bedroom and slammed his door behind him.

Was he dismissing me like I was just another one-night stand? Was he really treating me like one of the millions of whores he'd encountered just because I didn't want to be toyed with? Just because I knew it would turn for the worst if we were to turn into more than just friends? My mouth gaped open, disbelieving what he'd just said to me. He was brushing me off.

Damn it. He was the exact reason I didn't like to get comfortable with people. People expected too much from me and I couldn't live up to everyone's expectations. My mind was foggy, but I could remember him clearly saying I deserved someone better than him and Montana. Someone worthy of my time. What's more than friends anyway? Casual sex? Kissing and hugging? We did all that last night and had fun? Why want more? Why make it deeper when it would only be temporary?

Gage and I were no match. One: he had a girlfriend. And two: it wouldn't last between us. It would've been a complete waste of our time. As soon as the tour ended, I would be back in Virginia for school and he would continue doing what he normally did, which was having sex with random girls and then dismissing them the next morning for someone fresher.

I knew, as bad as I felt, I was right by telling him no. We had fun, but I wasn't about to get any closer to Gage just to have battered and fucked-up emotions when it's all over. I had enough problems I was still trying to look past.

Most would consider it being selfish or bitchy, but I had my reasons. I wasn't about to get fucked over because of him. It was best to play it safe.

After guarding my eyes from the blazing sun while walking across the parking lot, I was finally at my bus. As I boarded, no one was around, so I decided to hit the shower and get out of the filthy dress Gage bought for me. I wanted no part of it anymore. I just wanted to trash it and pretend the previous night never happened. I wanted to so badly, but instead, I stuffed it in the bottom of my suitcase.

As the warm water ran over me, I absorbed the soothing feel of it. It calmed me down a lot more than intended, so after I was done, I locked my bedroom door behind me and lounged around in just my pink bath towel. My hair was still wet, but it was opening my pores, relieving me of the minor headache I was still carrying. The coffee helped a ton, too. Along with the cup of water I took before storming off the FireNine bus.

I tried to distract my mind from Gage by going back to the bathroom and shaving my legs, painting my toes, my fingernails, and even braiding my hair, but none of it worked. I couldn't get over how rude he was to me. I mean, he had his reasons to be upset, but I couldn't understand why he wanted something with me so badly? I would have looked like the dumbest girl alive had I given Gage more of me. It was already a close one last night and I swore never to get that close again.

In the back of my mind, I knew it would probably be impossible.

During the process of girly-ing myself up, I couldn't help but relive the moments when Gage and I kissed—my first kiss, and it was better than I'd ever imagined. His lips molded with mine perfectly. His kisses always started off slow, tender, erotic, but then they would pick up and become slightly demanding, hungry, yet still a huge turn-on for me.

I noticed every time he kissed me, one of his hands would press against the small of my back; the other would cup my face. He wanted the kiss to drag on for however long, and I was willing. I never wanted to pull away from him. The only time we would stop was if we were interrupted and someone bumped into us or if we were running off to most likely find a new spot to make out.

The addition of his tongue made the kisses whole. He knew exactly how to play with mine—how to slide it around so I would become weak at the knees. Every time we tasted one another, I was reminded that his tongue had explored more places of my body than one. I didn't think it was possible to get so excited with someone like him and with the alcohol coursing through me, it made the night ten times more fun for us.

Gage and I talked a lot, but for some reason I couldn't remember about what. I knew a lot of the conversations were pointless, but some seemed so meaningful that I cursed at myself in the mirror for not remembering. Gage had opened up to me in some ways. He didn't give me much (otherwise, I would remember it), but it was enough for me to see that maybe he wasn't the arrogant rocker I thought he was.

I was frowning at myself in the mirror entirely too much that I didn't even notice someone had come inside the bus. Something heavy dropped on the floor and I gasped, spinning around and yanking the door open. I hurried down the hallway but paused in front of Cal's wide-open door.

He was standing above a stack of magazines, his gaze down and focused intently on them. I couldn't figure out what he was thinking, but as I cleared my throat, he looked up and at the sight of me he smiled sweetly.

"Oh, hi, Eliza," he said, tossing me a light wave and stepping in front of the magazines.

I waved back. "Hi. What are you doing?" Cal's eyes traveled southward and I looked with him, embarrassed that I was still walking around in only my towel.

"I see you're getting ready for the waterpark today." He chuckled.

I blushed. "Um... yeah." I took a step back, but he came toward me, his head tilted, a smile still on his lips.

"I was just going through some of the magazines for *It's Real*. Trying to figure out what should be included, taken out, etc."

"Oh." I nodded, my lips pressed.

He studied me for another moment, ogling my cleavage mainly and not bothering to hide it. "Everyone's partnering up for the waterpark today," Cal said, finally looking into my eyes. "Who's your partner?"

My eyebrows stitched. "I didn't think I had to have one."

"Well, of course you do." He laughed. "What fun would it be not to have a partner at a waterpark? Ben rented the whole park out for us anyway, and it would kind of suck if you got lost."

"What? Why would he rent out the whole thing?"

"I don't know." He ran a hand through his hair. "It might be because he doesn't want the boys to get trampled by hundreds of half-naked women."

I nodded, my lips pressing again. His reason was right on. "It's kind of weird that twenty-three and twenty-four-year-old men are going to a waterpark anyway." I laughed.

"FireNine is hilarious. They'll have fun anywhere. I heard it was Montana and Gage's idea. They have a few people coming along with them as well, so I'm sure they're already partnered up." Cal hesitated, looking me over. "I don't have a partner. I thought we could maybe... you know... partner up?"

I giggled. "We can, but what about Ben?"

"Ben's a great guy... I just don't think he's the kind of guy I should be hanging out with... at a waterpark. Not that he isn't cool to hang with, he's just—"

"Gay," I blurted, laughing.

"Uh... yeah," he said, rubbing the back of his neck nervously. "It would be kind of awkward to be half-naked with him the entire time—no offense. Besides, I think it'd be much better to see you that way—but don't tell him I said that."

I couldn't help but laugh at him. I knew he wasn't being offensive. "Okay. We can be partners. What time is everyone going?"

"I believe within the next hour. The band's just getting back in from their night out."

"Oh, okay." I took a step back and started down the hallway. "I'll be out in a bit."

"Can't wait." He winked.

I ducked into my room before he could catch me turning a bright shade of red. It was going to be a fun sight to see Cal Avery half-naked. I knew beneath the vintage T-shirts he wore, he had a glorious body. I was hoping it would be a six-pack I could drool all over. Oh, how delectable would that be?

I locked my door behind me before scrambling through my suitcase to find my bathing suits. I'd packed two of them. The last time I'd gone swimming was during my last semester of college. I swam at the community indoor pool as part of my workout. Ben gave me money every week, so I bought bathing suits and athletic clothes whenever I could. It was probably why it was so hard for me to find anything when we packed for the FireNine tour. All I had was shorts, tank tops, and sports bras. The clothes I'd packed for the tour were all bought with Ben, and he had to approve every single thing I picked out while shopping.

I came across my teal one-piece without a back and my pink-and-white striped two-piece that made my boobs seem bigger than they were. I also had the newest black-and-white suit I wore while jet skiing. I had to put it aside, though. I didn't want to repeat it.

My lips twisted as I held the teal and pink one up in front of me, debating on whether I wanted to be lame and simple with the one-piece or adventurous and mildly sex with the two-piece. I figured adventurous and mildly sexy was best while with the band. I couldn't afford to be laughed at. Plus, I would've rather had the boys drooling over me than chuckling over my choice of a one-piece. "Maybe next time, onesie," I mumbled, tucking the teal bathing suit back into the suitcase.

I strapped on my suit, grabbed a pair of ripped-up shorts to wear over my bottoms and a white tank to wear over my top. They didn't need to see me half-naked yet. It was bad that the one person I was most concerned about seeing me half-naked was Gage. Even though he'd more than seen the bottom half of me, I knew I was still going to be uncomfortable around him—especially since I'd just rejected him, flat-out.

I placed my sunglasses and camera into my extra white satchel, strapped on the bag, and then headed out. Cal was in the kitchen making a turkey sandwich. As his eyes swung up to look at me, he paused in spreading his mayonnaise and I blushed, forcing myself to keep my head up as I placed my satchel on the sofa. "I don't know how

I'm going to focus on the slides when you're stealing all my attention away," he teased.

I giggled, stepping behind him to get to the fridge. I pulled out a bottled water and then dug through one of the drawers for some pills. I finally came across a bottle of painkillers and dumped two into the palm of my hand.

"Had a rough night last night?" Cal asked.

I hesitated with my response. It didn't get rough until this morning. "No," I said.

"Oh, did you have fun?" He bit into his sandwich and I gulped down my pills, allowing the water to chase right after them for a smoother swallow. "I know how the band can get crazy. Didn't they go to a house party or something last night?"

"Yeah," I breathed. "It was pretty wild but fun. I didn't mind it."

"Oh. That's great." He smiled over his sandwich and then stepped out of the kitchen. "I'll be ready in just a sec."

I nodded, watching him trot off to his room before turning around to lean my lower back against the counter. I sighed, pressing my fingers against my temples and going over last night again and again. Why the hell couldn't I just get over it? It was one night of fun with Gage... one night with Gage I was never going to forget. One night with him that seemed to steam up and turn into something else entirely—something more than fun.

I hated facing the truth of it. The entire night of the house party I thought Gage was going to leave me to dance with another chick, but he didn't. In fact, he brushed off most of the girls who came our way. He was by my side the whole night. A few girls leaned into him, revealing their cleavage and hooking their arms around his neck, and he would flirt back, but it was only temporary. He would whisper something in their ear and they would nod, walk off, and then he would grab my hand to go somewhere quieter.

Darker.

Alone.

He spent more time with me than his band and that was speaking volumes. Montana kept trying to get Gage to join him in a session of hookah and even on the dance floor to see how many dances they could get, but Gage stuck with me. I kept insisting he go with them, but he would shrug it off. He would then whisper in my ear, "I have plenty of nights ahead of me to spend with them. I probably won't be having many more with you. I like being with you."

Of course I bubbled over, sparked with heat, intensity. I couldn't help myself. He was right. We only had two months on tour to be stuck together. He had the rest of his life to be with his band, unless they were to split up, but even then, I knew they would still be close.

"I was thinking maybe we could catch some smoothies before we hit the waterpark." Cal's voice thundered, interrupting my thoughts. I looked up quickly—maybe a little too quickly because at the sight of his body, my mouth gaped. I drank him in a little too fast and caught a dizzy spell on top of the minor headache I had.

I was right about the six-pack... and about the gloriousness of his body... and about me drooling over it. His skin was flawless and perfectly tanned. I wanted to slide my hands along his torso, pull him against me, and maybe kiss each pec, if he would've allowed me permission to do so. His nipples were perfect. Not too big or too small. Not too light of a pink, but just right against his smooth complexion. He'd even gelled his hair. Damn. Cal was hotter than hell.

"Uh…" I trailed off, gripping the edge of the counter. I tried to get myself to look up into his eyes, but it just wouldn't happen. I was too stuck on his body—on the curves and smooth, firm hills that stuck out most.

Finally, Cal chuckled and my eyes shot up to meet his. Another swarm of embarrassment consumed me and my face lit on fire. I couldn't believe myself. Was I really that weak? This proved I'd been around too many boys for too long. I was becoming an Eliza Smith with raging hormones. "Would you like smoothies?" he asked, laughing.

I nodded quickly. "Uh… yeah. Smoothies sound great."

"Good." He smirked, tying the drawstring of his green trunks. He had the deep creases on either side of his pelvis that trailed down to what I assumed was his rather large package. I called those creases on the pelvis the "Matthew McConaughey" creases. The deep V that every woman wanted to slide her tongue along repeatedly. Damn, it was so hot on Cal. "Let me get a shirt and we can go grab some."

I should've stopped him from grabbing a shirt. I wanted to stare at his body for the rest of the day. A part of me was actually glad he was my partner for the evening. I could stare from a distance; watch the way the muscles in his back rippled with each stride he took, just like I was at this very moment. I could imagine myself ripping his shirt off just to get another good look.

But I had to be patient. He wasn't going to have the shirt on long anyway. As soon as we were to grab our smoothies and head to the waterpark, his shirt would be off again and I could bask in his beauty. I could drink him whole and only hope he wouldn't notice.

It was a good thing a half-naked Cal was going to be my waterpark partner because at this very moment, I realized I wasn't even thinking about Gage or the previous night we shared. I was sort of glad my mind was too distracted by Cal to think about the stress between Grendel and me.

RISKS & TRUTHS

As we pulled into the parking lot of the waterpark, I could make out the tall waterslides in various colors. Some of them made me nervous. I was never a fan of heights so to know I had to go that high kind of freaked me out.

I stepped out of the truck, taking in the colorful sign with the title of the waterpark on it and then the woman waiting at the gates. As she saw the band hop out of their truck, she smiled eagerly, bouncing up and down.

"This should be fun, huh?" Cal asked, placing a hand against the small of my back.

I looked up at him and nodded. "It should. Just don't splash me too much," I teased.

"Oh, I think it'd be great to get you wet."

I bit on a smile as we walked toward the entrance. I could hear the message he was trying to deliver behind his sentence and he knew it just as well as I did because he laughed silently.

"Welcome to The Lagoon!" the woman chimed eagerly. "Oh, it's so great to have you all." She opened the gates and allowed Cal and me in, but she stepped in the way as FireNine came up. "Welcome!" she chimed again. "Listen, my daughter is a huge fan of you guys. She can never go a day without singing one of your songs, talking about Montana..."—Montana smirked at that—"or even about Roy back there." Oddly, Roy looked down at his feet, seeming uncomfortable. "After you're all worn out from hanging at The Lagoon, I would love it if you could autograph a few things for me. It would make her so happy."

"Of course." Montana grinned. "Anything for the kiddos."

The woman blushed. "Well, she's eighteen."

Montana simply smirked. "Anything for the ladies." He wiggled his eyebrows, but the woman didn't seem to catch his drift. Finally, after Ben and the crew started coming our way, she allowed the boys in.

"Don't forget!" she yelled as they got halfway in.

Gage and Deed laughed, but Roy shook his head, running a hand through his hair.

"The chicks really dig Roy, huh?" Cal asked, grinning at the boys.

Gage's eyes swung over to Cal and then his gaze shifted down to Cal's hand that was still on my back. His hazel eyes darkened a bit and then he looked into my eyes. Fidgeting, I took a small step away and luckily Cal didn't seem to notice.

"The ladies do love Roy," Gage said dryly.

"I don't know why," Roy muttered. Roy's voice was deep, heavy. It was weird to hear him actually speak, but his voice suited him. Roy saw me staring in disbelief and narrowed his eyes at me, his eyebrows drawn in.

"Where's everybody else?" he asked, looking at Montana.

"Coming," Montana sighed. "But for now I think we need to crack open some beers." Montana looked down at the cooler Deed had dragged in on its wheels. I was pretty sure it was illegal to have beer at a waterpark, but since we were the only ones around, I guess it didn't matter.

The boys stepped ahead of us to get to the nearest pool. As they walked by, Gage looked at me over his shoulder and shook his head. I frowned at him and then his lips curled into a knowing smirk. I shuddered before looking away.

"So," Cal sighed. I looked at him quickly. "Which slide would you like to go on first?"

"Um…" I took a look around. There were tons of waterslides. I couldn't decide alone. "I don't know. Which one would you like to go on first?" I asked, adjusting the strap of my satchel.

"We could try the one called *The Tunnel*. Sounds fun," he said, nodding his head at the large blue one only a few feet away.

"Sure."

Cal and I started our walk, but then Ben's voice called our names. I spun around quickly as he jogged toward us, a wide smile on his lips. "I hope you two aren't running off to do the do." He flashed a smile, wiggling his eyebrows.

I flushed and Cal laughed, looking down at me. "Not at all, Ben. Just going to catch a few water slides."

"Great. Liza, if you need me I'll be out tanning by the big pool. Far away from the boys and their nasty party they plan on throwing."

I frowned. "Party? You're letting them throw a party here?"

"They used their money to rent this place out. They call it being spontaneous. I call it bullshit. Any fines they get are on their hands." He pulled me in by the face to kiss my cheeks. "Later, dearest." With that, he turned around and walked with the crew to most likely find the largest pool.

I shook my head, turning to see where the band was. I could make out a glimpse of what they were doing. Gage and Montana were racing to see who could drink his beer the fastest. How glad was I to have Cal as my partner instead of any of them? I didn't want to be stuck with them again.

Cal hooked his arm across my shoulders and spun me around. "Don't worry. I'll be sure we have fun."

I smiled up at him and we started forward.

When we made it up the stairs to get to the top of the slide, a young man was already waiting up there. He smiled, looking us over and then looking behind us, as if more people were supposed to be coming. Perhaps he'd heard about FireNine renting the park out and was looking forward to seeing them as well, just to brag about it. I could see the spark die within his eyes once he realized we were the only ones.

The boy stepped out of our way and Cal asked me if I wanted to go down alone. I looked down the length of the slide and shook my head quickly. That was a *hell* to the no. I couldn't go down that slide alone. It was so high up and the pool at the bottom seemed so far away.

With a simple chuckle, Cal stepped out of his flip-flops, pulled his shirt over his head, and I gawked because I'd completely forgotten about his delicious body. I had to snap out of it, though. I was lucky he didn't catch me staring, so I shook my head and slipped out of my tank top and jeans. I kicked my flip-flops to the side and the boy told us he was going to take our things to the bottom so we wouldn't have to come back upstairs for it.

"All right," Cal said into my ear from behind me. "You ready?"

I melted from his voice. He was so close, and it was like he was trying to purposely make it deep and pleasurable. With his hard body near mine, I couldn't concentrate. When he placed both hands on either side of my waist, all focus had gone down the drain. He inched in closer and then whispered in my ear, telling me it was okay to sit. I sat down hastily, gripping the bar handles on the sides, and he sat behind me.

He moved in closer than expected, but it excited me and my heart raced. Hooking his arms around my middle, he placed his chin on my shoulder and I braced myself, taking in the wide pool at the bottom waiting for me.

"You sure you're ready?" he asked in my ear. He seemed to be saying it in more ways than one, but I nodded and he gripped me tighter. "Do you want to do a countdown or do you want me to push forward randomly?"

I bit on my lip, debating on the answer. Finally I said, "Randomly. The countdown will kill me."

Chuckling, his fingers splayed across my middle and I unnoticeably moved back to get between his legs more. I guess it wasn't as unnoticeable as I thought it would be because he laughed. "Eliza?" he said in my ear.

"Yeah?" I was about to turn and get a glimpse of him through the corner of my eye, but then he pushed forward and the cold water ran beneath my bottom. My heart lurched and I screamed as Cal laughed.

A tunnel appeared ahead and as soon as we were beneath it, it blocked my view of everything and I screamed even louder, ready for the darkness to fade. I guess there was a reason they called it *The Tunnel*. Cal laughed again as he held on to me, and I begged to the heavens that his grip wouldn't loosen.

The tunnel finally ended, but the slide looped and continued down. I finally settled a bit, realizing I was actually having fun and that I hadn't caught a panic attack yet. The slide was exciting and the cool water running beneath us felt good. I was too busy basking in the sun and enjoying the feel of the water that I wasn't expecting Cal's grip to slack and for a whole body of water to consume me.

As I hit the pool and sank beneath, I choked and gurgled and pushed my way up to surface, swallowing some of the chlorine-filled water on the way by accident. "Holy shit!" I sputtered, spotting Cal, who was just surfacing with droplets of water running off his blond hair and eyelashes. He met my gaze and laughed before swimming in my direction.

"See, wasn't too bad, right?" he breathed.

"No. That was fun! We should go again." I felt like a big-ass kid, but I was so excited and eager for the next. It was a thrill and I hated how I hadn't experienced it earlier than the age of twenty-one.

"We can go again, if you'd like," Cal said, pulling me in by my waist. "Did you think I was gonna let you go on the way down?"

I nodded, looking at him beneath my eyelashes bashfully.

"I wouldn't have let you go, Eliza." He gave me a crooked, heart-throbbing smile and I grinned, glad the water kept me cool. To avoid his beautiful green eyes, I took a look around to see which slide we could go on next. I pointed out a few in my head, but as I was about to look at Cal again, I caught sight of a pair of narrowed hazel eyes.

I gasped, staring right at Gage as he walked by, a beer in his hand, his eyes still hard on me. He stole glances between Cal and me, but I couldn't look away. I wanted to ignore him, but when he nodded slowly at me, his eyes still narrowed, I felt guilty. He was nodding as if he knew why I'd rejected him. But I didn't reject him for Cal. I just couldn't get caught up with someone like him. I knew he was assuming I'd chosen Cal over him, but I hadn't chosen either one. I wasn't about to choose at all.

Cal seemed to notice the frustration taking hold of my features and looked toward Gage, but Gage had turned around, his shoulders slightly hunched, while taking a sip of his beer. He had tattoos on his back as well. More tribal ink and Bible verses, I was sure. I'd even spotted a blue dragon on his right rib cage as he rounded a corner to start a new path. His back was perfectly creased and it was so hard to hate his presence yet feel excited by looking at his body. He wasn't too stocky or too lean; he was just right. He had the nice, athletic build, which proved he worked out just enough to keep himself in shape.

With a ragged sigh, I looked at Cal, who was already looking at me. "Trouble in paradise, I see," he said, smiling.

I shook my head quickly. "No. I'll never understand someone like Gage. He's his own person."

"That's a good thing, right?"

I shrugged.

"I think you deserve better anyway," Cal said.

I didn't want to talk about Gage at all so I grabbed Cal's hands beneath the water and grinned at him. "Let's go find us another slide." He nodded and we swam toward the ladder to climb out, collect our clothes, and then head to another tall water slide.

Spending time with Cal was pretty cool. Not only was his body pleasant to look at (especially when dripping with water), but also he was a sweet guy and actually made me laugh. It was odd that I was making comparisons between him and Gage and, sad to say, Gage was on the winning side in my mind. Even though we were drunk the night of the party, I had more of a connection with Gage than I had with Cal. As hot as Cal was, he was extremely corny but really sweet. I could only be friends with him. It just seemed like the type of relationship I was supposed to have with someone as kindhearted as he was.

Whenever we would take a break and grab a drink or some ice cream, Cal would always bring up his job for the magazine or how tough it was to get interviews with the boys when they were always on the go. He said his toughest so far was getting one with Roy, but he was determined to do so one way or another. I doubted him highly on that one. He also kept telling me I deserved better than Gage, but I always changed the subject.

We walked around the park for a while, basking in the sun and going from shop to shop. We stopped in a candy shop, a souvenir shop (where I bought a nice "I fucked Orlando good" shirt because Cal dared me to), and we even stopped by the mist zone to allow the soothing spray to cool our hot skin.

A shop was across from us with magazines and a newspaper stand on the outside. Some of the pictures on the magazines were of familiar people, but through the mist I couldn't make it out clearly. I looked at Cal, who was enjoying his mist, his eyes closed and his head thrown back as droplets dripped and caressed his beautiful body, and then took a step forward, wiping my face.

And then, as I approached the stand, I frowned. The reason the pictures were familiar was because it was a picture of *me* and Gage on the night of the party. "What the hell?" I hissed beneath my breath, snatching up the magazine. The front cover was a picture of Gage and me at the outlet, shopping for a decent outfit to wear to the house party. His arm was around me and I was smiling at him, but that's not what struck my nerves. It was the caption beside it.

Is our favorite rocker dating again?

I gritted my teeth, flipping through the pages to find the main topic of the magazine. I couldn't believe it. There were a whole two pages about Gage's secret love life and me being his new "girl toy." How the hell did they print this magazine so fast? And who the fuck said girl toy anyway? Corny-ass magazine.

A few more quotes stuck out at me, making my teeth grit even more:

Will this one last?

Is G.G. finally growing up?

Is she just another loose floosy?

The last line made me shut the magazine furiously and stuff it back onto its stand. I breathed through my nose, trying to calm down, but being called a floosy to a large portion of the world made me upset. Those people were judging me when they knew nothing about me or Gage or our friendship. *A loose floosy?* Seriously? That killed my joy even more. I was about to turn around, grab Cal, and go for some more fun, but then my eye caught them all.

There were three other magazines with Gage and me on the front. One with us at the club in the VIP section, another with us on our way to the hoedown, and the last of Gage and me talking in the parking lot of Cracker Barrel. On the Cracker Barrel cover, it had me flipping my middle finger at him and the line above it read, **"Trouble with love already?"** I scowled, cringed, and clenched my fist as if the magazine could somehow see my anger and make a run for it before it was too late.

"Hey," Cal said over my shoulder. I turned quickly, looking into Cal's soft green eyes. "Are you okay?" he asked, giving me a gentle smile.

"Uh… yeah," I said, shaking my head. "Yeah." I took a step forward so he couldn't see the real reason I was upset. "We should go catch some more slides," I said, forcing a smile. He agreed, and it was a good thing he didn't seem to notice my frustration.

After going on four more slides, we finally decided on grabbing some lunch. I was nearly starving, but my starvation seemed to subside as I saw Gage in the restaurant. I couldn't help but scowl at his back. I wanted to take Cal's hand and drag him to whatever else was around, but Cal caught sight of Gage before I could make a move and smiled eagerly, stepping inside.

"Gage!" Cal yelled from the door, holding his arms in the air.

Gage turned around slowly, and as the long-legged brunette stepped from in front of him to his side, my heart failed to beat. Gage noticed me pause in my tracks and smirked, completely satisfied with my shock. "S'up, Cal," Gage said, removing his arm from around Penelope to shake Cal's hand.

"This was a great idea. The waterpark," Cal said.

"Yeah, I agree," Penelope butted in. "Everyone's having so much fun." She hooked her arms around Gage's waist and he pulled her in closer, kissing her forehead twice. Those small forehead kisses were getting to me. I remembered how warm his lips were against my forehead, how he'd stroked the edges of my hair and kissed me so delicately that I could have been considered fragile. To top it all off and make it worse, he was half-naked and looked extremely delicious. Gage Grendel without a shirt would have caused me to salivate had I not been so aggravated by his presence.

"You guys should join us at our pool," Gage insisted smoothly. "We've got drinks and they'll be bringing food over in just a bit. We're ordering now."

I shook my head quickly. "No, thanks."

"Hold on now," Cal said, lifting his arm to hook it around my shoulders. I stiffened and if I wasn't mistaken, Gage did as well.

Penelope noticed and placed her hand on Gage's chest, looking up at him. "You okay, babe?"

"Fine," Gage mumbled, his shoulders lacking some of the tension. His eyes flickered to the arm around my shoulder and then back into Cal's eyes again.

"Eliza and I would love to meet you at the pool. All we have to do is grab our stuff." I frowned, slipping from beneath Cal's arm. I hated how he was using "we" and "our" as if we were a couple. It was kind of uncomfortable.

Grudgingly, I turned around and stepped out of the restaurant. I couldn't go to that damn pool. I didn't want to be around Gage, who I knew would purposely kiss and lick on his girlfriend in front me. I knew for sure he was planning on getting drunk, and a drunken Gage wasn't good to be around unless he was with me. While he was with Penelope, I wasn't too fond of the idea. It was selfish as hell, but what did I care?

Cal came bursting out the doors behind me and smiled, hooking an arm across my shoulders. "I should get a good scoop tonight, don't ya think?"

"You could." I sighed. I don't know why, but seeing Gage made me not want to be around Cal any longer. I didn't want to be around anyone. I just wanted to be left alone. On top of that, I was starving and almost exhausted. I was going to grow even more exhausted with trying to ignore and avoid Gage at the pool.

Cal and I grabbed our things as the sun was just setting. The sky was filled with splashes of pink, yellow, orange, and even a fierce red. It was a beautiful sight, but it wasn't the night to enjoy it.

Cal brought up some more small talk (more about the magazine and the band than anything else), and I was half relieved, half upset we'd finally gotten to the pool. Relieved because Cal finally stopped talking and upset because Gage was in the pool, so close to Penelope they could've been considered one person.

I kept stealing glances of them and with each one they were closer and closer, if that were even possible. Her back was against the wall and I knew her legs were wrapped around him beneath the water. She ran her fingers through his hair and he placed kisses on her neck, his beer resting on the concrete outside the pool, locked in his right hand. He would place a few kisses on her lips, but

I noticed how he didn't kiss her as much as he'd kissed me last night. These kisses weren't as passionate or deep. It was kind of strange, seeing as she was his "girlfriend" and all, but I shrugged it off.

Two beers appeared in front of my face and as I looked over my shoulder, I saw nothing beyond Montana's bright smile. "Come on," he begged as I scowled at the beers. "You've got to. You're sitting at the edge of this pool all pouty and shit." He stepped over to sit beside me. "Are you upset about Mr. Grendel?"

"No," I snapped quickly, looking around, glad no one could hear him. Cal was talking to Deed and the other people around were dancing to the boom box music playing loudly. My feet were in the water as I surveyed everyone from the opposite side of the pool.

"Drink one with me please, Miss Eliza," he insisted, lifting one of the beer bottles. Sighing, I grabbed it and he chuckled. "Atta girl."

I popped the cap and took a long draw. Montana did the same and I thought he was going to question my overzealous drinking, but he didn't. In fact, when we both finished our first bottle, he told me to wait while he went to get a few more. I could have rejected the drinks, but I refused to do so. I wanted to forget about Gage and the night we shared before.

I started thinking maybe that night wasn't real, but I knew I was to blame for him being with Penelope. I mean, I didn't want him, but I would much rather him be alone than with any other girl. That seemed so selfish, but it was just too soon for him to be rubbing and kissing another girl after what we shared less than twenty-four hours ago.

"I'm pretty sure you're upset about seeing him in there with her," Montana said, as if he'd just read my mind.

I looked at him and he smiled lazily. "I'm not," I lied.

"You sure?" He grinned, his head tilting.

"I'm…"

He raised an eyebrow, waiting on my response. Why was I being hesitant? Was it because I knew I was upset and would rather it were me he was against? I couldn't believe how stupid I was being. Why was I getting so upset over it? It was never like me to get upset over guys, but of course Gage was the one who had to be the exception. Gage, my high school crush and the guy that'd always haunted my dreams. Gage, the one I always happened to drool over whenever he made an appearance. Gage…

"Why don't you just go for something?" Montana inquired.

I looked at him, frowning as he took a sip of his beer. "What do you mean?"

"If you don't want to see him with her,"—he nearly cringed as he pointed at Penelope—"then why don't you just take her spot?"

"I don't wanna be his girlfriend."

"You don't have to be his girlfriend." He laughed. "And besides, Penelope *is not* his girlfriend. She just believes she is because she's known him for a while. She thinks after he's done partying and living life like a star, he'll finally settle down with her." Montana laughed again, placing his beer down. "Not likely. Not Gage."

"But even if that were true, she still allows him to do whatever he wants behind her back?"

"Sometimes he'll tell her." He smirked. I gaped. "She's crazy, I know. It's exactly what you're thinking. She's head over heels for Gage and I'm really not sure why he hasn't gotten rid of her yet. I'm not sure why he still leads her on. He can't stand that girl. None of us can."

"And you really expect me to 'go for something' with him?" I shook my head and laughed, placing the rim of my bottle against my lips.

"I look at it this way: you both have two months together on this trip and the more you try to avoid each other, the worse it'll be between you. He told me what happened this morning, and if we're being frank, it was really fucked up on your behalf."

I was about to protest, but he shook his head and his voice overpowered mine. "I'm pretty sure after the tour is over, you won't be seeing much of Gage. You won't have to worry about him because you'll be... wherever you are and Gage'll be too busy doing shit with the band. I say have at it. Have fun. Don't let any feelings get involved if you don't want to. I'm all up for having a friend with benefits—a hot friend at that. As long as she doesn't expect me to change or want to go through with something more, we're good. As long as she's all about fun, I can get down with that. Gage is the same way. He just wants some fun."

I pressed my lips together. "So you're saying I should have a casual fling with Gage?"

He nodded. "Or casual sex. No feelings, of course. Your choice." He smirked.

My cheeks sparked. That was going to be hard seeing how I was a virgin and all.

"Just a small fling," Montana said, placing the palms of his hands on the concrete behind him. "You can't lie and say you didn't have fun with him last night." I laughed as he raised a knowing eyebrow at me. "I saw it clearly and I was high as hell."

"I did," I admitted, "but we were drunk—"

"Doesn't matter. Fun is fun."

I looked from Montana to Gage, who was now sitting on the edge of the pool like us, his feet in the water. He was bobbing his head to the music and Penelope was still in the water between his legs. He seemed to be thinking about something else as she babbled on. Apparently the music was taking him away. He was staring right at Penelope, but he didn't seem to be listening to a word she said.

He then swung his gaze up and I stilled as our eyes locked. It was magnetic, powerful. I tried to blink and dared myself to look down, but I was stuck. Gage's face remained firm. His jaw ticked as he scanned me from head to toe and then looked at Montana who was only an inch away from me. He finally tore his gaze away, sighing and whispering something in Penelope's ear. She nodded and she and I both watched Gage walk away from the party with a beer in his hand.

I looked at Montana who was staring up at the stars, his palms still planted on the concrete behind him. "What if I actually start to… like him?"

He shrugged. "Try not to. Look, if you never take the risks, you'll never live. That's how I go about my life. We only have one to live, so why not make the most we can out of it? I'm sure since Gage is so 'hot' and 'charming,'"—he dramatically batted his eyelashes and I giggled—"then you might fall just a little, but you're a strong girl. I think you're smart enough to play it safe but still have some fun until it's time for you to go."

I nodded because he was right. Montana grunted as he pushed on his hands to stand. "I'm gonna get back with the people over there, but seriously," he said, eyeing me, "think about it. I'll catch you later, Miss Eliza."

He stumbled off and I watched him meet a blonde in a yellow and grey bikini. He kissed her and she melted in his arms, and I refused to watch his fingers slide into the bottoms of her bikini so I stared at the water.

I felt a pair of heavy eyes on me and I looked up, directly at Penelope glaring at me. Her lips were pinched tight and her dark eyes looked me over, as if she were trying to point out my flaws. Perhaps she'd caught sight of the magazines as well. At the thought of it, I gave her a smug smile and she snobbishly turned to meet with a brunette nearby.

I stumbled onto my feet and my head swayed. I'd obviously had too many beers. Montana kept bringing them back-to-back, but I had to admit they were easing my mind of the night before with Gage. I looked over at Cal who was still talking to Deed and decided not to interrupt. He was most likely interviewing him... again.

I figured taking a walk around the park was best. I would take a short trip alone to actually think about what Montana told me. Perhaps he was right. Gage and I could be a casual thing. A quick fling. I wasn't usually up for stuff like that, but it seemed like it would be fun with someone like Gage, especially after last night during the party.

Maybe it won't be so bad, I thought. The only thing bad about it was losing my virginity, but I was tired of holding it, and as bad as it seemed, I sort of wanted Gage to take it. My virginity had almost been taken one time. Back when I was eleven... by a man my mom was dating. Good thing she actually rescued me from that one. Thinking of it made me cringe inside, though. I hated reliving my past. It sucked so much and it wasn't easy to let most of it go.

The breeze picked up and I inhaled, allowing the air to fill my lungs. *Happy thoughts,* I told myself.

Breathe. Think happy thoughts. Breathe.

My eyes darted over to the trees and I spotted a bench... but it was occupied. With his elbows on his thighs and his gaze on the ground, Gage was sitting there looking nearly drained. He was hunched over, as if he'd drunk too much and was trying to sober himself up. "Gage?" I called cautiously.

At the sound of my voice, he looked up quickly, his eyes glazed over completely. Realizing it was only me, he scowled and looked down again. I stepped to his side and he tensed. He tensed even more as I sat beside him but not too closely. "Are you okay?" I asked.

"Fine," he muttered. "Just go back to Cal... or Montana... or whatever."

I couldn't ignore the slur in his tone. It was obvious he was drunk. I wanted to walk a bit more but knew he wasn't suited for walking, and if he were to pass out, I wouldn't have been able to support his weight. I remained seated, taking a deep sigh through my nostrils. It was silent between us. Crickets chirped and a few fireflies glowed around us.

The sun had set even more and the moon was hovering right above us. I could still make out the pink, red, orange, and yellow beneath the midnight purple of the sky, and it humbled me a bit.

"What do you see in them anyway?" Gage asked, catching me completely off guard.

My head whipped to look at him quickly and he was bent over even more, his forehead pressed on his folded arms.

"They're just friends."

"Oh, like I'm just a friend?" he slurred, aiming to be sarcastic. Unfortunately it didn't work to his advantage. His tone came off as harsh, insulting. "You really confuse me."

Shit, I confused myself. He wasn't the only one. "I've thought about it," I whispered.

He gave me a side-glance. "About what?"

"The 'more than friends' thing?"

"And?"

I bit my bottom lip, hesitant to answer. Was I sure about it? No. I didn't know how the hell I was only going to remain friends with Gage without feeling anything in return. It just wasn't me. I wasn't like the girls he slept with that could wake up the next morning and act like nothing ever happened. I was far from it. Plus, I was going to see him every day. What if something went wrong? What would happen if I wanted to continue our fun nights, but he got bored of them? Bored of me? I was an amateur at a lot of things, after all. It would make it that much easier for him to forget about me.

Before I could respond, Gage sat himself up and pulled me in by the waist. "I'm not forcing you to do anything with me, Eliza."

"I know you're not," I said, my eyebrows stitching.

"So why are you so hesitant? It's not like I'm asking you to... fall in love with me or anything."

I pressed my lips because he was right. I was just afraid of it possibly sneaking up on me.

When I didn't say anything, he sighed, running his fingers through his hair. The ink on his arms was bolder beneath the moonlight as his muscles locked. He swallowed noisily and I sighed, unsure of what to say to him. "How about we take a swim?"

I looked into his low, hazel eyes and he revealed a crooked, dazzling smile. With that, I was up for it. Gage wasn't as much of the stumbling, drunk idiot I thought he would be. He actually seemed to carry himself pretty well as we searched for another pool with no one around. We finally found one a bit smaller than the other.

Sighing, I stepped away from Gage and went for the steps to check the temperature. It was cooler than the other pool, but I didn't care. I slid out of my flip-flops, shorts, and tank top, stepping into the water and shivering with each step.

But then I realized Gage had been watching me attentively, even while I was undressing. I was embarrassed, but it was already over with so I lowered myself into the water. The light from the pool reflected onto him as he stood in his blue-and-black swimming trunks.

"Are you coming in?" I asked, smiling.

With haste, Gage stepped toward the edge of the pool and jumped in. As he surfaced, the water ran over his gorgeous face and my breath hitched as he brought a hand up to clear it all away. Noticing I was staring, he revealed a small smile and swam toward me.

As he neared me, he reeled me in, but I remained still, although I had the urge to hook my arms around his neck. My feet were kicking in the water to keep me afloat.

"I wanna kiss you again," he said, his breath warm as it tickled my cheek. He sluggishly licked his lips and I stared at them, slightly aching for those lips to touch mine.

"Weren't you just kissing Penelope?" I asked instead. I couldn't seem easy.

He laughed deeply, huskily. The sexy laugh that always made me melt. "It feels a whole lot better to kiss you."

"How?" I whispered. I don't know why I'd gotten so quiet. Perhaps it was because no one was around and I knew he was the only person who could hear me. Or maybe it was because I wanted to just shut the hell up already and kiss him. I couldn't figure it out.

"I can show you." His eyebrows rose and he pulled me in even closer. The water was still running from his hair to his plush, pink lips and he licked away each droplet. At the sight of his tongue, the pit of my belly heated. "I can show you a lot of things, if only you'd let me."

It wasn't worth it to stall anymore, especially as Gage inched closer. His hands moved up the small of my back to pull me in even tighter and first he kissed my cheek and then my neck. He kissed my neck in different areas, all sweet to the touch, and beneath the water my legs effortlessly circled around his waist. He moved forward so my back could press against the nearest wall, but his lips didn't stop teasing my skin. I was biting and nibbling on my bottom lip, heat bombarding my stomach and moisture building between my legs.

Lifting his hands, Gage gripped the edge of the pool and pressed his cock against me. When he was done tasting my neck, he devoured my lips, and I couldn't help it; I wrapped my arms around his neck. My legs squeezed tighter around him, wanting to feel the rock in his pants. It was turning me on in more ways than one. His silky tongue, although laced with alcohol, tasted sweet as it ran over mine.

He thrust against me and I moaned, running my fingers through his slick hair. His hard chest was pressed firmly against mine, no space between us. The little nibbles and bites he took of my lower lip were driving me insane. His fingers that snuck beneath my bathing suit to slide inside me caused my moans to grow louder and his lips to fall so he could grunt against my neck.

I was spiraling, bucking against him. "You like that?" he whispered gruffly in my ear. His other hand reached behind me and unhooked the top of my bathing suit. I could've stopped him, but I didn't. A growl came from the heart of his throat as he stared at my full, bare chest.

I nodded my head at his question, my body begging him to continue. Who knew his fingers could be so magical? He was pushing in and out of me, circling his thumb across my clit. I was so close. My fingernails bit into his skin and he went faster, faster, faster, sending me higher and higher... but then he just stopped. Right when I was about to reach the point of it all. Right when I'd just gotten wet and swollen.

"What the hell are you doing?" I breathed raggedly, aggravated.

He smirked, looking into my eyes and pulling his fingers out of my bottoms. I wanted to beg for his fingers not to leave, but I didn't. It would have been too embarrassing and shallow. "Since we're only 'friends,' I can't give you the full effect."

I scowled at him. "You're kidding." He raised an eyebrow. "Right?

"No, Ellie. This right here isn't what friends do to one another. Let's just do this shit. I swear it'll be fun. I'll make it worth it. You have my word."

"Gage, I—" *Damn, what do I say?*

"Nothing between us has to change," he assured me. "It doesn't have to be serious and I think if we try to continue this little battle going on between us, someone's gonna get hurt. I want you; you want me. Let's do it." He gave a lazy smirk, kissed my neck, and I snickered.

I thought it over, replaying the conversation Montana and I had just moments ago, knowing he was right. I wanted to do more things with Gage than I thought, and with him giving me an orgasm the night before, I was desperate and in need of more. Gage's touch was addicting, and I constantly craved more.

It was bad, but it felt good to be satisfied—to reach the point of bliss and not come down for hours. Gage was the closest I'd ever gotten to a guy and he was also my best bet, so I shrugged and thought to myself, *Fuck it.* Montana was right. I had to take risks and I was going to be taking a huge one with Gage Grendel.

"Okay," I said right before kissing him and allowing him to finish what he started.

CAREFUL

Although the boys had a small gig the following day for a few high school students, they performed better than usual, and I never thought it was possible. Okay... maybe *Gage* performed better than usual. He was so energetic, so full of life, and his voice was so powerful that I actually thought he was singing to me. His deep voice was alluring and I couldn't help but cheer and bounce on my toes when he would break down with a slower rhythm and his voice filled the stadium. The crowd (the girls especially) would go crazy, reaching their hands above for a feel of him. A blush crept up on me when I realized how bad I actually wanted to touch him myself.

The boys hooted and hollered as they stepped backstage, Gage coming back last and stealing a kiss from me. "You did great." I grinned at him.

He lit up, his hazel eyes wide with astonishment. "You think so?"

I nodded and he stole another kiss. I melted.

"Did it for you." Winking, he stepped around me and followed the boys, each of them going to separate dressing rooms. I couldn't help but notice the familiar man with the peppery hair and business suit following Deed into his. Once again, his face was stern and Deed took glances over his shoulder, as if the man was going to do something to him. It weirded me out a little, but then my mind circled back to Gage again. For a moment, I thought his statement about singing so well for me was true. Was he really glad I'd agreed to this fling thing with him?

I sighed, spinning around and heading for the exit door. There were a few things I had to grow accustomed to. For instance, the girls who would rush to the back, eagerly waiting to have their thigh, ass, or tit signed. I didn't want to be a witness to Gage signing boobs, so I stepped out and took in the steamy Orlando breeze. It was our last night, but we weren't going to be leaving until the next day, which meant another night for the boys to go out and get wild.

I needed to skip out on the fun this time. I missed painting and drawing and wanted to get back at it. My ideas were running wildly, all a mix of Gage, waterpark slides, and spark-filled kisses in the pool.

I knew it was going to take the boys a while, so instead of waiting up to try and tell Gage I was skipping out, I found the truck and told Marco to take me back to the bus. The sun was still sitting high in the sky, and I cracked the window, indulging in the warm, fresh breeze.

Marco pulled up to the front of the bus and I told him to wait while I gathered my supplies. As soon as I was packed, I told him to take me to the nearest beach, gave Ben a call to tell him where I was headed so he wouldn't panic, and then sat back to relax.

I arrived at the beach within an hour and found a good spot beside the pier with a perfect view of the setting sun. The wind was picking up, but it wasn't too much to blow away my papers. It was best to go with drawing. When my hand started, it wouldn't stop. It'd been a while and I felt rejuvenated.

After I was worn from drawing, I stood and snapped a few pictures of some of the seagulls at shore. Some were sitting perfectly in front of the rippling water and the setting sun, and I knew once I developed the pictures, it would be a beautiful sight to revisit. It would definitely be something to add to the collage of pictures I'd already taken.

The sun sank behind the horizon, making it harder for me to see. I packed my things, tucking them beneath my arm and walking along the shore. A few couples were walking by, hand-in-hand, and at the sight of them, I couldn't help but think of Gage.

I'd shocked myself last night when I told him we could try more. I swore up and down I would never do it, but I just couldn't say no. I was tired of lying to myself and tired of holding off. Plus, knowing no feelings had to be involved and that I could still do whatever I wanted was the best part. The worst part about it was Gage could still do what he wanted, and even though I knew it was going to upset me, I wasn't going to be able to do or say much about it. It was his life and I was just a minor part of it. I had to keep looking at it that way—just as he was a minor part of my life.

We said we wouldn't take it further than a casual fling, which involved kissing, hugging, maybe some cuddling, partying, and probably soon... *sex*. My cheeks sparked at the idea of having sex with Gage. Of course I knew it was going to be mind-blowing. What he could do with his mouth and hands was mind-blowing. I couldn't imagine how great it was going to be with the muscle he carried in his boxers.

Soon, the moon had risen and the sun was nowhere to be found. I turned slowly to look at the body of water in front of me. The gentle ripples of the ocean reflected the glow of the moon like dark, exotic jewels. It was a soothing sight—one I could appreciate.

I enjoyed the times I could be calm and not panic. I enjoyed smiling, even though at first it felt odd to do so. When I moved in with Ben, it was the hardest thing to adjust to. His warmness, his funkiness, his hugs, and the way he smiled at me as if I were actually a human being.

Ben was the first person I opened up to about a lot of things. It was tough the first couple of months, and at some points I wanted him to just stop trying to make small talk with me and leave me alone. I was bitter... sad... alone. I was so used to spending time alone that whenever someone actually tried to be nice to me, I thought they were making a mockery of me.

Around the fifth or sixth month of living with Ben, I finally opened up to him—not completely, but enough to see if I could trust him. I had no choice but to put my faith in him. Since then, I knew I could trust him with my life. With my happiness. He wanted to give me the universe and, even though some thought he was unfit to be a role model, he's the best damn father in the world to me. He gave me my space when I needed it—something my mom never gave me. He'd even given me my own room, and for that I was forever grateful.

I'd never had my own bedroom before, even though I was an only child. My mom rented a one-bedroom apartment and selfishly kept it all to herself. I had the rock-hard, lumpy sofa in the living room. The little bit of clothes I did have were folded neatly in the corners or hung in the living room closet.

Thinking about how low I started in life brought tears to the rims of my eyes, and the passageway between my lungs and mouth closed in, making it harder for me to breathe. It burned, but I blinked quickly, inhaling to get rid of the memories. I couldn't cry again. I hated crying because I was stronger now. It wasn't worth it to look back. As I'd told myself over and over again, it was the past and it was never going to happen again. *She* never again had to be a part of my life for as long as I lived. I knew with Ben by my side I would never have to look back. He promised me, and ever since, he was true to his word.

At the thought of the safety Ben provided, I inhaled again, breathing and nodding until I felt stable enough to take a step toward the water. *Breathe. Calm down and breathe, Eliza.*

"What are you doing out here by yourself?" a deep voice asked from behind me, causing me to spin around quickly.

I gasped as Gage took slow strides toward me, his head tilted and a soft smirk on his lips. The jeans he wore were snug but loose. His hair was perfectly and deliciously tousled. He had on a light-grey muscle T-shirt along with matching light-grey Chuck Taylors. Oh, how he loved his Chuck T's. Although his clothes were basic and casual, he looked completely irresistible. Amazingly delectable.

I cleared my throat softly, straightening myself, but the smile that had once been gracing his lips faded once he caught sight of my depressing features and glistening eyes. "Are you okay?" he asked, stepping closer.

"Fine." I waved him off, running my other hand across my nose. I tightened my grip around the bag of my art supplies and then looked into his concerned eyes. "How did you know where I was?"

He smiled faintly. "Benny boy."

"Of course," I sighed, returning the faint smile.

"Seriously, though," he said, gazing around at the empty beach, "why are you out here alone? I waited for you on your bus, but an hour passed and there was still no sign of you. After another two hours, I thought I'd come check up on you."

"I did some drawing and painting. It's been a while. Thought I'd get away from you and the boys for one night to do what I love." I shrugged, forcing a smile. "Why aren't you out partying with them anyway?"

Gage looked down at the art supplies tucked beneath my arm and then into my eyes again. "I thought it'd be more fun to hang with you. I thought maybe you would have wanted to join us, but seeing as you ran off without telling us anything, I guess I was wrong." He smirked.

"It's not that." I laughed, adjusting the heavy supplies beneath my arm. "I just had to clear my head, you know?"

Gage nodded, licking his dry bottom lip. He then took a slow step toward me to take the supplies from beneath my arm as if he felt my struggle. He placed the bag down on the sand and then gazed into my eyes, his meek and adorable. "Sometimes nights off are good." He inhaled, then exhaled, taking a look around. "How about we take a walk?"

I grinned, excited at the thought, but I didn't want to keep him from his fun. As much as I would've loved to walk with Gage, I sort of knew he would like partying with his band more. "Gage, I don't wanna hold you back. It's fine. Really. If you wanna hang with them, go ahead. I can't stop you."

"You aren't stopping me. If I really wanted to party tonight, I wouldn't have wasted time coming here." My lips twisted morosely and he chuckled. "But as I've said before, *we* only have a few weeks to share. I have pretty much the rest of my life with them. I'm sure it'll be just as fun with you as it is with them. I don't mind, Ellie."

Unwinding my lips, I smiled up at him and his head tilted adorably. He revealed a boyish grin and then, unexpectedly, bent down to untie his shoes. "What are you doing?" I giggled.

"Just bought these. Don't need 'em getting wet or dirty."

I smirked at him and as soon as his socks and shoes were off and I kicked my flip-flops to the side, I grabbed the hand he offered and we began our peaceful walk along the shore.

For the most part, my walk with Gage was entertaining. What amused me most was that his hand hardly left mine and if it did, it was so he could hook his arm around my shoulders and pull me in against him. It was comforting to be next to him—to laugh with him and tease him. The feeling was unfamiliar, but I enjoyed it. I was getting accustomed to smiling, grinning, blushing, and teasing.

He didn't seem to mind much, either.

I noticed one thing about Gage I thought was weird, though. Whenever I would ask him about his family or his past, he would brush me off and change the subject. I grew suspicious, but I wasn't one to pressure anyone into talking. I hated when people pressured me, so I just left it alone.

But then Gage asked something that completely caught me off guard...

"Are you still going to talk to Cal and Montana?"

I stared up at him blatantly, my eyes stretching. "Why would you assume I was talking to either of them?"

"You stare at them a lot. Talk to them a lot." He rubbed the back of his neck. "Probably more than me."

I laughed, thinking in the back of my mind how he had no clue how much I stared at him. There wasn't even a comparison in this situation. Had there been a chart, Gage's side would have skyrocketed and outshone both of theirs. Montana didn't even pique my interest. He was only a friend—almost like a long-lost brother. Although Cal did have a nice body, Gage had more for me to look at. "I don't stare," I corrected. "I admire."

"Well... admire. Whatever. Do you find them more interesting than me?"

"No," I blurted. Right after, I was embarrassed, especially when he grinned at me. "You're just being really silly right now. Montana and I are just friends, just like Cal."

"On a scale of one through ten, what am I to you, Ellie?"

"Ten being the hottest?" I asked, smiling at him.

He nodded, waiting for an answer.

"I'd have to give you a two. You're all right," I teased.

He laughed heartily. "Yet you *admire*. I must not be too shabby for those eyes."

I giggled as he circled his arms around my waist. "What about Penelope?" I asked as he inched in closer.

The inching stopped abruptly as he stared into my eyes, his suddenly hard. "What about her?"

"Are you going to keep talking to her?"

He shrugged. "No."

My head tilted. "How do I know that?"

"Because Penelope isn't as much fun as you are. She talks too much, whines too much. She asks for everything."

"And you think I wouldn't do the same?" I forced myself not to laugh at how aggravated his face had become.

"I know you wouldn't do the same. It may have only been a few days, but I can already see how you are."

"And how am I?" I urged. God, why was I being so demanding?

Instead of answering right away, Gage placed a kiss on my cheek. I sparked on the inside, bubbling over. The bubbling swelled as he kissed the left corner of my mouth. His tongue traced its way across the line of my lips and mine parted, begging for a taste of him, but he pulled back. "You're different—difficult to figure out sometimes, but different."

I could agree on that. Who wanted to be easy to figure out? I circled my arms around his neck, pulling him in closer, and his grip tightened around my waist. I was centered perfectly between his body and he towered over me, smiling so adorably that I couldn't help but admire him.

How could a man be so flawless, so gorgeous? If he had any imperfections, I couldn't see them. All I could see was this perfect man with the perfect hair and the perfect kisses. The perfect touch, perfect tongue. Thinking of his tongue caused a shiver to crawl along my spine, and my legs stiffened, but I held on to him. He didn't have the best personality, but at least he was done trying to get under my skin. All he wanted was my attention. I could give him that much.

"Let's make the next few weeks as fun as possible," Gage said, placing a kiss on the bend of my neck.

"How?" I breathed. It almost mixed with a moan. His lips on my neck always made me tingle. It was my spot— the perfect place to get me going.

"There are a million ways... Most of them can be done with your body and mine... together" His voice rumbled near my ear, so deep, so husky, and I spiraled as he kissed the lobe. "I want my hands all over you. Your skin on mine." His grip on my waist tightened even more and I yelped as he picked me up, and I circled my legs around his waist. He tasted the skin on my neck, licked, sucked, and licked some more with deep groans. I was biting on my lower lip fiercely, getting completely flushed as one of his hands cupped my ass. He was so strong. It was as if I were a feather in his arms.

Gage brought his lips to mine again and I devoured them greedily. That fast he'd turned me on. I was burning inside, craving something—anything to satisfy me. The most I had at the moment was his lips and his tongue, and his tongue worked wonders as it coaxed and stroked mine.

His arousal caved into me and he grunted, lowering his head to place another feverish kiss on my neck. "I can do so much to you, Sweet Ellie," he murmured, bringing his lips back up to touch my ear. "You just don't know it yet."

Little did he know how bad I wanted him to go through with his words. I wanted him to do anything with my body. Flashbacks of his tongue circling around my core, driving me higher and higher to a climax, came to mind, and I whimpered, pressing my cheek against his. All of a sudden I felt defeated, especially as he whispered, "Not here, though, Eliza." I would've given anything to feel that kind of pleasure again, but he was right. Not here. Not on a beach.

"Are you all right?" He placed me on my feet with a chuckle and I nodded, my lips pressing.

"I'm fine. Do you think we should go catch a little bit of that party?"

He looked me over, making sure I was being serious. "You're serious? You want to?"

"I don't mind."

"Penelope might be there, though... and you know how she can get whenever I'm around..."

I cringed as her name came out of his mouth, but I shook it off. I couldn't do much about her being around. Gage wasn't my property. I didn't own him. As far as I was concerned, we weren't anything other than friends... with benefits. I wasn't seeking much else and I sure as hell knew he wasn't. I finally nodded my head with a shrug and he sighed, bringing a hand up to run it through his hair. He pulled out his cell phone, his eyes a bit harder than before as he said, "I'll call Stan."

I wasn't sure what was wrong. Maybe he was worried he'd run into Penelope. Maybe he just really didn't want to go to that party. I was uncertain, so instead of making him feel guilty, I hooked my arm around his lean waist and smiled up at him, leading the way back to my art supplies. "It'll be fun, like you said," I assured him. "Nothing negative. I promise. And if she's there, we'll just leave."

He revealed a gentle, crooked smile, kissed my forehead, and I grinned as the sudden heat from his lips bombarded me with pleasure and contentment.

And for the rest of that night, luck was on our side because Penelope was nowhere to be found.

The next state was Kentucky. Being in Kentucky was different, not too sunny or too cloudy. The breezes were gentle, soothing. After the boys practiced beside the tour bus, it was time to head for the show. I couldn't help but stare as Gage sang without a microphone as he practiced. Surprisingly, even from sitting on the steps of my bus, I could hear him. His voice was loud and mesmerizing. I really couldn't figure out why I fell for his voice each and every time.

It could have been because he sang with so much emotion that it gave him more depth. He had so much soul, so much heart. He looked vulnerable when singing, like he was cut open and all his emotions were put on display for the whole world to see.

With my hand on my chin, my elbow on my lap, I found it hard to look away. I couldn't help but study him. The way he tapped the outside of his thigh with his hand. The way he snapped his fingers with the rhythm whenever his eyes were open and he was smiling behind the words. Something was letting me know that behind his lyrics, there was meaning, and I wanted so badly to find out. Who hurt him? Who broke his heart? I never thought any girl could break Gage Grendel's heart. He was too carefree and if anything, he was the one breaking hearts and messing with girl's emotions. Most of their songs were upbeat, but the lyrics were so sad.

As he sang, I saw the man with the peppery hair, suit, and clean face again—the one whose appearance always weirded me out. It was odd how he stared so intently at Deed as he played on the drums. I noticed how Deed would take nervous glances to his right at the man, and whenever Deed hit a certain beat, the man would nod, his fingers tucked into his pockets, and Deed's chest would sink and rise with relief. The guy seriously freaked me out, and it was weird how I didn't know who the hell he was, what he did, or what part of the crew he belonged to.

"Liza!" Ben called, snapping me out of my daze. I looked to my left quickly, seeing Ben standing with his hand at his hip, his eyes narrowed. "Did you not hear me calling you?"

"No… sorry. Are we ready to go?"

"Yes. We have to be there in twenty."

I nodded, clutching my bottle of water and grabbing my satchel. After strapping my bag around me, I made the turn for the truck but got caught in a pair of firm, masculine arms before I could make the complete spin. "Hey, Ellie," Gage murmured, his head tilting down to look at me.

My pulse paused, realizing how close he was. I still had to get used to this—to Gage touching me whenever he wanted, not that I minded it. "Hey," I breathed. "All ready for your show?"

"A little bit." He released me, running his fingers through his hair. "I don't think I'm completely ready yet, though."

My head tilted. "What do you mean? What's wrong?"

"Well… there's just this thing I wanted before stepping on stage."

"And what might that be?"

"A simple kiss on the cheek… from my Sweet Ellie."

I smirked at him, shaking my head and folding my arms. "You sure it isn't anything else?"

"Oh, trust me," he sighed. "I'd love more from you, Ellie, but since we're on a time crunch, a kiss on the cheek will do for now." Gage bent his knees a little and turned his head, pointing at his cheek. "Go ahead. Lay it on me. It's not asking for too much, is it?"

I giggled because it wasn't asking much at all. A kiss on the cheek would do, so I leaned forward and puckered my lips, ready to place them against his cheek, but then his head turned, right when I was close, and our lips collided. I gasped, smacking his shoulder playfully, and he laughed, reeling me in by the waist. "A kiss on the cheek? Yeah

WHO HE IS (BOOK #1 FIRENINE TRILOGY)

fucking right," he said, rolling his eyes. "I think those lips on mine are what I need in order to have a great show."

Grinning, I stood on my toes and kissed him swiftly but tenderly. "There. Good luck tonight."

"Uh… no." He pulled me in again, crushing my body against his. His arms were still circled around my waist and, tilting his head down, he leaned in and kissed me. The kiss was sweet, innocent, and simple at first, but then he added his tongue and I moaned into his mouth. My hand pressed against his chest to try and get him to release me and hurry before they ended up late, but it faltered and gave out on me as the intensity grew. I sank against him, and behind the kiss he smiled, pulling away slowly. "There," he said in a mocking tone. "That may just last me until the show's over."

I beamed at him and he unhooked his arms from my waist. "Good luck tonight," I said again, watching as he took gradual steps away. I couldn't look away from him. I wanted to kiss him again, and by the look in his hungry hazel irises, I knew he wanted it just as badly. He stopped walking quickly, his lips parting, eyes darting right down to my lips.

S. Q. WILLIAMS   311

"Just one more," he murmured, rushing for me and reeling me in. Giggling, I wrapped my arms around his neck and kissed him. It wasn't as long or as passion-filled as the previous one, but it made do.

With that, Gage tossed a light wave at me, rushed for the bus to grab his guitar and strap it around him, and then hurried for the truck. Before he hopped in all the way, he looked over his shoulder, noticing me still watching him. He then winked and climbed into the truck completely, shutting the door behind him. Their vehicle peeled off the instant he was inside, and I sighed, still smiling—wait... Why was I still smiling? It was just a kiss. Nothing other than that. It wasn't like we hadn't kissed before.

"All right, mesmerized damsel," Ben said, making me gasp. He hooked his arm around my shoulders and led the way toward the car. "I allowed you to have your little kiss, but we have to get going."

My cheeks burned as I looked up at him. "Oh, geez. You watched?"

"How could I not? You were standing right in front of me." He laughed a little and I smiled. "Just be careful with him, Liza," he added.

My head tilted a little, confused by the seriousness that just clouded his tone. "We aren't anything other than friends with benefits, Ben."

"I understand that, but…" Ben trailed off as we neared the truck and he opened the door for me.

"But what?" I asked as I climbed in, knowing he wasn't going to finish his sentence.

He looked me over, his brown eyes studying me cautiously. He then sighed, bringing his sunglasses up to place them over his eyes. "Nothing, Liza Bear. Just be careful, like I said. Have fun, but keep your heart to yourself while you're hanging with him."

He shut the door before I could ask him anything, and I slid back on the leather bench, sort of baffled. What exactly did he mean by that? Keep my heart to myself? Why would I give it to Gage, knowing he was one person who could crumble it to pieces? Handing it over would have been tremendously dumb of me.

Ben rounded the front of the car and hopped into the front seat. He told Marco we were all set and not once did he look back at me. It was as if he knew I had a million questions, but he didn't want to answer them. It made me kind of suspicious, but I told myself to drop it and stick with the plan Gage and I had. Friends with benefits and nothing more.

That was it.

WASHING MACHINE

The fans of Kentucky were rowdier than the other cities, but the band seemed to love their hollering and enthusiasm. It allowed them to play louder and for Gage to sing louder. I sang along to a few of the songs I knew, and it surprised me that every so often, Gage would steal glances to his left at me and wink. Smooth heat would creep up from my neck to my cheeks and I would wink back.

After the boys finished their performances, they decided to grab a bite to eat. I wasn't sure what they were going to be doing that night, but since I was going to be with Gage most of the time, I was kind of thrilled. I knew I shouldn't have been because he could still do whatever he wanted. I frowned when that thought came to mind.

I frowned even more as I slid into my booth across from Ben and Cal, who were talking about the boys' performances and the upcoming songs they had planned. The diner was connected to an arcade. The waiters and waitresses wore roller skates and bright colors. It was pretty spiffy.

After the boys downed their food, they rushed for the arcade in a heartbeat and hollered like idiots. If they all didn't have facial hair and nice bodies, I would've considered them a load of sixteen and seventeen-year-olds instead of twenty-three and twenty-four-year-olds.

A few girls were giggling in the corner, desperate for some attention. My gaze paused on Gage, who took a quick look over his shoulder and winked at one of them. They giggled even harder and my eyebrows drew in. I turned quickly. I couldn't become *that* girl... but then again, we did have to establish some rules if I wanted this to go correctly and be as fun as possible.

Ben and Cal finished their food and stood from the table to walk outside and meet with the crew, and I sighed, digging into my satchel for my book. I hadn't read a book in a while with all the partying, going out, and being stuck on… *him*. I figured a good romantic novel would do until it was time to go.

The only negative thing about books was I would get so sucked into them that I didn't pay much attention to anything outside of me. I didn't feel anyone moving up on me from behind. Usually I could feel the presence of another without even seeing them, but not this time. I didn't fully snap out of it until a pair of warm, damp lips pressed on the back of my neck, and I burned from head to toe. The hair on my back spiked and prickled at my skin. My legs clenched, heat bombarded my lower belly, and I gasped, holding back on a moan.

He kissed me again and this time there was a mixture of ice that made my toes curl. I gripped the edges of my book, his lips moving across my skin rather seductively up to the lobe of my ear, my jawline, and then down to the crook of my neck. I moaned and he chuckled deeply, sending another shot of heat between my legs.

"Hey, Ellie," Gage murmured, kissing my cheek. He stepped back to get into the booth with me and I sighed as he hooked an arm around my shoulders.

"Hey, Gage."

"Why are you sitting here alone?"

"I don't play video games… sorry." I shrugged.

"You read?" He pointed at my book.

"Yes," I blurted. I felt kind of stupid afterward because of my abruptness. "There's nothing wrong with reading. Maybe you should try it one day."

"Nah." He leaned back against the booth. "Reading was never my thing. I'll write without a problem, though."

"I guess that's just as good."

I looked into his eyes and he smirked at me. He inched in closer, but I backed away a little, pressing the palm of my hand against his firm chest. "What's wrong?" he asked, looking down at the hand on his chest and then into my eyes again.

"I think if we want this to be equally fun between us, with no drama, we have to make some things clear."

Gage looked me over briefly before clearing his throat. I dropped my arm as he sat up straight, stood, and moved to sit across from me. Leaning against his seat with his arms folded, he said, "Okay, let's hear it."

"Number one, just because we aren't involving more than benefits doesn't mean we should mess around with other people while we're hanging out. If we're really doing this for the next few weeks, our attention should be on each other... even if it's just for fun."

Gage raised an eyebrow. "Sounds like you're trying to make this sort of a... relationship."

"No." I shook my head quickly. "No, I don't want that. I just... It won't really be fun knowing you're sleeping with other girls when *we're* supposed to be having fun together. It'll make me wanna stop, ya know?"

"So you're pretty much saying I can only fuck you? Nobody else?"

I scowled as he smirked. "Gage, I'm being serious."

"Okay, okay." He chuckled, holding up his hands innocently. "All right, so no fucking around with other girls while we're doing this thing. Okay. I gotcha."

"Another thing... Penelope. What do you plan on doing with her?"

He looked me over, his eyes expanding. "I don't know. I'll most likely drop her... for you."

"Are you sure?"

His lips curled into another smirk. "Positive, Ellie. I've had more fun with you in one night than I've had with her in the past three years."

I smiled at his compliment. "All right. That's all. Besides those two things, we're good. Nothing too serious."

"I have one," he said, leaning forward and resting his arms on the table.

My eyebrows lifted. What could he have to ask me? I hardly ever did anything.

"Cal..." He trailed off and I grinned.

"What about him, Gage?"

"I notice how he flirts with you. He jokes around a lot with you and since you're on the same bus as him, it makes me think he might try something and eventually you'll give in."

"Cal's a nice guy. I'm sure he wouldn't try anything like that."

"He can be nice, but he's still a guy. A guy will do anything for some ass... especially an ass like yours."

I burned scarlet. "Oh, whatever." I waved him off.

"I'm serious." He grabbed the pepper and sprinkled some on the table. "I'd rather you not... flirt back with him if you can."

"How is it fair that you can flirt, but I can't?" I asked as he ran his finger through the pepper and spelled out his name.

"I sing for a band, Ellie. It's almost natural for me now."

I frowned, my eyes swinging down to my book again. I pretended to read the words and not become upset over his cocky, arrogant statement, but I couldn't think straight, especially by how quiet it became. Outside of hearing Montana, Roy, and Deed yelling from the arcade, it was dead silent between us.

Finally he sighed and placed his hand on top of mine. I looked up as he pulled my hand to his lips and kissed the flesh on top. "But if it really bothers you and you want me to calm down on it, I'll do it... for you... for now."

"Okay." I could deal with that. After I was gone from the tour, he could start his flirting again. At least he was going to try. It's all I was asking.

"We're going to a bonfire at the lake a little later." He sighed, releasing my hand. "They'll be roasting marshmallows, making s'mores, drinking a few beers, dancing... It'll be chill." He took a look down at my book and I lifted my elbow onto the table, placing the palm of my hand beneath my chin.

"And?" I urged.

His eyes hardened and I smirked. "Eliza, I'm not used to asking girls to come out with me. I'm telling you to."

"You're *telling* me I should come… with you?"

He nodded.

"What if I have plans?"

His lips pressed together, his eyes full of doubt. "Doing what exactly?"

"Reading. Maybe some painting."

"There're plenty of other nights to read and paint."

"Maybe if you *ask* nicely, I'll consider it." I teased him, but he wasn't smiling. I hated getting on his nerves, but I was getting a kick out of it. I wasn't about to be walked over like a doormat.

Here was another thing about Gage I'd noticed: how he always *told* me to join him. He never *asked* me and it kind of bothered me because he was so used to telling girls what to do that he probably became spoiled in his own kind of way.

"Eliza, you have to come with me—"

I held up my hand, stopping him. "I don't *have* to. If you want me to, why don't you just *ask* me?"

"'Cause then it'll feel like a date… We aren't dating, remember? Just flinging."

I laughed softly, focusing on my book again. He was definitely confusing me with the easy girls he usually dealt with.

"Eliza... please?"

I looked up slowly, staring into his eyes. He grabbed my hand again and squeezed it. "Is this what you want? For me to beg with puppy-dog eyes?" He grinned.

"Not beg." I giggled. "Just ask politely instead of *telling* me I'm gonna do something with you."

"All right," he sighed. "Can you please come to the bonfire with me tonight?"

"Yes, Gage." I beamed. "I *can* come with you to the bonfire tonight."

He laughed, pulling his hand away to rake his fingers through his tousled hair. A few pieces dropped onto his forehead, and I had the urge to reach forward and push them back. Unfortunately, before I could will myself to do it, he brushed them away. "You're seriously gonna make this tough for me, aren't you?"

"No, it won't be all tough." I smirked. "It'll be more fun than anything."

"You're trying to punk me out. It's cool. I can deal with it. Besides..." He sighed, sitting back. "Sooner or later you'll be the one begging *me*." He winked, sliding out of his bench to stand.

A few girls sitting at separate booths caught the sight of Gage and literally stopped eating. One of them was nearly salivating on her French fries while ogling him. Gage noticed and gave them a wink and they giggled girlishly, but I sighed, knowing his flirting wasn't going to stop completely. Not anytime soon, anyway.

Hooking his thumbs through his belt loops, he turned around and walked for the arcade but took a quick glance over his shoulder at me, winking again. Why was I still watching him? I sparked with heat, biting on a smile as I stared down at my book. I really had to get used to his charm.

The bonfire hadn't started yet, which left Gage and me lounging around inside the lake house. The house was huge, built with stone and expensive wrought iron, and I wasn't sure who it belonged to, but they were pretty lucky to have it.

Gage and I sat on the sofa in front of a tall arched window. He'd pushed the curtains back so we could watch the sunset. It was beautiful. A few streaks of yellow and orange cascaded beneath the hovering dark blue. The moon was just rising as the sun was sinking, creating a view of simplicity.

Gage shifted beneath me and I moved so he could hook his arm around my middle, the back of my head against his chest. He had a beer in his free hand and drank from it. A part of me wondered why he wasn't downstairs with his band brothers partying and drinking some more until it was time for the bonfire. I wanted to ask, but I didn't because it was too comfortable to sit like this.

As I turned in his arms and placed my cheek against his chest, he looked down at me, his hazel eyes sparkling from the sunset. He was calm, humble. I didn't want to destroy the mood so I kept my lips sealed... for a little while anyway...

"Have you ever had a real relationship before, Gage?" I asked. Immediately, I burned a fierce red but kept my gaze down, especially as he tensed against me, his grip slacking from my waist.

"No," he said, taking a sip of beer afterward.

"Why not, if you don't mind me asking?"

He shrugged. "I've never had the time for a real one."

I nodded as if I understood, but I really didn't and by his short responses, I knew he wasn't up for talking about it. "Montana told me you've been talking to Penelope for a long time. You said earlier you've known her for three years."

He looked down at me, his smile amused. "Did I?"

"Yeah."

"And?"

"And I was wondering why? Surely you feel something for her if you bring her back and forth from state to state. You pay for her plane tickets, don't you?"

"Yeah." He shrugged.

"Which means there's something there... for her."

Sighing, he unhooked his arm from around me and took a quick sip of his beer. "I have to keep Penelope close for certain reasons."

I frowned, doubting him because there was no reason at all to keep someone like her around unless it was just for sex. Instead of saying something negative, I asked, "Why?"

"Because… she knows a lot about me that I've never told anyone—not even the band. She was around during the wrong time. Eavesdropping and snooping when she wasn't supposed to."

"What, so you think she's going to use it as a weapon against you if you drop her?"

"Possibly. And it's nothing to take lightly. She's a dramatic girl. She'll do anything for attention. She'll blow it out of proportion if she has to. My reputation'll be fucked, along with the band's. Ever heard the saying 'keep your friends close but your enemies closer?'"

"Oh," was all I could manage. I wanted to know what Penelope knew, but by the look in his hard eyes, I didn't bother to ask. Instead, I slid in closer and wrapped my arm around his waist again. He sighed, kissing my hair, the tension seeping from his body. He finally leaned back against the sofa to relax, picking up his beer again.

"What about you?" he asked. "Have you ever had a real relationship before?"

I shook my head quickly. "No."

He smiled. "Why not?"

"I just don't think a real relationship is necessary right now."

"So you don't date? Is that what you're saying?" he asked, smirking down at me.

"No, Gage, I don't date. I don't have time for it right now." He let out a deep chuckle before chugging his beer, and I sat back to get a good look into his eyes. They smiled down at me and mine narrowed. "What's funny?"

"Nothing's funny. I just think you're worth much more than a fling. I guess I'm lucky."

"More than a fling with you?" I shook my head incredulously. "I don't think it would ever work between us."

"Do you doubt me that much?" he teased.

I laughed, folding my legs. I couldn't get started on that conversation with him, but as I turned to look at him again, he stared at me, his head tilted and his beer bottle a little ways from his lips, as if he were waiting on an answer. My heart pounded and it was just my luck that Montana capped his shoulder, getting him to turn his head and look his way.

"The bonfire's starting. Time to lick some marshmallows... and maybe some tits." Montana grinned devilishly. I snickered at him and he looked at me quickly. "You should let Gage lick yours. Let him suck the hell out of 'em, too. Heard it makes a woman feel good… along with a few other things." He wiggled his eyebrows.

My face burned scarlet and they both laughed heartily at my coy reaction. Gage then placed his beer bottle on the table and stood to stretch, his shirt rising and revealing the skin just above his waistband.

I resisted the urge to tug him back down on the couch and climb on top of him. Maybe even lick him. Instead, I took the hand he offered and allowed him to help me up. He didn't walk off right away, though. He pulled me into him and smiled down at me, his eyes deep and mischievous. "If you'd like me to lick them, I'd be honored," he said as soon as Montana was out of earshot.

My stomach coiled as he looked me over a dozen times, watching my body sink against his with each second. He placed a hand on the small of my back, the other cupping the nape of my neck. I bit my bottom lip and his head tilted to the other side as he inched in closer. My heartbeat climbed and clambered against my rib cage. His lips parted and he licked them slowly. I could smell the beer, but I wanted to lick it away, to suck the remainder of juice off his tongue.

He pulled me in by the back of my neck and I moved with his hand willingly. He lifted my leg, and soon the buzzing around us cleared. Everyone had gone downstairs to get outside and gather around the bonfire. Fortunately, Gage didn't seem to care much about it. He had enough fire igniting behind his eyes. He dropped his hand from around my neck, picking me up so I could circle my legs around him. He sucked on my skin greedily and I moaned, melting into his grasp. We stumbled toward the nearest wall and as soon as my back hit it, he delved into me.

After a few minutes of making out so hard our lips started swelling, he chuckled. "We don't want this to get carried away," he said, grinning behind his next kiss. I smiled, melting some more, and then nodded, climbing out of his arms.

Just as we'd turned for the stairs, thumping music came from outside. The bonfire was bright, enormous, and a few people were already sitting around it with drinks in hand. Two girls were on Montana's lap, another sitting beside him with her arm draped around his waist. All three of them were giggling at him, rubbing up and down his chest, his arms, and his face. He seemed to really love the attention.

Roy sat in front of the fire, taking long draws from his beer as he stared ahead. A few girls tried to brush against him, but he would frown at them and move away. Fortunately, the girls didn't pay much attention to it; otherwise, they would have taken offense. Deed stood with a group of people, including Cal, who was leisurely talking to a blonde with plump red lips and heavily mascaraed eyelashes. *When the hell did Cal get here?* He literally came out of nowhere.

"I'll go get us some drinks," Gage murmured into my ear.

I nodded, watching him walk toward a cooler near the fire. He gave a quick shout at Montana who grinned lazily, pointing at his crotch and then the three girls. Gage laughed and then went to talk to Roy briefly. I watched the entire time, waiting on his return, but then someone appeared behind him that I wasn't expecting at all. I could hear her annoying voice all the way by the door as she stood on her toes and covered his eyes. She was smiling eagerly, ready to surprise him.

"Guess who," she squeaked.

The corners of Gage's mouth turned down instantly and then he spun around, removing her hands. "Penelope?" he said, raising an eyebrow, his voice not as pleasant as the smile he forced.

"Yeah!" she squealed, hooking her arms around his waist and climbing into his arms. She kissed him passionately and Gage slowly wrapped his arms around her. "You didn't miss me?" she asked, pouting her bottom lip. "I sure as hell missed you."

Ice crawled down my spine, the hairs on my back rising at the sight of her all over him.

"Uh… yeah, babe. I missed you," Gage said. The ice filled my stomach, ran along my back. Gage took a quick glance at me, his eyes pleading, but I shook my head. I had to let myself know we were only a fling. Nothing more. But why the hell was Penelope around? Did he invite her? Something about it irked my nerves, but instead of being a party-pooper, I walked toward them. Penelope saw me approaching and smiled wickedly. Her evil grin made me shudder, but I smiled at her politely.

"Hi, guys," I said, my eyes swinging from hers to Gage's. His pale face was warmed only by the flames of the fire flickering nearby, his jaw ticking.

"Eliza." Penelope grinned, climbing out of his arms and facing me. "Oh my God, I love what you did to your hair!"

she screeched, reaching to twirl a curly strand around her finger. I smiled, but on the inside I cringed, hating her voice. "What kind of conditioner do you use? I mix *Suave* and *Wen*. It works sooo good for me. Wanna feel mine?" she asked eagerly.

I bit my tongue. What I really wanted to tell her was to shut the fuck up, but I held off on my acidity. I had to play nice. *She isn't worth it, Eliza.* I smiled sweetly at her as she took a step forward. "Sure." I touched her dark, straight hair, pretending to enjoy the feel of it before pulling away. "It's really soft and it smells good, too." I lied.

She smiled smugly at the compliment and took a step back, lacing her fingers with Gage's. I frowned at that, but she didn't notice. Of course Gage did because his head tilted and his eyes were hard on me, still pleading.

I finally gave him the question with my eyes: Was he going to spend the rest of his night with her or me? I didn't like competition, so it was up to him to decide. If he was to go with her, I was going to have to cut back on some of the flinging with him—possibly leaving it at just flirting.

The music got louder and Penelope squealed, pulling Gage in by his belt loop and grinning up at him. "Oh, babe! I love this song! We *have* to go dance."

Rigidly, Gage ran a hand through his hair and, sighing, said, "Sure."

What!? Was he serious? I scowled at him, taking a step back and turning my back to them. I stormed for the coolers, not daring to look back as I grabbed a beer. I popped the cap, took a long pull, but as I took another, I felt a pair of eyes on me. I turned to my right and Cal was sitting on a log, his smile amused as he watched me.

"Wanna sit with me?" he asked, patting the spot beside him. I blinked quickly, then took a glance over my shoulder at the crowd of dancing people by the bonfire. I spotted Gage with his head down, his focus on Penelope and her groove. She was dancing hard, his hands at her waist, his smile lazy as she looked over her shoulder to see if he was actually enjoying her. From what I saw, he seemed to be thoroughly enjoying himself.

I cringed but then remembered how upset Gage had gotten over me talking to Cal. At the wicked thoughts coming to mind, I grinned and leisurely took the seat on the log. I sat a little closer than he expected, but as my knee bumped against his, he only smiled.

"Having a rough night?" he asked.

"Nah." I lied. "Just need some real fun, you know?"

He raised a brow, confused. "What do you mean?"

"I don't know." I took another sip of my beer. I really didn't know what the hell I was talking about. I was a blubbering, furious mess and I despised myself for it.

"Ohh! You mean 'fun-fun?'" Cal asked, smiling at me.

I smiled, nodding slowly. "What exactly do you have in mind?"

Smirking, he finished his beer and placed his empty bottle down. I finished mine as well, but as I set the bottle down, Cal hooked his arm around me. "We can dance. It's been a while since I have."

I stilled, taking a glance at Gage again, but this time Penelope was in his arms, looking into his eyes with her arms locked around his neck. He was smiling down at her, his hand sneaking past her waist to most likely get to her ass. I looked at Cal before I could see him touch her there. "Sure, I'd love to."

Eagerly, he brought me to my feet, his arm still around my waist and allowing me to walk ahead of him. I held on to his hand, leading him toward the crowd of dancing people. I didn't want to dance near Gage, but I wanted to be somewhere he could see me. As soon as I found the perfect spot, I turned and faced Cal. His grin was goofy and wide, but I ignored his silliness and turned around again.

He placed both hands at my waist as I buried my ass into his groin. He stifled a groan, gripping me tight by the hips. The music had grown even louder with each dip, twist, shake, and grind. The crowd around the bonfire thickened and became sweatier, heavier. I opened my eyes slowly, allowing the back of my head to fall against Cal's shoulder.

He was obviously getting turned on because something hard and thick poked against my backside. I smiled. It was amazing how much power a woman could have over a man's body. And not only was I pleased by Cal's hard-on, but I was thrilled to see that between the bouncing bodies, waving arms, and bobbing heads, Gage was watching me, a beer in his hand. His hazel eyes were rock-hard, boring holes right through me. A line was drawn between his eyebrows, and with each sip of beer he took, his grip seemed to tighten around his bottle. The ink on his arms stood out along with his tense muscles. He seemed almost deadly as the flames flickered across his face.

Penelope was no longer by his side but running off with a friend of hers to walk along the shore of the lake. I saw her as I looked away briefly before meeting Gage's aggravated eyes again. With a ticking jaw, Gage turned his back to me and walked toward another crowd to busy himself.

Pleased by his annoyance, I turned in Cal's arms and he stared down at me, his eyes glazed over with lust. He'd sweated out his perfect blond hair, but it was sexy as it hung on his forehead. His lips parted and he inched in, but I tilted my head, pressing the palm of my hand against his chest as my eyebrows stitched. *Does he really think I'm going to kiss him?*

"I'm gonna go grab another beer. Will you wait here for me?" I asked.

He blinked quickly, swallowing and then nodding his head. "Sure. Would you grab one for me, too?"

"Yeah," I breathed, forcing a smile.

He smiled. "Don't be too long, Eliza!"

I pushed through the crowd, taking a glance over my shoulder as a girl came up to Cal, grinning up at him. She grabbed his hand and started dancing on him. He didn't object. Good. He was occupied with someone else. I needed to take a breather anyway. I needed to clear the fogginess in my brain.

I dug my hand into the cooler but frowned as I searched and searched only to find wine coolers. Shrugging, I grabbed one and downed it.

"Have fun?" a familiar, deep voice asked from behind me.

I frowned, spinning around quickly. Gage was staring at me, his head lowered, tilted, and his eyes darker than usual.

"I had a lot of fun, actually. Thanks for asking," I said smartly. "Have fun breaking your promise?"

"I didn't promise you anything," he countered.

I clamped my mouth shut, hating that he was right. It kind of felt like a promise. "Whatever." I waved him off, running the back of my hand across my sweaty forehead. "Go back to her. You don't have to bother yourself with me. It's obvious you aren't going to let her go anytime soon."

He smirked, placing his beer down in the sand and sliding the tips of his fingers into the front pockets of his cargo shorts. "You're upset," he pointed out.

I frowned. "No," I lied. *Ugh, what is up with me and lying tonight?* I took a step back, really not in the mood for arguing. It was clear who he wanted. Penelope. I began to walk off, but before I could, Gage grabbed my arm and hauled me against him.

"You're not going back to dance with him," he snapped through clamped teeth.

I snatched my arm out of his hand, scowling up at him. "I can dance with whomever I like. I've told you this before."

He stared at me, reliving the time when I actually did tell him I could dance with whomever I wanted. I wanted to leave him in the silence then. I wanted to feel superior—like a wiseass—so, I turned again, but he caught me, reeling me in by the waist. A few people that were chatting nearby turned to watch. He gripped my arm where it wasn't too tight to hurt me, but just enough so I couldn't pull away. He was pissing me off and by my fidgeting and trying to fight him off we were causing a scene.

"You're bringing attention our way," I hissed at him.

"Good, maybe it'll get you to stop acting out and cooperate."

"Fuck you, Gage."

His eyes widened, surprised by my crude words. Right after, he smirked and that pissed me off even more. "Anything else, Ellie?" he sighed.

I flared, yanking my arm free. "I told you less than two hours ago that if we were going to do this, you couldn't mess with anyone else. You told me you were going to drop her"—I pointed toward the crowd—"for me. You said it clearly!"

"I can't just drop her, Eliza!" His eyes widened when he realized how loud he was. He looked around slowly before running his fingers through his hair again. "I can't just pretend I don't know her," he hissed, his voice lower. "I told *you* less than ten minutes ago that she knows too much about me. I can't get on her bad side—"

I shook my head, waving him off. I didn't have time for his excuses. "Don't tell me you'll do one thing and then do the opposite," I snapped at him. I turned, ready to storm off and take a breather, but Gage caught me by the waist again. "Gage, stop!" I was so frustrated but glad I hadn't embarrassed myself too much by my screaming. The thumping music made my shout almost inaudible. "You're causing a scene," I snapped, clawing at his hand. "Get. Off. Me."

"No," he said, his voice a near growl.

I tried to push him away with my free hand, but he was like a brick wall. I tried again, but he smirked at me, his eyes saying, "You're not hurting me, Eliza." I flared, seeing nothing but red. If there was one thing I hated, it was people making a mockery of me. Laughing at me when I was really upset and was supposed to be taken seriously. Telling me they won't do one thing but doing it right after.

I shoved against Gage's large chest. He didn't budge. I finally gave a viscous blow to his gut with my elbow and he grunted, partially kneeling over, his eyes hard on me. His smirk faded; his eyes darkened. His lips pressed into a tight line as he inhaled deeply and a few people turned our way to see what he would do next, smirks on their lips.

"Let's fucking go," he snapped, reaching for me, picking me up, and tossing me over his shoulder.

"Put me down," I snarled, clawing at his back. Embarrassment flooded me as he marched for the house and a few people watched us, some laughing and some wondering what the hell Gage was going to do. Oddly, I was wondering the same thing. A part of me was afraid he was going to end our fling already—that he was going to tell me to leave him alone, and I didn't want that, yet I kept fighting him, beating his back to get him to put me down. I was letting my pride consume me.

A few people were chatting in the kitchen as we passed by, and soon we were heading up the stairs. I could feel his tension while bouncing on top of his shoulder and continuously growling for him to put me down.

Gage finally made a turn for the first room he came across and as soon as we were inside, he dropped me and flipped on the light switch. I took in the sight of the washing machine, the dryer, the detergent on the shelves above me, and the baskets of clothes in the corner. I then looked at him, a deep frown on my face. "I don't wanna be in here with you," I muttered.

"Yes, you do," he said matter-of-factly. He was still frowning, and the longer he stared at me, the harder it got for me to breathe. "The only reason you're mad is because you want my attention. Well, I'm giving it to you now, Eliza. You're so mad. Hit away," he said, holding his hands out to his sides, arms stretched. "Go ahead. Let it out."

I frowned. "I'm not hitting you, Gage."

"Oh, surely you wanna hit me again. You hit me the whole way upstairs when people were watching. You're mad, right? You were so fucking upset that you danced with *Cal*. I had no choice, Eliza! I had to pretend with her!"

"You didn't have to go with her, Gage! You had options."

"Eliza, I told you she knows too much. I can't get on her bad side. I have to act like I still care... like she means something to me. I have to keep her close. Otherwise, she'll become my enemy. I can't just disown her like she's a nobody. She has connections. She has ways of demolishing me."

"I don't care." I folded my arms stubbornly. "I don't care about *you* or Penelope or this stupid-ass bonfire. I shouldn't have even come with *you*. I shouldn't have even agreed to *this*! I knew you'd do something stupid. It's just a shame you've done it already."

He scowled at me, his eyes narrowing and his mouth thinning into a tight line. "I didn't do it to hurt you. I was doing it to protect myself. My past."

I kept silent, ready for him to just get out of my face. I wanted to ask about his past, but I was being too much of a stubborn bitch to even bother.

"So this is it?" he asked, dropping his hands to slap against his thighs. "This is it? You're so upset with me that you want to cancel *this* between us—already? You're just speaking out of anger right now, Eliza."

I was still quiet. I was being snobby—I knew it—but I didn't care. I couldn't do this when I knew he would constantly choose her whenever she came around. A part of me envied her because he needed her around in some kind of way and it made me sick.

"Eliza." His voice broke as he shook his head. I finally looked up at him and his eyes were sadder, guiltier. "Eliza, what do you wanna hear? An apology?" He took a step forward. "All right, I'm sorry. I'm sorry I went with her instead of you. I'm sorry for making you mad. You have to understand me, though. I would drop her for you... It's just... it would take some time. It won't be easy."

I shrugged. It was enough of the excuses. Had he not been blocking the door, I would've already taken off. He laughed dryly and my eyes swung up to meet his. "Don't do that," he muttered.

"Do what?" I snapped, frowning.

"Don't act like you don't care. You can't stand here in front of me and act like you don't fucking care."

"I don't care."

"You don't?" he asked, his tone rhetoric. "If you didn't care, you wouldn't be mad right now. If you didn't care, that stupid dance with Penelope wouldn't have gotten you this upset with me. If you didn't care, we wouldn't be standing in this Goddamn room, Eliza. I'll tell you something, though," he said, laughing humorlessly, running a hand through his hair yet again. I noticed he only did it when he was nervous or trying to keep his cool. "I care. *I want you*. I've wanted you since day one. I've wanted something from you—whatever it may have been. Whatever you were to give me, I would have taken it and accepted it, even if it were a simple hug or a kiss on the cheek. Anything—something. It doesn't matter as long as it was something with or from *you*."

My face softened, the ice surrounding my heart chipping away with each sentence.

"I've had too much fun with you not to care. I've spent too many nights with you that it would be impossible for me not to fucking care. You piss me off, make me smile, bring me up, aggravate me—I feel all these damn emotions when you're around, and if you can do that to me, then it means I care... maybe too much. I'm only human, Eliza. I have feelings, too, believe it or not. I just... I wanted *you*. I. Want. You." He ran a rigid hand over his face, blowing out a breath as if he had been holding that in forever and was glad he got it off his chest. "So don't do that," he mumbled. "Don't shrug your shoulders at me because there's no way in hell I can care this much—that I can adore you this much—and you not feel the same way. There's just no fucking way."

My frown transformed into a mask of sincerity. He was right. I wouldn't be mad if I didn't care… but I did. A little too much. And I hated it… No, I loved it. I was too wrapped up in it that I didn't even face the reality of it. We had some kind of connection and it wasn't safe… but I didn't mind it. I looked past it because I was enjoying it.

Gage's head tilted as he moved in closer. I bit my bottom lip, but he reached a finger up to stop me. He then picked me up to place me on top of the old-school washing machine. It was cold and hard beneath me, but I stayed in place, stuck in a deep trance by those mesmerizing hazel eyes.

As he pulled me in by the waist, I gasped. He sank between my legs, his body warm against mine; his chest was against my stomach, his mouth on my collarbone. He kissed below my collarbone and I shivered, biting my nails into his skin. "I hate how good you feel... but I can never seem to stop touching you. Why the hell do you feel so good?" he growled, kissing up my neck.

I smiled. How exactly was I supposed to answer that question? My head fell back as he continued his kisses. He unbuttoned my shirt and then slid his hand up my leg to get beneath my skirt. He smiled as he got closer to the heat between my legs and I whimpered as he skimmed over it to caress my other leg. He was such a damn tease and he knew it because he laughed deeply. "Yeah," he chuckled. "You care, all right." His statement annoyed me but turned me on at the same time.

Finally, he freed me from my shirt and tossed it beside us. I ran the palms of my hands over his chest before sneaking them beneath his shirt. He looked down quickly and then up into my eyes. His were more intense than before. He licked his lips and I inhaled, wanting them against mine.

Pulling him to me, I cupped the back of his neck, braiding my fingers through his silky hair as I kissed him deeply. He groaned, grabbing my skirt and unbuttoning it. I adjusted myself so he could slide down my skirt, and I heard it drop on the floor. He groaned again, tasting the skin on my neck. His hand still cupped the back of my neck and tingles rode along every inch of my spine. Making out wasn't enough. I needed more. I was sitting half-naked before him, aching for more of his touch, but he was already giving it all to me. He couldn't have kissed me any more deeply. His hands were skimming me everywhere. He was getting a taste of every part of my body.

His lips trailed down my chest and he freed one of my nipples. I bucked as he sucked one of them, pulling me in closer to get between my legs with a deep groan. His cock poked against my stomach, causing me to moan even more. His head moved over to my other nipple and he sucked it slowly, licking fiercely but delicately and groaning once again.

My fingers got tangled in his hair, my breath continuously catching. I was trying to keep up with myself, but his tongue worked miracles against me. I finally decided I'd had enough. I pushed him back by the shoulders and pulled his shirt over his head. The palms of my hands pressed against his firm, inked chest and slid down until I was at the button of his jeans.

I looked into his eyes quickly and he was staring at me, his eyes glazed over and longing but slightly worried. I ignored the worry and ran with the longing. I unbuttoned his jeans and then hopped from the washing machine to pull his pants down. He sucked in a breath through clenched teeth as I lowered his jeans and then stuck my hands beneath his boxers. His flesh was soft and at my first touch, his whole body tensed. I started pulling back, but he shook his head. "Don't," he murmured, pulling me against him, his breath running across my lips. "Don't stop. It feels good." His forehead touched mine and I nodded, continuing the strokes again.

He tilted my chin up with his forefinger, his lips only a sliver away from mine. He panted as he stared into my eyes while I continuously stroked him. I'd never done this before so I didn't know what the hell I was doing, but he was getting pleasure out of it so I kept it going. Some mild profanity slipped between his teeth, his lips extremely close. He cursed again and I couldn't take it anymore. I crushed his lips with my own, but I didn't stop stroking the length of him.

He was thicker than I imagined. He was long as well, and I knew with what was in my hands, he could provide nothing but satisfaction to a woman's body.

I moaned into his mouth and he cupped my face, deepening the kiss. His panting increased and a heavier, tighter ache built between my legs. I wanted him there. I wanted what was in my hands *inside me* already.

"Gage," I whispered.

"Eliza, please don't stop. I'm so close," he breathed against me, making my stomach spiral. I swallowed. I didn't want to stop and, in a freaky perspective, I liked seeing him this way. I liked how I provided his pleasure— how I had control over whether he was satisfied or not.

Gage turned and my back hit the wall. His chest pressed firmly on mine and he kissed me again as I slid my hand up and down his smooth hardness. He throbbed against my palms and groaned, deeply lodging his tongue into my mouth. His pleasure was burning and radiating into me. He growled against my lips before snatching his mouth away and lowering his head to kiss my neck. He hissed my name, tensing even more, and I knew it was coming.

I pumped harder, faster, and he gripped the back of my neck, digging his fingers into my skin. He cursed again, getting harder and harder until finally he growled loudly and sucked on my neck so hard I thought he'd bitten me. It was definitely going to leave a hickey. After a while, his sucking turned pleasurable and something hot and wet oozed down my hand. Knowing exactly what it was, I shook my head over his shoulder, my smile apprehensive.

Gage pulled back slowly, smirking down at me with lazy, infatuated eyes. "That was fucking great," he murmured. "My turn now." My eyes expanded, but I was left with no time to protest (I really didn't want to) because he kissed me fiercely and my knees quaked as he placed me on top of the washing machine again. He'd changed the roles in a heartbeat and by the end of our eagerness—after a few heavenly minutes of Gage's warm lips and tongue diving and licking the delicate, sweet nub between my legs—I was left completely satisfied.

SHOWER

Things moved at a faster pace after Gage and I
established that maybe we did care for each other more
than we were supposed to. A month and three weeks had
passed since our bonfire bonding, but it didn't feel like it'd
been that long. The days and nights turned into weeks and
it all started to become a messy blur. I knew it was
because I didn't have to worry over Gage or be a witness
to his mindlessness. We were on better, sexier terms, and
I was enjoying myself.

The cities passed by effortlessly and with each night
there was fun with the addition of kissing, hugging,
dancing, and laughing. On a few nights it would catch up to

me and in the mornings my head would be killing me, but as Gage always said, "Suck it up. At least you're still alive."

From state to state, I learned something new about Gage. I found out his favorite song he'd ever written was the song the band hated. He admitted it was juvenile and that he was never going to sing it publicly, but after begging him for fifteen minutes straight, he finally sang it to me and I fell in love with the lyrics. How could I not? They were adorable and with his voice, I melted with each word.

"You hate it, don't you?" he asked, unstrapping his guitar and placing it down.

I shook my head and climbed on his lap. Our touching was another thing that shocked a few, more so Ben, but he didn't question it. In fact, he would smile at us from a distance. He used to wonder why I never went out, why I never talked to any boys, so seeing me flirting and going out with Gage, he didn't complain much. I still couldn't get over what he'd said to me a few weeks ago about keeping my heart away from Gage. My mind was still boggled over it, but it was something I never wanted to talk about again.

"I don't hate it. I love it," I said. His lips curled into a smirk and then he kissed my cheek.

A few more things I learned about Gage (that I never would have expected) were, one: he loved to cuddle, and two: he loved to touch. Any time we were together, his hands had to be on me unless they were occupied. Whether it was the small of my back, around my waist, around my shoulders, or even holding my hand, he was touching me somehow. I didn't mind it. It was comforting and something I enjoyed because I'd never shared that with anyone before.

As for the cuddling part, whenever we were on the road and heading for another state, he would beg me to ride on the FireNine bus with him. I'd sleep in his bed after a night of laughing, giggling, flirting, play wrestling, and a few drinks in between. Roy and Deed tried their best to stay clear of us (which annoyed me) but Montana had become my best friend. I loved Montana's personality, his meekness. Although he was a party animal and a massive flirt, he was still a sweet guy and knew exactly how to have fun.

During one of the bus rides, we decided to play a small game of beer pong. Since the boys hardly ever ate or drank on the bus, we had to use coffee mugs because they didn't own any plastic cups. Montana filled each one with beer and pulled a white ball out of his suitcase.

"Don't tell me you've never played beer pong before either, Miss Eliza," Montana said, smirking at me over the bottle of beer in his hand.

"Nope, never." I shrugged.

Gage stepped to my side and laughed. "She's new to a lot of stuff."

"I can see that." Montana rolled the ball in his hand. "I guess to make it easier on her, you can be on her team. Don't need her crying on us or anything," he teased.

I laughed. "Oh, whatever. Explain to me how to play."

Montana explained and every so often Gage would say something in my ear about when to drink and how to throw. Once we'd started, I was a complete klutz. I threw the ball over the table quite a few times and Gage and Montana would laugh so hard at me while handing me a mug of beer to drink. Due to my suckiness, I drank most of the beers and became lightheaded.

"Oh, shit." Montana chuckled. "She's stumbling. Should we stop?"

I shook my head and Gage stepped to my side to hook his arm around my waist and keep me steady. Laughing at me, he said, "I think we should, Ellie."

My gaze swung up to his quickly. His eyes locked with mine and a warm smile curled his lips. I turned in his arms to lace mine around his neck. He wasn't surprised by the gesture. In fact, he pulled me in even tighter, his fingers curling around the belt loops of my shorts.

"All right." Montana laughed, grabbing one of the coffee mugs. "I'm off to my room. Night, freaks."

Gage and I ignored him. Montana's footsteps trailed off and his door clicked shut behind him, but my eyes remained focused on Gage's. I couldn't force myself to look away. One thing about being drunk was it made me vulnerable, and every time I was with Gage, I wanted to hook my legs around him and make out until I was out of breath.

He slowly licked his lips, his breathing even as he moved in closer. "I've got to stop getting you drunk," he murmured teasingly.

I smiled up at him, moving in closer. Heat radiated from his body to mine, and soon I pressed my cheek against his chest. Oh boy, my head was swimming badly. With the bus moving, it wasn't helping my stomach, either.

"Are you okay?" he asked into my hair.

"I should have told you I didn't eat much earlier."

Gage stiffened and pulled back a little. Tilting my chin with his finger, he gazed into my eyes, his head cocked. "Do you feel sick?"

"A little," I admitted.

He sighed, lifting me into his arms. I laid the side of my head against his chest and his heartbeat soothed me a little. He hurried to his room and placed me on the bed. He then bent down to take off my shoes.

"Don't stare at my feet." I giggled.

He laughed, removing my socks as well. He took a good look at my toes that were painted a metallic blue and then looked up at me. "They're cute." I rolled my eyes and he stood up straight. "Do you wanna take a quick shower? I can go find something for you eat while you're in there."

The shower sounded nice so I nodded and he helped me to my feet. I didn't know why I felt so weak. My knees were wobbly and as we stepped into the bathroom and the light turned on, I winced. Gage noticed me stiffen at his side and looked down at me, his eyes clouded with worry.

He lifted me up, placing me on the counter and stepping between my legs. I shut my eyes, craving to just lie against his chest. That's all I wanted. The warmth of his body. His small forehead kisses. "Eliza," he called. My eyelids fluttered open, and he lowered a bit, ducking his head to try and catch my droopy eyes. "You're really out of it," he laughed. "We're gonna have to cut back on some of the drinking. I always forget you're a lightweight."

I bit on a smile and then reached for the hem of my shirt. Not thinking, I pulled it over my head, the cotton blocking my view of him. As soon as I tossed my shirt on the floor, he was staring at me and had taken a step back. His eyes that were once smiling were now hard and his lips were pressed together into a thin line.

"I'll start the shower," he murmured. He stole a glance of my purple bra before turning and sliding open the shower door. I shut my eyes again and pressed my back against the mirror. It was cold against my back but felt good considering how flushed and heated I was becoming. My stomach was boiling over and I knew it was the beers, but I kept absolutely still. I refused to vomit in front of Gage. It would have been too unladylike of me.

The water from the shower spluttered and I heard Gage sigh. "Come on, Sweet Ellie." He grunted, helping me get down from the counter. I opened my eyes and looked at him, but he wasn't looking at me. He was too busy trying to unbutton my pants. A line drew between his eyebrows, showing how focused and determined he was to get them undone. Little did he know he had three more buttons to undo before I could slip out of them. I laughed at the thought and he looked up at me. "What?" he said, laughing back.

"Nothing," I murmured.

He shook his head with a small smile, lowering himself into a squat. He saw the three buttons and looked up at me, smiling even harder. "Sneaky girl."

I smirked as he finally undid the first button. Steam filled the bathroom, making me even more flushed. I could have helped him, but I liked that he had his hands on me. I liked seeing him concentrate. It was cute.

Finally undoing the last button, he slid my shorts down to my ankles. I was glad I had on a cute pair of lacey pink panties. Wearing granny panties in front of Gage wouldn't have been so appealing. But during my thought of granny panties, the bathroom had become completely silent. Outside of the running shower water, we were still, unmoving.

He took a look up at me beneath his long, thick eyelashes, sliding his hands up my thighs. His fingers slid around to the back of my legs and his breathing picked up. He was panting, and so was I. He slowly licked his lips, his eyes moving from mine to my bra and then down to my panties. The look in his eyes was driving me insane. I wanted to know so badly what he was thinking, but instead, I remained quiet.

Each passing second felt like an hour... and then he finally made a move, lowering his head, his gaze drifting from my body. "What's wrong?" I asked.

He shook his head and slowly stood up straight. There were a few things behind his eyes I could make out as he stared into mine. Pleasure. Longing. Annoyance. Guilt. Why did I spot annoyance and guilt? I was about to question it until he took a step back to get to the door. "Shower up, Ellie. I'll bring you a towel."

I zipped my lips, watching as the door shut behind him. Sighing, I slipped out of my bra and panties and stepped into the warm steam of the shower. As it ran over me, I exhaled, but out of nowhere, tightness crept up my throat. I turned quickly to find the drain, allowing vomit to splurge. Fire burned my stomach and throat. It hurt so badly. I'd never vomited from drinking before, but it was the worst feeling. At least I had the warm water to soothe me and at least the vomit wasn't thick and clumpy. It easily went down the drain and once my stomach was clear, I stood up straight and felt ten times better. I was still drunk without a doubt, but knowing my stomach was free of that mess made me a bit of a happy camper.

Grabbing the bar soap, I lathered it over me, my head tilted back in the running water until the bathroom door creaked open. My eyes widened, seeing Gage through the opaque glass door of the shower. His figure was solid, sexy. His strides toward the shower were cautious as he placed the towel on the rod.

He was about to turn around, but, surprisingly, I called his name and he stopped, taking a glance over his shoulder. A million thoughts were running through my drunken head. One of them was to tell him thanks... just because. Another was to ask for a kiss. It was odd, but I just wanted to feel him. The last was to tell him to come into the shower with me.

"Yeah?" Gage called, turning around.

I chewed on my bottom lip, the silence ringing between us. Finally, I asked, "Can you come in with me?"

He remained quiet for a few seconds. Through the opaque glass, he was perfectly still. Unmoving. Then, slowly and still quiet, he pulled his shirt over his head. He unbuttoned his jeans, kicked off his shoes, slid out of his boxers and jeans, and then walked toward the shower. My heart raced with each step closer. It raced even more as he grabbed the handle of the shower door and slid it open.

He stepped in without looking at me and I stepped beneath the water, as if it were going to hide my naked body. I held the bar of soap against my chest and as soon as Gage slid the shower door shut behind him, his heavy hazel eyes met mine.

For the most part, we were quiet. It wasn't awkward to stare because he had more than enough to stare at and keep me quiet. Although the features of his face were hard, his eyes were tranquil, admiring the naked aspects of my body. My eyes traveled from his face to his broad chest. There was a tattoo of a woman's name right below his left collarbone, almost where his heart would be. The name was *Chloe* and was in a flowing script.

The dragon on his ribs was defined; the blue and black stood out most. A splash of orange came out of its mouth and its head was tilted up, as if it were burning his armpit. My eyes continued traveling southward until they got to the main attraction. He wasn't soft. He was hard, probably harder than a rock. I had the urge to grab him, stroke him... maybe even get a taste of him, but I held off, suddenly realizing I was the reason he was getting turned on.

Gage finally made the first move. His actions were deliberate, but he was going for it. He cupped my face, taking the soap out of my hand, placing it down, and then pulling my lips to his and kissing me fiercely.

I drowned in his touch, my body sinking against his firm upper half. He swallowed my moans and his tongue ran over and slipped beneath mine. His panting increased, his whole body turned rigid. He then picked me up and I had no problem wrapping my legs around him. My back pressed against the cool shower wall, but our lips never parted.

Groaning, his head moved down and he licked the droplets off my neck. He kissed and sucked on me tenderly, his arousal digging into me. He was so close to my entrance that it frightened me yet turned me on at the same time. I wanted it more than I realized. My body was yearning, craving for him to just take me there. There'd been so much sexual tension between us that it was starting to kill me. It wasn't my fault, either. It was always Gage. He always held off whenever we would get too close to having sex. He was the one who always pulled away, knowing I wouldn't mind it. I would never question it and he would never explain it. Instead, he would do something else like take me out, *eat* me out, or cuddle with me until I would stop thinking about it.

This time I felt more than ready for it and he had no excuse.

"Gage… please," I begged into his ear, my voice raspy.

He tensed, his whole body stilling against mine. He pulled back a little, his lips leaving my neck so he could get a look into my eyes. I spotted the uneasiness behind them. What was so wrong with taking my virginity? Why was he feeling so guilty about it? We had to get it over with anyway. Why not hurry and do it?

"Eliza..." He shook his head. "I can't."

"Why not?"

His head lowered shamefully. Water splattered on us, some catching on his long eyelashes that were touching his cheekbones. "Is this really what you want? For *me* to take it?"

I nodded quickly. I couldn't think of anyone else I wanted to have it. "You told me to wait for the right time, Gage." I kissed his cheek and then cupped his jawline, lifting his head to meet his eyes. "This feels like the right time."

He stared into my eyes briefly. His were wide, taken off guard for just a moment, but then he grunted and moved in rapidly, his lips crushing mine as he turned around. His hand left my waist to shut off the water and he slid the shower door open, stepping out with me still bound around him. He stumbled toward the bedroom and luckily we didn't slip and fall on the bathroom floor because we were dripping wet.

His bed came into view and he laid me down. The lights were off, but the moon filtered in from the window above us. With the bus in motion, it made my head swim a little bit more. From the moonlight, Gage's features turned harder than steel. He slid me toward the top of the bed, and I rested my head on the pillows that smelled just like him.

He swallowed noisily, staring at me as I lay naked before him. I was slightly embarrassed, but with the alcohol still penetrating through my system, I couldn't look away. I didn't care, especially as he moved up, dividing my legs with his knee. He breathed onto me and I shuddered delightfully from the warmth against my slick skin. He climbed between my legs, his lips hovering above mine. I swallowed slowly, staring into the pool of hazel drinking me in.

"I don't wanna hurt you, Eliza," Gage whispered.

I craned my arms around his neck, refusing him to move away. "You won't, Gage. I know hurting me isn't your intention."

He blinked quickly, still looking into my eyes. He didn't speak again. Instead, he devoured my lips and glided his tongue into my mouth. His hands snuck down to my waist and his cock pressed even harder against me. I moaned into his mouth, ready for him to just take me. One of his hands left my waist to reach into the nightstand beside his bed. I didn't open my eyes. I was too indulged in the kiss.

He was multitasking and, damn it, he was good at it.

The crinkling of plastic filled the silence and Gage moved back a little, his lips leaving mine briefly as he looked down. When he was finished, he looked into my eyes and pulled my hips into his, forcing me to wrap my legs around him. "Are you sure?" he whispered, kissing my jawline. His kisses moved up to the lobe of my ear and I nodded as he throbbed against me. Apparently I wasn't the only one ready. "I'll be as gentle as I can," he whispered.

I froze as he said that, realizing this was my virginity he was taking. He was about to deflower me and make me into a real woman. With that there was pain and I wasn't too fond of pain. But, then again, I'd dealt with so much before that pain had become just a word to me. I'd overcome it all and this had to be nothing compared to what I'd gone through.

I nodded slowly, squeezing my arms around his neck. He stared down at me, his eyes concrete. As he stuck the tip inside me, I gasped and he paused. I shook my head at him, squeezing my arms around him tighter. "It's okay," I whispered.

"Are you sure? Am I... am I *hurting* you?"

"No."

He took a deep, rigid breath and then placed his lips on mine to most likely calm me down and loosen me up. The tip pressed into my entrance again and I hissed through my teeth, my fingernails biting into his skin. I refused for him to stop again. It's what I wanted it and I wanted to make it as unproblematic as possible for him, even if I was accepting all the pain.

I looked up slowly and he watched every emotion taking hold of my face. He slid into me some more, stretching me open, and I sucked in a breath through my teeth, biting my nails into his back once again. He didn't wince, but he was about to stop. I shook my head at him. Even though he was large and quite thick, I didn't want him to stop. We were pretty much there.

"Eliza, if I'm hurting you—"

I brought a hand forward to press my finger against the fold of his lips. "It's okay, Gage. Keep going." I smiled as warmly as I could beneath the moonlight and he nodded, his lips pressed. He continued sliding himself into me, watching me wince, blink hard, bite my lower lip, and then look into his eyes until finally the pain was gone. I could finally feel him without any kind of ache or stretching. He was fully inside me and once he noticed, he looked down at me and kissed me.

"Ready?" he whispered against my lips.

I nodded eagerly and his strokes deepened. He placed his face into my neck as he cupped my ass, burying himself within me. I never knew I could feel so pleasured, so excited. My moans grew louder and my fingernails kept clawing into his back. He grunted against my neck, gripping my hips so tightly I thought he was in pain. As he lifted up, I figured maybe he was.

Veins popped out of his neck as he tried to keep himself composed and gentle. He was holding back on me. I placed my hand on his chest, bringing my other hand up to cup his face. I brought his head down so we were nose-to-nose and whispered, "It's okay. I can handle it. Let go."

With those words alone, the intensity grew. I was nearly screaming as he began beating against me, circling his thumb around my clit, causing me to rise and sink against him. He was creating orgasm after orgasm, wave after wave, and I enjoyed it to the full extent.

His mouth devoured mine and my fingers ran through his hair, his hands cupping my ass as he slammed into me continuously. The headboard banged against the wall so loud it almost made my moaning and his groaning inaudible.

During the last few seconds, Gage picked up his speed, lifting my hips higher and pounding into me over and over again. I screamed wildly, thrilled but most of all turned on by his blazing eyes watching my every move. Finally, I bucked against him because it was coming. He growled deeply, bending down to bury his face into the crook of my neck. "I've wanted this from you for so long, Eliza," he breathed. "So. Fucking. Long."

I yelped, the pleasure coursing through me. Heat and pleasure raced between my legs and Gage groaned, allowing me to drench him with the flowing juices. Slamming and shuddering, he grunted some mild profanity as I squealed, pulling him down against me. He quaked a dozen times and within me I felt the heat through his condom. He shuddered again and again until finally his body lacked tension and he collapsed on top of me. We both panted into one another's ears, letting the silence ride. A few minutes passed and I still didn't want to move.

That was... amazing. Mind-blowing. Incredible. My first time and it was way better than I'd ever imagined. Unfortunately, my eyelids started getting droopy and

Gage's breathing evened out. He wasn't saying a thing, and I knew he was just as worn and tired as I was.

Sometime during our weariness, he'd pulled himself out of me, went to the bathroom to remove his condom, turn off the light, and then came back, pulling the blankets over our still-naked bodies. I didn't mind the thought of being naked in the same bed as him. He'd just given me that kind of freedom. It was a freedom I enjoyed. One I wanted to cherish.

Our bodies molded and I placed my arm over his waist, my cheek resting against his defined chest as I ran my fingers up and down his arm. Our legs were tangled, breaths entwining, as he stroked my cheek, my hair. His steady heartbeat soothed me again and he kissed my forehead before sighing deeply and allowing his head to fall back and his eyes to shut.

This night with Gage had to be one of the best nights we'd shared so far.

It was perfection.

I never wanted it to end.

SISTER

I woke up, still satisfied from the night before. I stretched, gazing up at the ceiling, feeling a slight twinge between my legs. I pulled the covers off to look down. There was some blood on the white sheets and I gasped, thinking maybe there really was a cherry down there.

Shrugging, I glanced where Gage had been sleeping, noticing his clothes and shoes still on the floor. I heard deep voices chatting a short distance away and figured he was out talking to one of his band brothers.

With a sigh, I hopped from the bed and grabbed the change of clothes I'd packed into a smaller bag. After taking a quick and thorough shower, I pulled my hair up into a tight ponytail and stared at Gage's messy sheets with my hand on my hip.

I couldn't leave them there and I definitely didn't want the blood to be a reminder to him of what he'd just taken. I wanted it to seem like casual, meaningless sex so I pulled the blankets off the bed. I took the sheets off and tossed everything into a corner before going for his closet and finding new bedding.

After making the bed, fluffing the pillows, and tossing the ruined sheets beside my bag, I slid my toes around the thongs of my flip-flops and opened the door. I inhaled deeply, the thick, rich aroma of coffee lingering in the air.

As I stepped around the corner, Gage and Roy were sitting at the table with pens in hand. Gage heard me and looked up quickly, a warm smile on his lips. Thank goodness he wasn't making things awkward for me. I told him over and over again during the middle of the night that it was only my virginity. It wasn't like he'd snatched it away from me. I wanted it to happen between us. I didn't mind it and if I weren't ready, I wouldn't have given it up. He finally became satisfied with my response and went back to sleep again.

"Good morning," I breathed, heading for the kitchen and rinsing out one of the mugs in the sink. It reeked of beer so I added soap to make sure it was thoroughly cleansed. Gage said good morning and Roy did as well, but his voice was barely a whisper and his eyes never left his paper.

Finding it odd, I kept my gaze on him for a brief second before grabbing the mug of coffee. I poured some into my cup, added crème, sugar, and then slid into the booth beside Gage. I kissed his cheek and he returned the kiss, but Roy stiffened, pulling his cup toward him and then picking it up to take a sip.

I brushed that off as well. I knew I would never figure Roy out, so I sipped my coffee while the boys continued writing. "Working on lyrics?" I asked.

"Yeah," Gage sighed. "It's best to work on them early when the animals like Montana and Deed are sleeping." He winked.

I nodded, sipping on my coffee again. I took a glance down at Gage's paper, spotting words like, "*pain, misery, it's all over, never look back,* and *newfound addiction.*" At the sight of *newfound addiction,* I looked up at him, but he sniffed and ran the back of his hand across his nose. *He isn't talking about me,* I thought to myself. *They're just lyrics anyway.*

I took a glance in Roy's direction but wasn't allowed enough time to see anything because he snatched up his paper. I looked into his eyes quickly, but his were dark, cold. His eyebrows knitted as he looked me over and then, picking up his coffee and still glaring at me, he turned to go for the living room. Gage didn't seem to think much of it, but I was pretty offended by his behavior. What had I ever done to make him hate me so much? I'd barely said two words to Roy and he was acting like I kneed him in the balls.

"Don't take it personally," Gage murmured into my ear, watching Roy sit on the sofa with his back facing us.

"What's wrong with him?" I whispered, hoping Roy couldn't hear me.

"He's just... not used to you being around us so much."

"And he hates me because I'm around you guys?" I frowned.

"He just has to warm up to you. That's all. He doesn't trust easily. He's very conservative."

"Yeah, I can see that," I scoffed, taking a look at Roy who was scribbling madly on his notepad.

Gage's hand ran over my thigh, stealing away my thoughts. I looked at him beneath my eyelashes and he smiled, gripping my hand. "Did I... um... hurt you last night? If so, I'm sorry. I've never—"

"No, Gage. I'm fine. It was good." I gave him a sweet smile and he nodded, tightening his grip around my hand. "Why were you so worried, anyway?"

He shrugged, pulling his hand away to pick up his pen again. He grabbed his coffee to sip it and then placed his mug down, his jaw ticking. "I don't know. Just not used to it I guess." He forced a smile, but I frowned, fixing my lips to speak. There was more to it than that. Unfortunately, before I could speak on it, Montana let out an exaggerated yawn from the hallway. We both looked up at him as he came walking in, scratching his bare chest.

Montana had a dragon on his ribs, too, but unlike Gage's blue and black one, his was red and black. The dragons were almost identical and I couldn't help but question it. "Did you two get the dragon tattoos together?" I asked.

Montana smirked as he stepped into the kitchen and pulled out the jug of milk. He drank straight from it and my nose crinkled while my mind made a mental note to never drink milk from the boys' bus. "We all have one," Gage said.

My eyebrows rose and my curiosity piqued. "Oh?"

"Yeah." Montana sighed, sitting across from me. "Mine is red and black, Gage got black and blue, Deed has green and black, and Roy over there has orange and black. It was a… drunk and crazy night. It was kind of like a band bonding thing."

"Oh." I grinned. That was kind of cute to hear. "Why dragons, though?"

"For one, dragons are the realest mythical creatures known to man," Montana said matter-of-factly. I smirked, pursing my lips at him with high amusement. "Plus, they aren't just ordinary dragons. They're *Chinese* dragons. Their meaning of the dragon is something much greater." I took a glance at Montana's ribs again, studying the graphics—the pointy tongue, fierce red eyes, extremely sharp teeth. I then thought back on how Gage's dragon looked. They did seem more Chinese than anything.

"Like happiness, immortality, the ability to ward off evil spirits," Gage added on. "We want all the luck we can get as a band and since Roy over there is a bit obsessed with them,"—Roy grunted, shrugging—"we figured we could just go for it. So far we've been doing great. We're all still happy, and by immortality, we mean that even if we are to split up or even die, we want the name of our band to live on—kind of like The Beatles or The Rolling Stones."

"Hmm." I nodded. "Cool. I never would have thought of that."

"See," Montana said, leaning back in his seat. "We aren't total dicks. We can still be on the caring side."

"You're all complete dicks." I laughed and for some reason, Roy laughed with me. I looked in his direction, but his back was still turned to us.

"Speaking of caring, I heard how well Gage took care of *you* last night." Montana burst out laughing while my heart skipped a beat, my eyes expanding. "Headboard and all." He laughed even harder and I turned crimson, stealing a glance at Gage, whose smile was amused. Of course he was used to being heard so he thought nothing of it, but since it was my first time, it made me squirm. Gage placed a hand on my thigh and I picked up my coffee, taking a huge swallow. I couldn't have been that loud... at least I hoped not.

"The bus is supposed to stop in a few minutes." Deed's deep voice came out of nowhere. He was no longer wearing his sunglasses, but I could see the hint of color beneath his eye. One would mistake it for a lack of sleep since there was bruising beneath both eyes, but I knew why it was really there.

"Okay?" Montana said, glancing over his shoulder with a slight frown.

"We have to be there early today."

Montana dropped his hands on the table, causing it to rattle. "Dude, what the fuck is up with you?" he asked, his eyebrows drawing in. "You've been acting like a bitch ever since the night you were late to the show."

Deed stepped into the kitchen and leaned his lower back against the counter, swinging his gaze from Montana to me. "I'm just saying. This time we can't be late, meaning the *visitors* should get going." I cringed inwardly, offended by Deed's menacing tone.

Gage stiffened at my side, taking in Deed's sullen mood. "Deed," he said, sliding away from me to stand to his feet. "Let's talk. *Now*." Gage cocked his head to his left and led the way down the hallway. I frowned, watching as Gage stole a quick glance over his shoulder at me, his eyes begging me not to get offended, before disappearing down the hallway.

The door shut behind them and not long after, there was yelling and grunting. Roy dropped his notepad in a flash and dashed down the hallway, and Montana hissed, "Oh shit," before following after him.

I jolted, placing my mug of coffee down and scurrying around the table to follow after as well, but at the sight of Gage pinning Deed down by the throat, I wished I hadn't. Anger was written all over Gage's face. His calm demeanor had vanished and turned into rage.

"Gage, chill." Montana help up his hands, trying to mediate. "Let him go. Chill."

Gage pulled away instantly, but I knew it wasn't because of Montana's calm voice. It was because I was watching. I knew because he looked straight into my eyes.

Deed sprang from the bed, shoving Gage against his chest with his hands. Gage hardly stumbled. Deed was about to swing, but Montana and Roy ran forward to break it up. Montana held Gage back; Roy held Deed back.

"She's fucking with the band!" Deed yelled.

I flinched because the only "she" around was me.

"Would you just shut the fuck up?" Gage snarled through his teeth. "The only one fucking with the band is you and your fucking attitude!"

"She's taking you away from the band, and you know it."

I swallowed the lump in my throat as Deed pulled away from Roy and stared at me briefly. Behind his grey eyes there was ice and anger. What had I done to him? Why was he so upset with me? Because I'd seen his black eye? Was it that serious? It's not like I told anyone about it.

"How, Deed?" Gage asked, his voice laced with frustration. "She's done nothing to you."

"Way before this tour even started, you told me you were going to be *my* partner and *my* wingman if you needed to be. You were supposed to be behind me, but instead you're fucking her and taking her out and shit. You've completely forgotten about who you're really supposed to be on this tour with."

"So you're mad because I'm spending time with her? Deed, you're a grown fucking man! You don't need me to have fun all the goddamn time."

"I'm a grown fucking man, but Bentley's been riding my ass. Because of you being with her all the time, Bentley's been—" Deed stopped talking abruptly, noticing he said too much. As he stopped, Gage's eyebrows furrowed, his eyes softening as if he just now registered the meaning behind Deed's words. I still had no clue.

Montana released Gage slowly, but everyone's eyes were on him, expecting him to clear the confusion. There was panic behind Gage's eyes. Panic, worry, a sliver of frustration, and even sympathy. *What the hell just happened?*

"Deed... shit, man, I'm so sorr—"

"I don't want your fucking apology, Gage. I don't need it. I see who's more important to you now, even when you've known me for pretty much your whole fucking life and you're just now getting to know her. Even when you gave me your fucking *word*." Deed huffed, grabbing a T-shirt and pulling it over his head. He stormed toward the door and I backed up a little, but not fast enough because he bumped into my shoulder, knocking me back a few steps.

I stared at Deed's back, my eyes wide with shock. He yanked one of the doors open up front and yelled for the driver to stop. The bus slowed down as soon as he met the front door, and he swung it open, shielding his eyes from the sun. He stepped down the stairs and out the door as the bus came to a complete stop, the door slamming behind him, causing me to flinch.

After he was gone, my gaze lowered to the ground. It was dead silent in the room and I didn't want to look, but I gave in and did anyway. Everyone was looking at me, their eyes full of sorrow, including Roy's. At least he was still capable of human emotions.

"Eliza, I'm sorry," Gage apologized, stepping past Montana to get to me. "I—he didn't mean it. I swear. He's just going through a rough time..."

He was about to say something else, but I didn't want to hear it anymore. As I looked around into each pair of eyes, I saw what I'd done. I lived through the moments again—mainly the night at the club. Gage was supposed to be hanging with Deed that night, not me. Deed was trying to make Gage jealous and it worked, but in the end, Gage spent his night alone. Montana warned me the day he went to the diner with me for breakfast. He didn't want anything to get ugly, but it did anyway.

I was coming between them. I told Gage over and over again it was okay to go out with his band and have fun without me, but he always refused. He always wanted me to come with him. We were together so much that he didn't even realize how much distance he put between him and his band.

While we were having fun, Deed was the one who would always end up missing. He was the one who would always leave early, and the reason for his attitude was because of my fling with Gage. Whenever I came around, he would look at Gage, expecting him to brush me off, but Gage would take me in and walk off with me. I hadn't noticed it before, but every time Gage walked away with me, Deed stormed away from the fun. It just seemed so immature of Deed, and I knew there had to be more behind it. I couldn't be the only reason for his frustration.

"I should probably go, Gage."

His eyes stretched, his head shaking. "No. Why, Eliza? It's fine. He didn't mean it. He just has to cool off. He'll be fine later."

I shrugged as if none of Deed's harsh words mattered, but deep down, it was killing me slowly. I swallowed to keep my throat from drying out. Montana took a step forward, his arms folded. "Eliza, you shouldn't let him get to you. We'll talk to him. We'll get him to apologize if you want us to."

"He doesn't have to apologize." I sighed. "I'll just be on my bus." I forced a smile at Gage, but he shook his head, grabbing my arm.

"Eliza, it's still early. You can stick around a little longer... can't you?"

"Gage." I smiled as warmly as I could, but it felt cold and meaningless to me. "It's okay. We can talk a little later. I have to go check in with Ben anyway." That was a lie. I just needed an excuse.

Gage's grip slacked from my arm slowly, and I took a few steps forward. "Are you sure you're okay?" he asked, walking down the hallway after me.

"I'm fine, Gage." I smiled again and, unexpectedly, he pulled me in against him. I warmed up to his embrace, inhaling deeply over his shoulder. "I'll see you in a bit. Go find Deed and talk to him. You can tell me about it later."

He pulled back slowly to get a look into my eyes. I remained strong, making sure a smile was still on my face when what I really wanted to do was curl up in my bed alone and sleep the rest of the day and night away.

Sighing, Gage kissed my cheek, my forehead, and then hugged me again. "Don't take what he said to heart," he whispered into my ear. "I swear he didn't mean it. I know

Deed. He speaks out of anger." He pulled back, his boyish smile warming my heart.

"I won't." Of course it was a lie because after I placed a swift kiss on Gage's cheek and stepped off the bus, I hurried for my bus and banged on the door, ready to dwell in my own gloom. Cal came to the door groggily, but at the sight of me, he smiled and his eyes brightened.

"Morning, Eliza."

"Good morning," I mumbled, stepping past him. I didn't need him in my way. I didn't need anyone in my way, and the last person I wanted to see was Ben. Good thing he was still in his room because I was sure facing him would have brought out the waterworks. I hated crying and I wasn't going to do it today. Instead, I shut and locked my door behind me and took the thought of curling into bed into consideration.

Ben came by my door twice and knocked, but I told him I wasn't feeling well each time. My voice was faint, feeble. I felt weak all over and I thought I was being dramatic, but I wasn't. This really bothered me. I was glad I locked the door because, knowing Ben, he would have barged in and demanded I talk to him, and that would have required me looking into his understanding eyes and probably crying.

No tears, I told myself. *No tears.*

Ben asked if I was going to attend the show, but I told him no. I didn't want to. I wanted to be left alone. My worrying exhausted me.

I knew the bus was going to be empty while everyone was out, so I went out and drew at the table. I made a few cups of coffee in between until I finally decided to stop and curl into bed again.

Night crept up on me and I sighed, turning onto my back to shut my eyes. I drifted into a light slumber, but my eyes opened widely at the sound of the door opening and closing. My heart sped as footsteps came down the hallway and my bedroom door creaked open. I cursed myself mentally for not locking the door behind me. I hoped it wasn't Ben or Cal. I didn't want to see either of them knowing they were always in chipper moods. Ben especially, who always wanted me to express my concerns. It just wasn't the night to express anything. I liked being alone, but a part of my body was longing and aching for Gage's touch. His presence. Anything from him.

The room stilled as I waited for whoever it was to turn on a light or say something. The bed sank beneath their weight and a hand touched my leg. Knowing the touch, I stirred and looked up. Gage smiled down at me, the moonlight shining on his handsome face. His eyes were tired, but other than that, he looked amazing. He had on all black; a few pieces of hair hung on his forehead. His cologne smelled nice as it whiffed past my nose and I inhaled, enjoying the scent of him.

"Hey, Ellie," he whispered.

"Hi," I whispered back.

"You didn't come to the show. Are you okay?"

I nodded, adjusting myself to get comfortable. "I just needed some time to myself." My lips twisted and I looked away from him. "Is… Deed okay?"

"He's fine." He sighed. "Just upset… and hurt. Now that I know why he was acting like that, I feel like the shittiest friend on the planet."

"Why?" I asked, sitting up against the headboard. "What happened?"

He shrugged and kicked off his shoes. "I would tell you, but it's kind of personal for him."

"I won't tell anyone."

"I know you won't, Ellie, but I have to respect his privacy." He smiled sweetly, his hand resting on my leg again. My lower lip pouted, but he leaned forward to kiss it. "It's nothing personal between us," he assured. "If he didn't care about people knowing, I would tell you."

I sighed because he was right and I wasn't pushing it. I didn't want my business buzzing around, either, so I sat up some more. Gage stared into my eyes briefly before leaning in again and pulling me against him. His arms circled around my waist and moved up my back, and I placed my chin on his shoulder, hugging him back. "I'm sorry, Ellie. I know he said some things that may have gotten to you, but he wants to apologize. He didn't mean it."

I swallowed, nodding my head. "It's okay. Maybe you should spend the rest of your night with him. It'll probably make him feel better."

He pulled away from me, a smile gracing his lips. "He's going to a strip club with Montana and a few others. Montana gave him a stack of money to cheer him up and, surprisingly, it worked."

I cringed at the thought of Gage going to a strip club and staring at other girls' tits and asses, but I slowly said, "Well, you should have joined them. I'm sure you wanted to anyway."

He chuckled softly, his broad shoulders shaking. "I could have, but I wanted to check up on you."

"Well, I'm okay," I sighed. "Really, you should go. I can just paint a little more tonight and then read until I fall asleep again."

Gage stared at me for a quick second before sighing and pulling away from me. Inwardly, I cringed as he stepped back to get out of the moonlight. He picked up his shoes and my gaze fell because although I said it, I really didn't want him to go. I hated how much I worried over him. I hated how I was starting to care more than necessary. We were taking this further than a fling and I knew it, but I didn't want to face it. Feelings were coming from somewhere and I couldn't deny it.

I lay on my side, listening as he rustled around a bit. Finally he blew out a sigh and the bed sank behind me. Heat smothered my backside and he hooked his arm around my middle, pulling me back to cuddle against me. "I'll just make you my stripper for tonight," he whispered in my ear. A smile spread across my lips and a heavy load of butterflies thrashed around in my tummy, but I remained content. I couldn't show too much emotion. We weren't involving emotions... or feelings.

Gage kissed my neck and my head fell back, allowing him to do so. I was sort of glad he stuck around because, in the back of my mind, I knew I wasn't going to paint or read after he left. I would have been up bothering myself about what he may have been doing or what stripper he may have possibly slept with.

His warm, plush lips moved up to my ear and he swirled his tongue around it, making the sweet heat between my legs clench. I gripped his hand that was on my stomach, smiling from ear to ear, knowing for the rest of the night I was going to have him to myself. I willingly turned in his arms and stared into his eyes. His were hard and his body tensed as he looked down at me, his smile transforming into an uneasy one. "Should I stop?" he asked.

"No." I shook my head quickly. "I like it. Keep going."

He smirked at my compliment and then kissed my neck again. With each one, I drowned more and more. At least I didn't have to worry about him holding off on me because of my V-card. I was no longer pocketing it so it made the casual sex that much better.

With each position, I was nearly in heaven. After a few moans, groans, and heavy panting between thick sweat and cavernous kisses, Gage and I took separate showers, tossed on our clothes, and decided to go to the nearest restaurant for a bite to eat.

I settled on a cheeseburger with fries and Gage went with two grilled cheese sandwiches and chili-cheese fries. "That's a lot of cheese." I giggled as he picked up a fry and popped it into his mouth.

He smirked. "I love cheese. My mom always used to make me a grilled cheese after school—" He stopped talking abruptly, leaving his sentence incomplete, and my head tilted curiously. "After a while, my sister started making them and then... I had to start making them myself."

"Oh," I said softly. "How old were you when you started making them yourself?"

"Twelve." He shrugged, keeping his eyes down.

I grew even more curious about Gage. He hardly talked about his family and I always wondered why. Even when we were younger, in Virginia, I never saw Gage with anyone outside of his band. No family, no other friends at all. Without much consideration, I asked him, "Who's Chloe and Kristina?"

He snapped his gaze on me, his hazel eyes darkening. He then licked his lips and reached for his glass of soda. "My mom and sister."

"Oh. Is your sister older or younger?"

"Older."

My mouth clamped shut, confused about why he gave me one and two-word answers. I was being nosey, that's for sure, but I was really trying to figure him out. After deciphering it in my head, I decided to go for it. Maybe I could exchange some info whenever he asked me about my family or my past life. I would do it just to get to know Gage a little bit more, even if it did hurt me to talk about. "What happened to them?" I asked.

He swallowed thickly, his Adam's apple working hard just to get the invisible lump down. Lifting his hand, he ran his fingers through his hair and lost all eye contact. He looked everywhere but into my eyes. "We should go," he said, dropping his napkin into his basket of fries.

"No… Gage." I reached for his hand, but he pulled away slowly. "Gage?" Silence again. I hated that he wasn't talking to me. I felt terrible and guilty for asking, especially as his eyes glistened. His eyes watered even more as I called his name again and he shook his head, pushing from the table. "Seriously, Eliza, come on."

"Gage, I—I'm sorry," I whispered, pushing out of my chair. He didn't look at me. Instead, he stared out the window behind me. I stepped forward, bringing my hand up to get him to look at me. He was stubborn at first, his neck stiffening so he couldn't see me, but I tried again until his eyes finally met mine. After I did it, I wished right away I hadn't. The rims of his eyes were red and glistening. Seeing his hurt made my heart snag. "Gage..."

I cupped his face. He shut his eyes briefly, shaking his head. "It's fine, Eliza," he whispered as a single tear fell. "It's fine. Come on... please."

I swallowed, conceding and nodding my head. To comfort him, I wrapped my arm around his waist and smiled up at him. He forced a smile back, hooking his arms around my shoulders and pulling me into him. My heart broke in two for him. I shouldn't have asked. I wasn't supposed to be getting in his business anyway. That wasn't me... but I wanted to know so badly. I knew it would take time for him to want to speak on it, so I let it go.

After a while, he warmed back up to me and we headed to the FireNine bus, cuddled on the sofa, and made out a little while a few movies played. I was sure he was still thinking about it because his eyes kept distancing. His gaze would lower and his jaw would tick, and instead of interrupting him or snapping him out of it, I'd watch him.

So many emotions were displayed on his face before he looked at me, and I forced a smile at him. Anger. Deception. Hurt. At one point he looked so feeble, so weak, that the guilt snuck up on me even more, causing my heart to crack for him. I'd obviously brought back horrid memories. Memories I was certain he didn't want to relive.

Damn it, Eliza! So stupid, I cursed myself.

I was worried for Gage, but I bit my tongue as much as I could and snuggled against him, kissing his cheek and his lips tenderly and hoping it would make him forget about it and feel better. He smiled at me and eventually, with each passing hour, he calmed down more and more and hugged and kissed me back like he really meant it.

I really wanted to know what happened. I just hoped he would tell me willingly before it was time for me to go back to Virginia. After that night, I refused to bring it up again unless he wanted to speak on it.

BREATHE

The cities were going by so fast I didn't even realize we were actually in Chicago. I figured it out as I heard the howling wind outside the window and remembered how many times Ben identified the newest state to me the previous afternoon. We'd been in the Windy City a little over twenty-four hours and I was just noticing. If it was becoming a blur for me, it had to be a blur to the band.

Gage and I ended up falling asleep on the couch. I was lying on top of him, my arm still around his waist and my other arm beneath him. He looked peaceful as he slept. His features were relaxed and no part of him seemed worried or upset about the night before. His lips were parted and by the dark circles beneath his eyes, I figured he needed the sleep. I didn't want to wake him so I pulled my arm from under him and slowly drew back. He shifted, groaning while gripping my arm and muttering something I couldn't make out.

Sighing, I freed my arm again and hopped off the couch. I turned, seeing if he would wake up or move again, but he remained perfectly still, his breath evening out again. Satisfied he was still sleeping, I turned and slipped on my flip-flops, hurried for the door, and stepped out, shutting it behind me quietly.

It was windier that day. The trees behind the buses were brushing with the howl of the wind. If I wasn't mistaken, a storm was coming. The clouds were grey and a light fog hovered in the parking lot, surrounding the buses and swarming all around me.

I shivered from the breeze, hurrying to my bus, but hearing someone yell, "GET UP!" caused me to flinch and stop in my tracks. I froze, gasping as I scanned my surroundings. No one was around; the parking lot was empty. I figured it was one of the security guards in the trailers being rowdy over a sports game, so I turned for my bus again, but this time I heard a loud *SMACK* and someone cried out in pain.

I gasped again, hurrying for the noise. The smacking and bone crunching happened over and over again, and as I got closer and closer, it sounded extremely painful. Grunting filled the silence and as soon as I rounded one of the trailers, I froze in my tracks, staring ahead in complete disbelief.

Bent over on his knees was Deed. His head hung low, blood running from his lips and dripping onto the pavement. His floppy, wet hair fell over his eyes and he was sniffling while clutching his middle. It surprised me that he was bending over, but what surprised me even more was seeing the man in the suit (whose presence always freaked me out) standing above him with nothing but hatred in his eyes. His large hand was balled into a fist and held in the air and his jaw was locked as he glared down at Deed. As they heard my gasp, both of them looked up at me, and the man lowered his hand slowly.

"W—what are you doing?" I tried to keep my voice stable... Unfortunately, I failed terribly at it.

The man in the suit ran a hand through his peppery hair. He looked at Deed once more and took a step back.

"It's none of your concern," he said, sliding his fingers into the pockets of his suit pants.

"Why are you hitting him?" I snapped. I then looked down at Deed, but his head was hanging in shame and he was still sniffling, his jaw locking while he clutched his middle. "Deed," I whispered. It sounded more like my voice had broken. "Are you okay?"

"Eliza... I'm fine. Just... leave," he murmured.

I flared instantly. Hearing his voice crack and fill with agony brought back harsh memories. Memories I didn't want to relive. *A smacking upside my head. A kick in the stomach. A blow to the chest. A slap on the face. Leather against my fragile skin.* It all came tunneling back to my mind, and I took a step forward. "You worthless piece of shit," I hissed at the man in the suit.

He chuckled, amused by my sudden rage, but I wasn't having it. I wanted to sock him right in his fucking jaw. Now I knew why Deed had such an attitude lately. It wasn't me. This man was to blame. I felt for Deed then because being tossed around and beaten up was never a good feeling. It hurt. I knew from experience.

Shoving past the man, I helped Deed to his feet, but he winced as I hooked my arm around his shoulder. Drizzle sprinkled over us as I grabbed his arm to keep him up. "Deed, look at me," I said, tilting his chin. "Are you hurt?"

He nodded once but kept his lips sealed. "You shouldn't be here, Eliza," he whispered to me. "You're just making it worse for me later on." Just as Deed spoke, there was a blow against his back and he crumpled. I didn't want him to fall and I couldn't support all his weight, so I ended up falling against the pavement with him.

"We aren't done talking, Dedrick," the man said, seeming entirely too intimidating for either one of us to handle. I scrambled back with Deed, but the man kept taking steps forward, his eyes dark, menacing.

He then pulled his leg back, lifting his foot higher in the air, and I knew what was coming. He was going to kick him. And by our proximity—by the way I was sitting in front of him, trying to defend him—I knew the kick might come at me first.

I winced, preparing for it. The higher his leg lifted, the more frightened I became—the heavier my heart banged against my chest. I squeezed my eyes shut. I would do it for Deed. He was hurting already. I would take the blow and tell Ben right away to toss this man in jail. Who the hell was he anyway?

Just as the thought surfaced, someone roared, "Bentley!" from a distance. I turned quickly, spotting Gage, whose eyebrows were stitched. His nostrils flared and his lips were pinched so tight that the skin around his mouth was pale. The skin over his knuckles was as white as snow because of his clenched fist.

"Look, all you fuckers are worried about me and my business. Mind your own," Bentley snapped, but before he could speak anymore, Gage stormed forward, punching him in the jaw. Bentley stumbled backward and started to fall but caught himself. Growling and grimacing at Gage, he charged forward, but it was too late. Gage widened his stance, his fists clenched and ready for him, but before he could get to Gage, a few large men stormed out from the trailers nearby and rushed for Bentley. Their grips locked around his arms and he tried to pull away, swing, and even shove, but they weren't having it.

Bentley then laughed sarcastically, looking around at each man, at Gage, and finally, Deed and me. Deed's head was still hanging down and he was breathing painfully hard behind me. *Who is Bentley to Deed?*

"This is funny," Bentley said, gazing around with a wide, eerie smile. "Truly funny." He yanked his arm free of the

men's grips and stormed for one of the trailers nearby.
The door slammed behind him and with a few grumbles
and concerned looks, the men were back in their trailers
as well. Gage was still standing, his eyebrows furrowed as
he stared at Bentley's trailer.

I stood slowly, struggling to bring Deed with me. Gage
heard me grunt and rushed for us, hooking Deed's arm
around his shoulders. "I got him." Gage sighed, taking him
away from me. "Go and get your day started, Ellie. We'll
meet up later."

I nodded, refusing to argue. I was terrified. I was so
close to being kicked—so close to being hurt and put back
into the nightmare I once lived, that I had to get away.
Shit. Bentley triggered it.

I started panicking, panting in and out my nose and
mouth a little too quickly. I rushed for the door of my bus
and banged on it. Ben appeared, fully dressed and smiling,
but as he took in my horrid, pale face and how fast I was
breathing, he panicked as well and helped me inside.

"Eliza, sweetie, what's wrong?" he asked, dragging me
toward the couch.

I heaved in a breath, but it didn't seem like enough. *Oh
no.* I was reliving it again. The flashbacks were coming. The

smacking. The beatings with leather belts. The shoving against my back. Her tormenting words as she laughed at me while it happened. It was painful, scary.

"Eliza, what did I tell you before?" Ben said, squatting down in front of me. "Breathe, Eliza. It's the past. Just... breathe, baby."

I nodded, taking in deep gulps of air. I started to calm down as I squeezed my hands together, my leg bouncing up and down to try and get rid of it. Unfortunately, it kept coming back and my breathing only increased. Soon I was hyperventilating and Ben cursed beneath his breath, pulling away from me. He stormed down the hallway and I clutched my chest, feeling my heart pounding a mile a minute.

I couldn't figure out why I couldn't get myself under control. I was older now and it was over with. It'd been a while since I thought about it, but being a witness to Bentley's abusive side brought back the harsh, terrifying memories. It dredged up the agony and sent my world crashing down around me. My ribs were closing in around my heart; my lungs were deprived of any oxygen.

The front door of the bus swung open, but I didn't bother to look up and see who it was. I couldn't. I was stuck.

"Eliza?" Gage called from the door.

I wanted to answer him. My heart had even skipped a beat at the sound of his voice. I was glad to hear it, but I couldn't stop. It was surprising that when he spoke, the worries vanished a little bit.

He came closer and bent down on one knee. "Eliza, what's wrong?" he asked, his voice shaky. I shook my head, still squeezing my fingers together. He looked down at my fingers, his eyes wide as they met mine. "Eliza, tell me what's wrong." He cupped my face, forcing me to look into his eyes. "Breathe, Eliza. Breathe. What's wrong?" he whispered.

He kissed my cheek and my heart skipped another beat. The heavy breathing slowed and I squeezed him, begging him to say something else to rid my mind of the memories. My fingernails bit into his arm as I squeezed him harder.

"What?" he asked, staring down at my vice grip on his arm. "What? Eliza, please say something." He pulled away slowly. "Shit, where's Ben?"

"Right here." Ben stormed around the corner with my inhaler in hand. "I had to dig around for her inhaler." He placed the inhaler in my hand and I brought it to my lips, gasping for dear life, sucking in and pressing the top to get as much medicine as I could. It would have been embarrassing had my life not been on the line, but I didn't care that Gage or Ben were watching me. I didn't even care when Cal came strolling into the living room fully dressed. He was humming but stopped immediately when he saw them standing in front of me with eyes full of concern.

"What's going on?" he asked, switching glances between all of us.

My heart steadied a little with each pump until finally I could breathe again. I inhaled one last time and breathed through my nose, pulling the inhaler away from my mouth.

"Are you okay, Liza Bear?" Ben asked. I nodded slowly, but my hands were shaking. Gage noticed and swallowed, shaking his head. "What the hell happened?" Ben hissed, smacking Gage on the shoulder.

"It wasn't me!" Gage snapped, standing to his feet. "Deed has warned you about Bentley since day one, yet you still keep him around. Why the hell can't you just dump his ass?"

Dump him? What did he mean dump him?

"Bentley is a huge part of this crew. He takes care of the drivers of the buses, handles the maps, and makes sure we get to each destination on time and safely."

Gage's frowned deepened. "Bentley is a fucking asshole." I finally noticed how shaky Ben's voice was before. Why did his voice waver? Gage shook his head, running his fingers through his hair. "Bentley almost... *kicked* Eliza."

I shuddered, begging my body not to relive it. Ben stilled at my side and sucked in a breath. "What do you mean *kicked* her? Why would he try to kick her?" There was rage in his voice.

Gage folded his arms, taking a step back and cocking his head at the door. "I don't know. How about you go ask him? You're the closest one to him besides Deed. If I see him, I'm fucking him up."

Ben shoved past Gage and rushed for the door.

"Gage," I croaked. I was still shaking. Gage looked down at me and, sitting beside me, pulled me into him. "Why would you say that to him? You shouldn't have told him. It might ruin the tour."

"Today's show probably has to be cancelled anyway. Might as well settle differences." He shrugged. "Besides, had he really kicked you, his ass would've been handed to him on a silver platter." He looked me over briefly, his eyes depressing. He grabbed my hands and kissed the tops of them. "Why didn't you come for me? He could've hurt you, Eliza."

I shrugged, shaking my head. It would have been too late. "I couldn't let him hit Deed again, Gage. Someone had to step in the way."

"You're so tiny, Eliza. He could have hurt you way more than he could've hurt Deed."

I sighed and that's when Cal cleared his throat. "So, no show today?" he asked.

Gage shook his head. "Most likely not."

Pressing his lips, Cal nodded and turned on his heels to get down the hallway again. Gage sighed, pulling me into him again and kissing my forehead. "What was that?" he asked.

"What?" I whispered, knowing exactly what he was talking about. It was better to play dumb.

"That… the wheezing and gasping. Were you having an anxiety attack?"

"Something like that." I sighed. I looked up and Gage smiled warmly, making me want to sink against him even more. "I have a small case of PTSD." His eyebrows lifted as if I'd spoken another language and I laughed at his twisted face, shaking my head. "Post traumatic stress disorder."

He frowned at that. "Why? What happened before?"

I bit on my lower lip, refusing to go there again. Going there meant thinking about the past and I didn't want to think about it. I didn't want the flashbacks to surface so I turned into his arms even more and shook my head.

"I get it." He sighed. "It's okay. We don't have to talk about it right now."

I was glad he understood. I didn't want to panic again. "Sorry your show got cancelled," I murmured as he hugged me.

"It's not your fault," he whispered, leaning against the sofa. "It's no one's fault but Bentley's. The security guards helped get Deed to a hospital. They think he has a fractured rib. He's pretty banged up. He won't even talk to me."

I shook my head, hating to hear that. Gage's grip tightened around me and soon he began panting unevenly through his nostrils. I looked up, confused about why his body had gotten so tense. "Gage, what's wrong?"

"I just..." He shook his head, pulling away from me. "I feel like it's my fault that Bentley kept getting that close to him. I was supposed to be with him—" He stopped talking again, sighing and running his hands over his face. "Every time Deed would leave from a party early, Bentley would find him. Deed told me last night. He thinks he can escape him, but it's like Bentley is constantly on the lookout for him. He gets mad when Deed isn't with the band.

"At first, Bentley started hitting him because he expected perfection. He'd told Deed a long time ago that if he wanted to be a part of the band, he had to act like the professional he wanted to be. That meant with drumming, he couldn't miss a beat. Bentley is a master at the drums and hearing Deed fuck up one time—one time... Bentley got on him for it. He got so upset that he gave him a black eye. Deed had to cover it up for weeks."

Gage stopped talking and my breathing stifled as I finally heard the truth about his black eye. So Gage knew why he'd had it all along. He knew since day one but kept it a secret. I wondered if Montana and Roy knew as well. When Deed wore sunglasses, I was sure most people thought of it as a fashion statement and looked past it, but not me. Not us. Not when I knew what was really behind those sunglasses. Gage played it off extremely well.

"Why haven't you guys told Ben?"

"Ben?" He shook his head, laughing dryly. "Ben's probably at Bentley's trailer kissing him as we speak."

I gasped, smacking his arm with no intentions of being playful. "Why would you say that?" I snapped.

"Because they date, Eliza. It isn't obvious? Ben isn't the only fruit in the vegetable garden." Gage revealed a small smile and I couldn't help but snicker at that. The snickering didn't last long for me, though. Not when I realized Ben had been hiding it from me.

Ben was very secretive about his love life. I didn't mind him being gay. It didn't steer me away or make me think less of him. I wouldn't have cared if he'd told me about Bentley. He didn't make it obvious that he was dating him, but I did notice how Ben always mentioned having a night out with a few friends. I put it all together then. By "friends" he meant a night out with his "friend" Bentley.

"So he hasn't gotten rid of Bentley because he likes him?"

"More like *love*." Gage sneered. "Ben and Bentley have been messing around for a while."

"Well, loves him. Whatever." I waved it off.

"Yeah," he sighed. "Bentley was around way before the band even got popular. He was our driver for a while and Deed hated it because it meant Bentley had no choice but to attend every show. Deed was always so stiff around him, so... out of it. He hardly talked while Bentley was around, and I picked up on it. Of course he would brush it off and say it was nothing, but I found out one day. I witnessed Deed's bruises and black eyes when I paid him a random visit. It's a shame that it's dragged on for this long. Bentley is better to Ben than he is to his own stepson. That's the sad part about it all."

"Stepson?" I questioned, my eyebrows shooting up. Perhaps Deed and I had more in common than I thought.

"Yeah." Gage cleared his throat, running the palms of his hands over his face again. "Just... don't say anything to anyone," he said, looking at me sternly.

"Why would I, Gage? I'd never stoop that low."

"I believe you. I'm just saying. Montana and Roy don't even know... at least not yet."

I shrugged off his statement and as soon as I felt stable enough, I stood to my feet and went for the kitchen. I grabbed a bottle of water and gulped it down and then Ben came bustling in, letting us know that the show was indeed cancelled for today and that he'd sent Bentley home. Ben made a call to the hospital a few minutes after and told us Deed had fractured a rib and was bruised up pretty badly. They had to stitch up his forehead and left hand.

I felt terribly sorry for Deed and wanted to visit, but Gage told me not to worry about it and that he and the band would send my condolences along with a few playful kisses. I tried to be happy after he left, but as I turned around, I felt even more terrible.

Ben sat at the table, sighing a dozen times over a short glass of Jack Daniels. I felt awful because a part of me knew I was the reason he had to tell Bentley to leave. It was the man he loved versus his daughter and his career. I was grateful he'd chosen his career and me because there were people I knew who would choose a man over their own child... over their own future. I couldn't fill the hole I knew was carved into his chest with my love. My daughterly love wasn't the kind of love he was seeking.

I hadn't seen Ben so down since my mom robbed us of everything. It was my senior year and Ben and I had taken a mini trip to Virginia Beach so he could take care of some business. When we got back home, the house was completely destroyed. Most of our valuables were gone— the TVs, the silverware, the chinaware, our couches... even our beds were stolen. Everything was missing and we knew it was my mom who'd done it. She was envious, angry that I'd finally decided to move in with Ben. She'd threatened us a million times, but we never thought she would actually go through with it.

The only thing that was left in that apartment the day we were robbed that made me actually think she cared about me were my art supplies. They were untouched, sitting in the same corner of the room, and seeing that made me break down.

Ben and I lived in a tiny one-bedroom apartment and didn't have much money after he was laid off his job, so losing all of that killed us. It killed *him*. He was out of employment and he hated how much he couldn't support me, but every little bit he got, he spent on me to make me happy. When he was offered the position of manager for FireNine a few weeks after, everything picked up. He worked hard and in the end got everything back. It took time, but he did it. He'd even bought a bigger house and since he'd given me the only bedroom of his apartment, I told him to take the master room of the new house. I insisted because he bought it and he deserved it. He simply declined, telling me he wanted to give me the world and more. After a while, I stopped bickering with him and accepted it. I could never thank Ben enough for his generosity.

I snapped out of my memories, hugging Ben as we talked about his situation with Bentley a little. He told me exactly what he said to Bentley:

"I'm tired of hearing about you hurting your son. You almost hurt my daughter. We can't do this anymore, Bentley. You have to go. It's hurting the band… I'm sorry, but… you're fired."

It hurt me to hear the words come out of his mouth because with each word his voice cracked. By the end of our talk, Ben had downed his fifth glass and hurried off to his room, slamming the door shut behind him before anyone could see his tears fall. I knew he was crying. I heard his sniffling and weeping as I went to the bathroom for a shower. Each sob hit against one of my nerves, making me feel guilty. In the back of my mind, I knew I really was to blame; he just didn't want it to seem like it was my fault.

If I never would have stepped in and helped Deed, Bentley would probably still be around and Deed would have just brushed it off like always. If I never would have joined the tour, Gage could have been around Deed more and Deed wouldn't have been getting hurt, abused. He would've had someone to cover him and be by his side each night. Bentley wouldn't have been looking for him because he knew he wouldn't be able to hit him while he was with the band. The boys could have been playing and the show never would have gotten cancelled. It hurt me more than anything to know that my dad was unhappy— to know that Gage made a promise to Deed but broke it to spend more time with *me*, a girl he'd just met. A girl he was just getting to know.

But what hurt me most of all was the bothersome fact that Ben didn't come out of his room until the following afternoon.

FEEL AGAIN

Everyone decided it was best to leave Chicago and get settled in New York City since the show had been cancelled. There were two things that bothered me a lot about being in New York. One was that we were going to be staying for a whole week since the band wasn't going to play until the weekend. The other thing, though I tried so hard to stop thinking about, was that it would be my last week on tour.

My first thoughts of the tour were that it was going to be shitty and a complete waste of my time. All of that changed for some reason. Maybe because for the first time, I had friends. For the first time, I enjoyed spending time with a guy—a really hot guy at that. He wasn't just an ordinary person. He considered himself one, but to me he wasn't. He was Gage Grendel. A rock god.

I noticed I wasn't being as open on going out with Gage as I had been before. For the first two nights, Gage didn't think much on it and didn't hesitate to leave. He'd kiss me good-bye and then he'd head out with Montana and Roy. Deed was stuck in the trailer, being taken care of by a few ladies Montana picked up for him, along with a real nurse. He had to get better by the weekend, and I was kind of glad for the girls by his side. At least he was a strong guy. At least he was smiling again.

Witnessing Deed being abused by his own stepdad kept taking me back. After so many years of forgetting about it, it registered that I'd gone through the same thing at one point, and thinking about it horrified me. I was forcing smiles at everyone and zoning out so much, hoping no one would notice. I'd sulk on the sofa when everyone would go out and when it got late and still no one was around, I'd sink into bed, curl into a ball, and do what I hated most.

Cry.

I hated crying. I hated feeling weak. I was strong. I knew I was, but I couldn't get over it. I couldn't get over how my mom could just let my stepdad have his way with me. How she could just allow a man to hurt her only little girl? Her own flesh and blood.

Sometimes she would defend me and only *sometimes*— only if she wanted something from me. If she wanted me to go "grab" something from the store or "pick up" a few bucks from my friends on the streets. I was terrible and I hated myself for it.

The tears kept falling, but I swiped at my face as hard as I could. I didn't want any trace of them on me. I didn't want the tears because of the pain she caused me. I just wanted to sleep and eventually, with the cool pillows and my tired eyes, I didn't fight it. I succumbed.

I stirred in my sleep as visions of Gage appeared. He was everywhere and at one point I swore I heard him speaking. Groggily twisting my body to try and rid myself of him, I heard him call my name again and my eyelids flew open. I gasped, spotting him bending over me, his hand on my waist, his hazel eyes narrowed with confusion.

"Eliza, what's wrong?"

I pulled away, shaking my head and pushing up to place my back against the headboard in a flash. Where the hell did he come from? My eyes were still tired and I noticed it was no longer dark. The sun was high in the sky, streaking in through the window and onto Gage's beautiful face. He blinked quickly, moving his hand up my waist, but I pulled away with a sigh and climbed out of bed.

"Eliza," he called as I kept my back to him. I was sure I looked like complete shit. I felt way worse than a pile of dog poop.

"Hmm?" I responded, bending down to unzip my suitcase.

Gage was quiet and I wanted to look over my shoulder to see him, but I knew the look on his face. I could feel his frustration. "Are you upset that I went out again last night?" he asked. "If so, we can go out tonight. I can make it up to you—"

"No." I shook my head but kept my gaze down. Great, he thought I was mad at him. I dug into my suitcase to find my most comfortable outfit. I came across a pair of dark-blue denim jeans along with a light-blue denim shirt. It would do for today.

Sighing, I stood and turned around but gasped as I got caught in Gage's arms. *When the hell did he get so close?*

"What's wrong, Eliza?" he asked, his gaze lowering to my lips.

I shook my head. "Nothing. I'm fine." I lied. We were close and I couldn't help but breathe unsteadily. I wanted his lips, but then again I didn't because by the end of this week, this fling between us would be over and I hated how quickly it was coming to an end. It was right around the corner and he'd be back to sleeping with random girls and partying with a different chick on his arm. *He might even go back to Penelope.*

"If you're upset with me about last night…"

"I'm not," I breathed. It was true. I wasn't. I really didn't even think about him last night. I was too worried about myself to even bring him to mind much. I was sure he popped in somewhere; I just didn't know where exactly.

"Then why are you avoiding me? You pulled away from me like…" His head lowered and he stared at the floor. His eyelashes touched his cheekbones and I had the urge to move in and kiss his cheek, but I didn't. I remained perfectly still.

It got so quiet that it became uncomfortable so I started pulling away again, but he tightened his arms around me, his eyes darting up to meet mine. "Why are you pulling away?" he asked, his breath running across my cheek.

I squeezed the back of his shirt, suddenly feeling weak at the knees because behind his question was a completely different meaning. He knew just as well as I did that our time was about to come to an end. He knew...

"Gage," I whispered, lowering my gaze. I couldn't look at him so I shut my eyes. "Gage, maybe we should just stop this now while—"

He stopped me from talking with his lips. My body sprang to life as his lips consumed mine. A surge of electricity struck my core as he kissed me harder, deeper, the passion coursing from his body to mine. I wrapped my arms around his neck, sinking into his firm chest. His fingers ran from my back to my hips. He pulled me in to him farther, and I moaned into his mouth, sparking with heat once again. He tasted like some kind of fruit. I wasn't sure what it was, maybe strawberry or raspberry? Whatever it was, it tasted fresh and divine as his tongue ran across mine and occasionally touched the roof of my mouth. I panted as he stepped forward, leaving me with no choice but to step backward and bump against the nearest wall.

He kept one hand on my waist, the other gradually pulling at my thigh so my leg could lift and wrap around him. His arousal strained against jeans, causing me to whimper uncontrollably against his lips. I wanted him, but I knew it wasn't good to take him. It would make it that much harder for me to let this go. To let *him* go.

"Gage," I whispered into his ear.

He stilled, but he didn't stop kissing me. "No," he growled.

I frowned. "No, what?"

"No, Eliza." He pulled his lips away from my neck and blinked quickly, but I noticed the tears burning in his hazy, sleep-deprived eyes. My heart ached, taking in the sight of him. His face was pained, hurt. Behind his eyes I saw the loneliness, the heartache. I couldn't wrap my mind around what he was thinking, but I knew whatever it was, was because of me.

Instead of speaking on it, I lowered my head and he dropped my leg. "Gage—"

"Stop saying my name like that, Eliza. I'm not..." His voice cracked, his head lowering. "I know what you're going to say. Not right now... Just please. Stop. Don't end it yet. Just... stop."

Tears burned my eyes, but I blinked quickly to get rid of them. "I'll have to leave eventually, Gage. I only have a few days left. You know this. We might as well stop while we can… before it gets too hard." My voice was breaking. I was breaking.

"I don't wanna stop," he said. "I like it too much. You do something to me. You make me think twice… You make me feel something. I feel alive with you around. I haven't felt anything this real in a long time. Not since…" He stopped talking again and I looked at him curiously.

"Since what, Gage?"

"Since… my sister."

He didn't look at me as he said it. I tried to get a good look into his eyes and figure him out, but he kept his head down, a few pieces of hair falling onto his forehead. Now he was making me feel even guiltier. Now he was making me want to take him just to make him happy again. I didn't know what else to do—what else to say. I didn't speak as I cupped his face in my hands and forced him to look at me. I pulled one hand away to run my fingers through his hair, pressing against his chest as our breaths caught and got tangled with each other's. I studied his sorrowed hazel eyes, the grief he'd been carrying for so long.

I didn't want to hurt him. I didn't want to lose the connection, so I told myself I would stay… for now. I could still remain casual, but that was it. I slowly brought his lips to mine, kissing him fervently, and he groaned, reeling me in by my hips so I could mold against him. I knew no one was on the bus. I heard Cal take off earlier and Ben left with his assistant Terri. It was only us, and I wanted to take advantage of it.

"Gage," I whispered as he picked me up in his arms. He stumbled forward to go for the bedroom door and shut it. He locked it and then my back pressed against it. "Gage," I said again.

"I'm not letting you go yet... You can't leave... We can't stop, Eliza." His lips touched my collarbone and my head fell back, enjoying his warm kisses on my skin. He moved up to my neck and kissed me, pressing his erection into my stomach. At the feel of him, I moaned, whimpered, ready for him to just rip off my clothes and go for it already. All thoughts were lost. All heartache seemed to disappear.

He kept me pinned against the door by his waist and reached up to help me remove my shirt. After tossing it on the floor, he reached behind me to unhook my bra, exposing my breasts. He tossed the bra, too, but his eyes never left my chest. He finally looked into my eyes again, scanning me intensely, hungrily. There was a fire behind his irises and it turned me on completely. Burned me on the inside with nothing but desire. My stomach coiled as his eyes locked on mine. It coiled even more as he leaned forward and sucked on my nipple greedily, his gaze never shifting. My breath hitched, enjoying the pleasure running through me, his hands at my waist, his tongue circling around my nipple until it was erect. He moved to the other and I rested the back of my head against the door, accepting it all.

I moaned, clutching his shoulders, ready for him. He didn't oblige. He continued sucking on me until that nipple had become a pebble and then he pulled down my shorts. He placed me down for only a second, and I helped him by stepping out of my shorts and panties. I was completely naked before him and my face burned scarlet, but his eyes remained hard, drinking in all of me. After staring at me for what seemed like hours, he attacked my lips and crushed my body to his.

I reached down to unbutton his jeans and he slid out of them with ease. Spinning me around in his arms, he placed my back on the bed and separated my legs, climbing between them. His lips found my neck and I gripped his back, my core throbbing as he got nearer. He was so close.

I could feel the heat of his cock. I throbbed for him again, aching, longing, desiring. I wanted it so much even though I knew I didn't need it. I shouldn't have, but I couldn't help it. I should have stopped it, but I gave in.

Gage pulled back in haste to dig into his jeans pocket for a condom. After sliding it on, he teased me some more with his tongue on my nipples. He ran his tongue down to the dip of my belly and I gasped, inhaling deeply at how far he'd gone and how close he was to my core.

"You can't stop this, Eliza," he said, kissing my thigh. "I need it." I tingled as he kissed the other and heat spiraled down between my legs. He kissed the skin outside my entrance, making me clench, tingle hard, and clutch at the sheets. "I've just gotten started with you," he whispered. "You can't stop this yet." Then he slid his tongue between my sweet, sensitive folds, and I bucked against his mouth.

The panting increased. I gripped at the sheets wildly, aiming to avoid scratching him up. One of my hands ran through his hair as his tongue licked, dove, and circled around my clit, causing me to screech at the top of my lungs. A rush ran through me as I moved against his mouth. He groaned and moaned, causing a vibration between my legs. *Oh, fuck.* He grabbed my waist to try and stop me from squirming and then he said, "Look at me, Eliza."

I shook my head. I couldn't look. Looking into his eyes was going to send me teetering over the edge completely. Gage's fingers dug into my side as he growled, his tongue swirling harder and flickering so quickly that it was driving me mad. I wasn't going to be able to keep up for long.

"Look at me, Eliza," he repeated. His mouth barely moved away from me. He was licking my nub as he spoke. He was so talented in bed and I hated how amateur I was. I dared a look and in return, I was sent into overdrive. The fire in his eyes, the heat as he watched me moan, the way his tongue circled and dipped and I felt it all, sent me shuddering. Shattering, crumpling into pieces. I squealed, my body quaking, legs trembling. In a heartbeat, Gage moved up quickly, kissing my nipples, each side of my collarbone, my neck. He hovered above my mouth, a small smile curling at the corner of his lips.

"Do you want me?" he asked.

I nodded, pressing my hand against his chest and squirming to get him as close to me as possible.

"You're sure? You want me?"

I nodded eagerly, moaning as his lips barely brushed mine.

"How much?" he asked.

"I want all of you, Gage," I whispered.

"All of me?" Before I could nod, he shoved his cock deep inside me. I sucked in a breath through my teeth as he hissed. "That's all of me, Eliza. Want me to go slow on you? Want me to *make love* to you?"

I looked up at him quickly, swallowing the heavy brick in my throat. Make love to me? How was that even possible when we weren't in love? My mind was boggled and soon Gage's strokes deepened, causing all worries to fade. His lips crushed mine, a saltiness taking over my taste buds. It was me I tasted, along with his personal taste.

Gage's forehead pressed on mine as he watched me, but I shut my eyes, wanting the feeling of him inside me to take over. His pace picked up as he gripped my hips, diving inside me, in and out, as my fingers bit into his skin. I groaned through my teeth as sweat built up between us and he lowered his head to bury his face into the hollow of my neck. He sucked on me tenderly, licking my neck and then the lobe of my ear, sending wave after wave of moisture to course through me and melt between my legs.

S. Q. WILLIAMS

I shuddered a dozen times, clenching around his thickness.

"You feel so good, Eliza. You make me feel good," he whispered. "You can't leave. You have to stay."

I didn't bother to speak. If I were to respond, I would have lied to him. We both knew I couldn't stay. I had a life to live, things to do. I had dreams to accomplish. Instead of speaking, I pulled him into me, leaving no space between us, and he went harder. His grunting grew heavier as he gripped my hips.

He then did something I didn't see coming: he lifted me up, still stroking and my chest still against his, but my back was no longer on the bed. I was being held upright against him, his arms circling around to hold me up by my back. He slammed into me some more and I stared into his eyes, enjoying the full feeling at the pit of my stomach.

"Ride me," he whispered.

I did as commanded. I had no idea what the hell I was doing, no idea which way to go, how fast to go, how slow to go, but I worked my hips as best as I could. His eyes were blazing, watching my pleasured face intently. He cupped my ass, allowing me to do all that I could. He kissed my neck, providing his own strokes and his own rhythm, which helped me out in return. He kept me steady, giving me a good balance, and after a while, I knew I'd gotten the hang of it because he grunted harder, hissing my name and cursing right after. I was moaning loudly, unable to hold back.

My hips grinded, still feeling him at the pit of my stomach. My core was tightening. I clenched around him, knowing another spiral of pleasure was on its way. He knew it as well because he brought his head up again to look into my eyes. "I want you to watch me as I watch you let go. I want your eyes on mine. Don't close them. Don't block me out."

His husky voice sent me higher. He stared into my eyes, his face oozing with just as much pleasure as mine. He groaned; I excessively moaned. My lips locked with his and my fingernails clenched into his skin, but I kept my eyes open. It was coming, and with each second, I kept getting hotter and hotter, but I didn't dare myself to look away. I couldn't. His eyes were doing something to me that I couldn't hold back on. They were low, heavy, watching every reaction.

Finally, I screeched, soaking the length of him, still grinding my hips, a bead of sweat trickling down my back. I was coming undone, falling apart. Melting. He growled against my chin and I couldn't help it anymore. I shut my eyes, shuddering and shattering. Trembling and quaking. My hips didn't stop moving. My head fell back and then he cursed beneath his breath, flipping me over. He gripped my ass, slamming into me from behind countlessly, grunting through his teeth, until finally he collapsed on top of me.

We breathed through the moment, the intensity still in the air, until I finally turned over to face him, tangling my fingers through his damp hair as he kissed my cheek.

So many thoughts were running through my mind. I had to stop this before I ended up even more torn than I already was. I had to just tell Gage straight. It wasn't like he couldn't replace me with another girl within a second. He could—I knew it—and as bad as I didn't want to be a part of his past, I knew we could never be more than a fling. We could never be more than casual because Gage lived the fast life. He lived a life that I could never live up to. We were two completely different people with completely different lives. I wanted a normal one. I couldn't tolerate being on the tabloids or the entertainment channels anymore. Most were calling me his girlfriend, but I wasn't that. We were just friends... with benefits.

I couldn't be the girl Gage wanted me to be. I had my own dreams to chase after and I knew I wouldn't be able to trust him once I was out of sight. Even if I were to ask for more, in the back of my mind I knew it would be dumb of me because he wasn't a faithful person. He didn't have to admit it for me to know. Sooner or later the distance would get in the way.

In between telling Gage good-bye so he could go practice with his band, taking a shower, brushing my teeth, detangling my hair, eating something light, getting dressed, and sulking on the couch all day with a book glued to my face, I finally settled with just letting life run its course. I didn't want to think about the end of the week any more than I needed to, so I slept it away and half-heartedly forgot about it.

STEPDAD

The following day, Ben and I went out to pick up flowers and balloons for Deed. No guy wanted flowers, but Ben insisted and irritably, I'd conceded and went with him. I should have known something was behind his little day out, though. He seemed much happier from the night when he was crying over Bentley. I refused to bring it up, especially when I knew it would most likely kill him to talk about.

We decided on grabbing some lunch after stuffing the flowers and balloons into the car with Marco. Marco rolled his eyes at us, but, as always, we thought nothing of him. The restaurant Ben chose was in the heart of New York

City. The city was bustling; bodies were everywhere. Steam drifted out of potholes, the color yellow crowded streets because of taxis. I would never understand why New York was so busy, but it truly was the city that never slept.

As we entered, a tall man with light-grey hair and a warm smile greeted us. He had on a chef's hat, a clean white smock, and black slacks. He was a decent-looking guy and knew who we were as we stepped into the restaurant. He called Ben by his first name and Ben blushed a few times, grinning at the man who he'd said to me a million times was a real "hottie." I smiled and laughed with him to keep his happy mood going, but I knew he was only trying to cover up his broken heart.

Thinking of broken hearts made me sick to my stomach. After last night, I was ripped in half. I could hardly sleep. I hadn't talked to Gage this morning and was slightly relieved he gave me some kind of space. I needed to clear my head. I needed to think.

Ben chatted with the man at the bar, but my gaze drifted to the busy streets. My eyes swung to the fleeting pedestrians, the food stands, the couples walking by hand-in-hand. I sighed, longing for Gage's hand in mine. Then again, I snapped out of it, knowing his hand wasn't what I needed. I only had three more days left. *Three more days*. I really didn't want to face the reality of it. Dreaming was better. Spending time with Gage was better. Laughing, joking around, teasing, cuddling, and even *sex* was better than being alone.

I wondered if he thought more of me, as I thought of him. He said a lot the other day, but everything was broken up. He didn't complete his sentences and it confused me even more. His face was torn, but I needed to hear it. I needed to know. I was hoping I wasn't overreacting to our fling that had transformed into more. I wasn't stupid. I could feel it between us. I just wanted so badly to ignore it. To just pretend it was nothing. Of course, that was nearly impossible.

"Eliza," Ben snapped, pulling me out of my daze. I dropped my hand from my chin, providing all my attention. "Eliza, talk to me," he sighed. "You've been zoning out on me all morning. Speak."

I sighed, shrugging and forcing a smile. "I'm fine. Just thinking... about school and classes and stuff."

I stole a glance at him and his eyes narrowed, full of doubt. "Gage," he said.

I frowned, my cheeks burning. "W—what?"

He smiled, oddly amused by my blush, and then sighed again, folding his arms. "You're thinking about him. I see it in your eyes. In your face. In your little red cheeks," he noted, reaching across the table to pinch them.

I brushed his hands away, smiling. "I'm not. I'm fine."

"Hmph." He snorted. "Whatever you say." Ben picked up his menu and I did the same, but his eyes never left me. "Liza, can I ask you something?"

I looked up, swallowing heavily. "Yeah, Ben. Anything."

"When it's time for you to go, what are you going to tell him exactly?"

I squeezed my hands together. "What do you mean?"

"I mean… how are you going to go about it without getting hurt? Without hurting him?"

"It's not going to hurt him," I assured, waving him off and staring at my menu. I was shrugging it off, but on the inside my heart was clambering and I could hear the beats in my eardrums.

"You think so? What about you?" he asked. "You didn't answer for yourself. How are *you* going to handle saying good-bye?"

I bit on my bottom lip. Tears stung my eyes, but I kept them down, reaching for my glass of water. "I don't know, Ben." My voice was faint, almost inaudible, but somehow he heard me.

Ben sighed, adjusting himself on his side of the table. I looked up and his eyes were empty, distant, but he was still staring at me. Worry crept behind those eyes and then he sighed again, reaching for my free hand that was on the table. I clutched my glass of water, hating how he'd set me up just to talk about it. I didn't want to talk about it. I just wanted to go through with it and get it over with already, no matter how much it tore me apart.

"I see the way he looks at you," he whispered. "I see the way you look at him. You told me it was just a fling— just a casual thing—but I see more than that, and you're fighting it. You're denying it so you won't be hurt by the end of this week."

My eyes burned and I looked down, no longer steady enough to look into his eyes. He squeezed my hand, rubbing his thumb along the back of it. "I'll be fine," I whispered.

"You always say that, Eliza. You swear you'll be fine, but that's when you're hurting the most." I hated how much he knew me. "Eliza, sweetie," he said, his voice wavering and causing me to look up. "Just don't lie to yourself. Don't lie to him. Do it the right way. Don't run from it. It'll kill you just as much as it'll kill him."

"Gage will be fine, Dad," I snapped. "He'll be doing just great without me, just like he was before. He'll move on. He'll be fine."

"And that's what bothers you most? The fact that he can move on with whomever he'd like and you can't."

"I can," I retorted. Suddenly, I was blinded with rage and hating this whole conversation. It all started to come to me again. After this week, he would be back at it and it would be like I never existed.

"You could, but you wouldn't want to," he said. "Eliza, be honest with me. Do you love him?"

I frowned, hesitating slightly. "No."

"Are you sure about that? Think about it. All the time you two have been spending together. All the nights you two have shared. All the smiling you've done. I've seen you smile more this summer than any other time of your life. He's made you happy and you've enjoyed the feeling."

I shook my head, pulling my hand away. It wasn't what I wanted to hear. "Why are you defending him now when you're the one who told me to be careful of my heart while we're together?"

"That was before I saw how much you really meant to him—before I noticed how much more time he was spending with you than his own band, the guys he grew up with. I notice these things, Eliza. I know love. I've been in it. You're in love, so stop lying to yourself. Stop wallowing about it."

"I'm not wallowing," I muttered. "And I'm not in love."

"You are and it's annoying as hell, sweetie." He was trying to be sympathetic, but I knew I was getting on his nerves. "You just don't wanna be 'cause you don't wanna get hurt. Because you know you'll have to go."

I finally caved in, drawing in a slow breath while staring at my menu again. Tears stung my eyes and I tried to fight against them, but one fell eventually and dropped onto my lap. "I know after I'm gone it won't be the same, Ben. Even if I do want more, I can't have it because we'll be separated. I'll be in school and he'll be... wherever. I'll be living a normal life and he'll still be living the fast life. Girls will continue throwing themselves at him and I'll start to fade into *nothing*. It's not like he's going to deny the girls that cross his path. I'll slip away from his memory. He'll drink, party, and forget about me and what we had because it's who he is and it's how he'll always be. It'll be like we were non-existent. That's how this fling was supposed to end… right?"

Ben was quiet for a moment, his lips pressed. His silence was really getting to me as he sipped his water, raked his wavy hair, and pursed his lips at me. I was about to yell at him to speak—to say something—but before I could, he said something to me that repeated in my mind for the rest of the evening. "Talk to him about it and see how he really feels. Don't assume. It'll only continue to bother you if you don't know the truth, Eliza."

It sucked that he was right.

Ben and I stopped by the FireNine tour bus. I decided to stick around with Deed while Ben left with Terri to check on the crew and make sure everything was going to be okay for the show on Saturday night. Deed was lying on the couch, playing a video game, his feet kicked up on the coffee table. I was sitting across from him, completely confused on how shooting zombies was so enjoyable. It kind of freaked me out.

"Do you watch *The Walking Dead*?" Deed asked, looking at my grimace toward the TV screen.

I shook my head. "No. What is it?"

"A kickass zombie show. Roy and me used to watch it all the time. We haven't had much time lately, but I swear it's the shit."

I shook my head again, laughing. "I hate zombies. They freak me out. A virus might break out one day and kill us all. Then we'll start eating each other and that's just... gross." I shuddered from the horrid thought.

Deed chuckled. "Funny, Eliza."

He clicked away at his game controller and I sighed, looking toward the kitchen. "Do you want me to make something to eat? I'm not sure what you guys have, but I can try and whip something up."

"You cook?" he asked, eyebrow raised, his eyes still on the TV screen.

"Yes," I laughed, pushing from the sofa. "I cook for Ben all the time when we're at home."

"Oh. You don't look like a cooker."

"Exactly how does a 'cooker' look?" I countered, teasing.

He shrugged and then snorted. "Like my mom."

I giggled, stepping around the sofa to get to the kitchen. I pulled the cabinets open, seeing what I had to work with. There were macaroni noodles in one cabinet, a bottle of wine in another, cheese in the fridge, a jar of honey, and a can of corn. I opened the freezer and there were frozen ham slices in a TV dinner box. It was odd seeing all the separate food, but I grabbed the macaroni noodles, the block of cheese, the corn, the honey, and the ham.

"How about macaroni and cheese with honey glazed ham slices and a side of corn?" After I asked, it sounded funny and Deed laughed the same time I did.

"Sure. Anything's fine, Eliza."

I nodded, turning to grab a pot beneath the counter and fill it with water. I dumped the noodles into it, added a few pinches of salt, and then scrambled around for a cheese grater. While grating the cheese, it became silent and I looked up quickly, but Deed was already looking at me, his head tilted to the side. I forced a smile, thinking he'd snap out of his stare and look away, but he didn't.

"Are you okay?" I asked, still forcing a smile.

He shook his head no. He continued staring at me until his eyes started glistening and he jerked away his gaze. He placed his game controller down, shaking his head and grunting as he stood from the sofa.

"Do you need help?" I asked, stopping my grating. He shook his head again.

"Just need to use the bathroom," he said, limping his way toward the hallway. I watched him until he was out of sight, my eyebrows drawn in with concern. Water ran in the bathroom so I started grating the cheese again.

After mixing some honey with brown sugar, I coated the slices of ham and stuck them in the oven. Now all I had to do was wait for the macaroni noodles to be done. I sighed, folding my arms and leaning against the counter. Deed came out of the bathroom seeming much better. His eyes weren't glistening.

As he entered the front room again, he met my gaze and smiled. Limping his way toward the kitchen table, he sank down into one of the seats, looking directly at me. "There's something I wanted to ask you," he said.

I swallowed, nodding as I tucked a lock of hair behind my ear. "Okay."

"I was so rude to you—mean to you when it wasn't even your fault. I'm sorry for that, seriously," he said, running a heavy hand through his dark hair.

"It's okay," I murmured.

He nodded, swallowing noisily. "Why'd you do it?" he asked.

"Do what?" It wasn't that I didn't know what he was talking about; I just didn't want to relive it again, for him or myself.

"Why did you step in?" he asked. "Why were you going to take the blow for me?"

I looked into his eyes thoughtfully and his were serious, desperate for an answer. Finally he blinked and I sighed, pressing my lips. "I just... I know how much it hurts to be... hurt by someone that you think loves you. I didn't want you to hurt anymore."

"So you stepped in the way and tried to take that hurt away from me?"

I nodded. "Yeah."

"Wow," he breathed, his head lowering. He stared at the table for a few minutes, and to find something to do to occupy myself, I checked the oven. I then checked the noodles and saw they were done. I grabbed a strainer, dumped the noodles, and ran some cold water over them. "Thank you, Eliza," Deed said from the table. I stopped the water, looking at him slowly. His eyes were soft, sincere. A few tears had run down his cheeks, but a small smile was on his lips.

I placed the noodles down hurriedly, rushing to his side to hug him. "You don't have to thank me, Deed." I sighed, hugging him tighter, but not enough to hurt his ribs. He sniffled, running the back of his hand across his nose and getting rid of the tears, but after a while he gave up on it because the tears kept streaming. We stayed that way for a while until he stopped crying. When he did, I pulled away and sat in the seat across from him.

"I just don't get why you've allowed him to hit you for this long. Why didn't you fight back?"

He shrugged, wiping his red nose again. "Because although Bentley is abusive, he was the only one who supported my dream. He was the only one who liked that I was following after my drumming career. My mom hated it, and I know she still hates it because whenever I call her, she hardly says a thing to me. I'm the youngest of the band, twenty-two, and when we started getting noticed, I was a senior in high school. It was a decision to go after my dreams or to get my diploma. I chose my dreams and she hated my decision. After she and Bentley split, I didn't hear from her for a while. Bentley gave up everything at home to join FireNine. I didn't know how to thank him so I thought it was best to let him tag along."

"But shouldn't he be proud of you? He shouldn't hit you," I said, getting even more upset about his past.

"I'll never understand Bentley." He ran a stitched hand across his face. "He has a different way of showing how proud of me he is. He's so strict and used to perfection that if I fuck up, he gets mad and hits me. He's been a part of this band for so long. We were his way of making money. As much as I may not like him, he raised me and I do love him. I wanted him to be taken care of and I didn't fight back because he's probably done more for me than my mom has. He was more of a dad to me than my biological one..."

"Oh," was all I could manage. He was torn. He didn't want Bentley to lose everything so he stuck through it. But sooner or later Deed could have been brutally injured, worse than now. Bentley seemed like he was going to keep hitting harder and harder the older Deed got. "What makes him so angry?" I asked.

He shrugged, running another hand through his hair. "Don't know. I think he had a fucked-up childhood. Saw some scars all over his back one time... It freaked me out. They were like scars from whippings. Not sure what happened, but I never wanna find out."

I nodded. That could be understood. Perhaps Bentley released his past aggressions on Deed. Maybe for once he felt superior to someone else and used it to his advantage. It happens.

"Seriously, though," Deed said, smiling softly and bringing me out of my crazy Bentley thoughts, "if there's anything you need from me, you ask me. I owe you big time. I really didn't know how I was going to get out of that one."

I smiled back. "Anytime, Deed."

We talked more about minor stuff like if he was going to be ready to play on Saturday and if he felt any better, and of course he was trying to man up and say he was more than ready, but by his limping, I knew he needed to heal a little more. I finished up cooking as we chatted and after the food was done, we talked over our meal and shared the bottle of wine that was in the cabinet.

WHO HE IS (BOOK #1 FIRENINE TRILOGY)

I learned a lot about Deed, which surprised me. He was hiding a burden for so long that he actually opened up to me in ways that created a better bridge for our friendship. He and Montana were similar in ways, only Montana was a bit goofier and more mindless than Deed. At least Deed thought about his picks before just dragging them onto the bus and sleeping with them.

I cleaned up after we finished eating and Deed hopped back to the couch to continue his game. During my cleaning, Gage came in with overly eager eyes.

As soon as he saw me, he smiled widely and rushed for me. "What are you doing tonight?" he asked.

I grinned as he pulled me close, reeling me in. "Nothing that I know of. Why? What do you have in mind? Another party?"

"No," he said, which caught me by surprise. "Something much better. A surprise."

"Where at?"

"It's a surprise, Sweet Ellie," he said, kissing my cheek. "You'll have to come with me to find out where and what we're doing it."

I kissed his cheek back, wrapping my arms around his neck. Finally, I nodded and finished up the cleaning, and

Gage told me to go pack some overnight clothes. I found that odd but did so anyway, refusing to miss out on any time with him. I was even more excited when he told me to bring a few art supplies. I wasn't sure which art supplies to bring so I went along with some paint, my sketchpad, and my drawing pencils.

I stuffed some shorts and tank tops into my small bag, my toiletries, and even a nice outfit consisting of skinny jeans, a sheer black blouse, and the Chuck Taylor's Gage bought me. I adored him for buying them for me. I'd even teased him and said we could be twins and match one day. I didn't know when that "one day" would be, but I tried to look over fitting the future into our present.

After I was all packed, I sent Ben a text telling him who I was spending my night with and he sent me a winky face along with another "be truthful and open up" reminder. I tried to not let it get to me as I tossed my bag onto my shoulder, headed for the front door of the bus, stepped out, and met Gage at Stan's truck.

"You all set?" he asked, taking my bag and art supplies from me and knocking on the glass of the trunk to get Stan to unlock it.

"Yep," I sighed. "All set."

After tossing in my bag, he stepped in close. "You know what I've just realized?" Gage asked, his nose skimming across my cheek.

"What?" I breathed.

"I haven't gotten a kiss from you all day, Ellie." His mouth hovered right above my lips. His voice had deepened and turned silky. I shivered, delighted by the nearness of his lips. It was fall, so it was a cool night in New York, but with him this close, my insides were set on fire. Warm tingles were running all over my skin.

"How about you take one from me?" I grinned wickedly.

He raised an eyebrow, his smile expanding. "Look how untamed you've become. I hope it isn't because of me," he teased, smirking.

I laughed as he chuckled, and soon our lips met. Fire sparked throughout my entire body, trailing down to my toes and causing them to curl. I breathed in his fresh, masculine cologne and sank my fingernails into his shirt, gripping onto him, never wanting to let go. There was urgency between us. It grew as he licked the curve of my upper lip and grinned devilishly behind it. I brought his tongue to my mouth, coaxing it with a few moans and delightful groans. He nibbled at my lower lip, his hand sneaking from my waist to my breast. He swallowed my next moan and I panted as he started kissing my neck. But then a loud horn beeped, snapping us out of our eager, fervent kiss.

"You have time for that later, you two!" Stan yelled out his window. "Get your asses in this truck. I ain't got all night!"

I giggled, glancing over my shoulder. Smirking, Gage smoothed his crumpled black T-shirt and then grabbed my hand, walking around to the passenger door behind Stan. "Sorry, Stan," Gage said, laughing as he opened the door and allowed me in first.

Stan only chuckled, cranking the car.

As soon as Gage was in the car, Stan pulled out of the parking lot and we were off to my "surprise" destination.

SINGLE DOVE

The hotel where Gage and I were dropped off was way more than luxurious. Tower after tower, lights over lights. It was beautiful and stood out next to the New York harbor. Of course Gage had to be fancy and go with the penthouse suite. As the elevator opened, I marveled at the scenery before me.

A spacious living room with a leather couch. Candles lit in every corner. A wide window took up one side of the room, and I rushed for it to gaze out. We were right beside the Atlantic Ocean. The water rippled and a few yachts and boats were parked near the shore. I gasped, completely in awe, and then heat smoldered my backside. Warm lips touched my neck and fire ran from my throat to my toes.

"You like it?" he asked, pulling my hair back to kiss the back of my neck. I smiled, realizing he meant his question in more ways than one. He moved in closer and my stomach pressed against the glass. His masculine scent filled my lungs and I breathed him in, lacing my fingers through his.

"This was sweet of you, Gage," I whispered.

He slowly stopped kissing me, pulling his hand away to grab mine and spin me around. "You think this is all?" he asked, a large smile on his face.

I looked around, frowning. "What's wrong with it? I love it."

He chuckled. "You're adorable, Ellie. This is only the warm-up. We have bigger plans for tonight." He kissed my cheek before pulling away from me and going for my bag. Making his way toward me, he smiled and handed it to me. "Go get changed. I know how you like to look 'presentable'"—he made quotation marks with his fingers—"as you put it."

I smiled, clutching my bag. "I do. And I'm glad you know it."

Gage tenderly kissed me on the lips before letting me go.

When I'd satisfied myself with how I looked and how I braided my hair to the side, I stepped out. He was waiting for me on the sofa, strumming his guitar. He heard me and looked up, smiling adorably. "You ready?"

"Yeah," I murmured.

He stood from the sofa, strapped his guitar around him, took my hand, and we were on our way.

Gage and I filled up on Italian food and wine. We laughed a lot and talked just enough. We flirted and held hands. Hugged and kissed. I was having so much fun and trying my hardest to block out my time limit with him. There were moments when I thought about it and it literally hurt my heart.

I hated it.

We strolled the city, gazing up at the high towers and twinkling lights. The stars were bright and seemed closer than normal. The streets were calm but somewhat busy. A few taxis were still raiding the streets, but it was soothing, especially having Gage by my side, hand-in-hand. We'd even passed a few people who knew Gage right on the spot and he autographed a few things for them. I was glad it was a group of calm teenagers. I don't think I could have handled girls revealing their tits that night. It would have killed my entire mood.

After Gage took a few goofy pictures with his fans, he hugged some of them and then came back to me. His smile stretched as he opened his arms wide and circled them around my waist. He kissed my cheek repeatedly, and I giggled, begging him to stop.

We continued our walk, hearing the occasional flickers and clicks of cameras. I thought about flipping some of them off, but Gage told me to act like they weren't even there. After a while, it became easier because he would steal away my attention, but it still aggravated me because we had no privacy whatsoever.

"I wanna take you somewhere," Gage said, smiling down at me.

"Where?" I asked curiously.

His eyes softened and he pecked my lips with his before flagging down a taxi. We climbed in and he leaned forward to whisper something to the driver. I couldn't make it out, but the driver nodded and Gage handed him a two hundred-dollar tip. The driver gratefully accepted it and pulled off quickly.

I snuggled up to Gage, wrapping my arms around him and enjoying his warmth. He always felt good against me. I enjoyed his forehead kisses during the ride, his arm casually draped around me. I didn't think he noticed, but I would always catch him staring and he'd smile at me as if he never had been. It was sweet. Innocent. Cute. I adored him.

Finally the taxi slowed down and we arrived at our destination. The driver thanked Gage for his tip, but Gage shrugged it off as if it were no big deal. Gripping my hand, he shut the door behind us and as soon as we turned around, I was struck with awe. I didn't know where we were, but the street was long and bright posters were everywhere. Lights of various colors shone for miles, bringing even more attention to the area. A few people walked by, some calling for a taxi and some enjoying the scenery just as much as I was.

"Where are we now?" I asked.

"Times Square," he murmured in my ear. My skin buzzed as he placed a hand on the small of my back. "Come on," he said, cocking his head to his left. We walked hand-in-hand down the street until he took a turn and we came across an area filled with bench seats. A few people were already sitting—a man reading a newspaper, a woman with a book and a cup of coffee. There were a few others around doing pretty much the same thing. Even a few couples were cuddled up.

"Gage," I whispered.

I looked at him and he smiled. "I wanted to do something here. My mom used to talk about it non-stop when I was a kid. It was always her dream to come to Times Square… just to sing to me."

I smiled, taking a seat on the front row. He sat beside me, grinning boyishly. He then pulled his guitar around him, setting it on his lap and adjusting his fingers along the strings. "You're going to sing?" I asked, excited.

"Mmhmm," he nodded. He looked down, focusing on his acoustic guitar. It was black, but the strings were blue. On the bottom was the band's name and Gage's was printed right above it in cursive. I figured it must have been custom made just for him. "You remember the song I was writing the other morning with Roy?"

I nodded. "Yeah."

"Can I sing it to you? You'll be the first to hear it."

I blushed ridiculously. "Of course, Gage. I'd love to hear."

He smirked, taking a brief glance into my eyes before focusing on his guitar again and clearing his throat. As he strummed, a few people walking by slowed down, wanting a good show. Some gasped, recognizing the stunning man with the guitar, and held still, ready for him to sing.

I watched the way his lips moved—absorbed the way his deep, silky voice filled me up and sent me on a high I'd never felt before. Each word was soft, caring. His voice made it much more intoxicating for me. It was lovely—he was lovely. He was singing from the depths of his soul. Sometimes he'd get higher; sometimes he'd get lower. Either way, I was thrilled by it. The final lyrics he sang were words I knew I would never forget for as long as I lived:

She was a single dove, a beauty,
A miraculous love, truly,
A new addiction I'd fight for,
My addiction, perhaps my heart and more.

BROKEN PROMISES

I couldn't resist the urge. I couldn't stop myself from allowing my fingers to crawl beneath Gage's shirt as we reached the very top floor in the elevator. Our eyes locked, intensity burned through us, and as soon as we reached our hotel door and he unlocked it, he dropped his guitar and took me in his arms.

He kissed me fiercely, deeply... passionately. I'd never felt a kiss so strong, and as much as I wanted to think nothing of it, I couldn't help it. I embraced it, drowned in his lips, his body. He cupped my face as we stumbled our way toward the nearest landing. My back gently landed on one of the sofas and he climbed on top of me. I stared up as he stared into my eyes, his hard, intense, and longing as he gazed at me. I saw something behind his eyes, but I couldn't figure out what it was. *It can't be love.* We weren't... were we?

The glass window was open wide revealing the high moon shining down on us. I looked at him again and he smiled. "I'm thinking, since we have all night, maybe we should take things slow," he murmured.

I swallowed but nodded my head anyway. He grabbed my hand, pulling me off the sofa and leading the way across the penthouse. I noticed the candles weren't melted. They looked like they'd just been lit. "Who was here?" I asked, smiling up at him.

"I have my ways," he said, taking note of the candles but still walking for the bedroom.

I smirked, remembering he had to make a phone call before we got back. He laced our fingers as we stepped into the bedroom. It was huge. A French window was above the king-sized bed against the north wall. A flat-screen TV was hung on the wall opposite the bed and two large dressers were against the east wall. The carpet was a light tan and looked extremely soft.

"Let's do something you love to do," Gage said, smiling.

I tilted my head. "What do you mean?"

"Paint... draw. Anything." He grinned, squeezing my hand.

I grinned back, nodding my head and going for my art supplies. I was thrilled he wanted to do the thing I loved most, with me. It was always a dream of mine—to paint with someone I really liked, so I eagerly gathered my things and rushed back to the room.

Gage was sitting on the edge of the bed, his shoes beside his feet and his head back, his hands planted behind him on the bed. The way he was leaning back gave definition to his chest beneath his shirt. I could make out the ripples, the lines and muscles. I wanted to hop on top of him and lick his entire body, but I held off, especially as he smiled innocently at me, making my thought process take an extremely wicked turn.

"So what are we doing?" he asked.

"Let's paint," I said, taking out a few sheets of paper. I pulled the paint out of the bag and told Gage to get some water for us. We sat on the floor after Gage spread out some newspapers and for the most part, painting with him was fun. We giggled as we painted our own silly pictures. He painted some odd-looking bird and named it Sweet

Ellie. I laughed at it and then he took a look at mine. I'd painted conjoining hearts, one blue and one red. His smile faltered a little bit as he looked from the painting to my eyes, but in an instant, he smiled warmly again.

Some paint from my brush splattered onto his arm and he declared war, swearing I did it on purpose. I laughed, begging him not to get paint on me (mainly in my hair), but of course he didn't listen. He didn't get it in my hair, but he did paint a thin purple line on my cheek. I placed my brush against the tip of his nose, leaving a bold green dot. His nose wiggled as he smeared it with his arm, chuckling, and then tackled me softly, nuzzling his nose in my neck.

"What do you say to a bath?" he whispered, taking my paintbrush from me and pulling me by the arm to help me sit upright. I looked down at the various colors of paint on me and agreed.

He took my hand, helping me to my feet and leading the way toward the bathroom. His walk was so seductive, so sexy, and I didn't think he realized it. His shoulders moved in swift but smooth movements. His hips swayed just enough to make me want to grab them and pull him against me. Ugh... he was just too damn beautiful.

As we stepped into the bathroom, the first thing I saw was the large Jacuzzi tub against one of the creamy walls. The wall behind it had a tall arched window above, revealing the enormous towers of New York City nearby. A few candles were set on the edge of the tub, flickering across the bathroom walls and creating a completely romantic atmosphere. I gazed in complete awe, taking in the off-white marble counters, the matching marble floors, the shower in the corner wall that had glass doors almost like the shower of the FireNine tour bus. I blushed, remembering the event that took place because of that shower.

Gage reached around me, kissing my neck tenderly. He circled his arms around my waist, reaching for the hem of my shirt. I allowed him to do what he wanted. We only had a few more days and I had a great night with him. Why not top it off with something steamy?

It wasn't until after he'd pulled my shirt over my head and tugged his off that I realized how quiet it'd gotten. Not that I minded; it just wasn't expected from him. I turned slowly to look into his eyes. He was already staring at me, his head tilted, eyes full of fire and passion. My eyes lowered to his chiseled upper half. I slowly ran the palms of my hands down his chest and he inhaled softly. He then nuzzled my neck and I giggled as his eyes softened and he kissed the tip of my nose.

His gaze then hardened a bit as he reached for the button of my jeans and slid them down my legs. I kicked them off and did the same for him. He smirked, standing before me in black boxers.

"You really don't get enough of black do you?" I teased.

He chuckled and my gaze fell down to the V hidden beneath the waistband of his boxers. The Matthew McConaughey V. I wanted to drool over it, but he laughed at me, snapping me out of my daze. "Bath, Ellie," he whispered, leaning forward to kiss my ear. I sparked with heat, nodding as I clutched his inked arms. "I'll go play some music."

I nodded, knowing he was only using the music as a distraction. What he really wanted was for me to run the water, add bubbles, and then wait for him. I thought it was best to do just that, so I watched him step out and shut the door behind him.

Sighing, I stepped in front of the mirror and ran a hand through my hair. It was odd that I was… smiling. *Why am I smiling?* I tried to drop the smile, but it kept returning. It kept showing up. I shook my head at myself, considering the Eliza in the mirror silly for her goofy grin.

I ran some bath water, making sure it was warm and satisfying, added bubbles, and then stripped out of my bra and panties. I sank into the tub, releasing a heavy sigh. It felt ten times nicer than it looked. I washed myself up, getting rid of the paint all over my face and arms, and not long after, music played. I couldn't believe my ears. Ed Sheeran, one of my favorite singers. Did he know? I wasn't sure, but hearing Ed singing about giving him love made me smile like an idiot.

Gage stepped into the bathroom moments later, raking a hand through his dark, tousled hair. He stepped behind me to get out of my view, and I heard uncomfortable shifting and rustling. Suddenly it felt awkward because I knew exactly what he was doing. I knew exactly what was wrong. He was nervous and he was most likely staring in the mirror, making sure he was stable enough to go through with the rest of this night. I took a peek over my shoulder to see him gripping the edges of the counter, staring directly at his reflection. His eyes were as hard as granite, his lips pressed into a tight line. Finally, he sighed and pulled back, and I turned forward quickly, sinking into the warmth of the water.

I waited for what seemed like hours before he finally sighed again and stepped into the bath. I didn't dare look at him. Ed Sheeran was on repeat, and hearing him sing about love was really getting to me. My heart banged against my chest and I grew nervous, wondering what Gage was going to do, say—anything. Whatever it was, I wasn't prepared for it. Ben kept saying over and over again to get the truth out of him, but I didn't want the truth. The truth was going to hurt both of us, so it was best to pretend nothing was here between us. It was safe to think we were still just a fling. But I knew we were way more than that... and I really didn't know what to do about it.

Gage shifted, clearing his throat. I looked up and his head was tilted, and he was smiling. "You okay?" he asked.

"Yeah," I breathed. Of course, it was a lie.

He smirked wholeheartedly and then moved to my side. I smiled at him as he grabbed my hand and brought it to his lips. Right after he pulled his lips away, he licked them. "You look tense. Want a massage?"

"Sure." I turned slowly, my heart beating a mile a minute. Gage sighed, reaching for my shoulders and circling his thumbs on my shoulder blades. I eased up after a while as the music played and his fingers kneaded into my back. It felt nice, different. "You're really good," I said, laughing a little.

"Yeah," he breathed. I tensed then, hearing the huskiness of his voice. He moved in slowly, and I slid back to get between his legs. He continued the massage for a few more moments before stopping slowly, pulling my hair away from my neck, and kissing it. I clutched my thigh, tensing again. He kissed between my shoulder blades and I shuddered, delighted by the warmth of his feathery-light lips. He continued down, one hand on my shoulder, the other reaching around to get to my middle and pull me against him.

Heat bombarded me and butterflies thrashed in the pit of my belly as he brought his lips back up and kissed the lobe of my ear. He then dropped his other hand from my shoulder to pull me against his body completely. He breathed into my hair, his whole body rigid. He was panting and his thick erection caved into my back. I moaned and he whispered my name faintly, begging me to turn around.

I turned around and sat on his lap. The water moved between us, but as I inched in closer, all I could feel was him against me. As I stared into his eyes, they were glazed over with passion, fire, yearning... I thought I caught *love,* but he blinked quickly and pulled my face to his. He kissed me, his tongue lapping over mine and his panting picking up with each coax of his tongue. He swallowed my moans, his hands still clasping my face. I laced my arms around his neck, moving against him as if it would get me any closer. I knew what I wanted. I knew the only way to feel completely near him was if he were inside me.

"God, Eliza," he breathed raggedly, pulling his lips away to kiss my neck. My head fell back so I could expose my neck and let him taste me eagerly. "I've never felt like this before," he whispered.

"Like what?"

"This," he said between kisses on my collarbone. "I've never... wanted a woman so much." He stopped kissing me slowly to get a look into my eyes, but I was already staring at him, shocked. I tried not to panic because I knew I wasn't mistaken. There *was* love behind those eyes. Whole, passionate, and incredibly deep love. And I couldn't ignore it.

He probably thought my silence was meant for him to keep talking, but I wished he hadn't. He pulled me in by my lower back, keeping us close as he spoke. Our eyes were locked. It was hard for me to look away from him. "I think about you day and night, Eliza. I wake up and wish every morning you were lying in my bed beside me. Every time I'm really smiling, it's because I'm with you or I'm thinking about you." He shook his head, his gaze lowering. "I've felt something between us for so long, Eliza. So long. I've tried blocking it, ignoring it, avoiding it, and just remaining casual, but... I can't anymore. Not with you. I know if I try to pretend this doesn't matter—that we don't matter—then I might end up hurting you, and the last thing I wanna do is hurt you. I could never hurt you because hurting you is... hurting me."

Tears stung my eyes as he pulled one arm away to run his hand over his face. "Gage." I choked, still not blinking.

"Eliza... don't. I told you, don't say my name like that. Don't try and deny it. I've known it before I took your virginity. I've known it since day one of the tour. You were different, unlike the rest. With the other girls, it's nothing. With you I feel something. With you I can actually be myself. Instead of forcing smiles, you allow me to do so freely. Instead of holding back, you allow me to give my all." He cupped my face, his hazel eyes hard on mine. "Don't leave me, Eliza. You can't... I need you too much. I love you too much."

I choked again and then I broke into a sob. He looked me over, his eyes just as sad as mine, stinging with tears. I tried to pull away, but he held on. I wanted him to let me go, but more than anything I wanted to stay in his arms. I just wanted him to hold me. I never wanted to leave him, but I knew in only three days I was going to have to and it was going to crush both of us. His thumbs brushed my cheeks and then he pulled me forward to kiss my cheek.

"I know you love me, Eliza," he whispered. "I love you. I'm *in love* with you. And tonight I wanna prove it."

More tears fell as Gage stood and picked me up with him. He stepped out of the tub with me in his arms and went for the bedroom. More candles were flickering in the large room. They danced across the walls behind my blurry eyes. I hated crying. I felt so weak. What I really wanted to do was smile and enjoy my night with him.

Gage laid me on the bed, kissing my forehead repeatedly as he parted my legs with his knee. He stared at my tearstained face, but his eyes adored me, as if he found me more beautiful than ever. His kisses started at my cheeks, my nose, and then my lips. He kissed my lips repeatedly, cupping my face. Ed Sheeran was still on repeat and my tears thickened, but he simply brushed them away with his thumb.

Damn it, why couldn't I stop crying? Was it because I knew what I felt wasn't fake? Was it because I knew that even though he wanted me to stay, I would have to leave anyway? Thinking about the last question brought more hot tears to my eyes. I had a scholarship. I couldn't lose it. I worked too hard for it.

He looked past my tears, placing his lips on mine over and over again. He then moved southward, kissing my collarbone, my chest, slowly licking each nipple, kissing the cave in stomach, my belly button. He got to my sweet area and kissed me there, too. My toes curled as he kissed my thighs, my knees, and even each toe. I giggled at that one, and soon my tears evaporated.

He stood from the bed, dug in his bag for a condom, slid it on, and then climbed between my legs again. I expected him to go straight for it, but he didn't. Instead, he kissed me deeply, delicately, as if I were fragile and he might break me. I ran my fingers over the ridges of his abdomen and the tight curves of his arms. He groaned, kissing my neck and causing my head to fall back.

"I'm making love to you tonight, Eliza," he whispered in my ear, his voice heavy and husky.

My throat tightened, but I swallowed all emotions and nodded my head, bringing his face to mine again. I kissed him, pulling his body against mine so no space could be between us. I wrapped my legs around him, clinging to him for dear life, as if he would just randomly leave me.

He slid inside me slowly, pulling his lips away to get a look into my eyes. I stared back as the full feeling consumed me, causing a moan to brush past my lips. His eyes were soft with an edge of steel as he focused on every emotion that took hold of my face. This wasn't like it was when he took my virginity. I thought that was the best time of my life, but I was wrong. This was better because this wasn't just sex. This was *love*. Fiery, intense love, and I was enjoying it. He groaned as he thrust into me, stroking as gently as he could and lifting my leg around him to bury himself deeper.

He lowered himself, his fingers sliding up my arm to get tangled with mine. His other hand was in my hair as he kissed me over and over again. I could tell he wanted to let go, that he wanted to just release. By the glazed look in his eyes, I saw it coming, but he squeezed my hand and continued until I was there. Until I screamed his name, dragged my fingernails through the creases of his back, and moaned into his mouth.

He emptied himself right after me, grunting against my neck and shuddering a dozen times. Sweat spilled from his body and onto mine as he fell on top of me, both of us breathing heavily. His fingers were still tangled with mine. His breath trickled onto my neck and my ear, and I was completely satisfied with him against me.

I tangled my fingers through his hair and after a few moments, he whispered something to me that almost made me cry again. It was heartfelt, deep, and I knew he meant it.

"I love you, Eliza."

"I love you, too, Gage. So much," I whispered.

He seemed content with my reply because he leaned up on his elbow, kissed me while cupping my face, and then fell onto his back beside me with a heavy sigh. He was staring at me for a while, and I grabbed his hand again. He brought up his hand, my fingers still entwined with his, to kiss my knuckles, his gaze deep.

Caring.

Sincere.

Loving.

I couldn't look away.

Finally, he turned his head, but his fingers were still laced with mine. He stared at the ceiling as if in deep thought, but then his eyelids grew heavy and soon they shut. His panting transformed into even breathing, his chest sinking and rising. I knew he was about to fall asleep, but I had one question I really needed an answer to.

"Gage?" I whispered.

"Hmm?" He sounded restless.

"Why was it so hard for you to take my virginity?"

His breathing picked up again as he tensed. I held on to him tighter, listening as his heartbeat sped up. "I don't know... My sister, I guess," he murmured. I remained quiet, hoping he would continue, and surprisingly he did. "She was raped when she was eighteen. I hated that it happened to her because all she used to talk about before it happened was how she couldn't wait to meet the right guy and give herself to him. She said it was going to be the best feeling in the world." His voice cracked and my heart ached for him, holding on even tighter. "There was one night when she was crying about it and I tried to comfort her. She told me to promise her to never take a girl's virginity unless I was planning on loving that girl." My heart skipped a beat, and then he kissed my forehead. "I didn't know if I was ready to face love with you, Eliza," he whispered.

I nodded my head, completely understanding. I didn't know either and now that he explained it, it made me feel much better. That night when he took my virginity, I knew he loved me. He was falling for me even more while taking my innocence away. It comforted me to know he loved me way before I'd even given thought to it.

Sighing, Gage kissed my forehead again. I knew he didn't want to talk about it anymore, so I kept quiet, listening as his breathing evened out again. Ten minutes had passed and he'd become completely still. The tension faded, letting me know he'd fallen asleep.

I turned on my back, staring up as the ceiling spun above me. More tears threatened to spill, but I bit them back, begging my body to hold off. Unfortunately, my body worked against me, knowing I needed to let it out. My heart knew just as much as my mind did that in less than seventy-two hours, Gage and I were going to go our separate ways. He was opening up to me so much and I didn't want to let it go.

It killed me to know I would be leaving all of this behind, and the tears grew heavier, but I made sure not to sob. I didn't want to wake him. I didn't want him to know I couldn't stay. I was getting his hopes up by not telling him, but... I just couldn't. The look in his pleading eyes squeezed my heart and tore me apart. He was going to expect me to stay with him for the rest of the tour, but that wasn't going to happen. I had to get back to my own life. To reality. I had to go back to school, study, and get my degree. I had to make a living for myself, and I couldn't do that with Gage—not when he was going to constantly be on the go. Not when he had his own dreams to chase and his own accomplishments to take care of. Maybe in the future we could work something real out, but right now, we weren't ready. I wasn't ready.

We lived two completely different lives and it was unfortunate that I couldn't be a part of his like he wanted me to be. I couldn't be by his side at all times, even though it was all I wanted. I had to put my priorities first and that was school. I refused to be like my mother, who dropped out of college. I wanted to be better than her and prove to myself that I could do it.

At least Ben was right about one thing between Gage and me. I'd found out the truth from Gage. I knew how he really felt about me. I knew how I felt about him as well. It was too strong not to feel. He pulled me in each day, with each smile and each hug. Each tender kiss and each moment we shared together. It sucked that at the end of all our fun, it was going to hurt him to watch me leave. I didn't want to hurt him and knowing we were going to have to part ways was already ripping me in two. I didn't know exactly what he would do, how he would handle my decision once I told him. I really didn't want to say good-bye at all. I just wanted to leave... but I knew that would hurt him and break his heart even more.

I broke down then, facing the truth. On Sunday, the morning after their show, I was leaving to work for my own future, and I didn't know when I was going to see Gage Grendel again.

And damn it, it killed me.

I watched Gage sleep for most of the night. He always looked so peaceful when he slept. He mumbled a few names in his sleep. One was mine (and at the sound of it my heart thumped rapidly with delight) and the others were Kris and Mom. I worried he was having a nightmare because he started shaking and grumbling beneath his breath. If I weren't mistaken, a tear had fallen while he was still sleeping.

I reached for him immediately, shaking him out of his slumber. He inhaled deeply, his eyelids fluttering open as he clutched my hand. "It's okay, Gage. I'm still here," I whispered, stroking his hair. He was still panting uneasily, staring into my eyes. His were glistening beneath the pale moonlight, and I sighed. "What's wrong?" I asked.

He shook his head, blinking rapidly as he pushed on his elbows to sit up. "Uh… nothing. Just a nightmare." He sighed, running a rough hand through his hair. I studied him thoughtfully, my head tilting.

"Do you wanna talk about it?"

"No. We should probably go back to sleep."

I frowned. "Gage, please tell me what that was about. You were crying in your sleep."

"It happens." He shrugged, his gaze drifting to avoid mine.

I reached for his face, forcing him to look at me. "Tell me," I whispered, kissing his lips. "Please. I swear I won't judge you. I have no room to judge anyone, Gage."

His eyebrows furrowed, his eyes glistening again. He pulled his face away and sighed again, swallowing noisily. He then reached for the sheets to pull them over us again. He pulled me against him and I wrapped my arm around his middle, pressing my cheek against his chest. "I'll tell you if you tell me why you have PTSD."

I swallowed but nodded because, even though he didn't know it, I'd promised him and myself a long time ago that I would spill something in exchange for some background on him. "Okay. I will. Promise," I whispered.

Gage sighed, bringing his free hand up to his face and running his palm over it. His back was against the headboard, and as I looked up, he was staring across the room, suddenly in deep thought.

"Just tell me what you want to know," he murmured.

"Tell me about Kristina."

He stilled for a minute, but I grabbed his hand, assuring him it was going to be okay. "Kristina," he breathed out, squeezing my hand. "She was my favorite person on Earth... after my mom died." He paused again, swallowing the emotion. "My mom died when I was four years old, but I swear I remember everything about her. She called me her little prince, her hero. Her miracle."

"Her miracle?" I questioned curiously. "Why?"

"When I was born, I was sick. I wasn't as healthy as they thought I'd be. I had heart problems and they'd even told her I probably wouldn't live past five..." He choked and I squeezed his hand, begging him not to stop. "It was my birthday. I was turning four and my mom threw a huge birthday party for me. She never told me I had a chance of dying—that I was sick. I didn't find out until I was twelve and the only reason I found out then is because my dad yelled it at me while he was drunk one night. Had I known why she was throwing such a huge party for me, I wouldn't have relished in it. I would have been bitter, angry at her."

I frowned. "Why?"

"That same night she came in and kissed me goodnight. She told me she loved me so much, and I thought she was just being an emotional mom. Her tears confused me, but I was young. I couldn't question it like I wanted to. If I would've known what she was going to do, I would've stopped her. I would've begged on my knees for her not to go."

Gage choked again, his grip tightening around my hand. I adjusted myself beside him to get a good look at his face. A tear had fallen down his cheek. I gasped, reaching to brush it away. "What happened to her?" I whispered.

He didn't answer right away. He seemed to be recollecting his breath. He was reliving the memory and I hated how torn he looked. "My mom died to give me her heart. So I could live on... She gave it to me. We had the same blood type and she was tired of waiting on someone else's heart, so she..."

I gasped again as more tears ran from his eyes. He shut his eyelids, lowering his head and most likely reliving the memory. "Gage, I'm so sorry," I whispered, pulling him against me to hug him.

He sobbed a little, swiped at his face, and then pulled away, inhaling deeply. "I would have done anything to stop her. My mom meant so much to me. When I found out she passed away, Kristina told me it was just her time to go. She never went into detail, and I didn't think on it when I'd gone into surgery two days later and came out a healthy boy. My mom told me over and over again that she would die for me. That she would give up everything for me. I used to believe her, but I never thought she'd literally do it."

"Oh," I mumbled. "So where is Kristina now?"

He shook his head and glared at his lap. "I don't know." I remained silent. How could he not know where his own sister was? Before I could ask, he spoke up again. "A few years after my surgery, we moved from Texas to Virginia. Kris begged my dad to get us an apartment so we could move out, and he did, but of course he didn't do it for free. Kris had to pay him back. My dad was and still is a huge dick, and the only reason I'm glad he's a part of my life is because he gave the band and me our breakthrough. He introduced us to Ben and Ben took it from there, setting us up on gigs, traveling for talent shows, singing at parties, until finally we were picked up and given a record deal."

"Ben knows your dad?" I frowned. That was news to me.

"Yeah. He met my dad at his... strip club." He looked at me sheepishly and I laughed a little. "My dad owns a chain of strip clubs, and I hated it. He worked late nights, went in early for no apparent reason. I don't like what my dad did to my mom before she died. He broke her heart in more ways than one. He cheated on her countlessly with women he didn't even know... At least that's what Kris told me. We traveled so much that no place seemed like home except Suffolk." Gage clamped his mouth shut, looking at me again. "I guess he's a part of the reason I thought it was okay to do it as well. He was the only man around when I was younger. I thought it was cool he always had chicks on his hip. When I was a teenager, I knew it was wrong, but it felt good to do."

I pursed my lips, shaking my head teasingly. "You're drifting from Kristina again."

"Oh, right." He adjusted himself against the headboard, clearing his throat. "Well, after Kris and I moved out, we used to stop by my dad's club every week so she could get some money from him to pay certain bills. Kris searched all over for a job, but no one would hire her because... Well, she's, like, a girl version of me—tattoos, bed hair, love for music, kinda careless. We had the same characteristics, and I think that's why I loved her so much—not only because she was my sister, but because she was like a best friend as well. After my mom died, Kris was the one who raised me. We hardly ever had a penny and she hated asking my dad for money but did so anyway because she knew he'd give it to us. He'd only give it after a lecture, though. He'd always ask her to join the strip club and dance for him. He would tell her over and over again that she wouldn't have to worry about a dime, but she always refused. She would tell him over and over again that she had responsibilities—taking care of me.

"It wasn't until I was ten years old when things started to change. When Kris started drifting from me. She'd leave me home alone sometimes. She'd leave a note on the counter telling me to fix a sandwich and chips for dinner and to go to bed on time. I broke the curfew a few times while waiting on her. One night I wished I hadn't." Gage's features hardened as he pressed his lips together. "She came home drunk with matted hair, wearing fishnet stockings and too much perfume. Her makeup was smeared; her breath reeked of alcohol—she just didn't look like the Kris I knew. This started happening after she'd gotten raped. I could understand her pain, but I was upset she was trashing herself.

"I helped her get undressed, helped her into the shower, and even helped her get into bed that night. She kept shivering and I didn't know what else to do, so I curled up against her side to try and keep her warm. She still quaked, but it wasn't as hard. I knew exactly what was happening to her, so that night I made her promise to stay away from Dad and his club. I made her promise she would find a real job and come home to me like she was supposed to. She was all I had. I didn't want to lose her, too."

I bit my bottom lip, thinking he'd continue, but he remained silent, his eyes distant. "Did she stop?"

He laughed humorlessly. "If she stopped, I wouldn't be so upset with her right now. I would know where she is. Who she's dating and what she's doing every day."

"Oh," I whispered. It was all I could manage. I could see the pain in his glistening eyes, but he was trying to fight it.

"I won't act like she didn't try, though. She did. That same night she kissed my forehead and said, 'Okay, kiddo.' She did well for the next five years. She found a job at a retail store and went to work every morning while I went to school. She'd pick me up after school and we'd go out to eat, to the park, or just go home and hang around the house and watch movies. We'd make songs together, play our guitars—she taught me how to play—and we'd be our own band. It was fun... but then she started disappearing again. When it happened again, I was fifteen. It was my freshman year and I'd just met Deed, Roy, and Montana. They occupied most of my time and sometimes I'd come home late from a night out with them... but she still wouldn't be home.

"Then one night, I knew I couldn't face her again. I came home from practicing guitars with Roy at the park. It was late when I got back—around three in the morning maybe. I remember it was the weekend. Shower water was running when I stepped in, so I knew she was home. It wasn't until after I'd eaten a bowl of cereal, changed into pajamas, and then slid between my sheets that I realized how long she'd actually been in the shower. I scrambled out of bed and rushed for the bathroom. To my luck, it was unlocked, but I hated what I saw. She was bent over in the tub, her head hanging beneath the shower water. It was cold. I felt it as I pulled her against me in a panic. She had vomit on her shirt, in her hair, on her too-short dress. She looked like complete shit and it freaked me out.

"The next morning, Kris was nowhere to be found. The next week, she was nowhere to be found. The next month, still nowhere to be found. I picked up two part-time jobs and in between those, I had school and then I would practice with the band. I was exhausted, ready for it all to end. I was on the verge of dropping out one time, but I didn't. It was hard not to do, but I motivated myself to keep going.

"I hated Kris for so long. She promised me she would give up on it. She promised she would always be here for me—that she'd always take care of me. She promised that she would be just as caring and sweet as Mom. She promised that when my dream happened, she would be backstage, rooting me on. She broke all her promises. I haven't seen Kris since I was nineteen years old. It kills me to know it's been five years.

"The last time I talked to her was when the band had just signed our record deal. We were happy, money was rolling in, and I'd even bought my own condo. I don't know how Kris found me, but she showed up at my doorstep one day. She looked terrible, Eliza. Sick," he said, his eyes horrified. "She was skinnier than I'd ever seen her before. Bags were beneath her eyes; her hair was matted; her lips were chapped. She said she was okay, but I knew she was doing every drug in the book. Of course I let her in. She was still my sister. I still loved her. I even let her stay at my place that night and begged her not to leave.

"She did anyway... and she took most of the money I had in my closet. She... robbed me. And I hated her. It took years for me to forgive her. I got drunk as hell one day and called my dad to ask for her number. It was stupid of me, but I ended up cursing her out. I was pissed. Unfortunately, Penelope showed up and heard every single word. She'd even found out my sister's name. Now you see why I have to keep her close. She knows too much. I don't want her ratting me or my family out, and as upset as I am with Kris, I don't want anyone figuring out who she is or where she is and blasting it. I'd rather her be a nobody than for the whole world to know I have a damn crackhead for a sister. I still love her."

I nodded, squeezing his hand.

He sighed, tears pricking at the rims of his eyes as he looked away. "I miss her... every day. I miss my mom. I miss them so much, and I wish my mom never sacrificed herself because if she hadn't, Kris never would have taken that route. She never would have gotten raped. Never would have turned into a stripper. A druggie."

"But you wouldn't be where you are now, Gage. Your mom loved you," I said.

He swallowed, shaking his head. "I know. It just... it hurts so fucking much. I would give it all up to be reunited with them again. I'd give up everything if my mom had a chance to come back."

Gage clutched the edge of the bed, a tear falling down his cheek. I reached to wipe it, but more continued to fall and, eventually, he started sobbing. I held on to him as he let it all out. Now I knew why it was so hard for him to talk about it. Gage used to have a hard life. A terrible past. We had a lot in common and that frightened me. Now I knew why he didn't want to let me go, why he always compared me to Kristina.

He went numb after she disappeared. While he was with her, he was happy, loved. His sister was his world; I knew it. He loved her deeply and I could tell by how much he was crying in my arms. Gage put all his emotions on hold until he met *me*. With me, he loved again, and knowing it made my heart ache even more. It was only getting harder for me to leave.

After a few minutes Gage finally settled down, clutching on to me as if I were going to let him go. His face was buried in my neck, his breathing light as it ran down my chest. I sighed, kissing his cheek. "You can tell me another time," he whispered.

I nodded, understanding his statement, glad because I wasn't up for freaking out and panicking. I had my inhaler in my bag, but I hated touching it because touching it meant I'd been thinking about my mom, the she-devil. Eventually we fell asleep in each other's arms. He'd fallen asleep before me and before I drifted, I was thinking way too much.

I was worried—afraid I'd hurt him again. I didn't want to hurt him like Kristina did, but I knew leaving was only going to rip his heart in half. I was torn, stuck between my life and my future and his heart. Each minute I thought on it, it got harder and harder for me to breathe, but I inhaled, holding him close and forcing myself to shut my eyes.

I didn't know what I was going to do and time was only winding down. I had to let him know sooner or later.

STAY

The following morning, Gage and I called room service for some breakfast. I went with cinnamon-flavored oatmeal and sliced bananas, while Gage went with a simple bowl of cold cereal.

While we were eating, it kind of bothered me that he wasn't saying much. Yes, he was still smiling and touching me, but it seemed a little off. I tried to think nothing of it, but every time I would look into his eyes, there were millions of questions behind them. There was also grief and hurt from last night.

"Are you okay?" I finally asked after finishing my cereal.

He looked at me over his bowl of cereal, his head nodding. "Fine, Ellie."

"Are you sure? You seem kind of... off."

He smirked, slurping down his milk before setting his bowl on the table. "I'm great, Ellie. I feel much better about last night, but... I wanted to ask you something."

"Okay." I straightened myself, dropping my spoon into my bowl. "Go ahead."

"There are two things I wanna talk about."

I nodded, gulping, and he sighed, running a hand through his wet hair.

"First thing is your PTSD. Tell me about it. Why it happens, how you control it... so on. You were trembling last night and whimpering. I didn't know whether to wake you or leave you, but you woke yourself."

"I did?" I whispered.

He nodded, but I couldn't remember waking up at all.

I swallowed again, folding my fingers on top of the table. Behind Gage there was the window that revealed the New York harbor and the boats and yachts at bay. A few seagulls stirred around the sails, flapping diligently, twisting and turning. Before the sunrise, it was truly a beautiful sight.

"My mom…" I trailed off, shutting my eyes briefly and seeing her face appear. Gage's chair scraped across the floor and I looked up just as he was standing to bring his chair beside me.

"What about her?" he asked.

"She was a bitch." I laughed dryly. He didn't smile, though. His face was stern, waiting for me to provide more. "Let's just say she's the worst mom on the planet. Since I've started storing memories, all the ones I have of her are terrible. She was manipulative, abusive, deceiving. She knew nothing about the value of family—nothing about protecting her own flesh and blood." I gripped my spoon, but he leaned forward, loosening my grip and lacing his fingers with mine. "Should I start with my worst memory of her?" I asked, forcing a smile.

"If that's what you'd like me to hear," he whispered, watching my face intently. I gripped his hand, forcing myself not to break down. I was told over and over again by Ben not to relive it—to just forget about it—but being with Gage was making me think about it all over again. My past. My pain. All of it.

"Well… I had just turned thirteen. I was no longer a child, but a teenager, and quite frankly, I was excited about it. I didn't expect my mom to get me anything for my birthday, but usually she would be a bit more lenient and leave me alone. At least she knew when my birthdays were." I shrugged. He smiled.

"I remember it like it was yesterday. The day my mom got married, it was a few weeks after my thirteenth birthday. Her husband's name was Jeremy. He had a beer belly, was balding; his teeth were rotten, and he had terrible body odor. I didn't know what my mom saw in him. She was a bitch, yes, but she's a spitting image of me. Pale skin and all. But she's gorgeous. Same light-blue eyes, same nose, mouth, cheeks, and dimples. The only difference is her hair is darker and sandier than mine, but we're complete opposites. I admit, I get my personality from Ben." I lifted a lock of my hair, twirling it around my finger. I could feel Gage staring at me, but I was no longer looking his way. I was zoned in on my empty bowl, my eyes completely distant, remembering it all.

"Jeremy was cool at first. We hardly talked to one another and that's why I thought he was a nice guy— because he didn't bother me. He worked for a plumbing company and worked early mornings and late nights. Sometimes he wouldn't come home and I would find my mom crying in her bedroom, most likely over him. He was a cheater... a liar. Then there was one night during my eighth-grade year when things turned... bad.

"I was drawing at our dining table. Jeremy came home around one that morning and his eyes were bloodshot red. His clothes were all sloppy and disgusting, and as soon as he stepped in, his gaze locked on mine. Only his was deadly. Mom sat up on the sofa and stared at him. She was groggy, but she knew just as well as I did what was about to happen. She stood up and looked directly at me. 'I told her,' she said, pointing at me. 'I told her exactly what you said and she didn't do it. She didn't wanna.'

"Jeremy slammed the door and I remember being scared shitless. 'Then I guess a punishment is necessary for disobeyin',' he said. I was terrified. I'd never heard him sound so dark or even seen my mom quake with fear over him that much. Jeremy came for me and gripped my arm, and I yelped because his grip was way too tight. I remember it leaving a bruise that I had to cover up for weeks. My heart was beating a mile a minute as he yanked me in front of him, gripped a lock of hair on the back of my head, and shoved me on the floor." I pressed my lips as my throat dried out. I squeezed my eyes shut, feeling Gage squeeze my hand in his. A few kisses were placed on my cheek, my temple, and my forehead, until he whispered to me that it was okay and to keep going. I nodded, swallowing down all the emotion.

"He dragged me to my mom's bedroom…" My voice broke as I squeezed my eyes tighter, but I couldn't fight the tears or the memories. "He… tossed me on the bed… and my mom was just standing there, watching everything. He kept repeating how he needed the money, how important it was to him and how he was going to teach me a lesson. Mom just smirked and folded her arms, shaking her head at me. I hated her so much for not helping, even when I was crying out to her—even when I begged her to protect me. What she said hurt me more than anything, and to this day I always hear her say it. 'I'm sorry, Liza, but you knew this was important. When we need money, it's not a joke. Should've done what was asked of you.'"

I hadn't realized I was sobbing, swiping at my face with my free hand. The memories burned me. They stirred my stomach and I felt like vomiting. My breathing turned into deep wheezing and Gage grabbed hold of either side of my face, making me look at him. "Eliza, breathe. Calm down and breathe, babe."

I swallowed, nodding my head and hoping it would work. I couldn't see him through the blur my tears created, but I knew his eyes were full of sorrow. His face had hardened, his jaw was ticking, but he nodded his head, telling me continuously to breathe for him. Surprisingly, as I watched his face, my panting decreased and my grip around his arm slacked. He noticed and smiled at me, leaning forward to kiss my tears away. "That's my sweet Ellie," he whispered, kissing my nose.

I smiled lightly, my eyes falling to stare at my lap. "It's just hard to think about again. He hit me so much, even after that night. Another night, he yanked me from the bed to toss me against the wall. I cried to my mom again, but she turned her back to me and walked off. After that night, I never trusted her again. He whipped me... He left marks that wouldn't heal for months. He left bruises from hitting me against the head, punching me in my stomach... shoving me against my back, making my nose bleed after I hit the ground." I sniffled as more tears shed.

"The worst part..." I choked out, "was that she never bothered to help me unless she got something in return.

Unless I stole from other people for her or unless I agreed to fight other girls my age in cage fights so she could make some extra cash. I guess that was a good thing, though. I learned how to fight for myself, even if I did end up with a black eye or busted lip. I started fighting against Jeremy when I was in high school, but he was always stronger. I would fight kids in the streets who talked about me or made fun of me. Most times I won... but that wasn't me. I wanted a normal childhood and a normal life. I didn't like how I was living for them, robbing for them, breaking bones and shedding blood for them.

"I was this shelled-in girl who didn't know what to do with her life, where to go, or even how to handle certain situations. After I moved in with Ben, things got better for me, but I didn't know how to act around him—or anybody—so I kept quiet. I didn't say anything to anyone, and I kept my distance as best as I could." I peered at Gage, who was already staring at me, his hazel eyes burning with sincerity. "I didn't start being myself until I started hanging around you."

He smiled widely at that, his teeth sparkling from the sun beaconing through the wide window. "Glad I could help, Eliza," he whispered and then kissed me. He cupped the back of my neck and I moaned, falling into his embrace. He then pulled away, kissing my cheek a few times before sitting back and exhaling. "Wow... that was... a lot to take in. I'm sorry that happened to you. If you want, we can find him and I can beat his ass for you."

I giggled, shaking my head. "No. That won't be necessary. They're both in my past now, and I'm never going back."

"But what about Ben? During all that, where was he?"

I shrugged. "When I first moved in with Ben, he told me he finally figured out he was gay when I was a baby. He stopped sleeping with my mom, stopped coming home, and he spent most of his time with some man named Franco. I guess there was a day he finally had the courage to tell her, and when he did, she kicked him out and threatened that if he ever showed his face again, she would take him to court and demand child support. From what I know, Ben was already living on a tight budget. He's told me plenty of times he would've taken me away, but he thought my mom was good. He never saw the abusive side in her. When I told him about how she watched Jeremy hit me, he was shocked. He didn't think she'd let anyone hurt me since I was all she had."

I sighed, shrugging again. "He was obviously wrong. I wanted to call Ben every time I felt hurt or alone, but I didn't know where he was. Mom moved across town, I went to a new school, and she changed our numbers. I found out Ben didn't live in the same place he told me about when I tried to visit him after school one day. Someone around there told me he'd gotten evicted. His phone was always off because he couldn't pay the bill, so we ended up losing contact until he visited every high school in Suffolk just to find me. He tells me every day he would have done anything to help me, but he felt I was in better hands with my mom. He didn't have anything going for himself. He was living off of friends. His choices back then were between food on the table or a roof over his head. He never had enough to have both. At least my mom had a job at one point. She paid bills. She fed me daily. Ben couldn't do that. His didn't get paid well enough."

Gage nodded, grabbing my hand to wrap his fingers around mine. "That's seriously fucked up of your mom."

"Yeah, I know. She's selfish. Always has been. I don't know how he didn't see it coming."

Gage sighed, shaking his head. He was quiet for a few seconds, but then he looked at me, forcing a smile. "So the other thing I wanted to ask was about you leaving..." He paused, running a heavy hand through his hair. "Is there any way I can get you to stay? You know I'd do anything for you, right?"

I lowered my gaze, biting the corner of my bottom lip. "Gage... I can't stay. School means too much to me. I have to build a life of my own. I was given a scholarship from University of Virginia. I have to keep working for my degree."

"But I can help you. I can give you whatever you want if you just tell me."

I shook my head. "I'm sure you'd do anything for me." I cupped his face. "*I know* you would do anything for me, but this is something I wanna do for myself. I wanna build my own life, not have someone try and build it for me. Just like you and the band worked hard to get where you are, I wanna work hard to be successful. I wanna be able to look back and see that I actually accomplished my own dreams. There'll always be time for us. Don't worry." I tried not to choke afterward. It was hurting me to say, especially as the rims of his eyes reddened and glistened, but after only a second, he nodded his head.

"The only thing I'm asking is for you to say good-bye to me the right way. I don't want this between us to die. I love it too much. I love *you* too damn much. I didn't think it was possible for me, but damn... It's un-fucking-believable." He smirked and I smiled sincerely as I pulled him in against me and held on. I wasn't sure how I was going to say good-bye, but at least he wasn't making it too hard for me. "Just think about it, Eliza. I know you're scared I might hurt you and forget about you, but I promise I'm trying. I promise I won't. I know I can give you the world and more if you want it. I'll work hard to keep you happy."

"I know," I whispered over his shoulder, but there was no need to think about it.

I had to go.

During the ride back to the buses, we cuddled and talked about how he thought his performance was going to go on Saturday. He told me he had it in the bag and that the boys had been practicing so much they had no choice but to be amazing. I agreed. The boys practiced most mornings or early afternoons. It was hard to do without Deed, but they made do. Deed practiced on the bus, trying to regain his strength. He still sounded awesome.

As we pulled into the parking lot, I hopped out and Gage kissed me good-bye. He had an interview at a radio station in thirty minutes and couldn't be late. Our fingers lingered on each other's as he took slow steps away, his smile gentle and loving. Finally, he stole another kiss and then hopped into the car. I watched him leave and sighed.

I didn't see Gage for the rest of the day. I knew he was with his band, so I took the time to paint. I painted Gage's beautiful face, of course. I'd even created a new logo for FireNine and thought it was pretty cool.

Then the fresh, beautiful memories came back. Putting paint all over Gage's glorious body. Watching the paint cover some of his tattoos. The way I giggled and he laughed as he tackled me just to put a dot of paint on the center of my forehead. I sighed because it was so vivid, so romantic... so *surreal*.

The next morning, I felt like I was going to hurl. It was Saturday, the day of the boys' show. Thinking about it made me sick to my stomach. It made me so sick that I didn't even attend the show. I knew I should have. I should have been there to support Gage, but my body refused for me to go. The entire day I was grabbing my stomach, a trash bin by my side. I hated how sick I felt, how lonely I felt. I thought I was overreacting... That is, until I finally vomited.

I drank some orange juice to sooth my tummy, then went to my room to do something I really didn't want to do. Pack. I packed up everything, made the bed, fluffed the pillows, and even cleaned the bathroom. I cleaned the living room as well, and when I was out of stuff to do, I slouched down on the couch and tears burned the rims of my eyes. I held back, swallowing and breathing through my nostrils.

Gage didn't show up that night either, and it hurt my heart, but I knew it was necessary. Maybe he knew I wasn't taking him up on his offer and I'd chosen to go home. Maybe he knew as much as I did that I had to go, even when he didn't want me to. I should have been satisfied with that... right? That should have made me happy because it meant it would be easier for me to leave. I wouldn't have to worry about hurting him.

Finally, the tears fell, as I realized maybe he was out doing something with another girl. Any girl. He could have been doing it just to forget. He probably knew he wouldn't be able to hold me back, so I broke down, sobbed into my hands until I couldn't cry anymore. I hated how much it hurt. How much *love* hurt. I was so used to being myself, avoiding boys, and doing my own thing, and then *bam*, there's Gage Grendel. He had my heart and I didn't even know I'd given it to him.

Full of sorrow, I stood and went to my room, nowhere near ready for Sunday. It was time; I knew. I had to let it go and tell myself that my life and career was more important... even if I did have an aching heart during the process.

I woke up early Sunday. I turned off the alarm on my phone, climbed out of bed grudgingly, brushed my teeth, got dressed, and then grabbed my bags. Ben was already waiting in the kitchen with a mug in his hand, which most likely contained coffee. I adjusted the strap of my bag on my shoulder, giving him a forced smile.

"Morning, sweetie," he whispered.

"Morning," I sighed, dropping my bags by the door. I slid my fingers into my back pockets, staring at Ben who was staring at me. "What?" I asked, suddenly self-conscious. I knew I looked horrible from my lack of sleep, but he didn't have to stare at me.

"Nothing," he said simply, then took a sip of his coffee.

"Is Marco already out?" I asked, reaching for my bags again. The sooner I was home, the better. I couldn't linger around because lingering meant wallowing again.

"Yeah, Liza. Go ahead." He forced a smile, but my eyebrows knitted, confused by his staring and short responses.

"Why are you looking at me like that?" I finally asked, twisting around to look at him.

He paused in taking a sip of his coffee as he stared into my swollen eyes. He then placed his coffee down on the counter and sighed, and I hated myself for taking my heartache out on him. "Liza," he murmured again, stepping out of the kitchen. He met up to me, pulled me in for a hug, and I squeezed my eyes shut, begging for no tears. "Sweetie, I know you're upset you have to go," he said, rubbing my back. "I'm sorry it has to be like this for you. I'm sorry it's so hard." He pushed me back by the shoulders and a tear fell down my cheek. "You know just as well as I do that school and your future comes first. It's all you've ever talked about. You come before any guy, no matter if he has your heart or not. There'll always be chances to see Gage again—"

"It won't be the same, Ben," I said, cutting him off midsentence.

"How will it not?"

"It just... won't. I know it. I haven't seen him in two nights. He knows it, too."

"Two nights?" His lips twisted as he pulled back. "Oh. I'm sorry, Liza Bear."

"It's fine. He just made it easier for me to go." I turned my back to Ben, bending down to reach for my bags again. "I'll be ready to go when you are."

His lips parted, as if he were going to say something, but he decided to hold off and nod his head instead. I swung the door open and as soon as I did, my breath caught at the sight of Gage. My heart skipped a beat, looking at his fist that was about to knock.

His gaze swung up quickly as the door opened, and as he saw me, his eyes softened. There were dark circles beneath them, like he hadn't slept in hours. His clothes looked worn and used, and his hair was messier than the norm but still unbelievably sexy. I took a look over my shoulder, glad Ben was making his way down the hallway.

I then looked at Gage who had taken a step down, his eyes pleading. "Eliza, can we talk?" he asked. Right after he asked, he took a glance at the bags in my hands and on my shoulder.

"There's nothing to talk about, Gage." I stepped down and walked past him to get across the parking lot and to Marco's truck, but before I could make it, he caught my arm and spun me around.

"Eliza, stop. I'm sorry. I got... I got caught up."

"With what, Gage?" I snapped, yanking my arm free. He swallowed, his head lowering. "With fucking your whores? The dozens of skanks who only want you for your stardom?" My tone was harsh, I knew it, but I was furious. I couldn't stop. "I thought we had fun. I actually wanted something more. I considered telling you good-bye the right way, but then you just... you disappeared on me." My eyes burned as my voice cracked. He lifted his head and reached for my face, but I pulled back. "Don't touch me. Just go away."

"Eliza, I'm sorry. I swear. I got caught up! Penelope wouldn't leave. She threatened me after seeing us together Friday night. She's been watching me. I don't know how she's been doing it, but she threatened to tell about Kris if I didn't spend time with her. I'm not letting her do that."

I scowled at him, jabbing a finger against his chest. "You were with *Penelope*?" I snarled. "Seriously!"

"I'm sorry! I told you about her. She knows too much. I tried calling Ben to get in contact with you, Eliza. I called almost every chance I could, but his phone kept going straight to voicemail—I even came here when I got a chance, but no one answered the fucking door!"

"You swore, Gage! You fucking swore you would leave her alone for me!"

"Eliza, I-I'm sorry."

I shook my head with incredulous eyes. I couldn't believe him. While I was alone and worried about him, he was with her. Vicious thoughts came to mind and I wanted to slap him so badly, but I held off, biting my lip.

"It's good you were with her, Gage," I said. "It's good."

His eyes struck with pain. "How? Why would you say that?"

"Because it makes it easier to leave. It makes it easier to forget about whatever it was between us. I knew it wouldn't work."

His mouth fell open, gaping. He took a step back, as if I'd just shot him right in the heart. Perhaps that's what it felt like because as I went over my words, I realized how harsh they sounded. But he hurt me. I couldn't let it go. The night we shared at the hotel... what was that to him?

"I don't know why I put so much trust in you. You warned me yourself. You're fucking selfish, Gage."

"Eliza, you don't mean any of this. I'm sorry, I swear." He reached for my hand, but I yanked back.

"Don't fucking touch me," I snarled.

He looked me over, baffled, and I wanted to leave him stumped. I was pissed. I couldn't face him anymore. He was a liar. He was my first at everything and he just...

demolished it. I thought we had more, but seeing as he was with Penelope for two whole days, perhaps I was wrong.

I decided not to say anything else. I had to go. Immediately.

I turned, pulling my bag on my shoulder and fighting tears, but Gage ran around me to stop me. "Eliza, don't leave me. Please," he whispered, grabbing my hands. Tears were building up in his eyes, but I shook my head. I couldn't look at him. I couldn't match his pain with my own. I would cave. I didn't need to cave; I just needed to go. "I was trying to find time to get you to change your mind, and I'm sorry I let her get in our way. I'm sorry I didn't spend the last two nights with you. It was all I wanted, but... she kept holding me back. She knew I was going to drop her for you, so she wailed on me. She threatened to expose me and Kris."

I shook my head. "I have to go, Gage."

"Eliza, no. Please," he begged, gripping my hands and placing his forehead against mine. "Eliza, you mean so much to me. You can't just leave like this."

I refused to open my eyes. I couldn't look at him. I couldn't break. I only shook my head, hoping he would let me go.

"Just think about it, Eliza. I can take care of you. I can set up that graphic design job for you. If you want me to, I'll set it up right now. I can buy you an apartment—uh... a house. I know how much you love to read... I can build you a ton of bookshelves... buy you a ton of books if it'll make you smile. I'll even give you your own studio to paint and draw in whenever you want to make your usual escapes. We can live together when this tour is over. I'll let you pick where we live—any state. Anywhere. It doesn't matter as long as we're together. Whenever I have to go somewhere, you can come with me. You can travel with me. We can continue being happy... We'll do good." His voice broke, causing my eyes to open. Tears were streaming down his cheeks, and I bit my bottom lip. He knew me so well and it was hurting me even more.

"I can do so much for you, Eliza. Just... don't leave what we have behind. Stay. Please. Don't go like this." A sudden guilt took hold of me. Tears continued running down his cheeks, and I bit my bottom lip, wanting to hold back, but it was impossible. Seeing him cry made me cry. Seeing him crack and break was making me break.

"Gage, I can't," I whispered. "I can't. I have to go back. I have to live my own life. I've told you this."

"You can. You love me, right? You can build your life with me." He cupped my face, bringing my lips to his. "You can, Eliza. Stay with me. I swear I'll drop Penelope. If that's what you're worried about, I'll call her right now and tell her we're done. I'll give it all up for you, Eliza. I'll let her tell the whole damn world about Kris and me as long as I can keep *you* in my arms. I don't give a fuck about her. *I love you*. Please..." he begged, tears gushing. I knew he was only saying this to keep me around. He didn't mean it. He wasn't going to let Penelope win that easily. "Please, don't leave me. Don't make me empty again. Don't let me break."

I swallowed a sob, dropping my bags. His eyes filled with relief at the sight of my bags on the ground, but I cupped his face, kissing him deeply, passionately. I don't know how long I kissed him, but I tried so hard to let go. It was hard to let go. I wanted to be in his embrace for the rest of my life. I wanted him to kiss me like this every hour of every day, but I knew we couldn't. Not yet. I had to go back. I had to go through with what I wanted. As much as it ripped me in half to think about—to go through—I had to.

"I love you, Gage, but I can't stay."

I stroked his cheek, but he shook his head, sobbing as his forehead fell onto my shoulder. He clutched me in his arms, refusing for me to leave. I tried to pull away, but each time he held on tighter, shaking his head. "Eliza... I'm begging you."

"I—I can't, Gage."

"You can!" he shouted, finally releasing me. "You can! You don't understand how much I need you around me. I need your smile, your grace... your love. I need everything about you in order to be happy. I won't be happy if you leave, and you know this! You won't be happy either, so just... stay with me. Please. Follow your heart, Eliza. You love me! Don't let this go."

I bit into my bottom lip, almost drawing blood. I shook my head. The longer I was to stand there crying with him, it was going to be harder and harder to go. "I have to go, Gage. I'm sorry. We'll see each other again," I assured him. "We'll work something out."

"Eliza, no! Fuck… no. Stop. I'm not letting you leave!" He stopped me from grabbing my bags. I stared into his hurt, angry eyes. Tears were still streaming and my vision became blurry again. Something loud came from behind him, almost like the slamming of a door, but I couldn't look away. Deep voices yelled his name, but neither of us averted our gazes. He grabbed me again and I slowly pulled away.

"Gage, you have to let me go," I whispered, shaking my head.

He didn't say anything. He just kept tugging on my arm. He was about to wrap his arms around me and I would have allowed him had someone not pulled me back by the shoulders to get me out of his grasp. My eyes were stuck on Gage, who was being hauled back by Montana and Roy. I wasn't sure who grabbed me at first, but by the hand that was rubbing circles on my back, I was certain it was Ben.

Gage was yelling my name fiercely, begging me not to leave. To stay. He yelled it repeatedly and I couldn't force myself to look away from his pain. Montana kept pushing him back by his chest, stealing glances at me, and Roy was holding Gage's arms, securing them behind his back so he wouldn't swing. "Eliza, you can't fucking leave like this!"

Gage yelled again. I flinched and soon I was pushed onto leather and the car door shut in my face… but I could still see him. And it was like he could still see me, even through the tinted windows. He was still glaring at me, veins popping out on his neck as Montana and Roy used all their strength to push him toward the FireNine bus. Soon, Deed came limping out, his eyes wide with shock as he rushed to help Montana and Roy.

But there was no need for Deed to help because Gage gave out. He stopped yelling and the boys tried to hold him up, but he ended up buckling to his knees. I gasped, tears falling down my face. I was sobbing and I hadn't even realized it. I was choking, desperate to get out of the car and comfort him, but I knew better. I couldn't bring myself to do it because I *had* to go.

But as Gage called my name one last time, something cracked inside me. I grabbed the door handle of the car and pushed out, rushing in Gage's direction. His head was still hanging down so he couldn't see me coming, but I wasn't stopping. I would clash into him if I had to. I would do whatever to let him know I loved him with all my heart. I was in love with him and distance would never change that.

I was almost there—just a few more steps—but before I could make it, one of the security guards grabbed me and I wailed as they rushed me back to the car. "Gage, I'm so sorry!" I yelled, fighting my hardest to get out of the guard's arms. "I'm so sorry. I love you."

He heard me, I knew, because he shook his head, keeping it down. The security guard stuffed me into the car, strapped my seatbelt around me, and then slammed the door before standing in front of it, making sure I wasn't going to get out again. I saw camera lights flickering and I wasn't sure where they were coming from. I turned and looked out the window past Gage. Cal was stepping out with a camera in hand, eyes wide as he stared at Gage on his knees. He then rushed back inside, pulling out his phone on the way. I didn't know what he was doing, and I didn't really care. I couldn't even think straight. I was hurting.

Breaking.

Obliterating.

As soon as Ben tossed the bags into the trunk, slammed it closed, and hopped into the backseat, ordering Marco to drive, he pulled me against him and stroked my hair, cooing to me that everything was going to be all right. But

I knew it wasn't. I was hurting, breaking on the inside, but it was best not to look back.

As soon as I sorrowfully kissed Ben good-bye and boarded the jet, I stared out the window and completely broke down. Sob after sob. Tear after heavy tear. I was lucky to be on the jet alone because I had all the time to myself to let it all go. To release the pain, the hurt, and grief. It literally killed me inside. I broke Gage. I took his happiness with me. I created a hole within him, leaving him empty once again.

The times when I couldn't stand him, I'd tell myself repeatedly it's who he is. His ways—the sleeping around, flirting, partying, drinking, and hurting girls... It was all him because it was the only way he could forget—the only way he wouldn't have to feel anything. The only way he wouldn't remember his past and how much Kristina actually took away from him.

But a part of him changed somehow. It wasn't a complete change, but it was enough, and the saddest, most heart-wrenching part about it was the changes were made for *me*. The changes were made so he could *love* me.

And since I was now on my way home—since I was leaving him behind, along with the relationship he wanted to continue and grow between us—I knew I'd destroyed him. I knew sooner or later his past doings, which I despised so much, would consume him all over again just so he wouldn't have to feel the pain, the hurt, and the heartache. Simply so he could try and forget about someone else who was close to his heart.

And I hated the ache within me.

I hated that—because of my priorities, my life, and my decision—I'd be the one to blame for Gage Grendel's shattered heart.

S. Q. WILLIAMS

There's more to Gage and Eliza's story in book two,

Who We Are
Coming September 2013

Until then, enjoy a little sneak peek...

Note:
The first two chapters are subject to change.
What you see now may or may not be in the published
copy.

HATRED

This is fucked up, Eliza. This is really fucked up of you.

I kept thinking it, but why the hell was I still walking forward with my roommate, the girl I couldn't stand most, Teala Morris.

"Gotta keep up if you're hanging with me, baby girl," she said, tugging on the hem of her skintight black dress. I had to pass on wearing one of her dresses. Instead, I went with some basic skinny jeans and a grey belly shirt.

It was instinct, really—going out with Teala of all people. I hated the girl with a passion and the only reason I dealt with her was because she was my roommate and it was too much of a hassle to try and move. Other than that,

I could have cared less about her. I was using her tonight because I was worried about being backstage alone, but being with her was just like being by myself. The plan was rather pointless.

Teala was the kind of girl who made fun of people like me. Simple girls. Girls who went to the library to read on weekends instead of parties. She was the kind of girl who mocked someone like me to my face and didn't think twice about whether she'd hurt my feelings or not. It's sad to say, but the only time I did like Teala was when she wasn't at the dorm, which was every night.

The music thumped louder, and with each step closer, my heart clambered against my chest. I knew what band was playing. I knew the song. I knew *every single* damn word, and the bad part about it was it was a song *he* named because of something I said. It was the song he sang to me three nights before I left him behind and a song that became extremely popular.

Every time I heard it on the radio, it was a constant reminder of what I'd actually done to him. I hated what I did and I was stupid for going with Teala to this damn concert, but I had to show up. It was my only way of getting back home. Ben (my dad and best friend) told me he would be waiting for me near the front gates. He was my only ride home and I didn't want to pass up the opportunity again. Going home meant relaxing for a few days before starting my internship.

During the internship, I was going to have my own apartment (bought by them) and the only thing I had to worry about was clothes, food, and transportation—but they paid for the transportation so I considered myself lucky to score the internship. It was for Arts Global, a gigantic art agency I'd fantasized about working for since I was a child. I was finally going to be living my dreams, painting, drawing, and meeting new people with similar interests.

There'd been plenty of times when Ben would call me and ask if I wanted to come home for a break. I would always tell him no because I knew exactly what he was trying to do. I knew who was always around him and I didn't want to face him again. I was a coward, I was selfish, but I couldn't help it. I literally ripped that boy's heart to shreds.

We neared the crest of the hill and long, silver gates appeared. I swallowed the lump in my throat as I spotted Ben standing near the ticket stand, checking his watch.

The line beside him was exceedingly long, and as I looked back to see where it led to, I shook my head. It was curving around the block and the show had already started. I guess the people were too amped for FireNine to leave.

Ben saw me coming, but as he spotted Teala, his eyebrows stitched. "It's about damn time, Liza," he snapped. "I have to get back there before the next song."

"Great to see you, too, Ben." I sighed, following him through the gates.

He slowed down to get to my side and then looked over his shoulder at Teala who was following behind us, ogling and batting her eyelashes at a few guys. "I'm sorry. You know I love you, sweetie." He looked at me again, kissing my cheek. "But did you have to bring that trailer trash with you?"

I bit on a laugh and he chuckled deeply as we neared another gate. The bald security guard standing in front of it nodded at Ben as we got closer and pressed a button for the gates to open. Teala clunked her way in behind us, her heels somewhat louder than the music. As we neared a door, the crowd screamed and I winced. It'd been so long since I heard a scream like that. A whole eight months to be exact.

Has it really been that long?

My palms became sweaty as Ben opened the door.

I was deathly afraid of what was going to happen tonight. I was left with no choice but to face Gage Grendel after his show. I was proud of Ben for being their successful manager, but during this one night, I wanted him to have nothing to do with Gage or FireNine.

"All right, Liza," Ben sighed. "Make yourself at home. Refreshments are on the table over there." I nodded and he kissed my cheek before walking toward a man in a suit near the curtains to watch the boys play. Teala came to my side, her perfume burning my nostrils. It was a mix of cherry and alcohol. Horrendous.

"This is fuckin' cool of you," she said, slapping my shoulder.

I buckled a bit from her blow but pressed my lips to smile. "Yeah."

"I can't wait to meet the band. They're total fuckin' hotties. That Montana... oh, he could so have me right now. Any day. Anywhere. And Gage!" She squealed, bouncing up and down. "Oh, fuck, I would let him sing to me while we're fuckin'. That would be amazing, right?"

I frowned at her. How many times could a person use the word "fuck?" Teala used it in every sentence and, quite frankly, it was unattractive... not that she wasn't already unattractive. She wore so much hairspray that I was surprised she hadn't choked on it. Her hair was a solid black, her lips plastered with bold, red lipstick, and she was on the skinnier side. I didn't want to know what she did to become so skinny, so I kept quiet and never asked. I was sure it had something to do with heavy drugs and working out too much... or her finger constantly being shoved down her throat.

"Teala, how about you go watch?" I insisted. I wanted her as far away from me as possible.

"Great idea!" She rushed away from me, her heels clomping as she pulled the curtain back and stared ahead in awe. I could tell she'd never been backstage before.

Sighing, I turned to face the refreshments and grabbed a bottle of water. I really wanted to bail. I couldn't face Gage again. I couldn't look into those hazel eyes or take in that casual smirk, his broad chest, firm shoulders... sexy figure. I didn't have to see him in order to know he looked hotter than hell. There was never a morning or night when he looked bad.

The crowd went wild as his voice echoed all across the stadium. I swallowed, hoping my knees wouldn't lock from the bliss of his deep bedroom voice. I shut my eyes, breathing through my nostrils and clutching my bottle of water. I had to be mature. I had to act like we were exactly what we'd started off as. A fling. I knew we were way more than that, but I told myself over and over again we weren't. It wasn't supposed to be more than that.

But then Gage said something that caused me to drop my bottle of water with a gasp. "I heard last night that one of the hottest girls I've ever met is supposed to be here right now." He chuckled and I halted my next breath, keeping my gaze focused on the table. Too bad I was all ears. "This girl... I know she's here right now. She really broke my fucking heart. I fucked up. She let me go. I opened up to her. She closed off on me. Has anyone in this crowd ever been in love?" he asked. As soon as he did, the crowd roared and there was even an "I'm in love with you, Gage!"

"That's great, y'all. That's great. I want her to know tonight how bad she fucked me over—how hurt I was when I watched her leave. Not only did she break my heart, but she took the pieces with her. This girl—

wherever she is—isn't gonna like this song, but..." I knew he was shrugging carelessly. "Oh well. I don't give a fuck. That's what this song is called tonight: 'We Don't Give A Fuck.' It's explicit, but y'all know how we are... If you don't, then bear with us." He laughed, but my heart did a spiral drop as I stared down.

I scrambled for my bottle of water as he sang loudly, his anger flowing through the microphone. Each word stabbed at my gut, making me want to double over, but I stayed grounded. I wanted to bolt for the exit, breathe in the crisp night air, but I knew I was still going to hear his lyrics. The bad part about hearing the song was he wrote it. He was the main lyricist and it killed me even more.

"*It was bad to let you in,*" he sang. "*It was hard to get over you. I was stupid to be with you. You hurt me when I never did anything to you. I'll scream 'fuck you' to the rooftops. I'll let everyone know I'm not... I'm not in love with you. Fuck you. Fuck us. Like the band always says... WE DON'T GIVE A FUCK!*"

I gasped again, hot tears creeping to the rims of my eyes. I blinked quickly, but I couldn't move. I was stuck in place, begging my body to leave—to just turn around and run for the door. I didn't have to face him. I was being nice and actually wanting to be mature, but he was singing *this*? He was lying—I knew. He told me over and over again how much he was in love with me. How much he needed me to stay before I was pulled away from him.

After hearing those words, though, I wanted to slap him.

A hand capped my shoulder and I whirled around, staring into Ben's bright brown eyes. "Liza, you okay?" he asked. "I'm sorry... You know how he is. He always sings songs that aren't planned."

"Y-you told him I was going to be here?" I asked faintly.

"No, Eliza. I would never do that." He sighed, running his fingers through his hair. "Look, Montana and I were talking last night about how you were doing in school. Gage overheard you were going to be backstage and I guess it led to... this." Ben's eyes softened as he pulled me in by the shoulders and held me, rubbing my back. "Don't let him get to you. He's still upset. You know he was in love with you. It's just an act."

"Well, his act seems real." I sighed over his shoulder.

He pulled back, glaring into my eyes. "It's not, Eliza. Keep your head up and whatever you do, don't let him get to you tonight. I mean it. You're coming home regardless."

I nodded, pressing my lips as I took a step back. Someone called Ben's name and he sighed, looking me over once more before turning around and meeting the same tall guy with blond hair.

The band sang three more songs before Gage finally told the fans of Virginia goodnight. I heard them gathering their things and then hooting and hollering as they rushed backstage. I searched for Ben, but he was nowhere to be found. I needed to get out of there. The show was over, I stayed and listened to his heartbreaking song, and now it was time for me to go.

I squeezed my hands together, eyeing everyone until the curtain drew open and the first two to come back were Deed P. and Montana. Deed caught sight of me first and his smile expanded as he rushed in my direction.

"Holy fucking hell!" Montana yelled, rushing for me as well. "Oh shit, we've got our Eliza back!"

I giggled as Deed gave me a warm hug and I giggled even harder as Montana picked me up in his arms and squeezed me while spinning in a circle. He then dropped me and gave a real hug, and I sighed because I knew who was coming back next, but I wanted to keep my composure. "Miss Eliza, it's been a while. How's everything going?"

"Great, Montana." I smiled, looking him over in his grey T-shirt and dark-blue jeans. He'd changed his lip and eyebrow piercings to silver hoops instead of the old silver studs and his blond mohawk was a few inches longer, the tips dyed a fierce orange. "You look great."

"Well... you know... I can never be ugly." He winked.

I laughed before looking at Deed, who was already smiling at me. "Deed, how are you feeling?"

"Great, Eliza. Never better." He winked as well, taking a step back. "I know we're supposed to get out of here in a few minutes so I'll go grab my stuff. Hopefully we can catch up later?"

"Yeah, for sure." I nodded, watching him take a slow step back.

He nodded back quickly, then spun around to get down the hallway, and Montana chuckled, bringing my attention back to him.

"I'm sure you caught Gage's performance," he said, still laughing.

I swallowed. "I did, actually. But it's whatever."

He frowned. "It's far from 'whatever.' I told him to chill, but when Gage wants something, he goes for it." He looked me over as I lowered my gaze. "You're okay… right? I know it's probably going to be weird seeing him again—"

"I'm fine, Montana. It's the past. I've gotten over it. I'm sure he has as well."

I stared into his light-blue eyes and he fixed his mouth to say something, but it took only a second for him to shut it and nod with a sigh. "Well, I'm just gonna head back and get my things. We can catch up later."

I nodded and he turned around, hurrying for his dressing room. Ben finally came down the hall with the blond-haired man in the suit, and I was more than relieved to see him. As I started walking his way, though, the curtain pulled back and my heart literally dropped. I don't know if it's possible to have your heart drop out of your ass, but that's what I felt was happening to me.

He was glorious, as always. His hair was still the same— maybe a few inches longer. More tousled than I'd ever seen it before and a few pieces were spiked up, but it looked amazing on him. He was lean in a black FireNine T-shirt with bright-red print. His dark-blue jeans were snug and as usual, he had Chuck Taylor's on his feet.

He saw me and paused on his next step, just as I had. His hazel eyes narrowed as he looked me over from head to toe. The smile that was on his lips from the raving crowd evaporated and the corners of his mouth turned down. His eyebrows stitched and then he folded his firm, creased arms, making his body ink as clear as day beneath the fluorescent lights. Roy stepped back last and stopped beside him, taking in the sight of me as well. He was about to say something to Gage, but before he could, Gage said something to him and Roy shook his head, walking away.

As soon as Roy was out of sight, I looked at Gage again, but he was still staring at me. His eyes were still narrowed, his chiseled jaw ticking. I knew he wasn't going to say anything first, so I murmured, "Hi, Gage."

"Eliza," he scoffed, dropping his arms and stepping around me to head for his dressing room. Some girls were already waiting backstage and as he passed them, he winked at them, blew kisses, and even pulled one of them in to wrap her in his arms while kissing the corner of her mouth. My throat burned, watching him walk away leisurely with the girls. Ben caught the little act between us and his eyes filled with guilt as he watched Gage step into his dressing room and slam his door behind him.

Ben looked at me with sorrow-filled eyes and I shrugged my shoulders as if I didn't care, but deep down, it hurt. Deep down, I felt like someone had just knifed me—twice. I knew this was going to be fucked up. I just knew it. I should've just told Ben to pick me up from my dorm… but either way, I would've had to see Gage. Ben rode with the band to get here and it sucked I had to ride back with them.

Teala came up to me, grinning like an idiot. "That Grendel… I swear he's so fuckin' hot."

I rolled my eyes, turning my back to her. I grabbed another water bottle from the table and shut my eyes briefly. I just wanted this night to be over with already. I wanted to go home and pretend I didn't see the hate in Gage's eyes.

I wanted to pretend, but it would have been impossible. The hate was clear. He was upset with me and he wasn't going to get over it… not until we talked. But I didn't want to talk. I just wanted to be friends…

Okay, that was a stupid thought, but I couldn't go back to what Gage and I were before. If I were to go back to it, it would be just like hurting him again. And I didn't want to hurt him. As much as I couldn't stand him for the song he sang or even his attitude toward me, it would've been wrong of me to bring more pain upon him.

In the back of my mind, I knew I deserved his hatred.

ANGRY LIPS

After Ben and I dropped Teala off at some after-party and grabbed my bags from the dorm, we were on our way back to the truck. During the whole ride back to the stadium to pick up the boys, Ben and I were silent. I was speechless. Seeing the anger in Gage's eyes made me relive all we'd gone through and how much he hated my decision. Ben knew it as well, which was why he kept quiet. He didn't know how to make me feel better, but he didn't need to. I didn't really care.

Lies.

The most awkward part about the night was riding home with the band. I shared a few laughs with Montana, but each time my laughter filled the car, Gage would shudder, his jaw would tick, or he would tell the driver to turn up the radio. I took in the small things he did. It was as if every single sound I made pissed him off. I was sure even my presence pissed him off.

"Try not to let him get to you," Montana whispered.

I shrugged him off, staring out the window, ready for the ride to be over. The times I wasn't staring out the window, I would unnoticeably stare at Gage. I was in the very back row with Montana and Deed. Deed had fallen asleep with headphones on, his forehead pressed against the window, and Montana was too busy with his nose in his phone to see me. Roy and Gage were sitting in the second row of the car. Ben was in the front seat with Stan, our driver.

I took the quiet time to study Gage all over again as the flickering lights from the passing cars danced across his face. His features were stern and aggravated, without a doubt, but all in all, he was breathtaking—his chiseled jaw, pointy, slightly crooked nose, full and plush pink lips, perfectly tousled hair. A light trace of stubble surrounded his mouth, and he would randomly lick his bottom lip while shifting and trying to get comfortable in his seat. As he rested his head on the window and stared out, his neck was exposed and I had the urge to lean forward and kiss it. His lightly tanned skin looked so smooth, so creamy. I wanted to touch it, caress it… maybe even lick it.

I was a fool, I know, but he was completely irresistible. It was hard not to stare at the man who'd taken my virginity and brought me into womanhood. The man who effortlessly made me smile, made countless butterflies thrash in my tummy, and the first man outside of my father who told me he *loved* me. There was no way in hell he hated me. The love I used to see in his eyes was all too strong and it'd only been eight months since the last time we saw each other. Love couldn't fade that fast… could it? I sure as hell loved him. The feeling had to be mutual.

It wasn't too long before we pulled up to our house and everyone groaned and stretched before hopping out. Gage and Roy stepped to the side as Montana, Deed, and I walked after Ben to get to the house.

As Ben unlocked the door and we stepped inside, I looked over my shoulder at Gage and Roy still standing outside the truck. They weren't talking, just leaning against it, arms folded. I frowned, wanting to blast the both of them, but I held off. It would have been awkward for him to come inside anyway.

"Glad we're here. I had to take a serious piss," Montana said, running his wet hands across his shirt as he reentered the living room.

I smiled, lowering myself onto the recliner, but before I could settle and get comfortable, it registered that my bags were still in the truck. I thought about asking for a favor from one of them, but Montana and Deed got comfortable on the sofas and Ben had trailed off into his bedroom. I sighed, hopping from the couch and stepping outside.

I left the door cracked, but my gaze was forward, staring at Roy and Gage who were standing at the curb, talking. *Good.* His back was facing me and he wasn't near the truck. It saved me a moment of awkwardness.

I quietly walked for the back door and gave another greeting to Stan, who only smiled, his eyes extremely tired. I told him I needed my things and after I'd grabbed them, Ben came out, yelling for Roy and Gage to stop standing outside like idiots.

I froze then, slowly unthawing and hooking the strap of my bag on my shoulder. I turned gradually and met Gage's hazel eyes, but unlike my confused glare, his was hard and intense. Ben came rushing my way, helping me with my bags and art supplies.

"They're staying the night?" I asked so only he could hear.

Ben's lips pressed, his gaze lowering. "I'm sorry, Liza. It's only for tonight. They thought it was best not to waste money on a hotel and to just stay at my place until it's time for them to go tomorrow."

I scowled, slamming the door and rushing for the house. It was a bitchy move on my part. I was never one to be selfish, but with Gage, it was a completely different scenario. I couldn't be under the same roof with him. We weren't on good terms and I wouldn't have been comfortable in my own home with him around watching me with angry eyes.

I slammed my bedroom door behind me, but moments after, there was a knock. "Just leave it in front of the door, Ben," I called, sighing as I slumped down on the edge of the bed.

I heard something drop outside the door, but after that it was silent. The TV was still on and the front door shut, letting me know Gage and Roy were inside. But then my stomach grumbled and I cursed myself over and over again for not eating before getting home.

Sighing, I slipped out of my outfit and found a pair of pink pajama shorts and a white tank. I tossed up my hair, wrapping a band around it, and then paced in front of my window for about ten minutes before clutching the doorknob. My heart beat a mile a minute as I twisted it and peered out into the dark hallway. I could see the flickering of the TV from the living room and I could also hear snoring. I hoped the snoring belonged to Gage.

As I shut my door behind me, I literally tiptoed my way toward the kitchen. Knowing he was around, the hallway seemed longer and darker than ever before. It was almost like it was closing me in and my lungs were forcing themselves to function. I felt like every step could be heard along with the banging of my heart. The worst part about it was in order to get to the kitchen, I had to pass the living room. Ugh. I loved that house, but at this moment, I hated the setup more than anything.

I passed the living room slowly and saw bundles of covers. I couldn't make out who was where with the flickering lights of the TV, but I did see four comforters and sheets with what looked like bodies beneath them. I sighed then, hoping they were all sleeping after an exhausting night of singing and playing instruments.

But then I stepped into the kitchen... and *he* was right there, sitting on a stool at the island counter. His elbows were planted on the tan marble counters, his hands on either side of his head, and he was staring down. He was hunched over, so I couldn't see his expression, but I could see him biting at his bottom lip.

I almost gasped, but I held it in. I was about to turn around, but heavy hazel eyes locked with mine and I stopped in my tracks. At the sight of me, his eyebrows drew in, creases forming in his forehead. The biting on his lower lip stopped and then he pushed from the counter, marching toward me with heavy steps.

A million things raced through my head. I thought he was going to grab me, shake me, and yell at me for what I did to him. I thought he was going to tell me I was the worst person on the planet and he hated me... but neither of those happened.

Instead, he cupped my face and our lips collided. His tongue immediately slid into my mouth and my lower back bumped against the nearest counter edge. I tangled my fingers in his hair and groaned as his grip around my face tightened, but it wasn't too tight to hurt me.

Pleasure burned through me and my arms locked around his neck, trying to pull him in closer, but it was impossible. We were so close; I could feel his cock growing harder by the second. His tongue traced the roof of my mouth, my upper lip. I didn't dare break the kiss because it had been so long. It'd been months since the last time I kissed anyone. Gage was the last person I had my lips on and I missed it so damn much.

His lips were so velvety, so smooth. As I gripped his face, it was baby soft except the stubble surrounding his mouth. He grunted as he squeezed me, pulling me into him, rocking his massive erection against me. He then lifted me up on the counter, breathing rigidly, uncontrollably. His fingers ran over my shoulders, my hips, my thighs. One of them found its way beneath my shorts and slid into me. I gasped, but our lips remained locked. God, I missed this. It felt so good.

Gage groaned, pumping his finger into me, adding another while circling his thumb across my throbbing clit. I was getting higher, my body begging for more. I wanted the arousal thrusting against my leg to be inside me, burying deep, pumping hard... punishing me. Accepting me. I no longer had any self-control and it was always like this with Gage. Whenever I was around him, he had complete control over my body. He could do anything to me and I would enjoy it. I wanted him in every way possible, but it was like he was trying to hold back.

But as all this pleasure burned through me, I realized something wasn't right. He pulled his fingers out and trembled, fighting with himself, until finally he snatched his lips away.

The fire in his eyes was intense, shocking. I could still see the aggravation behind them, the hurt, but then he blinked it all away and released me, taking a step back. He blinked again and then ran the top of his arm across his lips roughly, almost like he was getting rid of the hot kiss we'd just shared.

He opened his mouth as if he wanted to speak, but then it clamped shut instantly. Tears formed at the rims of his eyes as he shook his head, blinking hard. I couldn't help but notice the thin bags beneath his eyes, the redness surrounding his eyelids. It was almost like he'd been crying, but I wasn't too sure because it could have easily been a sign of a lack of sleep.

"I want that kiss to be a reminder of what we could've had but what you ended up leaving behind," he finally said, his voice deep, unfamiliar, and gravelly. "I still can't fucking believe you, Eliza. I—I... Fuck, man!"

I flinched as he went back for his alcohol and swallowed it down before slamming his glass down. He then walked past me, brushing my shoulder as his spicy cologne whiffed past my nostrils and filled my lungs. I hated how he led me on—got me worked up and anxious for his hard, delicious body—but nothing happened. Nothing came out of it.

But then I thought it was probably how he felt after opening up to me. After telling me things he never would have told anyone. After spending so much time together and falling deeply in love, it fell flat in the end and we went nowhere... because of me. I let him down and displeased him and he was returning the favor. He was showing me how it felt to be left wide open and end up with no kind of closure.

And the crazy part about it was I wanted to chase after him and drag him to my bedroom. I wanted to satisfy both him and myself. I wanted to apologize a million times between rough kisses, but I knew my apology would mean nothing to him. I was sure by now, he was pretty much done with me and it was best that way. It was best for him to move on because I wasn't done yet. I still had work to do and I was sure by the time I was finished and graduated with a well-paying job, he would be with someone else... someone worth his time.

That someone just wasn't me.

THANK YOU

I know I said before that this book was something completely new for me... well, not completely, but sort of. I guess the steaminess will always be with me. I love this book. I love Gage Grendel. I felt a connection with him and Eliza that I've never felt before. It's hard to explain, but let's just say I don't want their story to end... like, ever. I adore this couple to the max. I'm purposely working slowly on book two so it won't have to end. Eliza reminds me a lot of myself. A girl who puts her priorities first. A girl who feels wise enough to become responsible at a young age. I connected well with her and I think this is why she's my favorite lead female character I've created thus far.

I want to give all my honor to God for giving me this amazing talent. I can only get better, and He's proving this. He's blessed me tremendously at such a young age.

Thanks so much to Stina Rubio for reading my stories and falling in love with Gage just as much as me. For talking to me literally every day and allowing me to keep my head up, even when I feel down. I loved your reaction to this book—to Gage. It gave me a small boost of confidence about the whole book. I love you, chick!

Thank you Kim Bias of **Reviews by Tammy & Kim** for pointing out the minor flaws in WHI, telling me how much I was going to get drilled for the ending and making me nervous, and even giving me good feedback. I will never take your help for granted. It means so much to my characters and me, believe it or not. Thank you.

Cassie McCown, you're one kick-ass editor! You've taught me a lot and I can't thank you enough for dealing with me and my dorky side of writing.

Amanda Heath and Dawn Martens... such lovely, talented, and beautiful ladies. Thanks for making me even more nervous about the end and for being very supportive at the same time. I love you ladies dearly. You rock my damn world!

C.C. Brown... oh, goodness. Our daily talks keep me sane. Our talks gave me the courage to boost this book and get it out there. I love our little chats. They mean the world to me. We'll be sticking together FOEVA, that's for sure.

Thank you Ena Burnette of **Swoon Worthy Books** for being so awesome with these blog tours and sticking with me. You rock to the max, and you don't even know it. Thank you so much for everything!

To all the bloggers/reviewers who keep me on my toes, make me smile, and share my things willingly:

Kimberly Schaaf

Sarah Camargo of **S. Camargo's Book Addiction**

Mary Tatar of **Mary Elizabeth's Crazy Book Obsession**

Tamsyn Bester of **The Secret Book Brat**

Kim Bias of **Reviews by Tammy & Kim**

Kendall McCubbin of **Book Crazy**

Cassie Chavez of **Sassy Cassie's Reviews and Cassie's Crafty Creations**

Kristie Wittenberg of **Three Chicks and Their Books**

All admins of **First Class Books!**

Ren Reidy of **A Little Bit of R&R**

Karese Blackwell of **Kindred Souls Book Blog**

Kimberly Brower of **Book Reader Chronicles**

Kathy Womack of **Romantic Reading Escapes Book Blog**

These are in no specific order, but just know you ladies are all awesome. I know there are so many more, and if I didn't list you then, I'm so, so sorry, but know that I love you more than words can explain! I can't ask for anything or anyone better. I appreciate all you do for me—hell, reading my book means so much to me. I'll cherish each and every one of you.

Thanks to my family and my amazing boyfriend for supporting me through everything. Even though I'm sure they won't read the books, it's okay. Your encouragement is enough for me.

And last but not least, my readers. My fans. My adorable ladies who follow my every movement. It feels odd to say I have fans, but I won't deny it anymore. I do, and it makes me extremely happy. Thank you all so much for reading what I work so hard on. I couldn't ask for a better, more amazing group of enthusiasts.

"Heartbreak. Passion. Steaminess. LOVE."

About Shanora:

New York Times & USA Today Best Selling author, Shanora Williams considers herself one of the wondrous, down-to-earth authors who's all about romance and the paranormal... but of course she always makes room for the many other genres out there.

She's a huge lover of Starbucks and a big kid when it comes to Haribo Gummy Bears. If she could swim in Coca-Cola, she would. She's a very avid reader and a huge fan of many other independent authors.

Follow Shanora (S.Q. Williams) for the latest updates.

Facebook

Goodreads

Twitter

Website

I am always responding to emails from fans and readers. Don't be shy! If you want to contact me, feel free to do so. I love to connect with those who read my work, whether it is through Facebook, Twitter, email, or even my blog. I appreciate and love you all. Your support and feedback is beyond amazing.

Thank you,

Shanora

More books by Shanora:

The *New York Times* and *USA Today* best selling novel,

Hard to Resist

And it's sequel:

Hard to Hold On

Prequel:

Hard to Forget

Other books:

OBTAINED (BOOK ONE)

Find them on Amazon, Barnes & Noble, and Kobo today!

CPSIA information can be obtained
at www.ICGtesting.com
Printed in the USA
BVHW030158010419
544217BV00001B/122/P

9 781491 090565